ACCLAIM FOR SHELLEY GRAY

"Shelley Gray writes a well-paced story full of historical detail that will invite you into the romance, the glamour . . . and the mystery surrounding the Chicago World's Fair."

—Colleen Coble, *USA Today*
bestselling author of *Rosemary Cottage* and the Hope Beach series

"*Downton Abbey* comes to Chicago in Shelley Gray's delightful romantic suspense, *Secrets of Sloane House.* Gray's novel is rich in description and historical detail while asking thought-provoking questions about faith and one's place in society."

—Elizabeth Musser, novelist,
The Swan House, The Sweetest Thing,
The Secrets of the Cross Trilogy

"Full of vivid descriptions and beautiful prose, Gray has a way of making readers feel like they are actually in Chicago during the World's Fair . . . the mystery surrounding the 'Slasher' keeps the reader engaged throughout."

—*RT* Book Reviews, 4 star
review of *Deception on Sable Hill*

Whispers in the

READING ROOM

ALSO IN THE CHICAGO WORLD'S FAIR MYSTERY SERIES

Secrets of Sloane House
Deception on Sable Hill

Whispers in the

READING
ROOM

A Chicago World's Fair Mystery

SHELLEY GRAY

ZONDERVAN

Whispers in the Reading Room Copyright © 2015 by Shelley Gray

This title is also available as a Zondervan e-book. Visit www.zondervan.com.

Requests for information should be addressed to:

Zondervan, *Grand Rapids, Michigan 49546*

Gray, Shelley Shepard.
Whispers in the reading room : a Chicago World's Fair mystery / Shelley Gray.
pages ; cm
ISBN 978-0-310-33849-9 (softcover)
I. Title.
PS3607.R3966W364 2015
813'.6--dc23
2015020309

Scripture quotations are from the King James Version.

Any Internet addresses (websites, blogs, etc.) and telephone numbers in this book are offered as a resource. They are not intended in any way to be or imply an endorsement by Zondervan, nor does Zondervan vouch for the content of these sites and numbers for the life of this book.

Publisher's Note: This novel is a work of fiction. Names, characters, places, and incidents are either products of the author's imagination or used fictitiously. All characters are fictional, and any similarity to people living or dead is purely coincidental.

Interior design: Mallory Perkins

Printed in the United States of America

15 16 17 18 19 20 / RRD / 20 19 18 17 16 15 14 13 12 11 10 9 8 7 6 5 4 3 2 1

This novel is all about friendship. With that in mind, it's dedicated to Julie Stone. Thank you for being such a kind and steadfast friend! Thank you for touring Chicago with me . . . and then doing it again and again. Looking forward to years of collecting passport stamps together, wherever that may be!

Now faith is the substance of things hoped for, the evidence of things not seen.

—Hebrews 11:1

The astonishing Chicago—a city where they are always rubbing the lamp, and fetching up the genie, and contriving and achieving new impossibilities. It is hopeless for the occasional visitor to try to keep up with Chicago—she outgrows his prophecies faster than he can make them. She is always a novelty; for she is never the Chicago you saw when you passed through last time.

—Mark Twain, *Life on the Mississippi*, 1883

CHAPTER 1

CHICAGO TIMES-COURIER

From October 1893

Reported by Benson Gage

While the majority of the city basks in the glow of the Columbian Exposition's success, far more dark events are taking place in the city's underbelly. This publication has learned there has been a spike in attacks and murders deep in the heart of Camp Creek Alley. Has crime sought to take advantage of the fact that most everyone's eyes are on the bright Plaisance, allowing all sorts of criminals to run rampant?

This reporter can only advise for any reputable citizen with a care for both his purse and his life to stay far away from the area. It is very likely that even establishments that look reputable hide many dark secrets behind their beguiling façades.

MONDAY, JANUARY 8, 1894

He had returned.

Lydia Bancroft peeked over the stack of books she was cataloging, trying her best to see what new book her favorite patron was reading that afternoon.

For the past year, the debonair man had come into the reading room several times a week. And for the last three months, he'd sat in his favorite chair in the corner and kept his nose in a series of books detailing the adventures of Lewis and Clark.

She still remembered the expression on his face last week when he'd finished and closed the last tome. He'd looked pleased and just a bit melancholy. She knew those dual feelings well—the satisfaction of completing a well-written piece of literature while also coming to terms with the fact that those few moments of pure bliss would soon be replaced with a longing for more.

That was when she realized they were kindred spirits, even though she had no business observing him so intently. At long last, she was an engaged woman, and though Jason had never stepped foot in here, if he did, he undoubtedly would not appreciate the sight of her gazing upon another man.

But it seemed she couldn't help herself.

He intrigued her, even though she'd never uttered a single word to him, nor had he spoken to her. It remained a mystery why he had yet to ask for a library card or attempt to check out a book.

As Lydia continued to eye him, she wondered if perhaps she should offer help to obtain a library card. Perhaps he was unsure of the process. If that was the case, she would certainly be glad to be of assistance.

And, well, once they started talking, perhaps he'd be more apt to converse with her. At last.

"Excuse me, miss?"

Startled by a female voice, Lydia twisted around, disturbing the neat stack of books on the counter. They tumbled to the floor in a resounding crash, causing everyone around her to snap their attention her way.

Including her favorite patron. When she instinctively looked his way, he was gazing at her directly, not at the scattered books. His dark-brown eyes seeming to take in every freckle on her face and the flush she could feel rising on her neck.

Feeling like a little mouse caught in a trap, she stilled. For a split second, she gave in to temptation and allowed herself to meet his gaze. But when one of his eyebrows rose with a look of amusement, her embarrassment worsened.

Realizing that she had not improved his perception of her, she looked away.

"Miss?" The speaker's voice was sharp now. Irritated. Far from the low volume preferred in her reading room.

Finally facing the lady, Lydia gathered her wits. "Forgive me. How may I be of assistance?"

"I'm looking for the latest Sherlock Holmes mystery. Do you have it?"

"If we do, it would be on the shelf. Let's go see." She led the way to the fiction stacks, keeping her mind firmly on the task at hand. She smiled when she found the novel the woman was looking for in its place on the shelf.

Then, as she gathered the toppled books, she tried to hide her disappointment. Her favorite gentleman reader had gone.

And once again, he'd left the book he was reading on the table next to where he'd been sitting. Just like always. Carefully, she picked it up, noted the title, smiled, and placed it in a nearby cabinet. She knew from experience that he wouldn't return that day. But tomorrow she would set his selection out for him like she always did. She wanted him to have what he wanted here.

Even though she should not treat one patron more considerately than another—especially not a man who made her feel the loss of his presence.

Of course, there was always tomorrow or the next day. He would return. He always did. And the next time he did? She was going to approach him and offer a library card. Already her spirits lifted when she imagined how happy that would make him.

It took Sebastian Marks almost four blocks to shake off the cool feeling of serenity he'd enjoyed at the library. As the number of people around him doubled, then tripled, he forced himself to push away everything about his time at the Lincoln Lending Library. A gent like him was liable to get killed otherwise. After another block, he added a swagger to his step and a bit more menace to his expression.

It was just in time.

"Marks? Marks, yes. I thought that was you."

He turned and eyed Sergio Vlas, one of his longtime contemporaries, with a practiced look of contempt. "You weren't sure?"

"Not at first. No. There was something about your gait that didn't look right."

"Perhaps you should get your eyes examined."

"Yeah. Maybe." The Russian grinned as he fell in beside Sebastian, displaying a mouthful of gleaming but crooked teeth surrounding one gaping hole where an incisor had once been. "How's business?"

Sebastian shrugged. "Good enough. Why?"

"No reason." Vlas inhaled, then gave him a reason anyway. "With the recent rise in crime around here, the cops've been breathing down my neck lately something awful."

"Now that the fair is closed, the police seem to care about the number of suspicious deaths."

Sergio grunted. "It ain't the police who care, it's that blasted reporter from the *Chicago Times-Courier*. He's making it seem like every poor sod who's been mugged or stabbed is worth something." Illustrating his disdain for the reporter's interference, he spit on the ground.

Sebastian shrugged. "Murder is murder."

"Not at all. These men aren't society debutants. They're men who are gaming and drinking away their time. And worse."

Sebastian knew Sergio was referencing the Society Slasher, the man who had put the upper echelons of society on alert when he'd attacked some of the season's most eligible debutants. "Things will settle down soon. They have to."

"I imagine they will. I just was kind of hoping my place wasn't the only club that is suddenly swarming with police."

"It isn't."

What Sebastian didn't bother to point out, however, was that his club catered to a far different crowd from the Russian's. Sergio's gaming hall was a bit more than two rungs down from his own club and gambling institution. Sergio also dealt in women, which was something Sebastian never had the stomach for.

He far rather wished to put his efforts into making money from legal liquor and illegal poker tables. Somehow, becoming rich off of other men's vices didn't bother him. Making a cent at the expense of a desperate woman was a whole other story.

Besides, it was his luck that fools on the police force enjoyed visiting his gentlemen's club, not the Bear and Bull. Therefore, he was sure

Sergio's problems had nothing to do with him. "The police are always combing the backstreets. Pay 'em off."

"It ain't as easy as it used to be." Sergio sneered. "There's a fair contingent of cops who are on the straight and narrow."

Sebastian laughed. Partly because he didn't believe in anyone being completely on the straight and narrow, partly because he knew even if Sergio was indeed right, the cops would go after the Russian's business dealings before they'd touch his own. "Rotten luck."

They were now in the center of Camp Creek Alley, the aptly named path to both of their establishments. Old-timers said it was once the site of a number of brothels servicing trappers and frontiersmen back before Chicago was more than a swamp-infested town.

Now the alley was a main thoroughfare leading from booming businesses and socially acceptable sites to businesses better known to most in the dark. A left turn would eventually lead one to Sergio's Bear and Bull. Taking the second right led to his own club, the Silver Grotto.

"If I hear something about the coppers, I'll let you know," Sebastian said.

This time it was Sergio who smiled with disdain. "Yeah, right. I weren't born yesterday, Marks, and not even the day before. You're not gonna share anything you don't have to."

Sebastian didn't bother to deny that fact. "You're the same way. However, I don't blame you for that. We both know what happens to people who talk too much."

Abruptly, Sergio's grin vanished. "Don't get yourself killed today."

Sebastian nodded. That was something they all said to each other. It had started as a joke between two rivals. Now the joke was on all of them, since the recent crime wave had put many of their associates in danger or in the earth well before their time.

After they parted ways, Sebastian stopped a newsboy and purchased a paper, then entered the Grotto. All was quiet, seeing as it was still early in the day, not quite four o'clock.

Vincent Hunt, his personal assistant and club manager, greeted him at the door. After taking Sebastian's hat and coat, Vincent followed him through the main saloon, up two flights of narrow stairs, and at last into a spacious third-floor office. Once there, Sebastian took his chair behind a mahogany desk he'd won from a toff years ago. Then, at last, his manager presented the daily report.

For the next half hour, he listened as Vincent reported on everything from the kitchen staff, to menu choices, to items recently purchased for the poker rooms. As usual, Vincent waited until the very end to discuss any problems with recent customers or employees.

This was their usual routine, and they had perfected it into a fine art over the last two years—ever since Hunt's predecessor had been stabbed to death in the middle of a bar brawl and Sebastian had promoted Vincent to replace him.

Rarely did Sebastian take any notes. It was Vincent Hunt's job to analyze and investigate problems. Sebastian, on the other hand, decided matters quickly and concisely. He didn't want to spend any precious moments of his spare time pondering over decisions. As far as he was concerned, only fools procrastinated or fretted about things that had to be done or couldn't be changed.

At the end of their time together, Vincent looked up from his notes. "That's the extent of it, sir."

Sebastian looked at the gilded timepiece on his mantel. They had finished right on schedule. "Sounds fairly quiet."

Hunt nodded. "It has been. Well, except when Mr. Avondale paid us another visit."

Sebastian leaned forward, vaguely irritated Hunt hadn't mentioned this right away. "When was this?"

Hunt curled his lips in distaste. "Around two this morning, just in time to gamble before the rooms closed at three."

Sebastian didn't flinch, but he privately shared his manager's opinion of the man. If Avondale was on the property that time of night, he was no doubt three sheets to the wind. And while he didn't especially care how much his guests at the bar imbibed, with Avondale it continually meant only one thing. The gentleman would be loud, sloppy, unruly, and a sore loser. "Did he lose again?" he asked, thinking it was a rhetorical question.

"He did, sir."

"Did he cover all his losses for the night?"

Looking pleased, Hunt nodded. "He did. Of course, he still owes you thousands."

Of course he did—just as several wayward men from influential families did. He allowed it, to a point, because being indebted to him meant they would do his bidding should he need them in other matters.

But unless there was a problem Hunt couldn't—or shouldn't—handle himself, Sebastian didn't care to know anything about what men did in his club, not even the ones who owed him money. He paid Hunt to relay information that mattered to him, not to watch gents come and go and then report back to him like a gossiping old woman.

His blond-haired, too-often-wound-tight manager should know that.

And because he didn't, it tore a hole through Sebastian's carefully crafted and controlled diction. "Then what's yer problem?" The last thing he wanted was to start his workday reviewing gossip from the night before.

"Apparently he took out his displeasure about the night's losses on a girl."

"Girl?"

"Prostitute. Young one. Down at Jack's Last Stand." A pained look crossed his features. "He beat her severely. She almost died."

That was unfortunate.

However, he'd learned long ago that no good came to the man foolish enough to dwell on the darkness in life. And his control of those emotions let his diction settle once again. "You getting a soft heart, Hunt?"

"No, sir." He grimaced. "Maybe."

Sebastian raised his eyebrows.

"I have Mary, you know. The thought of someone beating her up is pretty hard to stomach."

Vincent was a single father, his wife having died of scarlet fever when his daughter was barely a year old. Now Mary was about four, and he knew Vincent was excessively fond of her.

But that didn't mean Hunt needed to let the child make him vulnerable. Summoning up his self-schooled vocabulary again, he warned, "Then don't think about it, Hunt. Just like with the recent beatings and murders around town, Avondale's proclivities and some Bear and Bull girl's misfortune don't affect us." He hardened his voice to make sure his point was taken. "At all."

Vincent shifted, lifting his shoulders as though they were suddenly stiff and sore. "It isn't always that easy to ignore when someone does something evil though."

A chill crept up Sebastian's spine. Was it because he'd done his share of shameful things in the past? Or because he was so used to turning a blind eye to evil that he'd forgotten what it was like to care?

"You're going to have to ignore things like this if you want to work here for any length of time, Hunt. I essentially told you that when you first interviewed." A memory surfaced of Vincent arriving three years ago, still grieving over the death of his wife, just let go from his job as a clerk in a law office. He'd been earnest and needy.

Sebastian hadn't been sure the man would last a full month, but he had been an exceptional employee.

That is, when he wasn't wearing his heart on his sleeve.

Hurt shone in his assistant's eyes. "Mr. Marks, surely some sympathy wouldn't be misplaced."

"It is not misplaced, but it's also not welcome."

"But have you never come across a woman you imagine being too good for the likes of Avondale?" Lowering his voice, he added, "A lady who is too good for the likes of any of us?"

A certain freckled, blue-eyed, auburn-haired librarian who favored silver-rimmed spectacles came to mind.

Ruthlessly, he pushed her image from his mind. "I don't think about women," he bit out, knowing it was almost the truth. "You know that."

Hunt looked as if he was barely suppressing the urge to roll his eyes.

"But if I did, I would only think of them in terms of pity. It's a woman's lot to be at the bidding of the men in her life." He would hate a life like that.

"It isn't always that way, sir," Hunt replied in his middle-class accent. "I treated my wife like she was a treasure."

A treasure. That was more than a bit effusive. Rather laughable. But even Sebastian wasn't cruel enough to make light of Vincent's love for his deceased wife.

Exhaling, he placed both hands on the surface of his desk, enjoying the satin-smoothness of the highly polished wood, as he always did. "My point, Hunt, is that many women, especially prostitutes, are at men's mercies. It's the way of the world, and there's nothing you nor I can do about that. But I will say that hearing about Avondale's latest misadventures makes me thank my lucky stars I don't deal in prostitutes just to make more money. They're more trouble than they're worth."

"Yes, sir. Do you need anything else now?"

Disappointment flickered in his manager's eyes before he lowered them. Sebastian knew Vincent didn't agree with everything he'd just said about some women's lot in life, but it didn't exactly matter. Only one person owned the Silver Grotto and that was him. That made him right. Always. "Not at the moment. Thank you for the report."

Only when he was alone again did Sebastian dare to let his mind drift back to Miss Lydia Bancroft. The way she rarely chattered on like most females of his acquaintance. The way she shelved books like they were old friends. How she seemed to be more at ease with a room full of books than with people.

Something about that little mouse spurred feelings of protectiveness he didn't even know he possessed.

He'd only recently learned her name, when he'd overheard one of the women borrowing books speak to her. He'd been surprised—not at her name, but at the realization that he'd even wanted to know it. That he needed to know it.

He was going to have to guard himself the next time he visited the library. He pigeonholed people in his life, and she needed to firmly stay in the small, very narrow expanse of his brain that focused on obtaining a few hours of peace in a worn and quiet reading room. He would not dwell on the faint scents of lavender and lemon that lingered there or the way he sometimes felt her steady gaze linger on his form.

It would not do for him to get to know her too well.

If that happened, she might seek him out. Attempt to talk to him. Worse, want to know his name.

And that would be a disaster. Few people knew how much he liked to read, and no one—besides her and that assistant of hers—knew just how much time he spent with his nose in books.

The lending library gave him some solace. For a few hours' time, he was able to be the man he had wished to become—back before he realized life in the slums wasn't about being smarter than the bullies on the street, but about being stronger. Meaner.

Now that he owned the Grotto, however, he knew success in his world meant he needed to be both—strong *and* smart.

Turning his chair, he stared out the window, watching the people below him hurry about their business. They all looked so busy. So intent. So purposeful.

Indeed, the regular populace, no matter in Camp Creek Alley or on Michigan Avenue, continued on their merry way during daylight hours, while he generally did all he could to merely while away the time until the sun went down and his club began to fill.

But when he saw two women walking in cheap, ill-fitting dresses on the way to the worst parts of Camp Creek, something inside of him twisted painfully.

Obviously, they were prostitutes. Very far from the refined Miss Lydia Bancroft. Far from Hunt's treasured, middle-class wife, even.

Now, perhaps because of Hunt's melodramatic story, he found himself viewing those harlots as something more than their occupation. As something more than a hurtful reminder of his own mother . . . and the way she'd been forced to ply her trade to keep him fed.

For the first time in, well, forever, he allowed his shields to fall, seeing the two prostitutes for what they truly were. To view them as women, as fragile beings in need of support.

Suddenly, he had no stomach for Avondale's transgressions. Or for being even inadvertently responsible for yet another woman's pain. Not anymore.

And right there and then he made a promise to himself. One day soon he was going to deliver some kind of payback to Mr. Avondale.

CHAPTER 2

ONE WEEK LATER

The sumptuous lobby of the Hartman Hotel was decked out in elegant Persian carpets that covered highly polished marble floors. Expensive artwork covering cherry-wood paneling decorated the walls. The exotic flowers displayed spread color throughout the area, attracting Lydia's eye and tingling her nose with perfumed scents.

All of it was so exquisite, so fragrant, so bright, and so . . . so *different* from her usual surroundings at the lending library that Lydia couldn't help but blink owlishly through her spectacles and hope she didn't look as out of place as she felt.

"I hope the Hartman meets your expectations?" her fiancé murmured at her side.

"Of course it does. How could you imagine that it wouldn't?"

"My only wish is for your happiness, my lamb."

Her cheeks heated, as they always did when he called her his lamb. She really didn't care for the pet name. She was rather tall, almost five foot seven. She was a bit clumsy too. Even when she was young, she'd never particularly felt very lamb-like—though she supposed a newborn lamb might be a bit wobbly.

His words were gallant. He was looking at her as if she was important to him. That was continually a mystery to her. She knew she was far away from the kind of woman a man dreamed to have on his arm. Beyond her glasses, she had freckles that seemed to multiply, no matter how much precious lemon juice she dabbed on her nose.

And then there was the unfortunate circumstance of her hair. Red.

Therefore, she felt "lamb" was rather unsuitable. Her logical mind had more than once considered begging him to substitute a better word. Owl, for example, would be more apt, though she'd never considered owls as particularly attractive birds.

But because telling him how she felt about his pet name would be terribly unkind, Lydia hoped she would grow into the endearment, rather like her mother's kid boots. Now, those were lamb-like.

She bit back a smile at the direction her thoughts had taken. Standing up straighter, she reminded herself that this was an important moment in their relationship. They were having tea out in public, just the two of them.

Essentially, her fiancé was putting her on display. She needed to make sure she did everything to make him proud.

Because, well, sometimes she couldn't quite understand how she'd gained Mr. Jason Avondale's devotion.

He was popular. Handsome. And wealthy.

Lydia, on the other hand, had few friends, none close, so no one would have considered her popular. She'd always been too bookish, she supposed. And though she realized she wasn't without good looks, she didn't need a mirror to know she would never be the beauty of, say, the diamond that was Eloisa Carstairs. As beautiful as she was wealthy, the young lady now married to the dashing police captain who had solved the Society Slasher mystery was still the talk of Chicago.

And last, she was only pretending to be wealthy.

"The Hartman Hotel is truly magnificent. Thank you for bringing me to tea this afternoon. It's a lovely treat, to be sure. Why, I've been looking forward to this afternoon ever since you invited me last week. Right away, I asked Priscilla to cover the reading room for me this afternoon."

Jason's lips pressed together. Making her realize she'd probably been a bit too enthusiastic in her response.

Releasing a sigh, she kept quiet and tried to look demure while Jason spoke to one of the hotel employees, who then motioned to the formal tea set up in the center of the lobby. If he had asked her, she could have told him where it was. She'd noticed it the moment they'd walked through the grand brass-and-glass doors.

After all, they were having an *early* tea—some might say a light luncheon—with very few others in the room this time of day. But she knew someone of her fiancé's station could ask for service whenever he wanted it.

As they were guided to the small table, Lydia took care to keep her expression serene. But inside she was remembering not to continually smile, not make eye contact with the hotel employees, to keep her chin up and posture straight.

And not let what would surely be her mother's disappointment at not being invited to tea as well fill her heart. When Lydia's father passed away three years ago, their circumstances had changed.

They lived simply now. Gone was the more lavish lifestyle they'd enjoyed. In its place was a carefully constructed act to ensure that Lydia married well. As soon as they realized how dire their finances were, they sold their house and moved into their brownstone townhouse.

"This house held too many memories," her mother had explained to a friend. That, at least, was true.

Then they sold some of their less valuable works of art displayed in private rooms. They sold their private carriage and team of horses, choosing to tell one and all they were adopting the modern travel conveniences of Chicago instead. They eventually let all their servants go, except their cook, Ethel, who shopped for food and came in each day.

Then her mother insisted they use their remaining but limited resources to ensure Lydia continued to attend parties and events so she could marry well. That was more important than ever. What else would restore them to the life they'd once had?

To complete the ruse, Lydia's mother let her circle believe she remained cloistered at home out of a widow's grief, rather than letting them see her wearing last season's clothes. They had even used the excuse of her prolonged grief to put Jason off from so much as having tea with them. What would he think if he saw their home so shabby and bare?

Unfortunately, as time went on, her mother had become not just disappointed but a complaining, depressed woman. And it seemed, despite the promise of Lydia's upcoming marriage, she was not going to change until she could return to the lifestyle she once knew.

Lydia realized that even if she hadn't made a good match, she and her mother could have lived for quite some time without going hungry. Her income from working at the lending library would see to that. But it wasn't enough. Her paltry earnings were nothing compared to the allowance her father used to make available for even incidentals.

There was a true pinch where there had once been none. Eventually, even the paintings in their foyer and stairwell had to be sold. Lydia might never marry, and it was time to be realistic.

Just when she had convinced her mother to begin exploring the possibility of moving to an even smaller, less prestigious address, Lydia caught Mr. Avondale's eye at a ball. And because she had no choice in the matter, she encouraged his advances.

Though they didn't have much in common, he was better—even wealthier—than any of the other men who'd shown the slightest interest. And she felt sure they would have a fine life together, even though she didn't understand why he had noticed her in the first place.

Of course, she might not have noticed him either. But it didn't necessarily matter that she didn't consider him all that smart. Or that he was strangely evasive about how he spent his evenings when not by her side. Her feelings toward him had no bearing.

He was everything she'd been taught to hope to find. He was from a good, influential family, had an excellent job in the banking district, and was well mannered. To her mother's delight, he proposed just last month, and now her mother's future was secure. That was all that was of importance.

She must soon tell him the truth, however, that she and her mother had no wealth of their own. It would be the right thing to do. Lydia wasn't worried. Jason did not need her money, just a wife with acceptable social status. Surely he would understand. And he seemed fond enough of her, as she had become fond enough of him.

He also seemed to find her bookish quirks amusing.

"I do hope they have both scones and sandwiches. I'm rather hungry," she blurted before remembering that she should never talk about food, especially food she was intending to consume.

"I imagine they will bring you your heart's desire, Lydia." Jason pulled out his rather large gold pocket watch, and after pressing a button with a single sapphire to open the cover, he scanned its face.

His glancing at his watch told Lydia he was a very busy man. "I'm glad you could clear your schedule at the bank to have time for tea."

"You are always worth my time."

He smiled at her before rubbing one finger along the magnificent gold watch. Then, with a look of regret, he slipped it back into his vest pocket.

Oh, he was so gentlemanly. So fussily proper! Surely with looks like his, God had been very smart to not give Jason all that much in his brain.

After all, the Lord could only give each of them so much.

She was still smiling about his gentlemanly comment minutes later when a pair of waiters arrived with tea and trays of delicacies.

Just as Lydia was about to remove her gloves so she could fill her plate, Jason excused himself to go speak rather intently to a man standing across the lobby, near the foyer.

Sitting alone, particularly taunted by the trays with watercress sandwiches and tarts but unable to begin without Jason, Lydia forced herself to give her attention to the paintings decorating the walls of the lobby.

She'd never been a great fan of either portraits or the heavy-handed works of the Dutch masters. She much preferred images her cherished works of literature created in her mind. That said, she could certainly appreciate the paintings by Rembrandt and Vermeer on display.

Her stomach growled.

Mortified, she picked up her teacup and took a large sip. And then another. After refilling her cup, she glanced Jason's way and noticed he was now talking to *two* gentlemen.

Peevishly, she wished he'd given her permission to begin without him. Of course, if he'd done so, she would have most likely already cleared her plate and would be hoping for seconds—which would have been just as embarrassing as a growling stomach.

And would, of course, have done nothing to reassure Jason that he'd made the right choice when he'd chosen her to be his bride.

Determined to sit quietly the way her mother had taught her,

Lydia allowed her gaze to skim over the ornately carved woodwork. She admired a debutante's daydress. The stained glass window.

And then she caught sight of him. Him!

It was all she could do not to gasp.

There he was, her favorite library patron. Lounging against a wall. Once more, he was staring at her with an expression that could only be described as amusement.

When their eyes met, his expression softened for the briefest of moments, then it flickered beyond her. And as his piercing regard settled on Jason and the men with him, his expression cooled. Considerably.

Did he know her fiancé?

Thankfully, Jason returned to her side a moment later. It was best not to think about the man right now, and she presented Jason with her best smile. Besides, at last it was time to eat.

"So sorry, lamb. I hate to leave you alone, but sometimes business rears its ugly head even here at the Hartman." A shadow moved into his eyes. "It couldn't be helped though."

"There is nothing to apologize for." She lifted her hand, intending to gently caress his arm, to show that she was always by his side, hoping to ease his concern, but at the last moment she changed her mind. It wasn't seemly to touch others in such familiar ways. She should know that. After all, she'd read it in her books time and again.

Instead, she took a moment to close her eyes and offer a brief prayer of thanks for the beautiful food and, truth be told, gave thanks for the fact that she was finally going to be able to eat.

Just before she finally started to remove her gloves so she could pick up one of the tiny, delectable sandwiches, she glanced back at her patron, her curiosity getting the better of her.

He was now glaring at both of them and not even attempting to be subtle about it. When they exchanged another look, his dark eyebrows lowered and his posture stiffened. Almost as if he was actively trying not to march over to their table.

The idea was so surprising, so very terribly unwelcome, that she stiffened.

Jason noticed. "Lydia? What is wrong?"

"I'm sorry. It is nothing. I just saw someone I recognize from the library."

His expression warmed as he leaned a little closer. "My little bookworm. Whatever are you going to do when you're a married woman?"

All thoughts of her patron—and her desperate hunger—evaporated as she began to guess his meaning. "What do you mean by that?"

"Only that you'll have to think of other things to occupy your time and interests."

What other interests? She liked reading. She also liked conversing with people who liked reading. "Jason, I enjoy working at the library." Just as important, she was good at it. Why, everyone said so!

"Of course you like your little job. But it wouldn't be appropriate for you to keep your hobby once you are wearing my name."

"You are expecting me to quit?" She pressed one hand to her mouth. She really was speaking altogether too loudly.

"Of course." His voice was clipped. Surprised. "You had to have known that."

"I don't know if I had ever thought about my life after we said our vows." Which was something she should have done, she realized.

Eyeing her like she was an unusual breed of gerbil, he chuckled softly. "Lydia, I know you like your head in the clouds, but it is time you returned to earth. Be realistic. We can't have anyone thinking I can't support you."

"No. Of course not."

"You will be too busy for books anyway, lamb. I intend for us to start our family right away."

Thinking just how he intended to start that family made her blush. And, well, feel a little troubled.

Afraid that anything she had to say about her job would convey her disappointment, Lydia took another sip of tea. Then she glanced her patron's way, just to see if he was still there.

And he was. He was also still staring at them.

Embarrassed that she was caught, she directed her attention back to the beautiful trays of food. And truly wished Jason would develop an appetite.

Immediately.

But instead of even once glancing at a trio of tiny meat pies, Jason continued to stare at her. "You still seem uneasy. Who is here that you know?"

Lydia elected not to tell Jason about her mystery patron. She liked to think he didn't want anyone to know he frequented her lending library. Some of her patrons were like that; they liked the anonymity of the quiet reading room. It was up to her to make sure they were granted such wishes.

She also secretly liked having this man to herself—even if she had no idea why he was glaring at them. It made her smile, liking the idea that she had a secret friend in the lobby, albeit he wasn't exactly a friend. And even though she shouldn't be thinking about him at all.

She needed to concentrate on her fiancé, the man who was going to help her mother return to her place in society. Surely if the other man knew Jason, he would have come to greet them by now.

She looked toward a rather haughty woman dressed in black

taffeta and with a bombastic hat adorned with purple feathers perched on her head. "That lady over there."

The lines around Jason's eyes eased. "Ah. Yes, I can see her visiting your library. Without a doubt."

She giggled. "What a thing to say. You've never stepped foot in there."

"I imagine I might . . . on your last day," he teased. He met her eyes briefly before looking beyond her. Then with a sharp intake of air, he stiffened.

Lydia turned to look at what—or who—had brought forth this change. But somehow she knew even before she looked. Jason and her patron stared at each other across the room in what could only be described as a contest of wills!

And then, to her shock and further discomfort, her patron turned his head slightly toward her and raised his eyebrows in a decidedly sardonic way.

She gasped. Jason turned back to her. "You know him."

Those three words were clipped and pointed, making her feel slightly afraid, though she wasn't sure why. "Of whom are you speaking?"

"Sebastian Marks."

"I've never heard of him." Thank goodness she was able to speak truthfully. Though, she did think his name had a decidedly beautiful cadence to it. Fitting.

"Are you certain? Look closer, lamb." Now the endearment rang false. It sounded degrading. "He is the man leaning against the wall in the black suit."

She forced herself to look in that direction again, and her patron's eyebrows rose in obvious amusement.

Feeling her cheeks heat, she whipped her head back to her fiancé. Jason leaned closer, reached for her arm, and clamped down on her wrist. "Do you recognize him now? Because he certainly seems to know you, Lydia. He is, after all, staring directly at you."

She forced herself to keep her tone light. "I'm sure you are imagining things."

"No. I am not." His grip tightened. "How do you know him, Lydia? Are you playing me for a fool?"

She winced in pain. "Jason! Release my wrist."

"Why is he here? Did you ask him to meet you here?" His voice lowered as his nails dug through her glove and into her skin. "Do you have plans together? Have you met here before?"

Jason's words were scandalous, filled with ugly insinuation. And though she'd been evading the truth, she was becoming too frightened to reveal her connection to this man now. She jerked her wrist again. "Jason, I beg of you. Please—"

"Not one more word unless you tell me the truth."

"Please loosen your grip. You are hurting me."

He lowered his voice as his grip tightened. "If you do feel pain, it is no less than you deserve."

She now feared all of the blood supply to her hand was being cut off. "I have done nothing to deserve this."

"Tell me. Now."

Her wrist was throbbing. Cold sweat formed on her brow. "Jason, please."

His gaze remained as hard as his hold on her wrist. "You're keeping something from me. I won't have that."

Just as a fresh wave of panic began to roll forward, she blurted, "Perhaps he is looking at me only because I am sitting by your side? You seem to know him better than I."

"Don't take me for a fool."

"I don't." Sparks of pain ran along her arm. Soon she would not be able to prevent tears from running down her cheeks. "Jason, people are watching."

However, it was doubtful that he heard her. He seemed to only be concerned with her patron's approach.

And her patron, Mr. Marks, was winding his way through the maze of chairs and tables with such a look of fury that Lydia feared the man was in danger of harming anyone in his path.

As he drew closer, Jason lurched to his feet, taking her with him since he was still clutching her wrist. She gasped as he pulled her in such a way she feared her wrist might break.

"Jason, please!"

At last, Jason released her. Waves of dizziness coursed through her as she attempted to right herself.

He stepped back, the clumsy movement shaking his chair and, consequently, the table. The cups and saucers clattered with the motion.

Crying out in alarm, she leaned down, attempting to still the fine china, but her shaking hands proved ineffectual. She'd hardly touched the teapot before it toppled.

Sinking into her chair, she watched in horrified dismay as the beautiful china piece fell to its side. "Oh!" she exclaimed, rather unnecessarily, all things considered.

Hot tea spilled out, some of it splashing onto her hands and arm. Startled by what had happened as much as her pain, she cried out.

"Silence," Jason said, hissing.

The tears that had formed earlier now fell, though she wasn't even sure what was more painful—the burn, the bruises, or her fiancé's terrible glare.

But before Lydia knew what she was about, she was pulled up into someone's arms. She landed in his warm embrace with a desperate *umph*.

She was confused and hurting. Feeling off-kilter and terribly frightened. And for a few seconds, the only thing she was aware of was the fact that no one was yelling at her, glaring at her, bruising her wrist, or causing hot tea to splash on her person.

Suddenly, all she felt was calm and secure. And that was such a welcome change, so very, very needed, that she did the unthinkable. She looked up at her rescuer in wonder.

"Easy now," a deep voice whispered into her neck as one of his arms carefully supported her while the other gently patted her back. "Everything is all right now, Lydia."

Nothing was all right. Her patron was holding her too close, too secure, and far too intimately. Her circumstances had certainly not just gotten better.

"You," she said in wonder. Even though what was happening made no sense.

CHAPTER 3

Lydia stared into his eyes, eyes that she'd only viewed from a distance but now was startled to see were not brown but a dark blue.

They were focused directly on her. As if there were not another person in the room.

"Me," he replied at last. His voice was thick, hoarse. "Don't worry, Miss Bancroft. I won't hurt you."

Instinctively, she believed him. For too long—ever since her father had passed away—she'd felt as if she'd been cast adrift. She'd been lonely and anxious, burdened by the knowledge that she had to obtain a wealthy husband to save her mother.

She'd been stumbling and fumbling through society's parties and events. For someone who had only felt comfortable within the pages of her books, she'd felt as lost as one of the German immigrants in the city.

But then she remembered where she was. She pulled away. "Please forgive me."

Her patron—Mr. Marks—released her without a moment's resistance. When she was free of his embrace, he guided her to another table a few feet from where she'd been sitting with Jason.

"Miss Bancroft, take this chair before you fall down." After he helped her sit, he pulled over the chair to her right and sat down as well.

Ignoring Jason, who was standing just a few feet away and breathing heavily, Mr. Marks reached for the arm whose wrist Jason had gripped so tightly. "We need to remove this glove immediately. Hot tea splashed on both of your hands, but I think the majority went on your right." His expression was hard as he gestured to one of the attendants now hovering around them. "Bridget, go fetch me a bowl of cool water and some fresh linens."

"Of course, Mr. Marks."

Lydia couldn't help herself. She remained half frozen, staring at this man who had come to her rescue and now seemed in no hurry to leave her side.

She was confused by his words and actions—after all, he'd spent the majority of the past year never saying as much as good afternoon to her. She stared at him instead of beginning the laborious task of unbuttoning her glove.

But rather than becoming impatient, he merely paused, his hand resting in midair. "Let me help you." As if her bones were as fragile as a bird's, he gently turned her hand over and began deftly unbuttoning her glove. "Tell me if I hurt you," he murmured, so low she wondered if she'd even imagined his words.

"Lydia," Jason blurted. "Come here. We are leaving."

With a jerk, Lydia looked up at her fiancé, who had stepped closer. He was now looming over her like a circling bird of prey.

Had she really forgotten Jason for a brief moment?

She inhaled, waiting to feel a rush of shame, wanting to feel as if she had a choice in the matter. But instead, only resignation coursed through her. Her mother needed this match. She had no choice. "Yes, Jason."

"I think not," Mr. Marks replied, stilling her movements. He didn't clutch her hand. Instead, he allowed it to rest on the table, but his presence was so powerful she felt caught in his embrace all over again.

"She is no concern of yours, Marks," Jason said through clenched teeth.

The man at her side turned to coolly stare up at him.

"I believe otherwise. It is obvious Miss Bancroft needs immediate attention."

"If she is actually injured, I will see to her needs. Help will not come from you." With a look of distaste, Jason added, "Never speak to her again."

"Or what? What will you do to me?" Mr. Marks' eyes fairly glittered. Why, he looked almost eager for a fight!

Fire lit Jason's gaze, but he said nothing as Mr. Marks turned his attention back to her glove.

And in that moment Lydia realized it was not hatred—jealous or otherwise—Jason felt toward Mr. Marks. It was fear.

"You may leave," her patron said to Jason, without even once glancing his way. "I will see her home."

Jason straightened his shoulders and narrowed his eyes. "Lydia, it is plain to see that you *do* know this man. You have been lying to me." Lydia's wrist was still throbbing, now from the burns as well as Jason's harsh grip. The rest of her felt numb and at a loss, and she didn't know what was happening between these two men.

Gazing at her patron, she shook her head. "No. I told you the truth, Jason. I have seen him before, but we have never actually met. We have never even spoken. I never knew his name."

"That means nothing. You have been playing me."

She felt Mr. Marks' body tighten beside her. "Avondale, I must ask that you desist with this tirade."

"Lydia, do as I say. Now," Jason barked.

Lydia knew she should stand up. She should follow Jason wherever he went. But if she did, he could hurt her again.

"Remain seated, Miss Bancroft. I will see to your injuries and then have someone escort you home. No harm will come to you."

It seemed as if her body knew something her mind hadn't yet grasped. She would be safe with him. She wouldn't be hurt. And so before she could think of what consequences her words would bring, she made her decision. It was rash. It would not be without consequences. But she could no more go to Jason's side than sprout wings and fly.

Looking her patron directly in the eye, she nodded. "All right."

"If you remain by his side, I will withdraw my suit," Jason warned.

"I understand." She would survive her mother's displeasure somehow.

Pure venom entered Jason's face. "No, I am quite sure you do not." He turned away, leaving her feeling as if her whole world had just turned upside down. Yet, for some reason, she'd had no earthly will to try to right it.

"Give me your hand once more, Miss Bancroft," Mr. Marks said.

Her mouth dry, she did as he asked. Then silently watched as he undressed her arm, deftly loosening the long row of buttons on her glove, one by one.

Feeling, as he did, that she was not only relinquishing herself to his aid but that she was allowing her whole life to change.

It didn't make sense. It wasn't logical. But for the first time in memory, she didn't care.

Not one bit.

CHAPTER 4

CHICAGO TIMES-COURIER

From October 1893

Reported by Benson Gage

Though many miraculous inventions have illuminated both our White City and Prairie Avenue, the streets surrounding Camp Creek Alley remain virtually the same. Few homes have plumbing, the streets are still filled with refuse, and the newfangled elevated train runs nowhere near the area. All this means that once a person discovers this place, virtually anything can happen, and it often does.

Sebastian Marks had quite a bit of practice removing select items of women's clothing. He'd even helped ladies remove their gloves a time or two.

But nothing in his experience had prepared him for what he was doing at the moment. His librarian was staring at him through lopsided spectacles, holding herself so still that he feared the slightest movement could threaten to break her in two.

A sixth sense told him that her discomfort had little to do with the fact that he was disrobing her gloved hand in the middle of the Hartman Hotel. Instead, she was trembling from the shock of being publicly abused by Jason Avondale.

Sebastian was torn between wanting to continue what he was doing and leaving her to her own devices while he beat Avondale to a bloody pulp.

The latter choice did have much in its favor. But of course, if he did that, he would suffer the loss of her company.

She trembled under his attentions, and once again he was torn between wishing he could hold her on his lap and comfort her or pick her up and take her to the nearest physician.

Instead, he did neither, simply continued the painstaking exercise of removing one wet kid glove from a very delicate-looking hand.

When at last he pulled the offending item away, she moaned under her breath. And he attempted to control a temper he hadn't tried to control in a very long time.

Her wrist was swollen and already black-and-blue from Avondale's harsh treatment. Above it, on the other side, her knuckles were bright red from the scalding tea. Faint blisters were already starting to form.

As she stared down at her injuries, she paled even further.

"Bridget?" he barked, belatedly realizing that he was letting his worry over Lydia become noticeable. "Where is that water?"

"Right here, sir."

He looked up to see his favorite employee standing at attention next to his side.

"I brought you a bowl of cool water, and towels, sir," she said after she was sure she had his attention. "I got you some ice too. In case you would be needin' it."

"Yes. That was a good idea. Thank you."

After flashing a pleased smile, Bridget set down the items, then stepped back. Once again, Sebastian was pleased that he'd hired Bridget to be his personal maid at the Hartman. He doubted even the experienced waitstaff in the restaurant could attend to him so well. He certainly didn't trust anyone else like he did her.

And he didn't need to wonder at her being in the lobby just when he needed her. It was her job to be available.

Turning back to Lydia, who was still sitting rather motionless, he gentled his voice. "Miss Bancroft, this should help. Give me your hand."

When she merely stared at him wide eyed through her lenses, he held out his hand, silently willing for Lydia to place her palm on his so he could see to her injuries.

But of course she did nothing of the sort.

He lifted his head to meet those completely striking pale-blue eyes. She didn't move.

Growing concerned that she was suffering from shock, Sebastian leaned closer. "Let me help you bathe your hand, my dear. The cool water will ease your pain."

It was his endearment, perhaps, that made her blink, then stare at him in surprise. "Thank you, but I can take care of this."

"Not very well, I wouldn't think. It's hard to do almost anything with only one hand."

"What?" After examining the shallow china bowl, cup of ice chips, and pair of towels, she blinked again. "Oh, perhaps you are right."

"I know I am. Hand, please?" he asked again, employing a tone he didn't even know he was capable of.

Without another moment's hesitation, she rested her palm in his. After he placed some ice chips on the towel and rested her wrist on it, he dipped the second cloth into the cool water, then bathed her red knuckles with it.

"This should help, though I fear you will be in some pain for the next day or two," he said.

"Yes." She closed her eyes then. Seconds later, a lone tear traipsed down, sliding under her glasses, at last stilling on her cheekbone.

Even though until this day he'd only known her from a distance, the sight of her tears hit him hard. He hated to see her cry. Hated the thought of anyone bringing her to tears.

He picked up another ice chip and ran it across her delicate skin. She flinched.

"Forgive me. I'll attempt to be gentler."

Behind him, he felt rather than heard Bridget inhale. He ignored her. Dampening the cloth, he smoothed it over the burns marking Lydia's blistered knuckles.

When she flinched again, he wished for the first time in his life that he could take someone else's pain. "Easy now, Miss Bancroft," he murmured. "This will help. I promise."

She lifted those remarkable eyes up to his. "How did you happen to be here?"

"You've seen me leave your library a time or two. It just so happens I sometimes visit other places."

Color splotched her cheeks. "I didn't mean that." She cleared her throat. "I mean, how did you happen to be here, at this hotel this afternoon? It feels quite coincidental."

"Not really. I live here."

"I wasn't aware a person could live in a hotel."

"It's possible. It's amazing what money allows a person to do," he said, joking.

But she didn't catch the jest. Instead, she continued to stare at him curiously. So much so that he was inclined to tell her his whole history. Almost.

Of how he'd grown up knowing his mother was forced to work as a prostitute to feed him. And how he'd been lucky to at least have a mattress on the floor to sleep on.

How he'd always yearned for a clean place to lay his head at night. How only the hotel enabled him to have that cleanliness but allowed him to keep his distance from most.

"Do you like living here?" She appeared to be grasping their conversation like a lifeline.

Against his better judgment, he let her. "I do."

She would never know it, but he usually took great pains to keep his unusual residence something of a secret. He slept better knowing that the majority of Chicago's citizens didn't realize the owner of the Silver Grotto lived at the top of the most fashionable hotel in the city.

"So Jason was wrong, of course," Lydia said. "You weren't here for me."

"He was indeed wrong." Because his living arrangements were taking her mind from her injuries, he continued. "Every once in a while, I loiter in the lobby." He shrugged. "It's a bad habit."

Again, he felt Bridget's amusement behind him.

He supposed it couldn't be helped. His life was a study in contrasts, of haves and have-nots. And though he'd tried his best to keep himself from getting to know Lydia Bancroft, it seemed inevitable. He wanted to know her. Just as important, he wanted her to know him.

At least the good parts.

Seeking to put Lydia more at ease, he said, "Now, if I had known you were going to be taking tea in the lobby, I would have taken great pains to be here just so our paths would cross again."

As he'd hoped, appreciation for his quip lit her eyes. "And here I was beginning to wonder if you even spoke."

"It's common knowledge that one should stay quiet in the reading room."

"I've always believed you took that to extremes. Conversation is allowed, of course—though primarily in whispers."

"I have had no need for conversation there. I visit for the books."

"Oh, I know, Mr. Marks. It's obvious that you are a bibliophile."

Suddenly, he felt curiously stripped bare. He'd held his efforts to learn close to his vest. From the time one of his mother's men spent an afternoon teaching him the basics of reading, Sebastian had devoured the written word the way he imagined other children devoured porridge.

And, little by little, he'd indeed worked on making himself into the person he wished to be. Austen and Brontë and Wilde taught him to speak. Dickens taught him about ills . . . and about what he had a hope of being.

Even the Bible had been utilized. He'd been a student of Jacob and Isaiah and Peter and Christ. The Bible with the God he occasionally thought to thank for any good that came his way.

In short, he'd read everything he could get from the library and attempted to glean as much as he could from the best of it.

But his self-taught education was never a thing of beauty or pride, for he now knew it contrasted sharply alongside the life that benefited real gentlemen.

That education was also his closely guarded secret. So much so, he knew he'd rather be stripped bare in this hotel lobby than be forced to admit how all of his learning had come from a poor boy's desire to become something he'd only witnessed in printed pages.

It wasn't his naked body that he feared showing—Lord knew, living on the streets, a man lost any hope or thought of modesty. Instead, it was his soul that he dare not reveal. That was something he feared could be far more easily shattered.

And even more easily ruined.

As if she sensed his dark thoughts, Lydia cleared her throat. "Mr. Marks, I believe my hand feels better now."

Looking down, he realized that he'd been unconsciously skimming his rough fingers along the delicate skin of her hand. "Are you sure?"

She looked down at the small bowl.

He raised his voice. "Bridget, did you think to bring a dry cloth?"

"Of course, sir." She handed him a neatly folded square of white linen.

With care, Sebastian lifted Lydia's hand from the bowl and patted it dry. Then he held her hand between the two of his and examined it carefully. "I think the swelling has eased, but you're going to need to keep your glove off the rest of today."

"Yes." She bit her lip. "Perhaps as I go home, I'll be able to keep it covered by my cloak and scarf. Then no one will notice I am not dressed properly."

He wanted to bark at her, say that it didn't matter one lick how people perceived her, but he refrained. It wasn't his place. Instead, he merely released her hand when she lightly tugged.

Immediately, he felt a loss.

After meeting his gaze again, color flooded her cheeks. "Well, thank you for your, um, care. However, I should be on my way now."

His reply was interrupted by her stomach growling. Behind him Bridget chuckled.

Lydia looked as if she'd just committed a mortal sin. "Please forgive me. I'm usually not so rude."

"Perhaps you're usually not so hungry? Miss Bancroft, please don't leave just yet. I believe Mr. Avondale never fed you. Allow me to see to your tea."

She turned to her old table. But of course the trays, soiled table-cloth, and cart were long gone. The Hartman Hotel's regular staff was nothing if not efficient. "I'm afraid the tea service is gone. I'll be fine. I'll eat something at home."

"Nonsense. It's no trouble to bring it out again." At least, it wouldn't be for him. "Bridget, remove these items and please bring Miss Bancroft a plate of tea sandwiches."

"Of course, Mr. Marks."

After picking up the bowl, cup, and towels, Bridget slipped out of sight.

Lydia shifted and placed her injured hand over her left one in her lap. "I honestly can't believe everything that happened here this after-noon. It's been very irregular."

He took care to keep his voice low and even. Desultory, as if they were discussing the weather. "Does Avondale treat you that way often?"

"What way?"

"Roughly manhandling you."

She averted her eyes. "That? Oh, no."

"You're sure?" Something in her voice didn't ring true.

"Oh, yes. Of course, I suppose we haven't found ourselves in many different situations yet. And this, um, was our first engagement without a chaperone," she said, practically tripping over her words. "But never before has he acted so, well, autocratic. I'm not sure what brought it on."

"I was under the impression that you were affianced."

"Ah, yes. We are. I mean, we were." She bit her lip. "Actually, I'm not sure if we are currently engaged or not."

"Forgive me for my bluntness, but I must say that it is better to find out now that he would hurt you." When she stilled, staring at him through her spectacles like a frightened deer, he continued.

"Before you give him your heart," he said gently, then wondered who in Sam Hill he had become. Men didn't speak of such things.

He, without a doubt, had never even entertained such fanciful thoughts before.

He knew nothing of hearts or breaking them. He certainly had no experience with tending to delicate fiancées. No, all he knew was from what he had read.

"I suppose that is true." She paused as Bridget set a silver tray filled with éclairs, cookies, scones, and tiny sandwiches in front of them. Another servant poured a cup of tea and carefully set it on Lydia's right.

"Tea, sir?" Bridget asked.

Sebastian shook his head at the offering. He did not drink tea.

He hid a smile as Lydia stared at the tray of offerings with something that could only be described as pure bliss and anticipation. "Don't wait for me, Miss Bancroft. Please begin."

"Will you not have any?"

"No. I have recently eaten."

"I see."

"I often eat early. It's a bad habit, I'm afraid," he murmured, and then fell silent before he started talking about his meals and his private life and his club. Before he started talking about everything that was his life and everything she should never know about.

"Oh." She smiled, then after pointing to a few of the sandwiches and one plump currant-filled scone, which Bridget placed on her china plate, she picked up the sandwich and took a rather unladylike bite.

John, one of the Hartman's longtime waiters, brought Sebastian a glass of what had to be lemonade. He studied it for a moment before raising it to his lips. The cold, sour-sweet mixture curled his tongue. Setting it down, he glared at the man-servant, who shrugged in an apologetic way.

It seemed even John was trying to help Sebastian look like a regular gentleman instead of the whiskey-drinking club owner he actually was.

"I see you enjoy cold beverages," Lydia said, as she picked up her second sandwich.

Gin and bourbon could be served cold. "I do."

"I suppose most men do."

Most men he knew did, indeed, enjoy spirits served cold. "Yes," he murmured as he watched her finish off a second delicate sandwich, then move to a thin watercress and turkey with gusto.

When she paused for breath, she said, "So, what book has taken your interest of late?"

He leaned back, far more comfortable talking about books than about anything of a personal nature. "I'm finding *The Wrecker* to be fascinating."

He suppressed a smile as well. If Miss Bancroft was going to pretend she didn't, without fail, safeguard his current selection at the reading room until his return, so would he.

A line formed between her brows. "Robert Louis Stevenson's works are tremendously popular. *The Wrecker* is reputed to be very exciting."

"So far, yes, I am finding it to be exciting as well."

"You should check it out, Mr. Marks, instead of simply reading books when you're in the library. Then you won't have to worry about it being there next time you stop in."

As though he had to worry now.

"I won't worry." He went to the library to read for pleasure, to lose himself in the allure of printed pages without anyone in his world taking note. Of late, he had also gone there to watch her. It seemed the stories told in the books were only part of the lending library's allure.

She frowned as she picked up a chocolate éclair. "Surely you didn't finish *The Wrecker* already? It's a rather large tome."

She knew very well he had only started reading the book a week ago, the day she'd spilled a stack of books all over the floor.

"If it isn't there, I'll make do with something else."

"But that makes no sense."

"Many things don't make sense, Miss Bancroft. But that doesn't mean they aren't done."

"I suppose you're right about that."

He watched her lean back and pop another éclair into her mouth, her expression turning to bliss as the custard and chocolate no doubt came in contact with her taste buds.

Just as his thoughts turned in that inappropriate direction, Vincent Hunt approached. He wore a determined expression, much the way he looked around three in the morning when they were closing the gambling for the night.

When he noticed Sebastian was not seated alone, Hunt looked completely brought up short. "Um, excuse me, sir. Miss."

"What is it, Hunt?"

"You asked me to get you if we heard from a, um, specific client. He arrived just minutes ago."

"Very good." He got to his feet, thinking that whatever had just come up had come at an opportune time. He was becoming entirely too comfortable with the young lady sitting across from him. "I'd best go see to that."

Lydia set the cup she'd just raised to her lips back down. Looking from him to Vincent, she said, "It is time for you to go?"

"I'm afraid I must."

Carefully, she folded her napkin and set it next to her plate. "I had better go as well."

"Forgive me. I seem to have lost my manners." While Hunt stared at him like he was a stranger, Sebastian continued, "Miss Bancroft, may I present my assistant, Mr. Vincent Hunt. Vincent, this is Miss Lydia Bancroft."

Hunt gave a small bow. "Miss Bancroft, a pleasure."

She inclined her head. "How do you do, Mr. Hunt."

"I was going to ask my maid, Bridget, but now that he's here, Mr. Hunt is going to escort you home."

Her blue eyes widened. "There is no need. I will be fine on my own."

"Definitely not. The streets aren't safe for young ladies like you."

"I don't think I will have any worries."

"Pray, don't tell me that you have already forgotten the fate of two ladies at the hands of the Slasher," he bit out.

Before his eyes, Lydia paled. "I . . . I haven't forgotten."

Next to him, Hunt groaned, reminding Sebastian that he'd just made a terrible faux pas.

Sebastian clamped down on the inside of his lip. "Forgive me. I, um, forget myself and my company from time to time."

"You forget your company?"

Now she was thinking that he hadn't even been thinking about her. "Never mind. Please do accept Hunt's escort."

"It would be my honor, miss."

"All right, then. Thank you, Mr. Hunt." She smiled softly. "And Mr. Marks, thank you for the tea, and for your assistance earlier. I am indebted."

The reminder drew his eyes to her bare right hand. "Please take care of your wrist and hand. If you have any need of assistance with . . . that, uh, problem, you need only leave a message for me here."

"Thank you."

He had to get out of there. He had to put as much space as possible between him and her innocence. "Hunt, I need a moment."

"Yes, sir."

Sebastian motioned for Bridget to stay near Lydia before leading Hunt to a shadowed alcove near the curved staircase. The moment they stopped, Vincent became all business.

"Sir, would you like to know about the problem? It seems Jeffrey Galvin has returned. You said if he did—"

"I'll deal with him when I get to the Grotto. I have something else you need to address."

"Sir?"

"You will escort Miss Bancroft all the way to her door," he ordered.

"Yes, sir."

"You will make sure she gets inside safely, and take special care to notice if she is favoring her right hand more than usual."

"Her hand?"

"She had a nasty altercation with a gentleman here. I put an end to it." At least he hoped so. And he saw no need to tell Hunt Lydia had had any association with the likes of Avondale.

"Anything else?"

"Yes. No matter what, you do not tell her anything about my line of work. Do you understand?"

Hunt's expression continued to remain impassive. "Yes, sir."

Just to make sure, he added, "Nothing about the Silver Grotto. Ladies like her don't know places like mine exist."

"Yes, sir. Anything else?"

Sebastian noticed a thread of hope in his voice. It was suddenly obvious to him that his assistant was finding this whole situation to be especially amusing. "Nothing else."

"Yes, sir."

Then, because he didn't dare speak to her again, he turned and walked up the stairs. But, perversely, he only waited at the edge of the landing. He wanted to watch her for just a little while longer. He wanted to see if she was in pain from Avondale's rough handling of her.

But all he did was watch Hunt very properly help her to her feet, offer his arm after helping her wrap her cloak around her shoulders, then smile at her softly while he walked her outside. Sebastian could see them through a window as they stopped for a moment on the sidewalk.

Lydia seemed to be perfectly at ease with him. Whatever Vincent Hunt was saying, it was everything proper—though, perhaps, he was standing just a tad too close and his fingers had brushed her shoulders a bit too intimately?

Sebastian felt the unfamiliar, curious grip of jealousy twist inside of him as he saw Lydia smile at Vincent before crossing the street by his side.

Irritated with himself, irritated with all of it, he stormed back down the stairs, intent on sliding out the back door of the hotel and going to his club.

He certainly hoped whatever was waiting for him was bad enough to use his fists. If he was lucky, perhaps a fight had broken out. It had been months since he'd worked up a sweat in a good fight.

"Excuse me, Mr. Marks?"

He paused, watching Bridget trot toward him, her uniform and brown hair tidy as usual. "Miss Bancroft forgot this." She held out one long white kid glove. Lydia's glove that he himself had peeled from her wrist. "Would you like me to try to catch Mr. Hunt and Miss Bancroft? I doubt they've gotten too far yet."

"No, don't bother."

"All right. Um, would you rather I leave it with the concierge?"

"No." He snatched it from her hand. "I'll make sure this is returned to her."

"Oh. Well then, very good, sir." She gave a small curtsy.

He stuffed the glove in his pocket. As he was walking toward the door, the persnickety proprietor of the hotel stopped him. "I trust everything was to your liking, sir?"

Nothing had been to his liking. "Good enough."

"Then if you would please tell us how to bill you for the tea?"

"You know you simply send the receipt to Hunt."

"No, sir. I mean the first tea." The man waved a cautious hand in the direction of the first table, where Lydia had been sitting with Avondale.

"Do you mean to tell me Avondale left without paying?"

"Regrettably, yes."

Why should he have been surprised? "Give that receipt to Hunt as well."

"Very good, sir."

At long last, Sebastian exited the Hartman Hotel, turned right, and descended into the back alleys. Fifteen minutes later, he was in sight of the Silver Grotto, and the streets were shadowed and narrow, smelling of trash and unwashed bodies.

The moment he strode through the tall, heavy, silver-plated doors, he gestured to Parker, his man standing guard at the entrance. "Hunt said Jeffrey Galvin is here. Where will I find him?"

"He left, sir. I suspect he knew Hunt went for you."

"Just as well. I'm in no mood to deliver my decision tonight. Find me a shot of gin. Keep it neat."

"Of course, Mr. Marks."

Feeling better already, Sebastian looked around, happy to see the bar starting to fill with customers.

Below, his workers were counting the hours until the sun set, when they'd open the doors to the basement gambling tables.

Here, Sebastian felt at home. He understood what was expected. He knew what should happen and what should not.

Most especially, there wasn't an auburn-haired librarian in the vicinity wanting to discuss books, enjoy the taste of éclairs, or who assumed he was a far better man than everyone here knew he was.

CHAPTER 5

After observing Mr. Hunt escort the librarian out the front door like she was made up of spun glass, then watching her employer stalk out the back door of the hotel like a swarm of bees was pursuing him, Bridget O'Connell slipped through one of the lobby's unmarked doors and into the servants' hall. As she took a deep breath and looked around, Bridget felt like Alice stepping through the looking glass.

Instead of being surrounded by priceless artwork and beautifully crafted furniture, she was face-to-face with painted brick, exposed pipes, utilitarian cabinets, and metal shelving. Instead of genteel voices speaking in well-modulated tones, she heard the rushing of feet and the barking orders of the chefs and head of housekeeping.

"Is *he* gone?" Harold, one of the longtime waitstaff, paused next to her, a tray of china cups and saucers in his hands.

Bridget knew the waiter was referring to Mr. Marks. All the hotel staff was slightly in awe of him, and usually only referred to him as *he* or *him.*

"Yes. Just."

He winked. "So you can take a few minutes rest now."

Bridget smiled. "Not likely. I've got other things to do."

Harold leaned forward, seemingly oblivious that he was holding a heavy tray. "Care to tell me what you're going to be doing?"

"You know I can't." She smiled when she spoke, hoping that smile would take the sting out of her words. It was a long-running joke that she was never quite a part of the other servants at the Hartman Hotel. "But I wish you luck with the rest of tea service."

He rolled his eyes. "Ever since the fair ended in October, we're getting fewer foreigners in the restaurant and a whole lot more cranky, bored ladies. Never thought I'd say it, but I'd give my right eyetooth to serve supper to another delegation from Germany or Austria." A dimple formed in his cheek. "They, at least, were lively."

"If I see any Germans out and about, I'll send them your way."

"Just make sure they tip." Harold winked again before lighting off, his smooth, easy glide making his job look far easier than it was. She'd seen some new workers still manage to make a racket when they were carrying half that much.

After nodding in the direction of two maids carrying silver candelabras, Bridget climbed three flights to the top floor, a good part of which was Mr. Marks' private quarters. After passing through another door, she was standing on a thick carpet runner and surrounded by gilt-framed mirrors. Taking care to step lively, she strode down the hall. Just as she rounded the corner, she spied Mabel and Gwen waiting for her.

She braced herself for their company.

By all accounts, she should consider them friends. And they were her friends, to a degree. However, her past and circumstances were far different from theirs. And her secrets kept her from lowering her guard too much around them. She had secrets that would shame her if revealed.

And nowhere else in the world would she feel as safe as her rather solitary existence as Mr. Marks' personal maid.

But still she pretended to be more open than she was.

"Hi, girls."

"Hi, yerself," Mabel replied with a saucy smile. "About time you came upstairs."

"Why were you waiting for me? Did you need something?"

"Only news," Gwen said. "We heard *he* had you attending him down in the lobby this afternoon."

She nodded. "Yes, Mr. Marks did."

"Why did you have to be there?" Mabel asked. "There's plenty of waiters to serve him tea."

"Well, you know . . ."

"No, I really don't," Gwen pressed. "Why did he need you there?" A brash grin played on her lips. "Or was it your idea?" she mused. "Bridget O'Connell, were you not able to keep yerself away from the illustrious Mr. Marks?"

"Hardly that," she said quickly, becoming flustered. "Mr. Marks asked me to fetch and carry for him. That is all."

"It weren't all," Mabel said with a pointed look. "I looked down from the stairwell and saw him tending to that poor, lost-looking lady. Who was she? She don't look near glamorous enough to be his sweetheart."

Bridget had seen her boss squire a number of young ladies about, but never one so plain as Miss Bancroft. Mr. Marks had been focused completely on the librarian though. And Bridget had felt more than a bit sorry for her, seeing that she was engaged to none other than Jason Avondale. Bridget knew his penchant for brutality far too well.

However, though it was on the tip of Bridget's tongue to correct Mabel's assumption, she did not.

The reason she had been in Mr. Marks' employ for two years was that she didn't divulge his secrets. Not ever. She did not comment on anything he did. Not even things he did in broad daylight.

"What are you two doing up here anyway?" She eyed the pair curiously. "I already cleaned Mr. Marks' suite."

"We were waiting for you. Obviously," Gwen said.

A mite cheekily, Bridget thought.

"I was telling Mabel here, if you have spare time, you always come up here. We have a couple of hours off, so we thought you might want to go out for a bit."

Though a part of her was warmed by the invitation, she didn't dare take them up on it. She would lose her job if Mr. Marks came back, needed something, and she wasn't available to procure it for him.

"I'm afraid I cannot. I need to iron Mr. Marks' shirts."

Mabel frowned. "Why don't he send them to the laundry? The girls do everyone else's."

At that moment another maid found the two women, asking about their afternoon plans. That gave Bridget time to think before answering—or evading—Mabel's question.

But that was the difference, Bridget reflected. Mr. Marks didn't want anything of his being touched by everyone else. He demanded privacy for both his personal life and his belongings.

As the maids' chatter became more animated, now focusing on a certain boot boy Bridget had never heard of, Bridget let her mind settle on her employer.

Just like it usually did.

Mr. Marks was not like anyone else. From the moment she'd walked into his office, begging for a job in his private club, and he'd stared at her in silence, she'd known that.

Especially since all he'd done was glare at her when he'd given her bedraggled, hungry self an audience and heard her whisper that she'd even be willing to work among the gentlemen gamblers.

She'd been sure he was about to send her on her way. And she knew when he did she was either going to be forced to go somewhere worse than the Silver Grotto or go to the workhouse. Tears had flooded her eyes.

He noticed. Then he did the most curious thing. He snapped his fingers.

Bridget still remembered how she'd jumped at the sound. But barely a second later, out came Vincent Hunt from a hidden panel in Mr. Marks' office. She later learned that Vincent Hunt was Mr. Marks' very own personal assistant and club manager.

"Take Miss O'Connell to the Hartman," he'd directed. "Once there, take her to the washroom in my suite."

"Um—" She'd attempted to interrupt.

He'd ignored her. "While she is bathing, locate some decent clothes for her."

Hunt hadn't looked dismayed by the request in the slightest. "Any special color or design, sir?"

"I don't care." Then, when he'd stared at Bridget with her brown hair and brown eyes, he reconsidered. "Maybe something in blue or green?"

"Green, sir?"

"Green. Like the meadow. Or violet."

"Yes, sir," Mr. Hunt had replied.

An awful, sick feeling had settled in her stomach when she'd heard Mr. Marks' wishes. She realized that not only did he plan to use her for his own base desires, he wanted to make sure she was clean before he touched her. She'd been more ashamed than she could ever remember.

Still ignoring her standing in front of him, Hunt asked, "What do you want me to do after I get her outfitted, sir?"

"Order her some food." Mr. Marks had looked her over like she'd been a flea-bitten dog. And a half-starved one at that. "See that she eats."

Mr. Hunt had nodded. "Of course."

Mr. Marks had then glared at her. "The skin under your eyes looks almost bruised. Have you slept?"

She hadn't known whether to apologize about her haggard appearance or merely answer. She opted to simply answer him honestly. "Not recently, sir."

"Get some rest then. You may have use of my private sitting room."

She was suddenly very, very confused. "Where do you want me to await you?" Deciding to stop pretending he saw her as anything but a fallen woman, she swallowed. "Do you want me to await you in your bed? Sir?"

His eyebrows had risen, and Mr. Hunt had uttered a noise that had sounded suspiciously like he was choking on his own tongue.

She'd felt her body flush with embarrassment but held her head high. After all, she knew her life would be forever changed when she walked through the doors of the Silver Grotto. Though she feared the future, it sounded as if she was going to have the opportunity to bathe, eat, and wear clean clothes for the first time in a long while.

Her life had been very hard after her employer had seen her slap Mr. Avondale when he tried to force his attentions on her. Rather than hold the cad accountable, Mr. Pinter had fired her without references.

She was smart enough—and desperate enough—to make sure she didn't lose a bath, clothes, and food right away.

But when Mr. Marks at last spoke, his voice was as gentle as if he were coaxing a newborn foal to its feet.

"Miss O'Connell, I beg your pardon. I am hiring you to be my personal maid at the Hartman Hotel, not to be my paramour. Hunt will secure your own room at the hotel. I simply wanted to go over my expectations after you had bathed, eaten, and rested in my suite until Hunt can make that arrangement. But I see we should begin here."

"Oh." She was so surprised, she couldn't think of another word to say.

"You will find I am not a difficult taskmaster as long as you adhere to my three basic tenets." Looking her over, he continued. "I don't put up with liars, thieves, or gossips."

"Yes, sir."

"That means you will not steal from me."

"No, sir."

"You will not make up stories about why you are late for work."

"I will not be late."

Impatiently, he brushed off her words. "If something spills, a dish breaks, a button gets lost and you are unable to replace it, tell me."

"Those things won't happen." She would make sure of it. "I was an excellent ladies' maid for the Pinter family."

"Quiet now," Mr. Hunt ordered from behind her back.

Embarrassed by her inability to refrain from blurting every little thing that popped into her head, she straightened and attempted to heed Mr. Hunt's advice as her new employer continued on.

"To continue, I am willing to hire you because I am weary of the hotel maids and attendants discussing my habits." Cool, dark indigo eyes met her own. "Do you feel you can avoid that, Miss O'Connell? Can you keep my secrets?"

His voice was silky. Filled with dreams of everything she hoped to have and hinting of things she'd never imagined. And in that moment, she knew she'd do whatever it took to keep this job. She would be fiercely loyal to one man and one man only. To Mr. Sebastian Marks.

She'd nodded slowly.

And in that quiet nod, his eyes had lit up with something that looked much like happiness. "Very well. You may go now. Hunt will discuss your pay and sleeping arrangements after you have an opportunity to bathe and eat and rest. On my couch," he added with the faintest of smiles.

"Yes, sir. Thank you very much."

Picking up a thick ledger, he nodded. It was obvious that to him, their discussion was over. But she hadn't been able to simply leave.

"Mr. Marks? I'm sorry. But, if I may?"

"Yes?" Already his voice was impatient.

"Why?" When his stare turned blank, she swallowed and forced herself to continue. "I mean, sir, um, why did you decide to have me be your servant instead of working in your club?" Her cheeks heated. Was she really such a ninny that she couldn't even say the word *prostitute*?

A muscle in his cheek twinged. "I rarely explain myself, Miss O'Connell."

"Oh. Um—"

"But even if I did have women working, as you say, in my club—which, unlike Mr. Vlas at Bear and Bull, I do *not*—I think you would be better suited to work for me in the capacity of a personal maid, Miss O'Connell. I trust you agree?"

After she'd nodded, Bridget had turned and scurried out of the room. Trailing behind Mr. Vincent Hunt and his polished good looks.

When they'd stepped outside, he'd slowed so that she could walk by his side. "Well, that's over."

"I still can't believe it."

Mr. Hunt had said nothing more. Only kept his hand on her elbow in a proprietary way the whole time they weaved their way through Camp Creek Alley, turned into a maze of even more back alleys, then at last veered onto a main street.

Only when they were on Michigan Avenue and standing in the fresh air and bright light did Mr. Hunt give her an answer to her unspoken question. "Mr. Marks does this from time to time. He takes in a poor, unfortunate soul and seeks to change his or her life."

"He's a benefactor."

Mr. Hunt had smiled, though it looked rather ironic instead of amused. "He is not that, miss. He doesn't do a single thing without a goal in mind or a reason behind it." Quietly he added, "And I promise you this. If you do steal, lie, or gossip, you will be back on the streets before you can say 'Bob's yer uncle.' He doesn't offer second chances. Ever. It would serve you well to commit that to memory."

A chill had crept up her spine. "I will."

"I pray you will." He frowned as he lazily scanned her too-thin figure. "Women don't live very long when they make their living on their backs."

She shivered at his crude reminder of what she'd offered herself up for. But perhaps she should never forget how close she'd come to being one of the many women forced to live that way.

"Well, he may not be a benefactor, but he certainly saved me."

"For now, he did."

"Did he save you as well, Mr. Hunt?"

He'd looked at her then, surprise and something like a guilt-ridden sadness slipping into his expression. "No. It was too late for that."

And it was right then and there that she became infatuated. Oh, not with Mr. Sebastian Marks. He only inspired her fear and awe.

But Vincent Hunt was different.

"Bridget? Bridget!" Mabel called out, waving a meaty hand in front of her. "What's wrong with ya? You looked like you were millions of miles away."

"I'm sorry. I guess I was."

"Well, answer my question. Why does *he* insist on only you seeing to his laundry? It don't make no sense."

"It does. Perfectly," she said, as she pulled out her key ring and unlocked Mr. Marks' door. She gave a weak smile to Gwen and Mabel before waving them off.

Only when she closed it firmly behind her and bolted both it and the extra latch, did she speak. "I do his laundry so then no one will ever know anything about him. So no one who can hurt him will ever know how much of a gentleman he actually is not. I do his laundry because I promised myself I would."

Taking a deep breath, she uttered her last confession. "I do his laundry and do anything he asks because he's a better person than anyone realizes."

Silently, she added, *And because I promised myself to never forget how it had felt to be at his mercy, to be willing to let him do his worst.*

Instead, Mr. Marks had given her the best he had.

CHAPTER 6

After escorting Miss Bancroft home, Vincent climbed aboard a grip car. By his estimation, he had four hours before he needed to return to the club and act as his employer's eyes and ears for the majority of the night.

That gave him two hours to spend with Mary, then two hours to nap. Working for Mr. Marks did not allow him the luxury of more than a few hours rest at any one time.

As the grip car rattled along, stopping frequently to let people off and even more people on, Vincent made sure to remain in the back corner. There was far less chance of being pick-pocketed there. It also allowed him to observe everyone without being too obvious.

Since he'd begun working for Sebastian Marks, he'd learned a great many things. He was no longer weak nor a fool.

As the grip car swung to a stop with a shriek, another dozen or so men and women climbed aboard, bringing with them the odors of pickles and heavy perfume. A rather rotund lady next to him pressed a fine linen handkerchief to her nose.

"Aboard!" the attendant called out.

More people hopped on as everyone else crushed together, making Vincent feel like a sardine in a tin. He took care to look straight ahead and not make eye contact with anyone he was pressed against. It was best to remain aloof.

As the car started forward with a sluggish jerk, a portly gentleman with a flowing gray mustache knocked into him. "Sorry, chap," he said with a friendly smile. "Can't be helped though."

After making sure the man hadn't just picked his pocket, Vincent treated him to a cool stare.

The gentleman's eyes widened. "Beg pardon," he wheezed before looking away.

Obviously, Vincent had frightened him.

He waited for the small feeling of satisfaction that used to rise up inside him when he'd inspired fear in others. The first time it had happened, Vincent had been so shocked, he'd almost started laughing. Until he realized it wasn't him who was feared, but his illustrious employer.

But Vincent had coveted that feeling of power.

When he'd first been hired by Mr. Marks, he'd been a lonely, downtrodden individual. His wife, Irene, had fallen ill and died, and he'd had to take time off from his law office to see to the funeral. And care for his baby.

The lawyers he clerked for, however, hadn't been pleased with his absences and had promptly fired him. The loss of his job had been yet another painful blow in an already excruciating month. He'd had little money, spending most of his savings on Irene's casket, headstone, and burial fees.

And though his sister, Janet, had taken Mary in, Vincent knew it wasn't fair to ask her to watch a baby for months or even years with no pay. He'd needed to make some money, and he'd needed to make as much as he could.

Then he had remembered the lawyers talking about the Silver Grotto and the owner, a man just about everyone in the city either knew or knew about. The proprietor had a fearsome reputation. But there was something in the lawyers' voices that had made Vincent gather just enough courage to walk down Camp Creek Alley and ultimately knock on the door of the infamous club.

One thing had propelled him. Not only had they feared Sebastian Marks, they'd respected him.

Vincent had needed respect in the worst way.

He still wasn't sure why Sebastian had hired him. Vincent would guess that the man had felt sorry for him, but *pity* wasn't in Sebastian Marks' vocabulary.

If Vincent had to take a guess, it was his answer to one of the interview questions that had gotten him the job.

"You're a quiet man, Hunt," Mr. Marks had said, looking over him as if he were a strange, scientific experiment. "You've also got no experience with drink, gambling, or the men who frequent my club. What makes you think you could offer me anything I need?"

Vincent had thought about that. Thought about it hard. Finally, he answered. "I don't drink or gamble or spend my evenings in the company of men who do. That is true. But it is precisely because of those reasons that you need me."

Mr. Marks' eyes had narrowed. "Why is that?"

"You need someone who will not be tempted by vices. You need someone you can trust."

"And you feel I'm going to be able to trust a man like you?" His voice had been thick with sarcasm.

Marks' disdain had hurt. At once, Vincent realized he wasn't very strong, and he wasn't very confident around men who used their muscles to get their way. He felt weak and useless.

But then he'd remembered what really mattered in life. "I don't steal or cheat, sir. I don't lie."

For the first time a spark of interest appeared in his eyes. "Ever?"

"Never. I can also keep secrets. I will keep your secrets, sir. If you are ever made aware that people are gossiping about you, you will know beyond a doubt that whatever rumor is circulating didn't begin with me."

Suddenly, Mr. Marks had looked at him with a spark of approval. "You're hired, Hunt." He then named a weekly pay that was more than Vincent had made working at the law office for a whole month.

Vincent had walked out of the club feeling empowered for the first time in his life. And until lately, he'd never looked back.

With a clang and a jerk, the car stopped, bringing Vincent back to the present. And, he realized, to his stop. He quickly moved forward, hardly noticing the other passengers as they squeezed aside to get out of his way.

After the car clanged again and shot down the street, he walked the two blocks home. Only when he got to the front walkway of his modest but well-appointed brownstone did he dare let down his guard.

A window upstairs opened. "Daddy!"

His sweet girl's dark-blonde curls matched his own. But her smile was the spitting image of Irene's. "Hi, Mary. Have a care now. Don't lean out so far. You're going to fall."

She giggled. "You say that every time." She giggled again before disappearing, only to burst through the front door mere seconds later. "You're home!"

"I am." After holding out his arms so she could launch herself into them, he hugged her tight. Breathed her sweet, clean, innocent scent. Enjoyed the feel of her little-girl arms wrapping around his sides.

After giving her cheek a kiss, Vincent sat down next to her on the stoop. "Where's Aunt Janet?"

"I'm right here," Janet said from the doorway. "You say that every time too."

He gave her a pointed look over his shoulder. "I simply want to make sure you're safe."

"You're silly, Daddy," Mary said, giggling again.

"Oh? And why is that?"

"We don't have to worry about being safe," she declared in that confident way he was learning only four-year-olds could. "You're the strongest and toughest man on the whole street."

"Is that so?"

"Oh yes," she replied, looking completely serious. "Everyone says so."

He attempted to laugh. "Little Mary, you've been telling tales about your old man?"

She shook her head solemnly. "No. I only heard some of the boys on the corner talk about you."

"Oh? What did they say?"

"That no one should disrespect you."

That made him mildly uncomfortable, though he wasn't sure why. "Well, remember how Daddy works for Mr. Marks? The man at the fancy building I told you about?" When she nodded, he explained, "That's why the boys said that. It's because I work for a very important man."

Mary giggled. "That's not why, silly. The boys said if they made you mad, you'd break their knees. Or worse." She giggled again before scampering back into the house.

As Vincent felt Janet's gaze settle on him, he shrugged. "Don't know what to say about that."

"Nothing you can say, Vincent. The boys were simply stating the truth." She raised an eyebrow, pretty much daring him to deny her words.

But because he couldn't, he kept his silence. He was a lot of things now. A lot of things he'd never dreamed he'd be or had ever wanted to become. But he still wasn't a liar.

At least, not most of the time.

CHAPTER 7

CHICAGO TIMES-COURIER

January 16, 1894

Reported by Benson Gage

It seems the police have been called down to Camp Creek Alley not once but twice in the last week. The bodies of two more men were discovered outside one of the most notorious clubs. It should be noted that at the time of this publication's printing, neither body has been identified. There have also been no leads.

It seems a man can be stabbed within the bowels of Camp Creek Alley without the crime being seen or properly investigated.

Lydia couldn't help but gape as she watched Mr. Marks approach the circulation desk from across the room, two days after the disastrous tea. When his gaze flickered to hers, she quickly closed her mouth and took care to keep her own expression as calm and serene as possible. A mask, for sure.

Standing by her side, her assistant, Priscilla, didn't even attempt to act indifferent. "He's approaching! He's going to speak to us."

"Priscilla, decorum."

Immediately Priscilla buttoned her lips. Her silence lasted a full three seconds before she chattered on again. "Oh. I mean, yes, of course, Miss Bancroft."

Lydia felt her cheeks heat just as Mr. Marks stopped in front of her. Staring directly ahead only gave her a close look at his chest. It was a very fine one.

But not at all what she should be looking at.

Inch by inch she raised her chin. As she studied him, Lydia was struck yet again by how intriguing his eyes were. Dark navy blue, so dark and magnetic they seemed almost black. And framed by thick lashes. Only the faint scar near the corner of his left eye marred their beauty.

Mentally, she shook herself. Men did not have beautiful eyes. "Good afternoon, Mr. Marks."

"Miss Bancroft." His gaze settled on her lips before drifting upward again.

She shifted awkwardly. "May I be of assistance to you in some way?"

He bowed slightly. "You may. I have recently discovered that I am in need of a library card."

She almost told him that what she'd warned would come to pass had happened. *The Wrecker* had been checked out on Monday. She'd forgotten to tell Priscilla why it was in the cabinet. When Priscilla found it, she not only put it back on its shelf but let another patron have it.

But there was something in his bearing that made her keep her distance. "This is Miss Johnstone. She will be happy to help you with that."

"I think not."

"Pardon?"

"I want your assistance. No one else's."

Well, this was completely irregular. While Priscilla made little distressed sounds, Lydia nodded. The truth was that she actually did want to be the one who helped him.

Pulling out a form and a pen, she leaned toward him. "First of all, I will need some information from you."

"I have no desire to talk to you from the other side of a counter. How about we do this over coffee or tea?"

She was tempted.

But duty prevailed. "I'm sorry, I cannot leave at the moment."

"Pity." He searched the room. "At least sit with me. I would rather not give my personal information out in such a public way."

There were currently seven people in her lending library. Two ladies at a desk, one gentleman reading periodicals, another gentleman perusing a collection of works by Dickens, and the three of them.

All of that meant, of course, there really was no need for the two of them to go anywhere in private.

But she couldn't have denied his wishes even if she wanted to. "Shall we go to where you were sitting the last time you visited?"

His voice warmed. "You remember where I was sitting, Miss Bancroft?"

Unfortunately, she remembered too much about him. "It's a habit of mine. I'm, uh, particularly good at remembering people and places."

"Lead on then."

She led the way to a collection of four chairs in the far corner. They were paired, like Noah's animals, and situated across from one another. She decided to take the one closest to the wall. Instead of electing to sit across from her, in the chair he always selected, Mr.

Marks took the chair next to her, bringing with him the scent of cigars and cold weather and something that she could only assume was the smell of spirits.

She didn't mind it though. Actually, she liked his scent. He smelled masculine and solid. Tempting.

"Miss Bancroft?"

"Hmm?" His coat was dark gray and looked very fine. She wondered if it was cashmere. She knew how soft the sheep's fleece was. And how exorbitantly expensive.

"Are you going to put my words to memory?"

Only then did she realize that she had neglected to bring over the form and pen. "Forgive me. I'll be right back."

But instead of allowing her to go, he reached out and curved two fingers around her left elbow. "Not yet."

"But—"

"I will get a card. But I came here to see how you are faring. How are your hand and wrist?" He nodded to her right hand, which she'd taken to practically hiding in the folds of her skirts.

Looking down at it, she said, "It is healing."

"May I see it?"

She didn't want to put it on display. Especially not in the reading room. But they were sitting in a corner. And they weren't attracting notice. The other patrons were either perusing the stacks or had their noses in books. Even Priscilla was busy helping the two women who had just walked in.

Without a word, she placed her right hand on the armrest of her chair. It was ungloved, of course. She was also wearing one of her more fussy blouses. Its frilled and lace cuffs helped conceal the dark bruises and healing blisters on her wrist and knuckles.

Mr. Marks reached out, and with a flick of his fingers unfastened three buttons, then smoothed back the linen. It seemed he wasn't deterred by a profusion of lace in the slightest.

Then, far more gently than she would have ever given him credit for, he ran his thumb along the faint outlines of the veins on the inside of her wrist.

It was highly inappropriate. She managed to hold her tremble at bay through a force of will.

He, on the other hand, had chosen not to remain impassive. As his calloused thumb made contact with her skin, a look of true anger flashed in his eyes. His lips hardened into a thin line. The muscles in his jaw clenched. He looked ready—if not eager—to injure someone.

She didn't have to ask why. Jason's grip had been so hard and abusive that her wrist was still swollen. But more noticeable than the swelling were the four dark fingertip bruises that marred the pale skin above her wrist.

On her knuckles two unattractive scabs had formed. Remnants from the blisters caused by the scalding tea. No doubt they would leave scars.

"He hurt you terribly." His voice was low. Thick. Almost a whisper.

"It isn't so bad."

"I beg to differ. What, pray tell, did you tell your parents?"

"About this? Nothing." She pulled her hand back to her lap. "I only have my mother, and luckily, she didn't notice."

"No?"

"She doesn't, um, have time to notice such things as my wrists."

"I see. What about your maid?"

"I don't have a ladies' maid." She felt her cheeks blush as she realized she'd given far too much away. "I mean, when my father died, I'm afraid he left us in something of a difficult financial situation."

"I see."

She doubted it. He had to be the richest man she'd ever met.

Only a man of extreme wealth could afford to live in a hotel like the Hartman. "Now, may I assist you with a library card?"

"Have you heard from Avondale again?"

"No."

He fired off another question. "Did you tell your mother about the broken engagement?"

"I have not. Though I don't believe it's any concern of yours."

His dark eyes searched her own. "You aren't still contemplating marriage to him, are you?"

"I don't know. My mother needs me to marry well."

"Jason Avondale's financial situation is precarious at best."

She pulled her hand away from his. "No, he has a carriage. He belongs to the best of society."

"His life is much like the White City. Outwardly impressive while structurally unsound."

"I'm afraid I do not understand."

"Much like an earnest debutant, Avondale is merely looking the part. He was looking for an heiress."

She pushed away the thought that she, too, had pretended wealth to marry a man with money.

"How do you know this?"

"It's my business to know such things."

"What is your job? Mr. Hunt wouldn't say a word about you." She stared at him, wishing that for once she could read his mind.

"I have varied interests."

"I see." But of course, she did not.

Just as she moved to rise, he held out his hand. "One moment. I need to button you back up."

Resigning herself to his assistance, she did as he asked. But as she watched his fingers carefully fasten the edges of her sleeve, Lydia couldn't help but notice how gentle he was. "Now you may get what you need to take down my information."

She darted back to her desk, pointedly ignored Priscilla's speculative look, and then returned to his side, a quill and her notebook firmly in hand. "Name?"

"Sebastian Marks. M-a-r-k-s."

"Address?"

"The Hartman Hotel on Michigan Avenue." She waited for him to expound upon this, perhaps give her his business address. But he added nothing more.

Feeling rather foolish, she asked him her standard questions. "Do you promise to treat well any books you borrow?"

His lips twitched. "I do."

"And to return them in a timely manner?"

"I will."

"And if for some reason you lose or damage one of the books, will you promise to pay for the book to be replaced?"

A new light burned in his eyes. "I promise."

"Very well then. You may have a library card."

He stood up. "Now that that's taken care of, when are you going to get *The Wrecker* for me?"

"I am afraid it has been loaned out. It should be returned in a week or two."

"What if the person who took it does not follow the instructions to the letter?"

"I've yet to meet anyone who doesn't follow through on their library promises."

"Very well then."

"Might I suggest another novel in the meantime?"

"Such as?"

She couldn't resist teasing him. "*Tess of the d'Urbervilles?*"

As she'd hoped, he looked completely affronted. "No matter how much I may enjoy Hardy, I will not be reading that."

"We just got in Wilde's *Lord Arthur Savile's Crime and Other Stories.*"

He leaned forward, lowering his voice. "Full of men who should not have been trusted, no doubt. Tell me, Miss Bancroft, do your books whisper warnings about befriending men like me?"

Now he was surely teasing her. Clearly, he was a gentleman, no one she need rebuff, especially in the safety of a public library.

"I am certain I can be friends with patrons such as you, Mr. Marks, despite any such whispers."

He leaned back into his chair. "Good. I'll look at Wilde's book. And then, I would like to escort you home."

The last note had been so smoothly interwoven, she was sure she'd misunderstood. "Beg pardon?"

"I thought I'd walk you home, then after you check in with your mother, take you out to supper."

"I . . . You have taken me by surprise."

"Have I?" He looked pleased. "I can't see why. My offer was a small thing."

Not to her. To her it was as momentous as when her fiancé had shown his true colors and hurt her in public. "I'm not sure if my mother would allow your escort."

"If your mother has not noticed your wrist and you have not told her about Avondale, I don't think you're really too concerned about what she might have to say." After the briefest of pauses, he stared hard at her. "Are you?"

"Well, I . . ."

"Besides," he said in his steady way, "some people even describe me as eminently suitable."

"No, they would describe you as eminently marriageable."

"Touché."

What she couldn't say was that he was suitable for someone else. She was neither beautiful nor wealthy. She had no illusions about her suitability to be a proper bride for a gentleman like him.

"Lydia, stop fighting me."

"I am not doing that," she sputtered, affected by his use of her first name but knowing she should protest his familiarity.

"No? Then allow me to be your friend."

His request caught her off guard. Both because of the idea of him wanting to be her friend and because she feared she wanted that too much.

Therefore, she attempted to stifle both of them with one pinched statement. "Women and men do not form friendships."

But instead of looking perturbed, his navy eyes glinted with amusement. "Why is that?"

She couldn't actually recall any specific reason. Especially since she'd just made that up. "Well . . ."

"We both enjoy books. I find you intriguing. Surely there is nothing wrong with allowing me to walk you home from work every now and then? Especially if I promise my intentions are true and innocent?"

"No. I mean, I can't think of any reason why that wouldn't be acceptable." Though, had she ever imagined that he would have any intentions that could be viewed as innocent?

His lips curved. "Very well then. It is settled."

Had it been? "I don't end my shift for another half hour."

"Which should give me plenty of time to determine if I actually wish to read Wilde's latest or not. He can be a bit wordy for my taste, you know."

She didn't know all his tastes. But she wished she did.

Suddenly feeling as if they were surely the focus of every other patron's scrutiny—though they might all be pretending not to observe them—Lydia elected to give Mr. Marks his way.

It would be foolish not to anyway, she decided. The fact of the matter was that she wanted to be near him. Wanted to get to know him better. Wanted a friend.

He would be as good a friend to have as any. And, she suspected, a better one than most.

CHAPTER 8

Sebastian had had only one goal in mind when he entered the reading room, and that had been to gain the trust of Lydia Bancroft. He needed her trust to gain more useful information about Jason Avondale. After everything that had happened in the lobby of the hotel, he was more determined than ever to see the man ruined both publicly and socially.

However, when he'd sat across from her and noticed how blue her eyes were, just how injured her wrist was, and just how, well, appealing she was, he'd realized he was going to have to think of any way he could to keep her near him. She appealed to him in a way he didn't know anyone could. Made him act a little less harsh. Made him want to be a little bit better.

Now, as he walked by her side toward her home, he found himself wondering more and more about her personal life.

He also couldn't help but wonder how a woman like her had become so educated. Most women of her station went to finishing school. He was also confounded by her apparent lack of admirers. Except for Avondale, it seemed she was ignored by the rest of society.

"My home isn't very fancy," she reminded him for the second

time as they turned right and ventured a little farther away from the most fashionable residences in Chicago. "It's actually a townhouse."

"Do you want a fancy residence?"

She blinked as if the idea had never occurred to her. "Goodness, no. Our townhouse suits me perfectly. I just, um, didn't want you to be shocked."

"I'm rarely shocked." Definitely never about one's living conditions.

"I misspoke," Lydia said in a rush. "Disappointed would be a better descriptor, perhaps."

"I will not be disappointed."

"I have a feeling it is far from what you are used to."

"You might be surprised about what I am used to," he countered. He knew he was confusing her, but he couldn't help himself. Just as she feared he might bolt if he knew her exact address, he feared Lydia would run if she knew how disreputable he actually was.

She said nothing, merely allowed a small pair of lines to mar the center of her forehead before she looked forward again and continued walking.

Sebastian kept his pace even with hers, taking care to glare at anyone who stepped too close to her person.

At last they arrived in front of a row of smallish-looking brownstones. "This is it," she announced as she stopped at the one in the middle.

She bit her lip as she looked at the empty flowerpots and some raggedy bushes on either side of the front door. "Like I said, it's nothing impressive."

"I want to be your friend, Miss Bancroft. Friends don't judge on appearances," he explained, just as if he were an authority on the subject. As if everything he knew about friendship hadn't been learned from the pages of books.

However, his words served to make the lines of worry around her eyes ease. "Give me your arm. Let's enter and inform your mother of your plans for supper."

"Yes, Mr. Marks." She tucked her hand in the curve of his elbow as they walked up the three steps to the front door.

Just as he was about to knock a second time on the door—obviously her servants were on the sluggish side—Lydia started, reached into her bag, and pulled out a key.

"Sorry," she said around an embarrassed smile. "For a moment I thought the door would simply open when I arrived."

He took the key from her and turned the bolt himself, then led her inside. He would ask later why she even possessed a key to her home. No woman of good birth handled such things.

When they entered, Sebastian was struck by the clean lines of the structure as well as the simplicity of the décor. It was by no means the height of fashion, but he couldn't say it lacked charm.

What it did lack was any servant at all.

Obviously, she didn't lack only a ladies' maid and a butler. No one greeted her, and no one stepped forward to take her coat. Actually, the house seemed as empty and quiet as a tomb.

To his dismay, she held out her hands to him to do the honors. "May I take your coat, Mr. Marks?"

"Allow me to assist you instead," he said, then leaned forward and began unfastening the three buttons on the front of her pelisse.

She tensed but he ignored her. After he pulled the pelisse from her frame, he glanced around for a coatrack, then ultimately decided to simply lay it on the table gracing the center of the small entryway. After a pause, he placed his own coat on top. He wasn't going to be staying long anyway.

"Lydia, where is your mother? Is she not at home?"

She blinked. "She often rests in her room." Gesturing in a vague way to a rather cramped-looking receiving room, she said, "Please, make yourself at home. I'll be right back."

Good manners meant that he should sit down and pretend her situation wasn't irregular in the slightest. He should patiently wait for her to go up the narrow staircase and wander about an empty house by herself.

But a lifetime of trusting no one led him to take her arm again. "I'll walk you upstairs."

"Mr. Marks, there is no need."

"I'm not going to allow you to wander around an empty house while I sit on a couch, Lydia."

"It is not empty. My mother is here."

He doubted that. "Then I am sure she will be happy to see you arrived in my care. Now, lead on."

With slow, grudging steps, she ascended the stairs. Following behind her, he took notice of the patches on the ceiling, the dark spots on the papered walls where paintings had once been hung. Sebastian began to fume.

Obviously she and her mother were in worse financial straits than he'd realized. Were there no men in their family to find Lydia a good match?

Had Jason Avondale—blackguard, abuser, gambler—truly been the best man her mother had been able to find for her daughter?

Once at the top of the stairs, Lydia looked at him helplessly, then turned to the first closed door and knocked twice.

When there was no answer, she knocked again. "Mother, are you awake?"

After a pause and rustling, her mother replied sleepily. "I am now, Lydia. Are you home already?"

"Yes," she said. "May I come in?"

"I suppose."

Sebastian clenched one of his hands. He knew enough about society's fresh girls to be affronted on Lydia's behalf. Did she have no one who put her needs first?

Still hesitating, her hand firmly gripping the doorknob, Lydia cast another awkward look his way. "I'll be right out, Mr. Marks. As I said downstairs, you really should go sit down."

"I'll be fine right here," he replied as he watched her brace herself, then open the door and slip inside. She left the door partway open.

Sebastian leaned against the opposite wall of the hallway, allowing himself to peek into the room.

And there he saw a thin woman reclined on a chaise lounge. "Lydia, you are home early."

"Yes. Mother, I thought you would be downstairs this time of day."

"There was no reason to get up."

"I think there is. I've brought a gentleman home."

"Oh? Is Mr. Avondale here?"

"No. Mother, this isn't the time to go into it, but . . . I suppose I have no choice but to tell you now. Um, he and I decided to not see each other anymore."

"Surely not."

"It is true. We are not after all . . . a suitable match."

Panic slid into her mother's voice. "Lydia, you must get him to take you back."

"I'd rather we didn't speak about this now. See, I brought a friend of mine whom I met at the library."

"A friend from the library." Her voice was thin. Full of consternation.

"Yes. His name is Mr. Marks. He is going to take me to supper."

"What about me? What am I going to eat?"

Finally forgetting that Mr. Marks lounged right outside the door, no doubt hearing every word of the conversation, Lydia winced as her mother's familiar whine tugged at her heart. "Didn't Cook come in today?"

"No. I had to let Ethel go."

"Pardon?"

"I wasn't able to pay her this week."

This was very bad—and made her wish once again that her mother would allow her to manage their finances. Lydia not only wanted to make sure her mother ate, but she needed to be sure a loyal servant like Ethel hadn't been let go like an old piece of furniture. "I'll visit Ethel and see that she gets paid."

"I hope you will not."

"We have to pay her."

"With what?" Wearily, her mother sat up, the pale peach silk of her nightdress cascading around her hips. "There's nothing left unless we sell more of our belongings, Lydia. Your salary will buy us food and not much else. We had one chance to secure our future and you ruined it. You needed that marriage to Mr. Avondale. I needed it."

"I'm sorry." Lydia felt terrible about that. She did. But with each hour that passed, she'd felt even more sure that ending the engagement had been the right thing to do. She couldn't allow herself to be abused.

"Mother—"

"I have a dreadful headache. Don't worry. We can pawn something else. There's still the painting in your room."

Lydia liked that painting. It was of the ocean, much like one of Turner's dramatic landscapes. It wasn't worth much, she didn't think, except in her heart. "Perhaps there's something else—"

"Now fix me something to eat. I've been so hungry all day, waiting for you to remember me."

"All right. I'll bring you a tray shortly. Is there anything else you need?"

———

As her mother gave Lydia more instructions, Sebastian remained motionless, wondering what Lydia would do or say next. He knew he shouldn't have been surprised by her mother's disinterest, but he still found himself disheartened by it.

With some surprise, he even found himself comparing her mother's actions to his own mother's. And while his own mother had been the lowest form of grace, selling herself to strangers, he suddenly realized that because of what she did, he had rarely gone hungry.

He couldn't imagine his mother lying about if she'd had a daughter as pretty and smart as Lydia.

When Lydia exited the room, her cheeks were bright red. She closed the door behind her. Then, to his immense satisfaction, she straightened and looked directly at him. He liked this hint of a backbone.

"My mother is under the weather at the moment. I think it would be best if we postponed our supper."

"No." If he allowed her to push him away now, he was sure he'd never be allowed to become close to her again.

She halted on the stairs. "Pardon?"

"You heard me, Miss Bancroft. I have no wish to reschedule. We will be going to supper this evening."

"I'm sorry, but I must—"

"But first I will help you see to your mother's supper."

She appeared flummoxed. "Help?"

"Assist. Work along with."

"I did not need your help defining the word, sir. I meant I cannot let you assist me in the kitchen."

Her tone was so tart he almost smiled. But he knew she would likely take it the wrong way. Therefore, he kept ordering her about. She responded to that.

"Miss Bancroft, I may live in a hotel, but believe it or not, I do know my way around a kitchen."

"Perhaps you do. However, I cannot in good conscience allow you to do that."

"Because?"

"You are my guest."

He'd had enough. "I'm hardly that. You need to learn to accept help when it is offered. And try to accept it with graciousness." Thoroughly irritated, he groused, "Didn't your fancy schooling teach you anything?"

"I learned enough."

"If that is the case, then you will realize I am right. Miss Bancroft, don't be so pigheaded."

Her eyes narrowed, telling him that he'd picked the absolute wrong thing to say. He followed her as she resolutely walked the rest of the way down the stairs and to the front door. "Thank you for seeing me home. And I do appreciate your invitation to supper. But I cannot accept it. My mother needs me."

"I heard what your mother said." He lowered his voice, and for the first time, he felt himself losing confidence. He wanted to help her, but he also knew much about saving face and feeling pride. "I realize now that you are in a far worse financial situation than I had originally thought."

"It is my business, not yours."

"Allow me to help you then."

"There is no need."

He pushed forward. "May I give you some money to pay your cook?"

"No."

"It would please me if you would change your mind. I don't like to think of you going hungry."

"We will not go hungry. I have my salary . . . Besides, I would be even more in your debt." She swallowed. "And that is why I feel certain that you will allow me to save at least a small bit of my dignity."

Because he couldn't fault that—because he knew he would want the same thing—he nodded. "I will see you soon at the library then, Miss Bancroft."

"Yes, Mr. Marks. Until we meet again."

Having to admire her spirit but still hating that she was forcing him to be so completely ineffectual, he stared at her one more time. Then he grabbed his coat and hat off the table. And as he strode out the door, practically marching down her front steps while glaring at anyone who looked his way curiously, Sebastian Marks knew one thing and one thing only.

This was the last time he was going to walk away from Lydia Bancroft when she was in need. In fact, an idea or two were already forming in the back of his mind.

But perhaps he should think things through, just this once. No matter how uncharacteristic for him. He didn't want her to keep refusing his help.

But no, no matter what happened between them in the future, he was not going to walk away again.

Not even if she insisted.

CHAPTER 9

Three days had passed since Mr. Marks had walked Lydia home from the library, witnessed her mother treating her like a servant, and then been asked to leave. Unfortunately, Lydia kept replaying that hour over and over in her head, making it constantly feel as if it had occurred mere moments ago.

Her circumstances hadn't changed much since his departure. She'd barely been able to scrape together enough money to give Ethel her back pay. On Thursday morning, she'd taken her pearls to the jeweler and pawned them for what she was sure was a third of their value.

Because she knew she needed to stretch each dollar as much as she could, she was resigning herself to cooking rather than trying to find some way to rehire Ethel.

She was such a fool. As Lydia walked back into the kitchen, she surveyed the rather bare cupboards, and she decided that pride really was a sin. If she had allowed Mr. Marks to take her to supper Wednesday night, she would have a little more food left over for a meal now that it was Saturday. She wouldn't be attempting to make two meals out of the pitiful number of ingredients that would barely make one. Not only would there be no shopping on a Sunday, but she would not be paid again soon enough to do them much good.

Perhaps the painting in her room was the next to go.

Now she was digging into the bottom of drawers for the last of their potatoes and onions and ruthlessly cutting off the spoiled ends. After that, she diced them as well as one could who had never had any formal kitchen training.

Which, unfortunately, wasn't very well. She found herself crying as she continued to chop onions, their harsh smell stinging her eyes.

At least, that was what she firmly told herself was happening. She certainly wasn't crying tears of frustration because she was in a difficult financial situation with no foreseeable way out. Or because she was going to keep from her mother the whole truth for breaking her engagement to Jason.

Or because she'd let her character flaw—too much pride— interfere with good sense.

With a new resolve, she poured the mixture of potatoes and onions into a cast-iron pan, turned up the gas flame, and added a few precious dots of butter and a heavy hand of salt to make the mixture palatable.

When she thought it was cooked through, Lydia spooned the mixture onto two plates, then cracked two eggs in the skillet and fried them as best she could. Finally, she carried two plates to her mother's room. It wasn't much, but it was certainly edible. And for that she was glad.

Her mother picked at the food with an expression of distaste. "This is all we have today?"

Lydia's spirits sank even further. "I am afraid so."

"But I thought you pawned your pearls?"

"I did. But I had to pay Ethel and a tax bill. As you know, our finances are rather pinched."

"Your pearls were very fine."

"Unfortunately, they didn't fetch a very fine price."

"Who was that man you brought by the other evening?"

Startled by the inquiry at last, Lydia replied before she considered the ramifications. "His name is Mr. Sebastian Marks. He's a gentleman I've met through the library."

She was so relieved a friend who still visited her mother had stopped by that morning, revealing the news that Jason had told his parents they were simply not a good match. Her mother had no choice but to finally let that dream go.

Lydia was also relieved Jason had apparently elected not to tell lies about her and Mr. Marks.

"Is he wealthy?"

"I believe him to be." A thread of doubt settled in and pulled tight. She actually didn't know him well, did she? But no, he was obviously wealthy.

Now ignoring her meal completely, her mother stared at her. "I only spied him from afar, but he seemed rather tall. And handsome. Do you find him attractive?"

"He is tall," Lydia murmured. "Easily more than six feet." Far better not to reflect on whether or not she found Mr. Marks attractive. She had only talked with him on two occasions, but he'd never given her any indication that he found her to be the type of woman he would seek in a wife.

Not that he would. He was indeed wealthy and high in the instep. She was a librarian.

"I did notice he had dark hair and eyes. Unusually dark."

"I suppose they are." It was best to keep her answers short and to the point. Otherwise she'd tell her mother that Mr. Marks actually had dark-blue eyes, the color of lapis lazuli. And that his dark hair sported a cowlick near his temple.

Her mother regarded her for a moment before taking another miniscule bite of potato and egg and setting her fork down again. "He really was rather hulking. And he seemed to be staring at you too. Staring and eavesdropping is rude."

"I didn't realize he could see us, but I suppose if you were able to see him, he could see us. I should have shut the door."

"Well, he's not terribly refined, is he? I mean, I'm not at all sure he looked the part of a wealthy man."

"Momma, his clothes are the latest fashion and very expensive. You were not close enough to see. But even if they weren't, there is nothing wrong with that," she retorted before remembering that Mr. Marks' appearance was certainly no business of hers anyway. "Don't forget, I wear glasses. Most people find that off-putting."

"You wouldn't if you tried harder to see."

No matter how much Lydia had tried to tell her mother that her poor vision was not something she could rectify on her own, her mother still was of the mind that her glasses were at the heart of her lack of success on the marriage market.

"Vanity is a sin," she declared piously. "Besides, I don't believe he minds my glasses."

"Altogether, he is unsuitable for any woman of means, don't you think?"

"No, I do not." Why wasn't her mother listening? Actually, she considered Mr. Marks to be one of the most handsome men she'd ever met. He was certainly the most intriguing. And the smartest. Those meant as much, if not more, to her as his wealth.

"You aren't thinking to see him again, are you?"

"I imagine I will see him from time to time. We are friends," she pointed out as soon as she swallowed another mouthful. "He frequents my reading room after all."

"It really is too bad that all the entertainments surrounding the fair are over. Perhaps you could have met more gentlemen that way."

"Mother, I wasn't invited to many of those events."

"You were invited to enough. If you had accepted *all* the invitations and comported yourself well, if you had tried to be a little more alluring, I feel certain you could have garnered even more invitations. Men like women who are enjoyable to be around. Who sparkle."

Lydia bit back a reply. She had accepted all the invitations. Her mother just could not accept that she was not a popular young woman. At times like this, she truly worried about her mother. It seemed her world was becoming smaller and smaller, that she was becoming less and less aware of reality, and far more comfortable with hazy memories of better days. Instead of uttering another retort, Lydia picked up their plates. Hers was practically licked bare. Her mother's was almost full. Disappointment coursed through her as she realized she'd managed to disappoint her mother this evening in not one way but two.

"I'm going to wash these and clean up the kitchen."

Her mother picked up her embroidery and nodded. "Very well. Yes, you may go do that."

As Lydia walked downstairs, she reflected again that her mother spoke to her as if she were a servant.

Something did need to change, she thought as she picked up her fork and ate the rest of the food on her mother's plate. While some might have thought the act repugnant, Lydia only knew that it would hold back her hunger for another few hours.

A half hour later, just as she was drying the last of the dishes, she heard a brusque knock on the front door.

She rushed to open it. Foolishly, she wondered if it could be Mr. Marks. He hadn't come into the library since she asked him to leave her home. But maybe he had by now forgiven her for her rudeness. Maybe he was still concerned about her.

But one quick look out the window had her feeling far less excited.

With a lump in her throat, she opened the door. "Mr. Avondale, it is very late. What are you doing here?"

"We need to talk."

"Now?"

"Let me in."

The other times he'd come calling, he'd only stood in the foyer. If she let him inside, he would see just how shabby the townhouse had become. She was tempted to close the door in his face, but his family was too influential. She couldn't afford to earn their disfavor.

"You may come in for a moment, but I'm afraid I don't have any refreshments to offer."

"I didn't come for refreshments. I came to speak to you about a private manner." He looked around. "Where is your mother?"

She was growing more confused. "My mother is upstairs in her room. Do you wish for her to be present?"

He shook his head. "I do not." He walked right into their receiving room and sat down. Two seconds later, he was on his feet again, pacing.

More confused than ever, she gazed at him curiously. "Jason, whatever is wrong?"

"I need to know just how well you know Sebastian Marks."

Mr. Marks seemed to be on everyone's mind that evening. "He is a friend."

"How good of one? You two seemed rather close at the hotel."

"He was seeing to my wrist. If you will remember, I burned my hand from the tea."

"Someone told me they saw you walking with him a few days

ago." He stared hard at her as she lowered herself into a chair. "What were you doing?"

She was as disconcerted by his question as his demanding tone. "I fail to see why that is any of your concern. You ended our engagement, if you will remember."

Instead of showing any reaction to that, he waved off her reminder, like it was nothing that mattered to him. Instead, he sat down across from her and leaned forward, bracing his elbows on his thighs. Crowding her space.

But it was the dark, panicked look in his eyes that caught her off guard. "Lydia, do you trust him?"

"I . . . I believe I do. Why?" Was he actually concerned for her welfare . . . or for his own?

"Have you ever seen any of his business partners? Any of the men who work with him?"

"Jason, he frequents my reading room. That is all." She had no idea what he did, and she would certainly have no idea if another gentleman would ever be one of his business partners or not.

Actually, all of this was becoming increasingly irregular. "Your manner is starting to worry me. What is wrong?"

"I feel as if I am being watched." He shuddered. "Usually I would call such suppositions nonsense. However, I could swear I saw the same man who was lurking about at my club last night standing outside my address this morning."

"Your club?" She knew men of his social circle frequented well-to-do gentlemen's clubs, but she had no idea which one or ones Jason claimed as his own. "What club is that?"

He did not answer, but she saw a muscle in his jaw jump as he looked away.

"Why would someone be doing that, Jason?"

He glanced at her before staring out the window.

He was hiding something. What she didn't know was what she wanted to do with what he was asking her. Did she care to get involved? *Should* she get involved?

She did not. She should not.

When she thought her only option for the future was Jason's like of her, she had been determined to keep his good will. But now that their engagement was a thing of the past, she felt she could be far more opinionated.

She had choices. Not too many in life, but she definitely did as it pertained to him.

Treading carefully, she said, "Again, I do not see how your suspicions affect me. There is nothing holding us together any longer." Just to set the record straight, she added, "And I must admit that I am no longer interested in your suit."

With obvious impatience, he brushed a stray lock of hair back from his forehead. "Lydia, this has nothing to do with you. I don't care what your feelings are."

"If you don't care, then perhaps you should go speak to someone else. I fail to see why you came to see me at this time of night."

"I'm here because I want you to talk to Marks on my behalf."

"I don't know him that well. And what would he have to do with someone watching you?"

Did this have something to do with what had happened in the hotel? Even if it did, even if she had known Mr. Marks well, she was absolutely sure now that she wouldn't do what Jason was asking anyway. His words were confusing and frightening. Nothing she wanted to become embroiled in.

He ignored her. "I want you to insist that he call off his watchdogs immediately. I am sure he is behind this."

It was becoming obvious that Jason was a bit confused. Yes, Mr. Marks had come to her rescue, and yes, he had been angry about Jason's behavior, but why would he care to have Jason followed? Mr. Marks lived in an expensive hotel and spent afternoons reading at her library. She was fairly certain he wouldn't know the first thing about spying on men.

Whatever Jason feared from Mr. Marks, this was taking it too far.

"Jason, forgive me, but you've let your imagination run away with you. Mr. Marks doesn't spy on people. Furthermore, he has no reason to do such things—not even after your despicable behavior at the hotel. Why would you think he would be behind this?"

A myriad of expressions—confusion, amusement, anger, despair—passed over Jason's features. Now Lydia felt sure he was struggling with something dire. She wondered if he was hiding a secret about himself or about Mr. Marks.

Then again, she remembered how instantly angry Jason had become when he saw Mr. Marks at the hotel. Was his first instinct really that there was something between her and Mr. Marks, or was there something between the two men that made him so suspicious? Something Mr. Marks didn't like but Jason actively feared.

It was time to uncover the truth, or at least move on. His pensive glares were becoming tiresome, and his accusations about Mr. Marks were giving her a headache. "Jason, I cannot help you if you are not honest with me," she chided. "Please either tell me what is the cause of your worry about Mr. Marks or bid me good evening."

"Honest? You want me to be honest?"

"Of course." She was becoming impatient. "Please be honest, if you can. It means candid. Straightforward. Sincere."

He scoffed. "You and your definitions. It's enough to make one ache to press a hand to your mouth, just to silence your superior attitude."

Remembering the way he'd gripped her wrist, she flinched. "Please leave."

He didn't budge. "Tell me, don't you ever get tired of being the smartest person in the room?"

His words were caustic. Cool. She knew his question was rhetorical as well. However, his criticism was just painful enough that she decided to pretend ignorance. "Actually, no, I do not tire of it. I *am* usually the smartest person in the room. I certainly am this evening."

His eyes turned cold. "One day you will wish you had minded your tongue."

That felt as though he were threatening her, but he did not make a move toward her. He only seemed to want to make her do his bidding, and she would not. Standing up on shaking legs, she said, "I will see you to the door. I believe this conversation has run its course."

Looking even more agitated, he got to his feet but didn't move a single inch. "You were right about one thing. Coming here was a mistake," he snapped as he looked around her small receiving room with disdain. "Though now that I am here, I see it. You are obviously extremely far from being a suitable bride."

Had Mr. Marks' warning been correct then? Jason had wanted her because he needed money? It made no sense since everyone knew his family was wealthy.

But if he had, indeed, only proposed because he'd assumed her dowry could ease his financial straits, how very disappointed he must be.

Almost as disappointed as herself.

Grabbing the top hat he'd thrown carelessly on the coffee table when he'd first sat down, he said, "I will leave you with one bit of advice. Sebastian Marks is not who you think he is. He is as far from the cream of Chicago society as one of the actors in Buffalo Bill

Cody's Wild West show. He is from the depths of the poorest class. Keeping his company should be avoided by ladies at all costs."

She knew he was wrong. He had to be. She recognized the fine cut of his suits and the expensive fabrics he wore. "I am sure you are mistaken."

"I am not. You may never imagine that I know more about anything than you, but I can promise you, in this instance, you are sadly out of your depth. Don't let your pride get in the way of common sense."

"Is he dangerous?"

"Of course he is," he bit out. "Most men in Chicago know who he is and fear him."

"I don't know—"

"Furthermore, most women who have the misfortune to know who he is make sure to never even meet his gaze."

"But—"

"Besides," he added darkly, "he eyes you in a peculiar way. I saw it in the lobby of the hotel. I saw it when he was staring at you from across the room."

"He is concerned for my welfare."

"No, he wants you in his life."

A chill inched up her spine. "We are merely friends." Actually, they weren't even that, no matter what she said. She didn't have friends. The invitations received to parties and balls had no doubt been sent in deference to her father's position and then out of pity for a widow and her daughter.

But she did know one or two afternoon's conversations did not a friendship make.

"He is not looking for a friend, Lydia. At least, not the type of *friend* you are thinking of. And let me tell you this. If you aren't careful, you are going to discover things about Marks that will mark you as well."

She imagined he used the word *mark* on purpose. As a play on words. It would have been mildly amusing if his words weren't so foreboding.

Though his warnings were scaring her, she wasn't about to give Jason the satisfaction of seeing her afraid of him again. "You are being rather dramatic, Jason."

"It would only be seen as dramatic by the naïve." He walked toward the door. "I promise you this, Lydia. If you don't break all ties with Marks, something is going to happen. And it won't be pleasant or easily removed. Actually, you might never recover from it."

Before she could ask him to explain himself, he set the hat on his head, strode to the door, and exited.

Closing the door behind him, Lydia looked around the quiet, dim foyer.

The artwork that used to decorate the walls was gone.

The servants who used to keep floors swept and the furniture glistening were gone.

She truly was alone. Responsible to secure her mother's future yet not knowing if she would ever marry. In the dark about what was and was not true about her new friend.

Soon, they were going to have to sell the chandelier in the dining room. After that? Her mother would be forced to give up even more of her jewelry. And how much longer could they afford even this townhouse?

Perhaps she would be forced to investigate other avenues for employment, not that she had any idea what she could do. Be a governess perhaps?

At the moment, all she had to trust were her treasured books and the stories inside that transported her to someplace far better.

Too tired to contemplate her mother's depression, her ex-fiancé's warnings about her new friend, the bills that needed to be paid, Lydia walked quietly up the stairs to her own bedroom. She lit her kerosene lamp, then opened the top book on the table by her favorite reading chair.

Running a hand along the leather spine, she sighed in blessed relief. At least her books hadn't failed her.

And for that, she took a fierce moment, closed her eyes, and gave thanks.

CHAPTER 10

CHICAGO TIMES-COURIER

From December 1893
Reported by Benson Gage

It is advised that all holiday revelers visit Camp
Creek Alley at their own risk. No less than five men
and one woman were attacked this past week. And
this is only what has been publicly reported.

Two raps followed by another three woke Bridget from her slumber
in her bedroom, which was really little more than a rather large closet
near the back stairs on the top floor of the Hartman Hotel.

Jolting to a sitting position, she gaped at her locked door. "Who
is there?"

"Vincent," the voice rasped. "I mean, Vincent Hunt."

Alarmed, she jumped out of bed and threw on her wrapper. Only
an emergency would have brought Mr. Marks' assistant to her door at
this time of night. Immediately, all the worst sorts of scenarios began
to dance in her head. What if some harm had befallen Mr. Marks?
What if he'd been attacked and was bleeding somewhere?

And if that was the case, if he were dead, what would become of her?

Aware that anyone could be lurking in her hallway, she paused with her hand on the door handle. If someone discovered her standing in her nightclothes while talking to a man, they would no doubt create such an outcry that Mr. Marks would be forced to release her. "Mr. Hunt, what is it? What's wrong?"

Pure frustration flavored each of his words. "I have no idea. Marks came to my office door barely twenty minutes ago and demanded that I bring you to him."

"He did?"

"Immediately."

She exhaled. The relief that Mr. Marks wasn't in danger came and went with the new knowledge that she might be. Hurriedly, she lifted the bolt on her door and opened it just enough for Vincent to see her. "You'd better come in."

He walked inside without a moment's hesitation, seemed to notice her state of undress, and abruptly faced the wall. "You shouldn't have invited me in, dressed as you are. It isn't proper."

His snippy words acted like a splash of cold water. "I am aware of that," she snapped. "I'm also aware that I shouldn't be allowing any men inside, even ones who show up uninvited. But if we woke up the rest of the house with you talking at me through the door, I know I'd get sent away for sure. Frankly, I'm surprised you were able to get upstairs without anyone stopping you. What time is it?"

"It's about one. And we both know none of the bellmen and desk clerks downstairs is going to say one word about what happens in Mr. Marks' rooms. I daresay his weekly payments keep half of them employed."

"You would be right about that."

He unbent his stalwart stance enough to glower at her over his shoulder. "You'd best get dressed. You may be right about me not loitering about in the hall. But still, it isn't proper for me to be in your bedroom."

She knew. Oh, she most definitely knew. But social rules and modesty were for people who could afford such things. She was a working girl and glad to have her job. "It will be all right. We both know I'm in no danger of ruining my fine reputation. No one here is mistaking me as an impressionable young miss."

"You're respectable."

"Of course I am. But it's at the very far edge of respectability." Before he could comment on that, she picked off her day dress from one of the pegs by her small desk. "Keep your back turned. I need to change."

"Absolutely not. Wait until I go back outside to disrobe."

If Bridget hadn't been so surprised by Vincent's dismayed expression, she would have laughed. Honestly, she would have thought nothing could shock him after working for Mr. Marks for as long as he had. After all, women loitered outside the Silver Grotto in all forms of dress.

"Mr. Hunt, you may not loiter in my hallway. If you left this room, you'd have to go out into the alley, and then I'd have to go out there to find you. Just stand there and give me a few seconds, if you please?"

"I don't like this."

"For goodness' sake. You have a young daughter. You were married. I'm sure I have nothing you haven't seen before."

"I'll do as you wish, but I'm not happy about it," he said as he stood motionless, staring at the wall. "And it's bad form to speak of such personal things."

"Duly noted." As she quickly unfastened the row of buttons down the front of her nightgown, it occurred to her to wonder why she wasn't more nervous about changing clothes while in the same room with him. She should be uncomfortable.

But instead of any of that, she felt completely safe.

Was it because she knew he feared the wrath of Mr. Marks?

Or was it because Vincent Hunt was the only man besides Mr. Marks she was coming to trust?

"Are you almost done?"

"I'm hurrying," she called out as she pulled the stays on her corset as tightly as she could. "You were married," she reminded him again. "Women's clothes, as you know, are made up of entirely too many fussy layers."

He blew out an impatient burst of air. "I don't need to hear about your garments, Miss O'Connell."

"It won't take me much longer now."

Vincent sighed. "Never thought I'd end up doing this tonight."

She wondered what he thought he would be doing. Did he expect to still be working? Or had he had his own plans?

After a pause, she secured her stockings, then pulled a chemise over her head, followed by a petticoat and a small bustle. After smoothing all the fabrics into order as best she could, she stepped into her gray dress.

Vincent planted one hand on his waist. "Are you almost done? Please say you are."

"Not yet. I still have to fasten my gown."

"This is taking too long. One would have thought you'd be used to getting dressed more quickly, what with you being a maid and all."

"Usually I can move around the room. You being here takes up quite a bit of my space."

"I did offer to leave."

"I did ask you to be patient."

He didn't deign to reply. Merely grunted.

Now that her dress was on, she said, "You can look now. All I have to do is fasten my boots."

"Good. He's not going to be liking us taking so long."

Bridget noticed he was watching as she fastened her boots. She supposed he was biting his tongue, since she was showing him her ankles and all.

After smoothing back her hair and fashioning it into a low chignon, she grabbed her keys and coat. "I'm ready."

"Almost." To her surprise, he deftly took the coat from her hands and held it for her to slip her arms in. Just like a gentleman would for a lady.

Also to her surprise—and secret amusement—she found she still remembered how to accept a gentleman's help. She wondered how he'd ever learned.

She didn't have any time to reflect on it, however, because he was already peeking out her door and gesturing with one hand to follow him.

Five minutes later she was following him down the alleyway. She was confused. "Where are we meeting Mr. Marks?"

"At the club, of course."

"Really? At this time of night?" She hoped he didn't hear the tremors in her voice.

"Yes. Where else? He wanted me to bring you to the Grotto as quickly as possible. Therefore, I am."

"Did he say why he wanted to see me so urgently?"

Vincent frowned at her. "Of course not."

"He gave you no sign?" She really wanted to be prepared for the meeting.

"No. You know how things go with Mr. Marks. He doesn't deign to explain himself."

"No." She learned some time ago he did not. Realizing that Vincent was waiting for her to finish her thought, she blurted, "I mean, of course he does not."

Vincent nodded. They picked up their pace, darting around the few men who were about. Most looked exhausted and were obviously coming home from late hours working at the factories, but there were a few men who seemed to only be dallying. A couple of them glanced her way with an interested expression. But when they caught sight of Vincent, with his cold eyes and large, muscular frame, they promptly skittered away.

Just before they turned into the narrow, winding street that would eventually lead them to Camp Creek Alley, they passed under the steady glow of a burning gaslight that illuminated much of the block they were on.

Bridget saw two men she recognized.

One was Sergio Vlas, Mr. Marks' competition. He owned the Bear and Bull and had approached her once or twice when she'd delivered something for Mr. Marks at the Grotto. He'd offered her both his protection and a job, apparently unafraid of any retaliation from Mr. Marks. Though he'd actually seemed kind, she would never want to work for him. Unlike her employer, Vlas made money using women.

He was standing alone, and as if he felt her gaze resting on him, he lifted his chin, looked directly at her, and smiled. She averted her eyes. He seemed more intimidating at night than in broad daylight.

Which brought her to notice Jason Avondale. He was standing not far from Vlas with a man she thought, though Bridget couldn't be absolutely sure, was Mr. Galvin. She'd heard him speak to Mr. Marks once or twice outside the Hartman. She could just make out the gold pocket watch clutched in Avondale's hand, a sapphire catch gleaming under the streetlamp's glow. She remembered seeing him with it at the Pinter home.

Bridget couldn't help but wonder if he was courting his demise, holding that expensive watch in plain sight in such a place.

Before he could catch her staring at him, Bridget averted her eyes again, choosing to focus on Vincent's profile instead. He seemed unconcerned about any of the men she'd seen, and she supposed he was relieved she'd finally stopped asking him questions he couldn't answer.

Suddenly, she knew. It was perfectly clear. Now she understood why he sent Mr. Hunt to get her in the dead of night. Why he'd summoned her to the club.

She was no longer going to be Mr. Marks' maidservant. She was going to be asked—no, told—to do what she'd once offered but always had feared the most. Mr. Marks had changed his mind. Like Sergio Vlas, he had decided to use women for profit at the Silver Grotto.

And somehow she had earned his disfavor, and he was sending her there.

A slow, sick feeling knotted her stomach when she realized she had no choice about it either. She had nowhere else to go and no one to look to for help. She had to do whatever he asked. Even though the area seemed to be in the middle of a terrible crime spree, making the thought of working there all the more frightening, the consequences for refusing Mr. Marks' directives were too dear.

It was simply too bad that she was different than she'd been when she first shakily stood in front of Mr. Marks' desk. Over the past two years, she'd become used to being treated with respect. She'd become used to feeling safe.

Worse, she'd begun to have expectations.

When she'd shown up at the Silver Grotto for the first time, she'd been traumatized by thoughts of being fired. She'd experienced the sharp tang of fear that could only come after spending a night alone on the streets of Chicago.

She'd been willing to do almost anything to have some protection.

But now "almost anything" brought forth more feelings of dread than hope. She had begun to feel as though she was someone of worth. She had begun to foolishly imagine that she was something more.

No doubt many women in the city could have reminded her. No good ever comes to girls like her who dare to dream.

For better or worse, they lived with the consequences of their choices every single day.

More than ever, it seemed she was completely alone. Even Vincent Hunt did not seem to care at all about her fate.

CHAPTER 11

Sebastian was indulging in one of his favorite pastimes—standing on the third-floor balcony of the Grotto and watching the guests below spend money—when Vincent arrived with Bridget.

Their arrival drew no notice. He was glad to see Bridget was wearing her plainest, darkest gray dress and that her hair was styled plainly as well. She looked drab against the Grotto's gold walls, vivid paintings, and dark woodwork.

He was pleased about that.

While it wasn't common for women to frequent the Grotto, it wasn't unheard of either. Vincent employed several women to serve drinks and food in the gambling den. Every now and then one of the gambler's ladybirds visited as well.

Most of the Grotto's customers knew better than to accost a woman on the property. The women in Sebastian's employ were at his beck and call, not the customers'.

Vincent, of course, drew no notice whatsoever.

Sebastian's assistant had on his serviceable, thick black overcoat. It was well cut and obviously expensive, being fashioned of a particularly fine wool fabric. So much so, the quality of the article of clothing was apparent even from two floors above.

And reminded Sebastian that the insecure, fumbling man who was down on his luck when he'd entered Sebastian's life was much changed.

Now Vincent looked almost as well-heeled as the majority of the men who frequented the establishment. Only his rather tight expression and business-like manners gave away the fact that he came to the Grotto for business and not pleasure.

After spying Sebastian leaning on the railing, Vincent started walking up the back staircase. Bridget following behind.

He met them at the landing. "Good evening, Bridget," he said quietly before facing Hunt. "Took you long enough. I expected you to arrive fifteen minutes ago."

Bridget blanched. "I'm sorry, sir. It was my fault."

He was rather surprised to see that she looked scared to death. Gentling his voice, he said, "No worries, Bridget. You, of all people, know my bark is worse than my bite." At least with her, it was. "Wait in my office, will you?"

Looking rather relieved to be allowed out of sight, Bridget scurried off down the hall. Only when he heard his office door open and shut did Sebastian raise a brow toward Vincent. "What happened?"

"I'm sorry you were waiting, sir. She was asleep when I knocked on her door. I had to wait for her to get dressed."

She'd been asleep? He pulled out his pocket watch, then inwardly winced. It was now half past one in the morning. Action barely began at the Silver Grotto before eleven. But he should have recalled that the real world kept a far different schedule.

And that most people required far more sleep than his usual four hours. Still contemplating Bridget's odd behavior, he asked, "Did something untoward happen on the way here? She seems out of sorts."

"No, sir. Though she did seem taken aback by your request to see her here."

He was at a loss. "Where would we have met if not here?"

"I could not say, sir."

Sebastian should have known better than to ask such a thing. It was obvious that the whims of women were just as foreign to his assistant as himself. "Thank you for fetching her. Go downstairs and check in with the floor managers. Tables were running high an hour ago."

"Yes, sir." Hunt nodded, then headed back down the stairs. After walking toward the railing and watching a few of the executives from one of the packing companies head down to the basement level, obviously in search of a poker game, Marks strode to his office.

There he found Bridget nervously standing in the middle of the room, wringing her hands. "Bridget, why are you standing there looking scared to death?"

She paled. "Sir?"

"You should have sat down. Sit."

"If you don't mind, I, um, don't much feel like sitting, sir."

Her words hit him as he was about to sit down behind his desk. Her tone was just agitated enough that he decided to sit in one of the uncomfortable chairs that flanked the front of his desk instead. "Join me over here. If you please." He kept his voice firm and his request a command.

"Yes, sir." Not looking at him, she sat, then plucked at her skirts.

He supposed some kind of explanation was in order. "I'm sorry to have disturbed your sleep."

"It's all right."

It wasn't, really. He had no boundaries, but even he knew that. "It isn't all right. I should have been more considerate. I fear these hours I keep sometimes make me forget how the rest of the world lives."

"Don't worry about it, sir."

He scanned her face, noticing the strain around her eyes. Her pursed lips. And decided that no good was going to come from delaying the inevitable. "Bridget, I asked you to come here this evening because I want to talk to you about your job."

She seemed to brace herself. "Yes, sir?"

Thinking about what he wanted her to do, he decided the best course of action would be to speak bluntly. "Starting tomorrow, you will no longer be working for me at the hotel."

She bit her lip. Then, to his dismay, he realized she was actively struggling to hold back her tears.

This was absolutely something he could not bear. While he usually had no patience for women's weaknesses, he felt a wave of tenderness for his reclusive employee. "Bridget, please do not say you are crying."

After swiping at her eyes with the side of her hand, she shook her head. "Of course not, sir."

"As much as I would like to believe you, I'm fairly certain those are tears."

"It's nothing. I'll be all right."

"Your reaction astounds me. I wasn't aware you enjoyed laundering my shirts so much."

"It's not that," she said quickly. "It's, um . . . I'm, uh . . . apprehensive about working in the club." Suddenly looking determined, she straightened her spine. "I'll get over it though."

"The club?" He struggled to understand. "Are you under the assumption that I want you to spend time *here*? At the Silver Grotto?"

"Well, yes, sir."

He would never understand a woman's mind. "Why on earth would you think I would want that?"

"Um. Well, I assumed . . . if you don't want me at the hotel, where else would I be?"

Cutting her off, he glowered at her. "I never have a shortage of women to serve, so how could you think . . . Bridget, do you think I want you to *whore* for me?"

The skin around her mouth turned white, causing him to recall that while she might not be a society lady, she certainly was a far cry from the girls he'd grown up beside. They'd all grown up talking about things in the coarsest of ways. Very little shocked them.

But Bridget was from a middle-class background, raised in church—so he'd overheard her say one day—and no doubt unused to such language. She'd been a ladies' maid before being released from service.

"Forgive me. At times I fear I revert to my baser self." He didn't mention that he usually only slipped when he was ill at ease. She no doubt had surmised that.

Sitting ramrod straight, Bridget stared at him, wide eyed.

Which made him even more ill at ease. Trying again, he decided to simply tell her how he felt. "I can see that is exactly what you thought. The fact is I am rather shocked that you'd think I would ask such a thing of you. I thought you knew me better."

"Sir?"

Restless, he stood. "Bridget, later on this morning, I would like you to accompany me to Miss Lydia Bancroft's home. She's a woman of good character who, I'm afraid, has fallen on some hard times."

"She's the librarian you helped in the lobby of the Hartman, isn't she?"

"Actually, yes, she is." Sebastian was surprised Bridget remembered, even though she obviously had overheard enough to know Lydia worked in a reading room. But he supposed he shouldn't have been. She didn't gossip, but it would be naïve of him to imagine that everything he did wasn't of notice—and perhaps of interest—to much of the staff at the hotel.

"Bridget, I would like you to become her ladies' maid and be . . . well, my eyes and ears, if you would."

"Sir?"

"If you recall me tending to her hand, you no doubt will recall Avondale's rough treatment. I fear this gentleman hasn't been convinced yet to leave her alone. In fact, I have learned he visited her earlier this evening. I can't have that. If you see him near her, I'll want to know about it."

"I understand."

He doubted that. Because *he* didn't even understand what he was seeing when he looked at Lydia. By all accounts, she should be nothing more than a spectacle-wearing, quiet librarian, possessing a beautiful pair of blue eyes and a rather beguiling figure.

Who was well read, quick thinking, and so sweet and naïve he was constantly tempted to be at his best around her to save her from herself.

Yes, that is all she is to me, he mocked himself. *Nearly everything. Nothing more, nothing less.*

"In addition, Bridget, you are going to need to make sure she has food in her house. I'll give you money for that, of course." After she nodded her understanding, he added, "Next, make sure her mother doesn't take too much advantage of her."

For the first time since she'd arrived, Bridget's posture relaxed. "And how would you like me to do that?"

"I couldn't begin to imagine." He waved a hand in the air. "You're a woman. I'm sure you'll find a way."

"Yes, sir. I expect I shall."

Her voice was everything respectful and obedient. But he did happen to notice that she seemed to be hiding a smile.

"Do you have any questions?"

"Only one."

"Yes?"

"Um, who will see to your laundry now?"

He hadn't thought that far. Actually, he had a feeling he was going to miss Bridget's competent ways. To cover up this lack of foresight, he said, "My shirts are no longer your concern. All you will need to do is appear on the sidewalk outside the Hartman at nine o'clock tomorrow morning."

"Very well." She stood up. "All right, Mr. Marks. I'll be ready at nine in the morning."

"Thank you, Bridget." Now that he had his way, he smiled slightly. "Who knows? Perhaps you might even like this job better. Working with two ladies has got to be better than looking after a reprobate such as myself."

"It hasn't been so bad," she replied with a small smile. "After all, I'm used to you."

He walked her out, staying by her side as they descended the back staircase. When they reached the ground floor, they parted ways.

Hunt was waiting for him when he entered the club. "I checked with all the floor managers. All is running smoothly, sir."

"Good. You may go home now. You need an early night once in a while."

"Yes, Mr. Marks. Thank you." He turned his head slightly and looked down the hall. "Um, sir, if I may? Where is Miss O'Connell now?"

"I sent her on her way."

"Alone?"

"Yes." He almost smiled. "Don't worry, man. Everyone knows she's under my protection."

"I will still offer my escort."

"If you intend to do that, then you'd best catch her."

Only after Vincent tore out of the club did Sebastian allow himself to smile.

Just in time to see Avondale enter the club with Jeffrey Galvin. Though Sebastian was tempted to throw them both out, he edged closer to the shadows and decided to watch them for a while. He could always make his intentions clear to Galvin later. And at least if Avondale was here, he wouldn't have to wonder what he was up to.

The devil you knew and all that.

———

Bridget had barely gone half a block when she heard Vincent call her name.

With a feeling of dread, she turned and waited for him to approach.

"I'm glad I caught you," he said with a hint of a smile. "I was afraid I wouldn't."

"Why were you searching for me? Does Mr. Marks need to speak with me again?" She was so tired, but she would do whatever he needed.

"No, of course not."

"Oh." She glanced around apprehensively. The streets were beginning to thin, and the people left were looking at her far too intently. "Well, then, I wish you a good evening."

"I wanted to walk you home."

"That is so kind of you. Thank you. But I'll be fine."

His light-blue eyes softened in the dim light. "I'm sure you will. But still, things happen. Things no one ever imagines."

He was right. "Thank you, Mr. Hunt. I will appreciate your escort." She was so relieved that, like Mr. Marks, he did have respect and concern for her.

He smiled. As they crossed an intersection, he stayed close, even grasped her elbow when she slipped on a patch of slick mud. "Easy now," he murmured. "There's no hurry."

His kindness soothed her enough to share her news. "I'm going to be Miss Bancroft's new maid. That is why he summoned me tonight. I start in the morning."

He glanced at her in surprise. "That will be quite the change."

Bridget shivered dramatically. "Indeed. I'll go from ironing Mr. Marks' shirts in the morning and making sure the chef sends up his coffee to being at the beck and call of a lady."

He laughed. "At least from what we've seen of Miss Bancroft, she doesn't seem to be a difficult person."

"That may be how she is. Or how she wants the world to see her. Don't forget, I have been a ladies' maid before."

"I hope you will find her to be an agreeable mistress."

"I hope so too." His words were just the balm she needed. After smiling briefly at him, she glanced around again. "We're almost at the Hartman."

"Three more blocks."

"I hope this isn't too far out of your way." Looking at him in shock, she said, "Goodness, I've known you for years now, but I've yet to ask you where you live."

"Not too far. Only about ten blocks north. I'll be home in no time."

"And then you will collapse."

He laughed. "Yes. Then I will collapse at last. Luckily I can go to sleep at a moment's notice."

His words made her realize just how much she really didn't know about him. Though both of their jobs revolved around the needs of one man, they'd rarely had the occasion to converse with each other.

Or, perhaps, they'd both consciously strived to keep their

distance? "Your hours are so irregular. Coming home so late is your norm, isn't it?"

"It's the job." He reached out and placed a hand on her arm, preventing her from stepping into the street. "Careful, Miss O'Connell. Even at night one must keep an eye out for traffic."

She shivered as a team of four horses raced by, the carriage careening slightly before it straightened out. "Thank you, Mr. Hunt. You are my savior tonight."

"Then I will count today as a success. I rarely get to help young ladies anymore."

His words reminded her of his past. "How old is your little daughter now?"

"Four. She is four." He softened. "She has my heart. She is adorable."

"I bet she is. What is her name again?" Bridget had heard the little girl's name, but she didn't want to sound too familiar.

"Mary." He sighed. "I don't get to see her all that much. My sister, Janet, is basically raising her."

"You don't have much choice. You must miss your wife at times like this."

"I miss her all the time. My Irene was a good woman."

"I'm sorry I brought her up."

"Don't be. I never want the day to come that I forget to thank God for my blessings. She was one of them." He stared at her. Smiled, then shook it off. "Look at that. We're here."

The Hartman loomed tall behind her. Gaslights cast a gorgeous glow on its grand marble entry. "Thank you for seeing me home."

"It was my pleasure. Sleep well, Miss O'Connell. And best of luck tomorrow."

"Pray for me." She teased, though it pleased her to learn he acknowledged God in his life. Perhaps he, too, had been raised to believe.

"I will," he said in all seriousness. "I will pray for all of us."

On that note, he turned and walked away. Moments later, he blended into the dark shadows of the streets.

When she blinked, Bridget had the strange sensation that he had practically vanished into the night. She also suddenly felt compelled to pray in earnest. It was starting to feel as if everything in their lives was about to change.

The feeling of foreboding settled in and gave her pause. Making her wonder if she suddenly had far more to fear than ever working in a gentlemen's club.

CHAPTER 12

Lydia discovered Mr. Marks lounging in her kitchen at half past nine in the morning. Next to him was a woman about her age, holding a cloak and overnight bag, and dressed in a plain black dress. She looked far less at ease than Mr. Marks.

As for herself? Well, she was barely able to stifle her scream. "Mr. Marks? What are you doing here?"

He looked rather unperturbed as he got to his feet. "There you are. At last," he drawled as he looked her over. "We've been waiting on you at least a quarter of an hour. I feared I was going to have to send Bridget upstairs to awaken you. I must admit that I'm rather surprised to discover that you sleep so late."

"I've been awake," she retorted before remembering that she should be asking him why he had broken into her house with a woman dressed as a maid.

"Didn't seem that way."

Recovering, she glared at him. "How did you get inside?"

"Picked the lock." He frowned as he sat back down. "You've got a poor one, I'll tell you that." With a scowl, he said, "You might as well have left the door open or placed a sign out front inviting everyone in."

"The locks stood up to everyone but you."

He had the nerve to look pleased about that. "I'll send someone by later to install a better one."

"Mr. Marks. Please. Do not."

He leaned back, having the audacity to place one polished shoe on his opposite knee. "Though you haven't asked, this is Bridget O'Connell. She works for me."

"How do you do, Miss Bancroft," Bridget said.

Lydia yearned to rail at Mr. Marks, but for some reason good manners prevailed. Instead, she inclined her head. "Miss O'Connell, good morning." Suddenly, she remembered seeing her at the Hartman that day. She had assisted Mr. Marks. "You helped when I hurt my hand, didn't you?"

"Yes, miss."

Sebastian frowned. "You didn't hurt your hand, Lydia. Avondale hurt you." He cleared his throat. "In any case, Bridget here is going to be working for you from now on. I noticed you needed a maid, and I trust there is a room somewhere in the house for her."

It took a moment for his words to sink in. Feeling the weight of both Bridget's and Mr. Marks' stares, Lydia smoothed her hair back before realizing that she was giving herself away. She was quickly learning that it was best to never let Mr. Marks see when she was nervous or unsure. "I, uh, am afraid that is not all right with me."

He looked nonplussed. "I'll be paying her salary, of course. Don't worry about that."

"That is not exactly—"

Completely ignoring her, he motioned to a box of items on the kitchen counter. "Bridget never had cause to do much cooking for me, but she says she does know how to make a few things until we decide about a cook."

Lydia glanced from Bridget to Mr. Marks to Bridget again. Though the maid was sitting quietly, there was a look in her eyes that told Lydia she knew exactly how Lydia was feeling.

Seeing that helped embolden her.

"Ah, no. Mr. Marks, you may not simply begin managing me."

"You said we were friends, didn't you?"

"Yes. Yes, of course. But not the kind who would—"

"Then I am doing this for you in friendship. That's the conclusion I have come to, and the least you can do is tell me thank you."

"Sir. Forgive me, but I fear you are misunderstanding the definition of friendship."

"I understand the meaning of the word well. Friendship is the mutual affectionate relationship between two or more people."

"I was referring to our actual relationship, not the definition found in Webster's dictionary."

His statement stung because it reminded her of how much she hadn't actually been making friends, instead memorizing definitions and reading about characters.

However, even though she might not have had much actual experience in making friends, even she knew his high-handedness was beyond the pale. "We need to talk, Mr. Marks."

He looked her over, seemed to contemplate that for a moment, then turned to the maid. "Bridget, go upstairs and check on Lydia's mother."

After standing and giving him a brief curtsey, she asked, "Will there be anything else?"

"I imagine Mrs. Bancroft will let you know what she would like done."

"Very well."

"But, please do inform Hunt if you have need of anything else. He should be stopping by in three hours or so."

After nodding to Mr. Marks, Bridget sent a sympathetic smile Lydia's way before heading up the stairs.

The moment they were alone, Lydia glared at her new, unsolicited benefactor, who was far exceeding the kind of help she had thought to accept when she imagined he might have returned the night before. "Mr. Marks, I must point out that your heavy-handed ways are particularly inappropriate."

"It's Sebastian, remember?"

"Fine. Sebastian, this is most irregular. I simply cannot accept this kind of help."

"Lydia, now that your engagement is over, you need to have a plan. At least as much of one as you can afford to have. You made it clear the other night that you did not want my assistance, but I am sure you are over that by now. Let me help."

"I will formulate a plan of action," she countered, hardly caring that she sounded particularly supercilious. "But in my own time. Not yours."

"The way I see it, you don't have that kind of time. You need to work at the library, pay your bills, not lose any more of your mother's possessions—"

"I know all that. Of course I know that."

"Your mother expects things to be like they used to be. And how much more can you afford to pawn or sell without your walls being completely bare?"

She felt herself pale at his words. Perhaps it was because they were so brutally honest. Perhaps it was the process of actually hearing her circumstances uttered in the bright light of day.

Whatever the reason, she felt dizzy.

He patted her on the back. Rather forcefully too. "For goodness' sake, breathe."

Obediently, she inhaled. It helped her flow of air, but not the way she felt about the conversation.

With his eyes focused intently on her, Sebastian waited for her to gain her bearings.

Only then did he bark a question. "Am I right, Lydia? Did I surmise your circumstances correctly?"

She ached to throw him out again. To tell him that he was absolutely wrong. But more than either of those things, she ached for her life to get easier.

And, it seemed, the only way that was going to happen was if she decided to accept his help. After all, no one else had been running forward to do that. And she had felt so alone.

"What is this Bridget like?"

"Like?" He blinked. "She's a good woman and hard worker. Intensely loyal."

"I hope my mother finds her satisfactory."

"You had best make sure your mother minds her tongue. I won't have her hurting my favorite maid's feelings."

He sounded so protective. "You sound as if you know her well." She wondered what, exactly, Bridget was to him. Did she even want to know?

"She has been my personal maid for two years now. I value her judgment and her discretion."

"If she is so valued, why are you asking her to work for me?"

"Because you are in need, Lydia. Young ladies of your station should not be venturing about without a proper escort or, at the very least, a maid."

"But still—"

"Lydia, don't be so stubborn. Accept Bridget's help. At least temporarily."

"What will you do? Do you have another woman in your employ whom you can trust?"

Something flickered in his eyes. "You truly care about that, don't you?"

She dared not contemplate as to why she was so intrigued by his feelings. "Yes, I think I do."

He smiled. "Because we are friends."

"Yes. Because, I suppose, we are friends." It was becoming terribly apparent that arguing any further about Bridget's employ was neither going to make anything change nor change her circumstances. He was right. Most ladies of her station did employ at least one housemaid.

She might as well accept Bridget's presence with grace.

"Then, well, I suppose I should accept your offer. Thank you. I will do my best to see that Bridget is treated kindly."

"Thank you." He smiled. "Now, please tell me. When are you going to the library today?"

"Um, I wasn't. This is Sunday, remember? The library isn't open. I was about to make a pot of tea . . ." She didn't want to admit her mother no longer attended church services, too embarrassed to go without new clothes. Lydia's wardrobe had been kept updated, but she did not care to face any stares given her broken engagement.

"I'll make you some tea. Go tell your mother good-bye. Then we'll go for a walk. Fresh air will do you good."

He was bossy. And too forward. And too, well, everything. Except what Jason had said he was—trouble. Surely her ex-fiancé could not have been more wrong. And she certainly wasn't going to tell Sebastian about Jason's bizarre visit last night.

Besides, she'd given up wondering why this man was in her life. Too much had happened to look a gift horse in the mouth.

And, well, Mr. Sebastian Marks was growing on her. If she were to be honest with herself, he'd been growing on her for quite some time. They were much alike, and few people were much like her. It was time to let down her guard and accept his friendship. To do anything else would be a mistake.

And with that, she went upstairs to check on her mother, introduce herself more fully to Bridget, and get ready for a walk on the arm of her handsome benefactor.

CHAPTER 13

CHICAGO TIMES-COURIER

From Mid-January 1894
Reported by Benson Gage

This reporter has become aware of more than one
gentleman who has been seen leaving Camp Creek
Alley with roughed-up clothing and visible bruises.
Either the area is even more unsafe than previously
thought, or the clubs that abound have become
even more dangerous than previously suspected.
Perhaps it is both.

She was charming," Lydia proclaimed with a laugh. "Charming and
inventive."

"She was a busybody and inappropriate," Sebastian countered
as they walked out of the library three days later. The cloudy day
hinted of snow, and the temperatures, combined with the wind, made
Lydia long to stay inside with vats of hot tea and a down quilt. "Jane
Austen's Emma was not a woman of character."

"Of course she was," she countered, just as a burst of wind rushed through the buildings and practically pulled off her hat. "Oh!" She reached up and planted one hand on the back of it, hoping to keep it in place.

"Has your hat pin become loose?" He glanced around. Perhaps he could pull her back into the library and help her resituate it.

As if she could read his mind, she shook her head. "My bonnet is secure."

"I think that is wishful thinking in this wind."

"I'll be fine and my hat will be too." A teasing glint appeared in her eyes. "I find the wind refreshing."

"Indeed. Much like Emma," he said sarcastically.

"She wasn't that bad."

Sebastian noticed that her lips twitched. "You may say that, but we both know you are giving her qualities she didn't possess." He raised his eyebrows. "You know I'm right. Simply agree with me so that we may end this conversation."

"Very well. I agree." As usual, she looked put upon.

He stood by her side as she carefully locked the library's door before placing the keys securely back into her purse. "Sebastian, do you still want to have supper together?"

Tender feelings he hadn't known he possessed filtered through him as he stepped forward to fasten the top two buttons of her cloak. As he felt the material, he wished it were of better quality and thicker.

He wished that she would accept a gift of a cloak even more. But of course she would not.

He was going to have to feel hopeful about what she had given him over the past three days. Her smiles, her time. And, little by little, her trust. Since he was a man who usually trusted no one, earning her trust felt like a wondrous gift.

"Of course I still want to have supper with you," he said as he held out his arm for her to take. "Why else would I be here?"

"For the last two days, you simply escorted me home."

"It was on my way."

"I think not."

"I wanted to check on Bridget," he said as he took care to be on the outside of the sidewalk, near the worst of the ice and grime that was piled on the streets.

"Really?" One eyebrow arched. "You barely spoke with her five minutes."

"Bridget and I are not in the habit of entering into lengthy conversations."

"Your conversation still seemed particularly short."

He was tired of trying to think of reasons that made no sense. "Didn't you say you were pleased with her work?"

"Of course I did. She is wonderful. So organized and pleasant, and she is even able to keep my mother in line."

"Perhaps I should give her a raise. It sounds as if she deserves one."

She laughed before quickly covering her mouth. "Don't make me smile at such things. It isn't right."

"I will try not to." He was prevented from teasing her further when they passed Sergio Vlas. Grinning at Sebastian, he stepped closer. Sebastian tensed, wondering what he was doing in this neighborhood, ready to intervene if the other man dared to speak to Lydia.

However, Sergio only inclined his head and walked by.

Sebastian relaxed. He didn't think Sergio would ever be disrespectful to a lady of quality, but he did fear that he might let slip something about the Silver Grotto. He wasn't ready for Lydia to know anything beyond what he'd told her—that he was in business downtown.

After they entered the Hartman, he escorted Lydia to the dining room. With much fanfare, the staff seated them at the best table, causing several of the other diners to turn their way.

Usually Sebastian simply had a tray delivered to his room. He didn't like to feel eyes on him while he ate, and he rarely wanted to take the time to enjoy a leisurely meal.

For that matter, until lately—very lately—he hadn't even been in the hotel at this time of the early evening. Usually he was working hard at the club and eagerly waiting for the sun to set so business would begin.

Therefore, he was of a mind to savor the rare, leisurely meal in public. He enjoyed seeing the twin spots of color appear on Lydia's cheeks as the maître d' placed a napkin in her lap and the assistant servers filled their glasses with water.

After he ordered beef filets for the both of them, accompanied by a course of soup and fish, Lydia looked more relaxed and was smiling at him in a direct way.

"You spoil me."

"Hardly." She had no idea the things he wished to do for her.

She dimpled. "I'm not going to argue with you because I've learned that it is a futile exercise."

"It seems I am making progress in our relationship."

"I've learned that it's easier to simply let you have your way."

"That's what I said," he replied, unable to keep from smiling smugly. "We have made progress."

"May I simply tell you thank you?"

He inclined his head as their waiter brought them delicate bowls filled with French onion soup laced with sherry. As far as he was concerned, seeing her smile was all the thanks he needed.

"Eat, Lydia. The chef's soup is usually delicious."

He watched her delicately spoon a small portion, blow on it, then taste. When she closed her eyes in appreciation, he picked up his own spoon. He wasn't especially hungry, but it wouldn't do to simply stare while she ate.

"Excuse me, Marks. We need to have a word."

Sebastian stilled as he turned to the voice. It was Jeffrey Galvin, and Vincent had obviously delivered the message Sebastian had become too distracted by Lydia to deliver himself. "I think not."

"It won't take but a moment."

"This is neither the time nor the place," Sebastian warned.

"I have no choice but to speak with you here and now. You won't let me back into your club."

As he felt Lydia's attention move from her soup to Galvin's words, a slow pain pierced his chest. It seemed no matter how hard he tried, his life was always, always going to infringe upon his wants.

He forced himself to answer Galvin as quietly and concisely as possible. "You have been refused admittance because you now owe a substantial amount of money, one over any limit I allow. I am sure my man Hunt told you that on my behalf. When your debt is paid, you will be welcomed again," he lied. Galvin would never be welcomed back to the Grotto after daring to speak to him in front of Lydia.

"I could pay you back if you'd let me play the tables."

"That strategy has not proven to be successful."

Galvin's voice turned louder and filled with loathing. "You certainly seem to have an answer for everything."

"I only speak the truth."

"No, you twist things to your benefit." Galvin waved a hand. "As if you have that right. As if you were my equal. I can't believe I'm reduced to speaking to you out in the open like this."

"Reduced?" Sebastian arched a brow. He certainly knew he was no gentleman. But he drew the line at being talked down to. He was no longer a scamp scrounging for pennies, and he didn't take kindly to any man treating him that way again.

"Even having to talk to you in a public place, you sit here acting like some king. Ruling lives. *Ruining them.*" He glared with disdain. "It's all an act, of course. We both know you are nothing."

Lydia was clenching her napkin in her hands. The other diners weren't even pretending to do anything but eavesdrop.

"I think not." Anxious to get Galvin away from their table, away from the curious eyes and ears in the room, away from Lydia, Sebastian said, "I will make an exception for you. Come to the club at eleven tonight. We will talk then."

Galvin's usually attractive features darkened with pure loathing. "As if I would ever trust you now. What do you plan to do to me in the back rooms of your club, Marks?" he asked, raising his voice. "Have me beaten up?"

Hearing Lydia's stifled gasp, Sebastian decided to accept that their friendship was most likely at an end. His only recourse was to deflect Galvin's lies and innuendos.

He got to his feet. "I'm afraid you have confused me with someone else," he bit out. Though, of course, Galvin hadn't. There had been many times in his past when only his fists gave him power.

However, for someone like Galvin, threats and loss of social standing were what mattered the most.

"I have you confused with no one. I saw Jason Avondale two nights ago, Marks. I saw what you did to him."

Sebastian heard Lydia gasp.

"I have no idea to what you are referring."

"The man was beaten black-and-blue. It was obvious that you had pulled in some markers to ensure that."

"This discussion is over."

Galvin turned to Lydia, his expression filled with arrogance. "You look like you've seen a ghost, Miss Bancroft."

When she froze, he smiled. "Yes, I know who you are. Jason's friends all know you threw him aside for the most notorious club owner in Chicago."

Sebastian didn't dare look at Lydia again. He didn't dare speak. He simply stood there, hands fisted, hoping to summon enough control to refrain from grabbing Galvin by the shoulders and escorting him out of the hotel. Actually, at the moment he was even considering the benefits of using his fists to force his submission.

Only when he regained control did he speak.

"Your accusations bore me. I suggest you leave before I make sure you are escorted off the premises by force."

"What about tonight?"

"I feel we have nothing left to say to each other. This conversation is finished."

"But—"

"Flannery, please help Mr. Galvin leave the premises."

"Very well, sir," the burly hotel employee said as he approached Galvin. His expression was impassive, but Sebastian knew the man's build and obvious strength spoke volumes for him.

"You are going to regret this, Marks," Galvin stated.

Sebastian said nothing. Because there was nothing to say. He very much regretted what had just happened.

And when he finally forced himself to turn to Lydia and saw her wide, pale-blue eyes gaze at him in an awful turn of hurt and amazement, Sebastian Marks felt the kind of despair he used to know when he was in his tenement and hoping that his mother would return alone.

It was the type of feeling he'd foolishly believed he would never encounter again. He'd been so utterly wrong.

CHAPTER 14

I am sorry you had to witness that," Sebastian said before picking up his glass of water and drinking it deeply.

Lydia watched the muscles in his throat contract as he gulped. She found it easier to concentrate on that instead of the conversation that had just taken place.

With a shaking hand, she picked up her glass and drank deeply too. However, instead of feeling refreshing, she rather thought the water tasted stale. She'd never been one for spirits, but she couldn't deny that a glass of sherry sounded like it might be helpful.

Because as everything that she'd just heard sank in, Lydia realized the gentleman sitting across from her was not the man he'd led her to believe.

Sebastian was staring at her intently. "Are you all right?"

Blunt questions called for honest answers. "No, I don't believe I am."

He said nothing as two waiters carefully removed their bowls of soup before placing plates of fish in front of them. The chef had left both the fish heads and tails intact. Only the middle had been prepared for consumption.

After meeting the fish's vacant eye, Lydia further lost her appetite. She was fairly sure she'd never seen anything that looked so repugnant. "I think I would like to leave now."

He carefully placed his fork on the side of his plate. "You haven't touched your meal."

"I find I am no longer hungry."

"I see." He pressed his lips together. "We need to talk about what just happened."

"I am not ready to listen. I need to go."

"Stay anyway."

"Mr. Marks, I think not."

"We're back to Mr. Marks now?"

"Yes. I . . . I need some time to reflect on what I just heard."

The lines around his mouth deepened. It was obvious he was trying his best to not only explain himself, but temper his voice. "You don't need time. You need to hear what I have to say."

Aware that several pairs of eyes in the room were still intently watching them, she picked up her fork and carefully flaked off a miniscule portion. "Who are you, really?"

"I am who you know me to be."

"I'd prefer that you stop speaking in ridiculous riddles. Tell me what that man was talking about. What in the world is a 'grotto'?"

"It is an artificial structure or recess built to resemble a cave."

Her temper flared. "I know what a grotto is. I want to know why you have one. And why he wants to visit."

"The Grotto is the name of my club." His chin lifted. "Actually, it is called the Silver Grotto."

"The Silver Grotto," she repeated, more confused than ever. "What kind of club is this?"

"It is a gathering place for gentlemen." After a pause, he averted

127

his eyes, looking just beyond her. "Men frequent the Grotto when they are in search of spirits. And gambling."

She was shocked. "Isn't gambling illegal?"

"Supposedly."

"Supposedly isn't an answer. Either it is or it isn't."

"A lot of powerful men come to the nether regions of my club to gamble, Miss Bancroft. The police who patrol the area have long looked the other way."

"They do? That doesn't seem right."

He shrugged. "Even Irish cops can use a bit of financial incentive now and again."

She wondered what that meant. She was finding his short answers insufficient. Only his obvious unease—and the sense that he would be disappointed if she left—was preventing her from getting up and exiting the dining room.

"What did that man mean about Jason? Does he frequent your club?"

"Yes." The word sounded as if it had been forced out between his teeth.

She pushed harder. "And he lost money there?"

His expression became harder. "He did."

His reticence was frustrating. But even more disturbing, to her at least, was the way she was reacting to the news. Instead of focusing on the revelations about Jason, or even her curiosity about why Mr. Marks was running a gentlemen's club in the first place, Lydia kept dwelling on her own hurts and insecurities.

How had she so misread Sebastian Marks' character? She'd believed he was her friend.

She'd even imagined that perhaps one day he would be able to overlook her spectacles, red hair, freckles, and bookish nature and see something of value in her.

No, she'd wanted more than that, she firmly reprimanded herself. She'd secretly wanted him to fall in love with her. Yes, even to desire her.

To her great embarrassment, she'd sometimes even dreamed that one day he'd want to marry her.

Until the first day he strode into the reading room, she hadn't believed such fanciful notions existed. She certainly had never imagined she could have a romance of her own.

Now she wished she'd never let those dreams take flight.

"You look upset," he stated. "I apologize if you feel as if I've betrayed you."

"'As if I've betrayed you'? As if?" she sputtered. Pressing her hands together in her lap, she leaned toward him. "Mr. Marks, you misrepresented your entire identity to me."

"I did not. You never specifically asked me what I did."

"You are splitting hairs."

"No, I am stating the facts. You may not accuse me of lying to you about occupations and habits you had no knowledge of."

"I didn't think I needed to ask you," she protested. "I thought you were a gentleman. I thought you lived here, at the Hartman."

"I didn't lie. I do live here."

"And Bridget? What is she to you?" she recklessly asked. "Is she one of your . . . your women?"

His dark eyes turned icy. "Be careful, Miss Bancroft. You are about to harm a very decent woman's character. And she has been nothing but kind to you."

"I disagree. She had to have known that I thought you were simply a rich man. She knew I thought you were upstanding. I can't believe you put someone in my home with instructions to lie to me and my mother."

He had the audacity to roll his eyes. "Oh, for heaven's sake, Lydia. You are being increasingly dramatic. Please, why don't you show me where I've stabbed you in the heart?"

His words were so hurtful, his attitude so blasé, it was taking Lydia everything she had to keep her composure. Any concerns she had about his feelings fell to the wayside. "Do you have anything to add before I leave?"

Sebastian stared at her for what felt like a solid ten minutes, though it was most likely only a few seconds. "Yes," he said around an exhale. "Please know that I am sorry. I never meant for things between us to become so convoluted. If you want to know the truth, I liked knowing there was at least one person in the world who thought I was decent."

Each word he spoke seemed pulled from the recesses of his heart. Each word was filled with emotion—and a terrible thread of disappointment.

It made her regret her harsh words. "Sebastian—"

He ignored her. "Lydia, I needed this relationship with you. I liked how you thought I was reputable. Worthy."

Her lip trembled. "I'm sorry."

He still was staring straight ahead. "After we got to know each other better, I wanted to protect you. I didn't want the other parts of my life to sully you. And now it seems as if everything I've tried so hard to keep to one side has bubbled over into your life. I hope, in time, you will find a way to forgive me."

His expression was so full of regret, his tone so sincere, it burst her bubble of pain. "Sebastian, I am sorry if you thought I needed to be cosseted, but I don't. I'd much rather know the real you than a make-believe version. Who are you, really?"

"I am not a gentleman." He frowned. "I am far from that. I grew up poor, just outside the slums and tenements near the docks." He lowered his voice. "My mother did not know who my father was."

She didn't understand. "How can that be?"

"She . . . she sold herself to men. For money." Still not meeting her gaze, he lowered his voice to something very close to a whisper. "She continued to do that until she died."

Lydia knew she was naïve. She knew she hadn't experienced too many things. But she read a lot. And she was observant too. Somehow, he'd reworked himself from being the poor son of a prostitute to a well-read gentleman of considerable wealth. "Mr. Marks, Sebastian, you are so polished and debonair. How did you become the way you are? What was it like for you, growing up?"

"Lydia, I am sorry, but I cannot speak to you about that."

"I think you owe me the truth."

"Trust me. It is better if you don't know the truth. It is not pretty, particularly interesting, or the least bit heartwarming."

She set her fork down on her plate, her food half-eaten. She was surprised. She hadn't realized she'd been eating while he'd been laying his heart on the table.

When the white-jacketed waiter appeared at her side, she motioned for him to remove her plate.

"I wish you would eat more."

"I can't at the moment."

"Please try for me."

His words, his caring tone, could very easily melt her resolve. But then where would she be? "My eating habits are none of your concern," she said. But when she noticed a look of hurt flash in his eyes, she realized she could no more hurt him intentionally than it seemed he could face her with the truth.

"Sebastian, I know you said you wanted me to see a different side of you, but why were you not honest with me from the start? After all, I am nobody special. I'm no one you would have needed to impress."

"I thought differently."

"But I am only a librarian. I promise I wouldn't have cared who you were when you visited. If you wanted books, I would have still lent them to you. It's my job to provide books to the citizens of Chicago, not pass judgments on behavior or morality."

"Truth?"

"Of course."

"I do value you. I like how smart you are. I value that very much. Lydia, I really did want there to be one person in the world who thought I was everything I longed to be. I didn't want to lose that."

She knew what he meant. She, too, had always dreamed of being something more than herself. Something like the women in her books, with their many admirers and incomparable beauty. And even though she knew her dreams were never going to come true, she could understand someone wanting that.

It seemed even a rich and powerful and exceptionally handsome man like Sebastian Marks had dreams too.

She didn't know if that made her feel better or worse.

But she did know she believed Jason and Galvin were gamblers and angry, vindictive men because they lost and owed money. If Jason had been beaten, however—though she did not like to think of anyone being hurt—she did not believe Sebastian had anything to do with it.

Perhaps whoever Jason was convinced had been following him had also beaten him.

She didn't know. There was so much she didn't know.

"How can I make this up to you, Lydia? I don't want to lose your friendship."

"You can take me to your Grotto."

His eyes widened. "You don't know what you're asking."

"I am asking to know the place that helped you become the man you are. I am asking to see the place where Jason became a desperate man."

"It is no place for ladies."

"We both know I'm not much of a lady."

"You are."

"That Mr. Galvin thought I was your mistress."

"His words were meant to hurt me, not you."

"Mr. Marks, take me there tonight, or I will go home, tell Bridget to leave my house, and ask you never to enter my reading room again." Of course, the moment she heard her threat, she felt her skin flush. What kind of threat was that, really?

"You will go hungry—or at least lose everything you have."

The fact that he focused on her circumstances instead of her feelings broke her heart. Did he really think his disappearance from her life would be easy for her to recover from? "I would make do. What do you say, Mr. Marks? Are you feeling brave enough to show me your club tonight?"

"You drive a hard bargain, Miss Bancroft."

"Does that mean you will?"

Time became suspended between them again as waiters arrived with the meat course. "First, you must eat."

Now that she'd gotten her way and was feeling the novel excitement of being just an hour or so away from somewhere a little dangerous and forbidden, her appetite was back.

Picking up her fork, she said, "I will clean my plate, Mr. Marks. Suddenly I've found I'm almost ravenous."

"Suddenly I'm finding that you are incorrigible."

When she popped a piece of steak in her mouth, he stood up. "Please excuse me for one moment."

Seeing that Mr. Hunt was lurking over by the dining room's entrance, she nodded. "Of course, Sebastian."

"Absolutely incorrigible," he muttered under his breath as he strode over to the man who was staring at him with a solemn expression.

———

Sebastian greeted Vincent Hunt, then led him to a quiet spot down the hallway. "Glad you're here, Hunt," he blurted. "Something has come up. I need you—"

But instead of looking attentive, Hunt looked pained. "Sir, I am sorry to interrupt, but there has been a new development. Another gambler was stabbed last night."

"So? People are dying like flies these days."

"This one was a foreigner, someone well-known in Belgium. The police are combing the area for suspects, and for some reason they seem focused on the Grotto."

Sebastian barely refrained from rolling his eyes. "Perhaps because we are the finest establishment, one well-off foreigners know. They'll either find nothing or commandeer some poor sod no one will miss even as he is hanging from the gallows. The fact is, we have more important things to focus on."

Hunt stilled. "What is it, sir?"

"I need you to go to Miss Bancroft's home, summon Bridget, and bring her here. Immediately."

To his surprise, Hunt's posture changed. If Sebastian didn't know better, he could have sworn that Hunt looked a bit disappointed with the request.

"Is Bridget returning to work for you at the hotel?" he asked.

"No. The two of you are going to accompany me and Miss Bancroft to the Silver Grotto tonight."

Hunt stared at him incredulously. "Sir?"

"Do you now require explanation to do as I bid?"

"No, sir."

"Good. Now, go get Bridget and bring her here. Immediately."

Staring directly in front of him, Hunt nodded. "Yes, sir." He then turned and walked away, his gait stiff and indignant.

Obviously his assistant did not approve of Sebastian's treatment of Bridget. It was interesting. Worth noting.

But as he crossed back into the dining room, where Lydia was sitting, looking more lost than ever, Sebastian realized he was going to have to wait to have that conversation with Vincent as well.

Currently, there was only one person on his mind, and that was a lady with auburn hair, perfectly proportioned lips, and a better vocabulary than the average man.

The lady who had not even asked if he was responsible for Avondale's beating.

"Forgive me for leaving you," he said as he returned to his chair.

"Is something wrong?"

"Perhaps." Everything was wrong. "You remember Hunt. He went to get Bridget so you will have a chaperone this evening."

For the first time since that idiot Galvin arrived, Lydia smiled.

"So you really are going to let me go see your club tonight. Go to the Silver Grotto."

"I suppose I am." Suddenly, he hated the name. Whereas it used to amuse him and make him think of all things dark and otherworldly, the thought of viewing it through her eyes made it seem rather sordid.

Her pretty eyes shone. "I'm so glad."

"I can imagine. You got your way." Where was his little mouse?

"You know that's not the only reason I want to see it, Sebastian. I am eager to learn more about you."

"You may regret that goal. But if you do, pray, don't remind me. After all, you didn't give me much choice in the matter." Still feeling rather put upon, he added, "Rather none at all."

But instead of looking appropriately chastised, a smile played on her lips. "I think I would like some coffee now, Mr. Marks. I need to be at my best because it's going to be a busy night."

"Of course." He gestured to the waiter to bring coffee for the both of them and a chocolate soufflé for Lydia. The soufflé would occupy her until Hunt returned with Bridget.

And she did enjoy her sweets.

She pressed her hand to his arm then. "Please don't worry, Sebastian. I know my visit will be slightly inappropriate, but everything is going to be all right."

"You sound so certain."

"I am, because you will be with me." Her voice suddenly sounded musical. Light and sweet.

The selfish survivor in him knew he should bask in the sweetness of the comment. After all, when she knew the whole truth about him, she wasn't going to be thinking anything other than the need to stay away from him.

Far, far away.

In the meantime, he needed to keep her inquisitive mind at bay and her beautiful figure in one piece.

Right in the middle of Camp Creek Alley. Most likely until the wee hours of the morning.

It was going to be a very, very long night. He was also sure he was going to regret every moment of it.

CHAPTER 15

Hearing a brisk knock at the door of the Bancrofts' townhouse was unusual. Hearing it after dark, at almost nine o'clock at night, was unheard of.

During the few days since she'd become Lydia's maid and her mother's nurse, Bridget had already learned quite a bit about the regular routines of the two women.

It seemed they lived just about the quietest existence in the city of Chicago. Lydia arose early, insisted on seeing to her own needs for her first hour, then after a solitary cup of coffee or tea began preparing for her day. Her breakfast consisted of toast.

She often read to her mother for a few minutes before getting dressed. Her voice melodic and sure, she would read each page with great enthusiasm. Bridget was fairly sure Lydia enjoyed the story time with her mother far more than Mrs. Bancroft did.

After she read, Lydia would dart into her bedroom and hastily don one of her four rather plain shirtwaist dresses if she was going to the reading room. Unlike her mother, she had several fashionable day and evening gowns. They were of good quality but not especially notable. However, Bridget assumed they had kept up Lydia's appearances in her search for a husband. Knowing what Mr. Marks expected, Bridget vowed to keep Lydia's clothes pressed and mended. She had even offered to update an old evening gown she'd seen in Miss Bancroft's wardrobe, though Bridget feared any efforts she made would be wasted. Miss Bancroft had merely stared at her blankly when Bridget had suggested an addition of lace. Perhaps her mother had chosen all her clothes.

After she dressed, Lydia would grab her coat and tote bag, and because it was what Mr. Marks wanted, Bridget accompanied her to the library before returning to see to Mrs. Bancroft.

The evenings were quiet as well. Though she was having supper out with Mr. Marks this evening, on previous evenings Lydia had read a chapter from a book while Bridget made supper for the ladies. Then Bridget helped both Bancroft ladies brush out their hair before bed.

Other than light cleaning and catering to Mrs. Bancroft, who liked to complain but wasn't especially demanding, that was the extent of Bridget's days and evenings.

She had not received a single visitor yet.

When the knock came again, Bridget was brought back to the present and opened the door. Perhaps Lydia had forgotten her key? Or perhaps Miss Bancroft at last had a caller?

She hoped it was not Avondale—though Mr. Marks seemed to think he could show up.

Instead, she came face-to-face with Mr. Marks' personal assistant. He also happened to be her own special brand of purgatory. Ever since he'd walked her from the Grotto back to the hotel, he had made her think about her former life. Made her remember when she'd thought she had choices and could one day have a relationship. A husband. Children.

Immediately her cheeks flushed. "Mr. Hunt!"

"Miss O'Connell," he said as he walked right inside. "I need to speak to you."

"What happened? Is something wrong with Miss Bancroft?" A new fear bubbled forth. "Is it Mr. Marks? Has something happened to him?"

Vincent's lips thinned. "Not exactly."

Before she stopped herself, she reached out and gripped his arm. "Please tell me. Don't make me think the worst. Is he all right? Is he hurt?"

He stared hard at her hand before his gaze skimmed her body, at last resting on her face. She might have imagined it, but he looked a bit hurt. "He is fine, Bridget. Don't worry so."

Feeling foolish, she swallowed. Then remembered she was still holding on to him and hurriedly pulled her hand away. "Why are you here?"

"Marks wants us to accompany him and Miss Bancroft to the Silver Grotto."

She blinked. "I'm sorry. I believe I misunderstood what you just said?"

"I don't joke about our employer's whims and wishes," he said stiffly. "You know that."

"So you came here to retrieve me?"

He nodded. "Time is ticking away. Go do whatever you need to do to get ready."

Glancing down at her plain gray dress, she wondered why he thought anyone would notice what she was wearing. But instead of pestering him with more questions and comments, she nodded. "I'll be right back."

She turned and ascended the staircase, stopping briefly outside of Mrs. Bancroft's door, but ultimately deciding to keep her departure secret. Chances were good that she wouldn't even wake up and would therefore never know Bridget had left the house.

If she was awake, then Bridget would be forced to lie about her errand. She didn't want Miss Bancroft to feel as if she were being betrayed. More importantly, she didn't want Mr. Marks to imagine that she was talking freely about his private interests.

Once she got to her small and tidy yet comfortable room in the attic, Bridget changed into one of her old evening gowns, grateful that Mr. Marks had had the rest of her belongings sent over. It wasn't anywhere near fashionable, but the fabric was good and the cut flattered the slim lines of her figure. With gloves, she could fit in most anywhere. At the Grotto, no one would be looking at her dress, only the rest of her person.

After taking down her hair, she pinned it up again, smoothing it carefully and securing it with a couple of jet-embedded combs that had been her grandmother's. They were pretty but had never been considered valuable enough to fetch a pretty penny.

After picking up her carefully cleaned and neatly mended gloves, she slipped them on as she descended the stairs.

The moment she came into view, Vincent stood up. As he watched her approach, she was enough of a woman to notice that true appreciation glowed in his eyes.

"Need help?" He reached out a hand, obviously intent on fastening the trio of buttons at her wrist.

"Thank you." She placed her hands in his and watched as he carefully fastened the buttons. "When I lived at the Hartman, I would simply get one of the girls there to help me."

Obviously, it wasn't the first time she'd been so close to him. But it was definitely the first time he'd performed such a service for her. The intimate chore made her cheeks heat and her mind drift.

What if he had come to see her by choice? What if he yearned to make their relationship about more than duty and obligation? Then she'd feel like a woman of worth again. Not because of money or status or privilege. But because a good man had decided that she was worth his time and attention.

She could only imagine what that would feel like.

"Ready?" He was standing at the door. Not holding it open. And that small gesture reminded her to get her head out of the clouds and remember who she had become. She was the servant of a very infamous man in Chicago. That was what she had become. It didn't matter if she remembered how it had felt to be a sheltered young girl. In Vincent Hunt's eyes she was no one.

After pulling her cloak from the hall table, she slipped it around her shoulders, secured the enclosure, and strode to the door. "Of course."

"Let's go on then. You know how Mr. Marks is when he is kept waiting."

Nothing more needed to be said about that. Mr. Marks liked his way, and since she worked for him, she figured he had that right. "Why is he taking Miss Bancroft to the Grotto? She has no business stepping into the club, let alone making that trek down Camp Creek Alley."

"I couldn't begin to guess why."

His voice was icy cold. "You sound as if you are angry."

"I am not."

She couldn't resist needling him. "But you sound like it."

"It is not for me to make judgments."

Ah. "I didn't mention judgments. With whom are you angry? Mr. Marks or Miss Bancroft?"

His lips pursed, and as they picked up the pace, she realized there was a very good chance that he was going to refuse to answer her. She didn't blame him. His future was just as dependent on Mr. Marks' good will as hers was.

And though he'd never said a thing, she had a feeling that he had

had a good dose of living in far worse situations and knew better than to wreak havoc on the very thing that had brought about the change in those circumstances.

Because she could still feel the tension flowing through his arm, she gave him an out. "I'm sorry for pushing for more information than you can share. I, uh, need to learn to be more circumspect."

She laughed, realizing that she was speaking from the heart. "Actually, I should try to be more like you, I'm afraid. It's best not to speak of the hand that feeds me. I know what it feels like to go hungry."

"I'm displeased with both of them, if you want to know the truth," he blurted.

"Why?"

"Why?" He looked flummoxed before saying caustically, "Because they go through their lives without a thought for consequences."

"They?"

He nodded, the action stiff. "In her own way, Miss Bancroft goes through her days much the way Mr. Marks does. Neither tries to fit in with what society expects. Furthermore, they spend their days wishing for things they don't have or can't do instead of appreciating what they do have. Worse, they always seem to get them."

Though she could see his point, she also thought he was being a bit harsh, especially when his criticism referred to Mr. Marks. Bridget knew for a fact that their employer worked long hours and didn't spend much time—if any—daydreaming. "Well, now—"

"And look what has happened!" he exclaimed.

Because he looked so expectant, and because she had no idea to what he referred, she stared at him blankly. "I have no idea. What has happened?"

He gripped her elbow with one hand and curved the other around her back as a trio of gentlemen approached.

After they passed, he said, "Whatever their reason for going, their impetuousness has caused *him* to send *me* out to retrieve *you*. Like some fool errand boy."

"Um. Well . . ."

"And now, here you are."

"Yes—"

"Walking in the cold and dark, on the street late at night instead of safe in your room."

This was true, but she wasn't upset . . .

"Once more, he is going to make you escort *her* to the very last place you ever want to see again."

His continued use of pronouns was becoming amusing. "Vincent, while it is true that I don't care to work at the Silver Grotto, I really don't mind this errand."

"You should," he retorted. "Bridget, you should resent the intrusion." His voice rose. "You should be back at the Bancroft townhouse, sipping chamomile tea and resting. You should be comfortable and warm and dry."

Bridget decided not to mention that since it wasn't snowing or raining, she wasn't in danger of becoming wet. Instead, she pointed out the obvious. "Please don't distress yourself. My job is to take care of Miss Bancroft. You know Mr. Marks is paying me to be at her service. Every maid knows her lady's schedule and whims are her own."

"I'm sure Miss Bancroft knows it too," he retorted. "I saw her face, Bridget. She was glowing. She was excited that I was getting sent to retrieve you. She gave no thought to your welfare or wants."

As his words sank in, as she realized he had called her Bridget, the meaning of his rant became clear. "Vincent, you're concerned about me."

"Well, of course I am," he bit out as they approached the front of the Hartman Hotel, then stopped.

Its marble façade gleamed in the moonlight, making it look magical. Bridget realized then how rarely she'd seen it at night. She also had to privately admit that she was glad she was getting the opportunity. It was a thing of beauty. If Mr. Marks had never called for her, if Miss Bancroft had never accepted Bridget's appearance in her life, Bridget would have missed chances like this.

And it would have been one more item in a list of many that she would have never, or rarely, experienced if she hadn't gathered her courage, approached Mr. Marks, and asked him for a job.

Perhaps she was being naïve, but she wasn't going to start finding fault with the world or how the social classes treated each other. Bridget hadn't grown up privileged, but her family had certainly been steps above her current station. She knew that if her mother had asked for their one maid to accompany her somewhere, all of them would have been shocked if the maid had shown reluctance. It simply wasn't done.

"Thank you for your concern. However, I promise I am not upset about being sent for. I am well aware who butters my toast. For what it's worth, I like my toast buttered. I've had it plain."

Vincent rocked on his heels, a sure sign he was not happy. He was such a physical man, she thought. Taller even than Mr. Marks, and carrying at least an additional twenty or thirty pounds of muscle on his frame. Being around him made her feel safe.

But at the moment, with his looking like he'd just bit into a sour lemon rind, Bridget couldn't help but reflect that he also amused her. In some ways, he was as out of place in the world as she was.

"You should not be taken advantage of."

"I'm not being taken advantage of. I'm doing my job. As are you," she added quietly when he looked prepared to protest.

He swallowed, looked like he was about to divulge a secret, then sighed. "Let us go in then. Time and tide waits for no man. And neither does Mr. Marks."

———

Lydia had just taken her fourth bite of the most sumptuous dessert ever created when she heard Mr. Marks give a sigh of relief. "At last."

Turning, she saw his assistant and Bridget standing just outside the restaurant. "They made it." With regret, she put down her fork. It was a shame to pass up the opportunity to eat a little bit more of the chocolate soufflé, but her waistline would probably not appreciate it. Corsets were uncomfortable enough without punishing her body by eating too many calories.

"Are you done already?"

"Yes. Are you ready to leave now, sir?"

He glanced at the soufflé again before looking at her directly. "What is wrong with it?"

"Nothing. Of course it is wonderful. Truly one of the most wonderful things I've ever enjoyed."

"Then why didn't you finish it?"

"I know you are ready to go."

"Eat, Lydia. We will wait."

"I hate the thought of inconveniencing you."

"It's not an inconvenience to watch you enjoy a treat," he said quietly. "Eat a little bit more, Miss Bancroft. The chef will be disappointed if you don't do justice to his efforts."

His words were no doubt painting the truth a bit bright. But they also were persuasive enough to be all she needed to take another few bites.

It was extremely doubtful that she'd ever have the opportunity to eat this again anyway.

Things being what they were, she had a feeling that after Mr. Marks allowed her to see a little bit more into his inner sanctum, he wasn't going to want to know her anymore.

She knew from experience that letting a person in meant becoming vulnerable. She also knew what happened then, at least to her. When people knew how bookish and socially awkward she was, they turned away.

She was sure Mr. Marks would be no different. Actually, the only difference would be how his rejection would make her feel.

More alone than ever before.

CHAPTER 16

CHICAGO TIMES-COURIER

From Mid-January 1894

Reported by Benson Gage

One should note that ladies of good breeding should never consider visiting Camp Creek Alley. Of course, one would assume that any lady of good breeding would never desire to go near such an area in the first place.

They made an unusual quartet, walking as they did down the dark alleys and backstreets of Chicago.

Lydia was flanked by Mr. Marks on her left and Bridget on her right. Mr. Hunt, it seemed, was serving as their lookout. He by turns walked in front or behind them, depending on the corner they were on and how many people were around.

Though the streets were dark, there was enough light shining from the moon and gaslights and kerosene lamps glowing from the occasional window to allow Lydia to see sights she'd never known existed in her hometown.

Men in natty suits spewing coarse language loitered outside of taverns. Women, some looking world-weary, others far more scantily clad, walked furtively next to buildings. Groups of boys, each one made braver by the company of his cohorts, laughed and tipped hats at passersby.

And everyone, truly *everyone*, seemed not only to notice them but to treat Sebastian Marks with a healthy dose of respect.

As for her escort, the deeper they traveled into the recesses of the slums, the more Mr. Marks' posture and gait changed. Gone was his perfect posture and accommodating gait. Instead, he walked with a confident swagger. And when he wasn't checking to make sure she was all right, seeming to forget that he was holding her elbow in a death grip, Mr. Marks was staring at every person they passed directly in the eye.

Lydia found his transformation fascinating.

So much so, she continually found herself watching him instead of their surroundings. The only drawback she could ascertain was that she had no idea where she was. She'd neglected to take note of a single landmark, street name, or corner store.

Though she'd lived in Chicago her whole life, she had become a stranger in a strange land.

Now that Mr. Marks had released her arm, she slowed, gazed into the empty storefronts, let herself watch a poor man stuff another piece of newsprint under his clothes for added warmth. He wore an eye patch and was missing part of one leg. She wondered if he had been a soldier.

"Please, Miss Bancroft," Hunt pleaded as he stepped closer. "Try to be at least a little more aware of your surroundings."

Though she was tempted to relay that she had been actively trying to do that, Lydia knew he was attempting to keep her safe. "Yes, Mr. Hunt."

"You must stay in step with us," he cautioned. "It's for your safety."

"I'm doing just that. I wanted a better idea of where I am going in case I get lost."

"That is not going to happen," Mr. Marks muttered under his breath. "The only time you will ever need to find your way through Camp Creek Alley is if Hunt, Bridget, and I all became incapacitated. And that would be a shame."

"To be sure, sir," Mr. Hunt agreed. But he punctuated his comment with another most meaningful glance her way.

"I'll stay by your side, Sebastian," she said quietly.

When his eyes met hers and he smiled, she thought she'd never seen a man so handsome.

"Look who the cat dragged in," a voice called out, sounding both drowsy and amused. "Fancy you being here."

It was enough to divert her contemplation of Sebastian's cheeks and jaw.

When she turned to the newcomer, Lydia was taken aback. The man who approached was like nothing she'd seen before, outside of the carnival barkers along the World's Fair Midway. He was outfitted in a tight-fitting, shiny black suit. Almost a parody of gentlemen's evening wear.

But instead of remaining in unrelieved black and white, he'd added a splash of color in a magnificently embroidered vest composed of turquoise, magenta, orange, and azure blue. It drew her eye in the dark recesses of the alley, then upward to a man with slicked-back hair, piercing eyes, and olive skin.

To her shame, he watched her inspection with something that looked much like pleasure. His smile turned into a broad grin.

"Now, whom do we have here?"

Mr. Marks said nothing, merely glared.

"Come now. Surely you aren't going to ignore me, are you, Marks?" the man continued, picking up his pace to stay by Sebastian's side. "I would think twice about that. You know I don't give up easily. If you don't pay attention to me now, why, who knows where I'll show up next?"

"I'd think twice about that, Vlas," Mr. Marks said. "The consequences could prove foolhardy."

"Don't you mean deadly?"

Lydia gasped.

Beside her, Bridget stiffened, then pulled Lydia close to her side.

"Hunt," Sebastian barked, before abandoning them completely.

Worried that he was in possible danger, she called out for him. "Sebastian?"

"Probably not the best time to be calling his name, miss," Bridget said. "Around here it's best to not make much of a scene."

"I see." Though she really didn't. She thought the four of them already stuck out like sore thumbs.

Looking even more agitated, Bridget stepped closer. "We need to get out of here. Immediately."

The warning sounded ominous. As did the great number of men who seemed to suddenly slip through the shadows and surround Sebastian. Oh, it looked very dire, indeed. "But I fear—"

Hunt grabbed her elbow and motioned her forward. "Let's continue, miss. Quick-like, if you please."

His grip caused Lydia to stumble.

Immediately his grip loosened. "Beg pardon," he murmured, but he still held on to her in a death grip.

Abandoning Mr. Marks to the angry-looking crowd.

"But he looks like he is about to be attacked! We can't leave him alone."

"Rest easy now, Miss Bancroft," Bridget cautioned. "Mr. Marks will be all right. I promise, the last thing you want to do at the moment is make more of a ruckus than we already have. You'll distract him."

"You mean cause more of a disturbance than she already has," Mr. Hunt said darkly as he pulled her forward.

Now they were walking too quickly. Lydia understood the motivation, but she was tempted to remind Mr. Hunt that she was wearing tightly buttoned kid boots, a very narrow-fitted long gown, and an especially snug corset. Practically running anywhere wasn't an option. Then, of course, was the fact that the streets were narrow and dark. And there was, at times, a proliferation of debris on the ground.

That, alone, necessitated that one should tread carefully.

But because she was beginning to get the sense that Mr. Hunt didn't like her much right now, she stuck to the one topic she was sure he would respond to. She stopped and looked up at him.

"Forgive me for pointing out the obvious, but wouldn't it be wise for us to wait for Mr. Marks?"

"It would be foolhardy to stay," Mr. Hunt muttered under his breath.

"It isn't a good idea to stop along Camp Creek Alley," Bridget warned. "Not if one can help it."

"I appreciate your concern for my welfare, but isn't Sebastian in danger? Those men looked like rather rough characters. And there were a lot of them."

Hunt laughed then. "You really are as naïve as you look, aren't you?"

"Mr. Hunt, mind your manners," Bridget warned.

"I'm not going to say anything that she shouldn't already know."

"You leave that to Mr. Marks."

"What is it you're hiding?" Lydia asked, growing tired of their repartee.

"I'm not hiding a thing. At least not something that pretty much everyone in Chicago knows. Except for you, it seems."

She was sure there was another put-down in there somewhere. "What do I not know?"

"That it isn't those burly men you were describing who are the problem, Miss Bancroft. It's Sebastian Marks."

"What? I . . . I'm afraid I don't understand."

"Mr. Marks is the toughest man in these parts, and everyone knows it. He doesn't fear a soul."

"Of course he does."

"Not him. You see, he's the person everyone in the city fears, not the other way around."

Lydia halted immediately and stared at him in shock. "Surely you jest?"

"Not about this, miss," Hunt said with a grim look.

Just as a gang of hoodlums approached.

"Now you've gone and done it, Vincent," Bridget whispered as they were surrounded. "Mr. Marks is going to be mad at you, for sure."

As the men stepped even closer, their comments to one another growing ribald, Lydia shivered.

Under his breath, Mr. Hunt cursed. "I'm going to be lucky if he lets me live."

"What do we have here?" one of the burly men said as he stepped so close to Lydia that she could smell his sour breath. "Slumming tonight, pet?"

Pet? Oh, she did so hate that name, almost as much as "lamb." But instead of telling him that, for the first time in recent memory, Lydia elected to stay completely silent.

But her silence only seemed to please the men. "What's wrong, girl? Cat got your tongue?"

Mr. Hunt cleared his throat. "I should inform you that this lady is under Mr. Marks' protection. He will not take kindly to your interest in her."

"But he ain't here." A swarthy man with a hole pierced in his ear looked around. "A woman like you? No man who owned you would be letting you out of his sight. Not around these parts, leastways . . ." His voice drifted off in a meaningful way.

Then, to Lydia's dismay, he turned to Bridget. "Now, *you* are obviously in no man's protection."

Bridget flushed but remained silent.

Mr. Hunt cleared his throat, then said in the most aloof tone, "We really must be going. I suggest you move along."

"You can move along with the lady here. I know my place. Her family would have me in a cell for sullying her by morning." He wrapped his thick hand around Bridget's upper arm. "But I'll take this one."

As Bridget tried to pull away, Lydia gasped.

It was then that Mr. Hunt looked positively lethal. "She is under my protection. Unhand her."

"Or what? You might work for Marks, but you ain't him."

"Drop your hand."

As Bridget struggled against the man's grip, Lydia began to panic. She would have screamed for help except that no one around looked like he would either listen or lend a helping hand.

Just as Mr. Hunt slammed his fist into the assailant's nose with a jarring crack, Mr. Marks and Mr. Vlas joined the fray. Within seconds, their attacker was lying on the ground, his nose bleeding, his eye swollen, and a dazed look on the rest of his face. Mr. Marks barely had a smudge of dust decorating his trousers.

"You have made a very foolish mistake," Sebastian said with a fierce scowl. "I see you. I know your face. And I will soon know where you live."

The man's face went slack as he held up a hand. "Now, see here, Mr. Marks—"

Sebastian continued as if he hadn't said a word. "You won't have to wait long for retribution. Of that I can assure you."

Mr. Vlas laughed in a dark way. "And if he don't find you, never worry, I will."

At that the man went deathly pale.

Then, before the other men in the alley could do anything more than stare at Mr. Marks and Mr. Vlas in fear, Sebastian faced Bridget. "You all right?"

She nodded. "Yes, sir."

"Good." Turning to Lydia, he gently pressed his palm in the center of her back. His touch instantly made her feel more reassured. "Let's go now, dear. It's time we got you off of the streets. Past time."

Lydia knew the opportune time to ask questions had long since passed. She was still trembling from what had happened and feeling light-headed whenever she imagined what would have happened if that man had taken Bridget.

Meekly, she stayed by his side as he spurred her along. She knew Mr. Hunt and Bridget were directly behind them, could even hear them whispering to each other. However, she was too flustered to attempt to listen to what they were saying. Therefore, she kept her eyes on the ground, choosing to notice the irregular patterns of the damp brick and cobblestones under their feet.

Twenty minutes later—or it might have been only two—they arrived at a rather nondescript building built out of white limestone bricks. Nothing about it was remarkable except for the large, glistening double doors that look like silver. They were so shiny, so intricately designed, so, so enchanting, Lydia felt awed by their beauty.

Which was how she saw a fairly small silver sign embedded in the brick: The Silver Grotto.

They had arrived.

Without a word, Sebastian opened one extravagant door and waved her inside.

As Lydia looked around at the black-and-white-checkered marble floor, at the Grecian columns, at the murals of nude women on the ceiling, she knew she'd never imagined such a place existed. "Oh, my goodness, Sebastian. I have never seen the like."

He turned to Bridget as if Lydia had never said a word. "See that she gets upstairs without any further trouble. If that is even possible."

"Yes, sir. Come along, miss," Bridget said quietly, positioning herself in between Lydia and the occupants in the room.

Lydia let herself be led. She let herself be guided toward a set of back steps without pausing to look around, without meeting another person's eyes, without saying another word.

Up they went. Up a set of narrow stairs, turning down a narrow hallway whose only purpose was to look at the revelers below. She did peek over the side for the barest of seconds, only enough to view the cloud of fragrant, hazy smoke that billowed up like tangled plumes from a forgotten lady's hat.

"Almost there, Miss Bancroft," Bridget said. "Step lively, if you please."

Obediently, Lydia followed up another staircase, down a rather plain hallway that looked like it would be better situated in a university building or law office instead of a gentlemen's den.

At last, Bridget opened the door. "This is it."

Glad to at last be someplace where she could stop for a moment and regroup, Lydia looked around eagerly.

She didn't even try to conceal her surprise.

Bridget smiled. "It's a far cry from the Hartman, isn't it? One wouldn't even imagine that the same man could be at home in so many places. But he is."

"Except for that beautiful desk, it's very plain. Utilitarian."

"It is that, indeed." Looking around, she noticed the bare floor swept clean. Across from the desk were two rather uncomfortable-looking chairs. Wooden and ladderbacked, Lydia imagined they would be more at home in a kitchen than in a gentleman's office.

Ah, but that was the point, wasn't it?

Mr. Marks was not actually a gentleman. From what she could discern, he was just as rough and tumble a fellow as any of the men she'd encountered in the alley.

Thinking of those terrible, scary men again, she wrapped her arms around herself and hugged tight. She'd never been embraced by a man before, but she suddenly wished to have the experience. It was doubtful that she'd ever be warm again.

"Miss Bancroft, I think you should sit down."

"Thank you," she said quietly. "I believe I will." Warily, she eyed the chairs. Hopefully they weren't so small as to prevent her from sitting easily.

"Not there, miss. Over here."

Lydia turned, then barely managed to stifle her gasp. There, against the back wall, was a sumptuous couch, upholstered in bronze-colored velvet. The cushions were plump, and the sheer number of them practically invited a person to relax among them.

"This is beautiful."

"Hunt said they had a devil of a time getting it up through the windows. Rumor has it that it took at least six men between hoisting it up and pushing it behind."

"I can only imagine," she said as she sat down. Belatedly realizing she was sitting smack in the middle of it, she moved to one side. "Won't you join me?"

Bridget's expression softened before she shook her head. "Thank you, but no. That isn't my place."

"This place is obviously not mine either," Lydia said. "I fear Mr. Marks will never forgive me."

"What happened outside wasn't your fault, miss."

"If not mine, whose? I'm the one who begged to visit. I'm also the one who stopped even though both you and Mr. Hunt warned against it."

"It wasn't your fault," she said again. "You didn't know what Camp Creek Alley was like, did you?"

Lydia shook her head. "I had no idea." To herself, she was more blunt. For all her knowledge and perceived independence, she'd had no idea that there was an area so close to her home that was filled with dangerous people.

"Mr. Marks is a very smart man. Brilliant, he is. But he wasn't too smart tonight." Bridget paused, as if she was weighing her words, then blurted, "He knew better than to bring you here. It was foolhardy, it was."

"I cajoled him."

"He could have said no. And even if he had found himself agreeing, he certainly should have never left your side."

Lydia didn't want to put all the blame on Sebastian's shoulders. "I dare say he thought I would have handled things a far sight better."

Bridget tilted her head. "Do you? How so?"

"Well, um, I am well-read, you see. I know a lot of information."

"Beg pardon, miss, but I'm afraid I must point out that reading about something is never the same as experiencing it. Some things cannot be adequately described." Her face looking a bit melancholy, she shrugged. "It's the way of the world, don't you think?" She turned the handle on the door. "I need to go find Mr. Hunt and tell him you are settled up here. I'll be back soon." She looked doubtful for a moment. "I trust you will be okay?"

"I won't leave, Bridget. I promise, I'll stay right here until you or Mr. Marks returns."

"Thank you, miss. That will ease everyone's mind."

She quickly exited then, leaving Lydia alone on the top floor of a gentlemen's club, in the private offices of a gambler. She'd almost been attacked tonight. Worse, she'd put Bridget at risk as well.

All because she'd been eager to experience life. To get to know the elusive Sebastian Marks better. To have something besides her books and her mother and the burden of making a good-enough match to pull them out of their financial struggles.

But she'd only put many people in jeopardy. Mr. Hunt was mad at her, Bridget seemed disappointed . . . and Sebastian? Well, he would likely never speak to her again.

This, she supposed, should be a good thing. After all, she'd learned too much about him for them to ever remain friends. Hadn't she?

But as she sat alone in the room, tears pricked her eyes. This had been a horrible experience.

But the only thing worse was knowing that it would never—in all likelihood—be repeated.

CHAPTER 17

After throwing back a sizable amount of rye whiskey, Sebastian stepped back in the corner between the quickly filling bar and the rest of the room. When he'd first opened the Silver Grotto, before he'd learned to trust Hunt completely, he stood in this spot for hours at a time.

It afforded him an excellent view of the main room of the club but also was enough in the shadows that most never even glanced his way.

Back in those days, he'd lived his life in a haze of bitterness mixed in with paranoia that it was all going to go away within hours. He'd made friends with the cops who patrolled the area and soon learned they were understaffed and underpaid. They had no true desire to arrest a man for enjoying a few card games when so many more serious crimes occurred just outside the club. Sebastian had found that a couple of dollars, laced with a word or two of kindness, went a long way.

He'd also given generously to the widows and orphans fund.

Because of that, Sebastian had ruled the Silver Grotto with a mixture of care and disdain. He'd watched men drink themselves silly, count change to see if they had enough to venture downstairs. Or if their pockets were empty, they'd eye the infamous silver doors with a growing sense of defeat.

Sebastian had soon learned which men—even some on the police force—spent all of their paychecks on drink, forgoing the needs of their wives and children for a few hours of oblivion.

After hearing about the conditions in the various slaughterhouses, docks, and other factories, Sebastian had never blamed them. Men were maimed or died on the job every day, and no one but their family cared.

He had vowed that he would never be one of them.

That was why he'd used as much of his brain as he could to outsmart and trick any men in his way. He'd stayed up late, with only the cheapest candles for company, not only laboriously attempting to improve his reading, but practicing reciting the words he heard gentlemen saying on the streets.

That had been some time ago—almost a lifetime ago.

But not quite.

After he'd hired Hunt, after he'd hired floor managers to report to Hunt, he had spent far less time in the bar and more time walking among the gamblers down below. But of late, even watching that action had grown stale. For the last year, he'd begun to spend even more time in his private office in the back of the third floor.

He'd even begun to pretend that his life was much different than it used to be. It had become almost easy to forget how it felt to be cold and hungry, dirty and illiterate.

Now he slept in the best suite at the Hartman. His clothes were custom tailored, his hair trimmed by a private barber who visited his suite every three weeks.

He employed a woman to tend to his clothes and his room so he could keep his privacy.

Every so often, when he lounged in a fine dining restaurant or when he was visiting the Columbian Exposition, he'd known that to one and all, his transformation was complete. No longer was he the poor boy named Samuel Marx, sleeping on a flea-bitten mattress. Instead, he was the gentleman Sebastian Marks, the man who lived on the edge of polite society. Who sometimes was seen escorting ladies languishing in the fringes of society.

And had developed an unlikely but mutually satisfying relationship with a rather shy, rather beautiful librarian.

But this evening's short walk from the hotel to the Grotto had been nothing if not a revelation. He'd suddenly seen his life and its surroundings through her wide, scared eyes, and he had been the one who had been afraid.

It was time he remembered the truth. He was only a sham, a propped-up figment of a pitiful boy's hopes and dreams.

Looking at the factory worker standing at the bar, his clothes smelling faintly of blood and sweat, his ragged expression and desolate eyes revealing that tomorrow he would be doing the same things yet again, Sebastian knew without a doubt which of them was the better man.

At least that man was honest and could sleep at night, knowing he hadn't been living a lie. And worse, subjecting innocent women to that lie.

He was about to offer to buy the man a drink, or even pass him a few dollars to pass on to his wife, when he spied Hunt striding his way.

He pushed off from his spot and met him in the center of the room. "Do you have a report?"

Hunt nodded, his eyes as alert as they always were, carefully scanning each person, looking for trouble. Again and again, he met other men's looks directly, never flinching, always cool and calculating.

Once he seemed satisfied with what he saw, he turned to Sebastian. "The gambling is going well. Tables are filled and bets are high. You should be pleased with this evening's profits. Turner is doing a fine job of keeping a handle on things. It was right to promote him."

Sebastian was pleased with the news, though he could barely summon the interest in the tables. "What about Miss Bancroft? How is she faring?"

"Her?" he asked in a dismissive way. "Bridget told me Miss Bancroft is no worse for wear." His lips twisted. "She's also promised to stay in your office and out of trouble."

The tone in his assistant's voice was troublesome. With a jerk of his head, he directed Hunt to follow him toward a quiet place near the front door. "What is it that bothers you about her, Hunt?"

"What doesn't? That woman is far too impetuous and naïve. She doesn't listen either."

That woman? "All those things are true. But I still fail to understand the basis for your tone."

"Sir?" Vincent's lips curved up in a tentative smile, glanced Sebastian's way, then turned appreciatively more somber. "You know I meant no disrespect to you, sir. It's just that, well, it's obvious she is playing you."

Hunt's new desire to have an opinion on most everything was beginning to grate on his nerves. "I, for one, don't believe it was obvious, or that she was doing anything of the kind. In fact, I'm afraid you need to reevaluate your opinion of Miss Bancroft."

Vincent's eyes widened. "Yes, sir."

"Good. I don't want to ever hear you refer to her as 'that woman' again."

"I understand, Mr. Marks."

"If I ever get the sense that she feels that you are not her friend, you and I will have a problem."

His eyebrows rose. "You wish me to be her friend?"

"She needs one. She needs more than one, Hunt."

As his assistant was staring at him, his skin now tinged with gray, Sebastian noticed that Bridget was standing with two of the girls who served drinks and food in the basement. He had no idea why she was now standing in the middle of the room when he'd taken such pains to keep her from the club.

Worse, if Bridget, Hunt, and he were here, that meant Lydia was upstairs in his office by herself. Completely by herself.

Anyone could accost her, and he would have no knowledge of the fact.

"See to Bridget."

"What do you want me to do with her? Send her to your office?"

"No. I am going to see to Miss Bancroft. I want to make sure she is all right. We will not need a chaperone. Instead, take Bridget down to the kitchens and see that she is fed."

"Fed."

Pleased with the idea, Sebastian nodded. "Yes. Feed yourself, too, if you're hungry."

"And then?"

"Then keep her by your side," he continued, thinking quickly. It was too crowded to allow Hunt to leave. "I'll decide when it's time for you to escort them both home."

"Yes, sir."

Sebastian turned away without another word. After fishing in his pocket for a few dollars, he walked to the bar and pressed them into the slaughterhouse worker's hand.

"What's this for?" The man looked at him suspiciously.

"Take it home to yer missus," Sebastian said. "Let her use it on coal or food for a change."

The worker rolled his eyes. "What would you know about needing coal or food?"

The bartender coughed. "Watch it, Pete. That's Mr. Marks."

The man paled. "Beg yer pardon."

Sebastian shrugged. "I learned over the years not to question good fortune. But do as I say. That money is no good here."

"Yeah. Thanks."

Sebastian brushed off the thanks and quickly strode up the stairs. As he walked up each step, his heart started to pound. What if someone knew Lydia was alone?

What if she hadn't decided to listen to Bridget and ventured out on her own?

What if he lost her? What if she was hurt?

He fairly raced up each step, ignoring a pair of his workers as he rushed past them in the hall.

Only when he was outside his office door did he take a fortifying, calming breath. It would be foolhardy to enter in the state he was in. She was so intuitive; she would notice his unease immediately.

After closing his eyes and relaxing the muscles in his neck and shoulders, he opened the door.

"Lydia, forgive me," he began, intentionally keeping his voice light and easy. "I didn't mean to keep you sitting alone up here for so long."

As he closed the door behind him, he listened for her light laugh.

But he heard nothing.

Warily, he glanced at his desk, half thinking she would have decided to occupy his desk chair. But there was no one. Neither were the chairs facing the desk occupied.

The sense of panic he'd barely been able to control reared forth, causing a trickle of sweat to slide down his back. "Lydia?" he called out more loudly. He turned on his heel, scanning the rest of the room.

Then, miraculously, he rested his gaze on his lovely librarian. She'd somehow found his hidden stash of novels in the wooden crate under the couch and had opened a copy of what looked like *Robinson Crusoe*. Then, she'd fallen asleep.

Her spectacles were perched lopsided on her nose, and more than a few strands of her glorious auburn hair had fallen from her combs. One hand was hanging down, the other curved around the tome protectively, as if that book was all that was important.

A lump formed in his throat.

Stealth-like, he approached. Crouching on his knees, he gently pried the book from her grip and placed it back in its crate. Then, he pulled off her spectacles, folded the wire arms, and slipped them inside his suit pocket. That way he would know where they were at all times, in no danger of getting lost or damaged.

After debating the pros and cons of rearranging her figure, he decided not to move her. He didn't want to risk waking her. Instead, he walked to his coat rack, pulled off one of his older overcoats that he kept for whenever he felt the need to roam the area streets, and carefully laid it over her.

She mumbled under her breath, sighed, and to his amusement, curled into a ball.

Contentedly, he watched her sleep for a long moment. Happy that she was safe and sleeping soundly. Happy that he could watch her without her observing him staring too long.

A bump sounded down the hall. He stared at the door, half expecting Hunt to pound on it, alerting him to yet another fight or drunk or the appearance of someone too disreputable.

But the noise drifted off in a sigh, leaving the area quiet.

Sebastian walked to his desk and pulled out the day's folder of messages and receipts. After getting out his ledger, he settled in for three hours of paperwork.

As far as he was concerned, there was no place else to go. There was certainly nowhere else he'd rather be.

—

"You need to stay by my side," Vincent said as he approached.

Vincent looked so ill at ease, so different from his usual implacable self, Bridget eyed him curiously. "Why?"

"Because Mr. Marks ordered it, that's why."

"What is wrong with you? Has something else upset you?"

He blew out a harsh breath of air. "Why would anything be wrong? Other than, you know, we've got a lady librarian in our midst." To her surprise, his voice turned even more caustic. "In a few hours, we're going to have to go fetch her and escort her back home."

"All right."

"All right?" he snarled. "Aren't you just the least bit resentful of the fact that you should be sleeping right now?"

"I'm not tired." She shrugged. "To be honest, I'm having a good time."

"You shouldn't be here. Especially not in here."

"Mr. Marks must be thinking otherwise if he told you to stick to my side." She scanned the area, but saw no trace of his indomitable presence. "Where is he, by the way?"

Hunt motioned to the dark entryway of the back stairs. "He went to go check on her."

Bridget sighed, glad her instincts about the two of them had been correct. "Ah. Well, that's telling, don't you think?"

"Not really." He scoffed. "I bet Marks is afraid she ran off. I am."

"That is doubtful."

"Or is about to start wandering about the place like it's one of those white palaces at the fair."

"Those burned down," she retorted, unafraid to keep both her skepticism and a healthy amount of tartness from her voice.

Hunt waved off her protests with a hand. "For Pete's sake, Bridget. You know what I mean. She doesn't belong here."

"I daresay you are right. But what I think matters even more is that he didn't send me back up to sit with Miss Bancroft."

"He probably is feeling sorry for you."

"Mr. Marks doesn't feel sorry for his workers. He pays them to do a good job." Lowering her voice, she added, "Listen to what I am saying, Vincent. Mr. Marks is upstairs himself keeping her company. He wants to be with her. He cares about her."

"Don't know why. Or do you think there's more to her than meets the eye?" He waggled his eyebrows.

She deliberately chose to misunderstand. "Miss Bancroft is not stuffy at all. She's actually really very kind. And she has quite a nice sense of humor. You would like her, if you ever decided to unbend enough to give her half a chance." After a pause, she warned, "And you should really give her a chance. Mr. Marks is not going to take kindly to you being disrespectful to her."

"That is not what I was talking about." He smirked. "Maybe she's more of a light skirt than she lets on?"

Bridget glared at him, slightly shocked that he was determined to think poorly of Miss Bancroft. "Of course not. She is a lady, Mr. Hunt."

"Ladies don't always act like ladies. Surely you've seen enough at the hotel to know that."

"What do you know?" she taunted.

"I know more than you might think."

Her cheeks heated as she began to get the idea he was implying that he was experienced. Very experienced. Suddenly, she thought less of him.

And, in doing so, she thought less of herself for ever imagining that he could be something special to her. She stepped a bit away from him, needing that physical distance to remind her of why the two of them ever having a relationship of the romantic kind would be so very wrong. "Whatever you are insinuating, you would be wrong. I promise you that Miss Bancroft is everything proper. And you have got yourself an attitude about her that you should consider readjusting."

"You and Mr. Marks," he scoffed. "He practically bit my head off just now when I didn't act like she caused the sun to shine."

"What did you say?"

"Nothing that wasn't the truth."

She shook her head. "And here I thought you were a smart man."

"I am smart. And in this instance, I'm smarter than our boss. He's blinded by her tomfoolery, and he's going to pay for it, he is. She's going to get him hurt or killed."

"I fear that is your fault, Vincent," she replied, realizing they had both been using Christian names. "You are blinded by a prejudice against a woman who has done nothing to you."

"But—"

"Furthermore, we are not Mr. Marks' friends. Or his equals. We are his employees."

"We are just as worthy as he is."

"I know that. You know that. He knows that. But *that* is not the point. The point is he didn't hire you to be his conscience. He hired you to do what he wants you to do. When you start forgetting, that is when you are going to get into trouble."

"Maybe I already have."

Fear burned inside her. "What if that is the case? Have you saved so much money that you want to get fired? And how will you get rehired without a reference? No one is going to hire a man whose employment was terminated because he disapproved of his employer's romantic interests."

Bridget held her breath, certain that she had been so disapproving that he would never forgive her.

Or that he would never, at the very least, feel he could confide in her again.

She watched him gather himself, take a deep breath, then at last stare at her blankly.

"Excuse me, Miss O'Connell. I have some business I need to take care of. Mr. Marks wanted you to go down to the kitchens and get something to drink and eat and rest a bit. I trust you can see to yourself without my assistance? You are, of course, just the maid."

Though it was completely true, each word felt like a slap in the face. Instead of arguing, Bridget stared directly at him until he flashed her yet another cool look and turned away.

As the next few hours passed, she at first tried to help out the bartender, but that proved to be a mistake when the men surrounding the bar either ceaselessly cajoled her to keep them company or questioned her presence.

She ended up going to the small storage area in the back of the first floor, underneath the staircase. She found a small chair there, as well as a table, a lamp, and an old deck of cards. Obviously, this was some employee's secret area to relax and while away his break time.

After thumbing the cards for a while, she attempted to shuffle them, failed helplessly, picked them all up from the floor, and at last neatly rearranged them according to suit and number.

When she finished that small project, Bridget leaned her head back against the rough wall behind her head and closed her eyes. While doing so, she firmly resolved to think about everything and anything instead of replaying the awful conversation she'd had with Vincent.

She'd said things she shouldn't have said. No doubt, he was feeling just as guilty. Therefore, she promised herself that before the night was over, she would make every attempt to make things right.

Just as soon as she rested her eyes. She was more tired than she'd let on to Vincent. But she would not rest for more than ten minutes' time. Definitely no more than twenty.

But the feeling of warmth and security in that small closet was hard to ignore. As was the opportunity to completely relax. For the next couple of minutes, no one wanted her, no one needed her. She could worry only about herself.

Only herself.

She didn't know how long she had been asleep when the scream tore through the building. Heart racing, she rushed out of the closet when another scream erupted, followed by the low rumble of men's voices. Following the noise, she saw at least a dozen men and a few women crowded around the front doors.

Their voices were angry, concerned, in distress. She glanced around, quickly looking for Mr. Marks or Vincent.

She saw neither.

She let her natural instincts take over, pushed her way into the fray, and then had to press the edge of her palm to her mouth to stifle a gasp.

The trademark silver doors were flung wide open, and she could see policemen running toward the building. Lying on the front steps was a man, bleeding from what looked like multiple stab wounds. He was staring blankly at them all through unseeing eyes.

Bridget stifled a cry as she recognized him. It was none other than Jason Avondale. And kneeling at his side was Jeffrey Galvin.

She backed away so quickly, she wasn't thinking about anything other than removing the sight of the bloody body from her memory.

"Hold on, miss. Don't faint on me," a rough voice whispered in her ear as he held her by the waist.

It seemed things had just gone from bad to worse.

CHAPTER 18

A steady pounding on the stairs jarred Sebastian from the page he'd been rereading for the last twenty minutes. As authoritative voices joined the din, along with brisk knocks on doors, Sebastian strode to his office door, barely checking on the sleeping Lydia before grasping the handle. He intended to chew out the employees responsible for letting the revelers make their way into the club's private spaces.

But before he could throw open the door and take care of the problem, three sharp, staccato raps pounded against the wood.

The jarring noise woke Lydia, who sat upright with a cry of alarm. "Sebastian?"

He had no time to calm her.

He opened the door to two men in suits and one very agitated Vincent Hunt. Luckily, he'd had a lifetime of concealing his emotions. "Hunt, what is going on?"

"The police are here, sir. They have discovered a body." He looked the complete opposite of his normal, unflappable self.

With effort, he tamped down his shock. "I see," he said. Though, of course, he really didn't see anything at all.

One of the men, his brown eyes perceptive and his blond hair expertly groomed, spoke. "Sir, I'm Lieutenant Detective Owen Howard. I regret to inform you that a man has just been discovered murdered outside your club."

Some of the tension in his shoulders eased. "That is sad news, indeed, though not exactly a surprise. This area is a rather violent one."

"Yes, it is. We were investigating another report only two blocks over when we heard screams coming from the direction of the Grotto. The dead man looks to be a gentleman, sir. And his murder looks to have been a particularly violent one as well. In addition, he seems to have received a recent beating."

Behind him, Lydia gasped.

Inwardly, Sebastian winced. Never would he have wanted her to be in the midst of this. Gripping the door's handle, he said, "Thank you for letting me know, Detective. I'll be downstairs shortly."

Howard reached out and gripped the side of the door. "Not so fast, sir. I have some questions for you."

"Which I will answer presently."

The second man, who until that moment had been simply standing and observing, pushed his way to face Sebastian. "Our business would be best taken care of now. And out of the hall. If we may come in, sir?"

The man's hazel eyes were piercing, his dark hair far more clumsily cut than Lieutenant Howard's. His voice held the faint suggestion of an Irish accent. Sebastian was fairly sure who he was looking at: Sean Ryan, the luckiest cop on the face of the earth. The new husband of the elusive, beautiful Eloisa Carstairs.

"I'd rather you did not. I have company."

"I'm afraid I must insist that we enter, sir. Immediately."

Sebastian glanced Vincent's way. His assistant had a bit of color back in his cheeks but otherwise appeared flummoxed. It was now becoming evident that they weren't here to go through the motions of investigating another poor sod who'd faced his end in Camp Creek Alley. No, this death seemed to matter.

Howard stepped forward. "Mr. Marks, if we may?"

Sebastian ignored him but stared at the other officer and took care to speak in his most bored tone. "With whom am I speaking?"

"Captain Sean Ryan. Please forgive my sorry manners."

Knowing it was inevitable, Sebastian stepped backward and allowed the three men inside. Immediately, the two policemen directed their attention to Lydia, who was standing nervously next to the sofa, one hand curved around the plush velvet, the other clenching a fold in the skirt of her gown.

"Miss Bancroft." Howard nodded.

Lydia paled.

Worried that she was on the verge of fainting, Sebastian walked to her side. "Sit down, Lydia," he murmured. "Everything will be sorted out in no time."

"All right." She smiled hesitantly. "Forgive me, but my glasses? Have you seen them?"

Remembering he had slipped them into his coat pocket, he fished them out and pressed them into her palm. "Here you are. You fell asleep with them on. I took them off so they wouldn't get broken."

Howard and Ryan said nothing through the exchange. Actually, Sebastian was rather surprised to see that they seemed content to merely listen to them. Both men's expressions had softened.

Hunt, on the other hand, eyed her with an ill-concealed disdain.

Hunt's blatant disrespect made his hackles rise and his voice turn sharp. "Hunt, is there a reason you accompanied Lieutenant Howard and Captain Ryan to my offices?"

Vincent flinched. "Yes, sir. They asked me to take them to you. I . . . I thought you may need my assistance as well."

The last thing he wanted or Lydia needed was his assistant glaring at her as if she was less than worthy. "Do you wish him to remain?" he asked the officers.

Ryan glanced from Hunt to Marks. "Not at this time. But don't leave the premises."

"I won't. It would be fairly hard to leave, anyhow, what with the swarm of officers you have milling around downstairs," Hunt reported.

Sebastian's stomach sank. "There are more officers here?"

Howard answered. "We have a lot of folks to interview and even more to deal with the evidence. We would appreciate your staff's assistance in this. However, we will make sure we get our answers one way or another."

Sebastian heard the not-so-subtle warning in the lieutenant's voice. They were in charge; he was not. Furthermore, they could make this shift in power painfully evident if he gave them any trouble. "My staff will do everything in their power to assist you." He meant every word too. They were nothing if not loyal and trustworthy. Hardening his voice, he added, "See to it, Hunt."

"Of course, Mr. Marks." Hunt's expression was respectful, the light in his eyes indicating he was pleased with both Sebastian's authority and the job he was given to do.

At last, he and Vincent seemed back on familiar ground. His assistant smartly nodded and exited the room, both opening and shutting the door behind him in such a way that it could hardly be heard.

Only then did Sebastian turn to Lydia and perform introductions. "Miss Bancroft and Lieutenant Howard, I surmise that you already know each other?"

"That is correct," Lieutenant Howard replied.

"In that case, Lydia, may I present Captain Sean Ryan? As you heard, there seems to have been a disturbance downstairs that they are investigating."

She stood up. "Lieutenant Howard, Captain Ryan."

"Miss Bancroft, I believe our paths crossed at some of the parties surrounding the fair," Lieutenant Howard said.

"I am sure you are right." She smiled softly, and Sebastian noticed that some of the unease in her shoulders dissipated. Sebastian had never thought much of the gentleman detective's chosen profession, but at the moment he was thankful for Howard's social status.

"Miss Bancroft." Ryan inclined his head. "I'm sorry to disturb you at this late hour."

"I fear it is the early morning now." She bit her bottom lip as her face turned bright red. "I, uh, fell asleep on the couch. This is, um, not my usual place." Looking even more flustered, she added, "I really don't know what happened. I shouldn't have come here at all."

Howard's expression was carefully blank. "Oh? Where do you usually meet Mr. Marks?"

Her blush deepened. Looking as if she was intent to avoid Sebastian's eye at all costs, she murmured, "I don't. I mean, he and I are friends. I mean . . ." She pressed both hands to her face. "Oh, but this is awful."

Sebastian stepped to her side, effectively blocking the other men's view of Lydia. Though it did nothing to shield her from their insinuations or her embarrassment, he was willing to do whatever he could to attempt to salvage her reputation, though it was surely a moot point now.

"Easy, Lydia. You have done nothing to be ashamed of."

"I beg to differ. I am currently sitting in a private room in a gentlemen's club."

"You have done nothing wrong."

"Oh, Sebastian," she whispered. Her eyes, so luminescent under the hint of tears, looked back at him.

He saw a trust there that knocked him deep in his soul. How he had earned such a gift from her, he would never know. He wished they were alone. He wished he could wrap his arms around her and hold her protectively against his side twenty-four hours a day. He would like nothing better than to be the person who shielded her from harm.

Ryan cleared his throat. "Mr. Marks, care to tell us why Miss Bancroft is here this evening?"

He did not. "Would you care to tell me why my private life is a concern of yours?" he shot back.

Ryan exchanged a look with Howard, then said, "Jason Avondale was just found stabbed to death outside the silver doors of your club."

Behind him, Lydia gasped once more. "Jason?"

Sebastian forced himself to ignore her cries, knowing he needed to keep his emotions firmly in check. "Avondale, you say?"

"Yes, sir," Ryan said, keeping his expression blank. And firmly fixated on Sebastian's face. His look was so intent, Sebastian felt that his every thought was being perceived. "From what we can surmise, he was attacked just outside the Silver Grotto. He was either left on the front steps or that is as far as he was able to get before collapsing. By the time he was discovered by a man and woman about to leave your establishment, he was already dead."

Lieutenant Howard leaned forward slightly. "Am I to understand that Avondale's murder comes as a surprise?"

"It is a shock," Sebastian corrected. Lydia sniffed and swiped at her cheek with the side of her hand.

Before Sebastian could reach for a handkerchief, Howard stepped forward and handed his to Lydia. "Please, take mine, Miss Bancroft," he offered before eyeing Sebastian again. "Yes, sir. I imagine this news about Avondale is coming as quite a shock."

Sebastian turned to Lydia, who was looking on the verge of collapsing into a dead faint. "Give us a moment," he barked to the two officers before rushing to her side and pressing one palm on the middle of her back. "Please, do sit back down, dear."

"I-I can't." Her face was white, her body completely stiff.

He realized then that she was so distraught she was holding her breath. "Breathe," he ordered, giving her a good pat on the back to encourage the motion.

When she gasped, he felt the tension he didn't even know he carried release.

"Now, breathe in. Out," he whispered, wishing with all his might that she would regain her composure so she wouldn't have to suffer the further injustice of his reaching for her corset stays.

Both of her hands gripped his arms. "Sebastian, this is so terrible!"

"I know." Impatiently, he turned to the two policemen. "Surely your questions could wait for another time? It is obvious that Miss Bancroft is in severe emotional distress."

Captain Ryan looked compassionate but unaffected. "Take your time."

Sebastian's temper flared. "I don't need to take my time. I need to see her home."

"I'm afraid that will not be possible," Ryan returned.

"What will not?"

"You and Miss Bancroft need to stay and answer some questions."

"Whatever questions you have for Miss Bancroft can wait until tomorrow."

"Definitely not."

"At least until later this morning." Sebastian honestly couldn't remember the last time he'd been treated like he was nothing. No better than the lowliest street sweeper.

"I think not," Ryan said. "You see, we need to know where each of you was this evening." He pulled out a worn-looking notebook and the stub of a pencil. "If you could recount things to the best of your memory, it would be most helpful."

"Are you seeking our alibis?" He didn't even attempt to hide his incredulousness.

"We have no choice, Mr. Marks. Of all the people in the building, the two of you might have had the most reason to wish Mr. Avondale harm," Lieutenant Howard replied. "You see, Avondale's friend Jeffrey Galvin arrived just as the couple discovered Avondale. He says he and Avondale planned to meet here and discuss a few things with you, Marks, despite an earlier warning from you to Galvin to stay away. They believed you are the one who had Avondale beaten a few nights ago, perhaps because of the money he owed you."

"Many people owe me money," Sebastian said. "That doesn't mean I beat them. And how do you know Galvin did not murder Avondale?"

Looking unfazed, Howard continued. "We already have evidence to the contrary, but that is none of your concern. And Avondale had just jilted you, Miss Bancroft. As far as we are concerned, there is a very good chance we are staring at Mr. Avondale's murderer right at this moment."

As the shock of the words penetrated, Sebastian suddenly felt dizzy. Only his pure irritation caused him to remain impassive.

It wasn't so easy for Miss Bancroft, though. She collapsed in a dead faint.

Obviously she had forgotten to breathe again, and he had forgotten to make sure she did.

He had failed her yet again.

CHAPTER 19

Lydia. Come now, Lydia, it's time. Lydia, come back to me."

Lydia slowly opened her eyes to see Sebastian Marks' face hovering over her own. His expression was tender, filled with worry. His mouth set in a grim line.

"Sebastian?"

He reached out and ran one callused finger along her cheek. "Easy now, sweetheart. You fainted."

His voice was rough and his consonants were softened, giving a hint of what he must have sounded like when he was young and growing up on the city streets. Staring into his dark eyes, she wished she knew everything about him.

And hoped he'd call her sweetheart again very soon.

Then, like a splash of cold water, the reality of their situation hit her hard. She attempted to push away from him. They were sitting far too intimately together.

But instead of budging, he simply held her in place with one hand. "Easy, now," he repeated. "Catch your bearings first."

"What happened?" Of course, the minute she asked the inane question, she knew.

She was in Sebastian's private office at his club. It was the middle of the night. Her ex-fiancé had been found murdered downstairs!

And the police had been there. Questioning them both.

Tensing, she scanned the room. It was empty except for the two of them. "Where are the policemen?"

"I sent them away."

"How did you manage that? They didn't want to leave."

"I managed to convince them."

"What did you do?"

"Nothing you need to be concerned with," he soothed. "Lydia, answer me, now. Are you feeling better?"

"Yes." She sat up farther, then gasped when she noticed that the bodice of her dress gaped open. "Did . . . did you undress me?"

He seemed amused by her outrage. "I unbuttoned your shirtwaist and loosened your corset. That is all."

"That was certainly too much!"

"Forgive me for being crass, but surely you didn't expect me to let your modesty take precedence over your ability to breathe?"

"I suppose not." She moaned. "I suppose the detectives saw you undress me?" Her reputation was now completely ruined.

He scowled. "Of course not. I told them to leave before seeing to you."

She felt flustered, both by his actions and the police officers' accusations. Needing more time, she said, "I need to put myself back together."

"Of course. Turn around and let me fasten your stays."

"I couldn't let you."

"I can't summon a maid right now, Lydia. Things are a little busy downstairs." When she groaned, he continued with a thinly veiled, exaggerated impatience. "Either let me help you or remain in your current state of dishabille. It's all the same to me."

Thinking back to some of the heroines she'd read about, most specifically Joan of Arc, Lydia stood up, gathered her courage, and with her back to him, lowered the top of her dress.

The moment she did, she felt him reach for the ends of her corset. "Inhale."

When she did, she felt him expertly pull at her stays and fasten the hooks he'd earlier detached. "Finished."

She pulled the bodice back up, fastened the six buttons in the front, and smoothed her gown. "Thank you."

"My pleasure." When she turned, she noticed that a hint of a smile played on his lips. "I've never thought much about it, but as it is now well past the time you would normally retire for the night, I would surmise that being in that contraption for so long can be painful."

"You would be correct. But I will survive. It's nothing, comparatively speaking. Joan of Arc was burned at the stake, you know."

He looked at her appreciatively. "She was a saint and a martyr, indeed."

"Sebastian, what happens next?"

"I think we had better go downstairs. As much as I'd love to let you remain here where you would be able to have a modicum of privacy, I'm afraid I am more concerned about you being alone. I don't want to alarm you, but until we know exactly what happened to Avondale, I don't like the idea of you being anywhere alone."

She shivered. "I don't want to be alone."

Looking as if it pained him, he reached out and clasped her hand. "Please know I will look after you."

She didn't know why he would make such a promise. Beyond the fact that he'd come to her reading room for almost a year, they had little connecting them. Only their burgeoning friendship.

It wasn't like she'd had a lot of close friends anyway. Not close friends she could trust.

Of course, that made her think about Jason and how she'd pinned so many hopes and dreams on a future with him. And how he hadn't hesitated to show her his true colors the first time she'd angered him.

She didn't regret that their engagement ended, but she never had wished him harm. "I still can't believe Jason is dead."

His mouth tightened. "It is unfortunate. The police will discover who did it however. He is important enough for them to care."

"Do you think they wouldn't care otherwise?"

"Of course not. Haven't you been reading the latest editions of the *Chicago Courier-Times*? That rag hasn't missed announcing a single death around here. I'm beginning to think their star reporter, Benson Gage, must live in one of the tenements down the street."

"I have read Gage's reports, if you can call them that. His stories and comments are so sensational, I've often considered them to be exaggerated."

"They weren't, well, not all that much. However, whether they were sensationalized or not, it didn't matter. Nothing was ever investigated."

"Nothing?"

"Lydia, surely even you realize that no one pays too much attention to what happens to the poor or downtrodden. Especially not the majority of the men and women living on Camp Creek Alley."

His tone had changed. Became rougher and, she thought, threaded with a bit of disappointment. "Were you born here, Sebastian?"

"That, Miss Bancroft, is none of your concern."

She heard the resolve in his voice, and she supposed she couldn't blame him. Everyone needed something that was just their own. Who was she to say his secrets weren't worth guarding?

Besides, they had more important problems than his past or the specifics of their relationship. "Sebastian, what if the police don't discover who murdered Jason?" Before he could reply, a new, terrible thought entered her mind. "I can hardly believe they think you or I did it, even if Jason did owe you money and he did call off our engage-ment. But if they learn Jason manhandled me at the Hartman, they'll consider that a motive too—for both of us."

"Lydia, we did not harm Avondale. Remember, you were asleep and I was in here with you working. Even if either of us did do something nefarious, they couldn't investigate. After all, we are each other's alibi."

"But what if the police don't believe us?"

"They will. You are a woman of worth. Of course they would never think anything like that of you. I am sure they are merely observing protocol."

She knew he was trying to ease her troubled mind. Unfortunately, he was failing miserably. "What if we are sent to prison?"

"That is not going to happen."

"You sound so sure."

"I will allow nothing to happen to you, Lydia." As he gathered his next words, he stared hard at her. The intensity in his gaze both slightly alarming and a little endearing too. In that moment, Lydia knew she did trust him. Probably more than anyone else in her life.

"If you believe in nothing else I say, please believe that," he added.

"I'll try." After all, what else could she do?

"Try harder." He snapped his fingers. "Now, go to the basin and splash some water on your face. It is time we went downstairs. I need to see what is happening."

"Yes, sir," she said. She wouldn't have thought she could summon her usual tart tongue, but she did.

As she hoped, her quip eased the fine lines of tension around his mouth and eyes. "Watch yerself, Miss Bancroft," he retorted in a voice that sounded as if he had been living his whole life on the streets. "If you aren't careful, you're going to turn into quite the tartar."

"Ah, but that was my intention. I've decided to live the rest of my life as a tartar. All will fear me and give me a wide berth." She lifted her chin in what she hoped was a haughty way. "Perhaps I'll move to one of the lighthouses dotting the Great Lakes. I'll spend my days watching the ships sail around."

"If you did that, I would lose my librarian, Miss Bancroft," he said gently. "And we both know I would never allow that to happen."

She grinned. "I suppose not."

After she saw to her ablutions in the beautiful bathing room, she walked by his side down the stairwell.

Now that there was no music drifting upward, no raucous, ribald talk, no laughter, the Silver Grotto seemed far less full of flair.

The farther down they went, the greater her apprehension grew. She wasn't sure what her relationship with Sebastian was. It wasn't like they actually knew each other all that well. Beyond their recent acquaintance, she wasn't sure if their tenuous friendship could survive a situation like they were in.

What was even more surprising was how much she already had come to appreciate his presence in her life. She would surely miss him if this tragedy parted their ways.

"Chin up, Lydia," he murmured. "Come, take my arm. We'll get through these next few minutes together."

She curved her hand around his elbow with relief. She needed his sturdy presence in her life.

They reached the first landing. He paused. "Are you still well?"

"Yes. Thank you."

"All right then." They continued downward.

However, she couldn't hold back her gasp when she saw the scene below. At least forty men—and a couple of women—from all walks of life were standing around the area. Some looked irritated, others tired, others angry and on the verge of losing their tempers.

No fewer than six uniformed police officers were scattered around the perimeter. They seemed to be both guarding the exits and doing their best to calm the crowd.

Off to one side stood a nervous-looking Bridget and Mr. Hunt. Bridget was staring off into the distance, the expression of shock and dismay on her face mirroring how Lydia felt inside. In contrast, Mr. Hunt was looking intently at Sebastian.

Lydia didn't know either man well enough to determine if Mr. Hunt looked worried about himself, concerned for his employer, or was merely attempting to learn what Mr. Marks wanted him to do next.

Finally, Lydia allowed herself to look directly into the center of the room. Lieutenant Howard and Captain Ryan were standing close together, having a conversation with a rather worn-looking man in a white coat.

And directly at their feet was a body. Shiny black shoes were sticking out from underneath what looked to be a white tablecloth.

Lydia started shaking as she realized that, of course, she was staring at the remains of Jason Avondale.

"Looks like they brought him inside," Sebastian muttered under his breath. "Makes sense; it's well below freezing."

His casual observation didn't make her feel any better.

Immediately Sebastian placed an arm around her waist and took her arm with his other hand. His position essentially enveloped her, and though it might have been awkward for him, she'd never felt more safe.

He refused to let her stop. "Lydia, I know you're distressed. I know this is unpleasant. But I need you to press on. I cannot get you home until the officers finish here. And for that they need our cooperation."

"Yes, Sebastian."

"Thank you," he said right as they came to a stop.

Before Sebastian could say a word, voices began calling out to him.

"Marks, I need to be getting home. When are you going to release us?"

"Marks, leave your ladylove alone and fix this. Whatever is keeping me here?"

"Marks, do something!"

As the crowd's voices seemed to intensify, Sebastian dropped his hands from her side and raised a hand to the crowd. "Silence," he said.

Immediately everyone in the room did as he bid.

Lydia was amazed. He hadn't yelled. He hadn't even repeated himself. But everyone took his word to be the voice of authority.

"Gentlemen, I beg your pardon, but I imagine even you all will agree that there are some things more important than our petty desires. Death is one of them." Glaring at Captain Ryan, he added, "I'm sure these officers will take your statements and send you on your way as quickly as possible."

Captain Ryan walked toward them, nodded to Sebastian, then ascended the first flight of stairs, stopping on the landing so everyone could see him. "Mr. Marks is correct. We are doing our best to take names and statements. Matter of fact, my officers have told me they are finished. Therefore, with the exception of Mr. Marks, Mr. Hunt, Miss Bancroft, and Miss O'Connell, all of you may leave."

Seconds later, the heavy front doors opened and the crowd exited.

A woman approached Mr. Marks. "Excuse me, sir. What would you be needin' us to do?"

"You head on home as well, Gretchen." Raising his voice, he said, "All of my employees may leave. Stay home until further notice."

After a few wary looks at him, more people left. Soon, only a handful of uniformed officers, Lieutenant Howard, Captain Ryan, Mr. Hunt and Bridget, the medical examiner, Mr. Marks and herself—and the body of Jason Avondale—were left in the room. Lydia averted her eyes when the medical examiner looked as if he were about to begin preparing Jason's body for transport.

Mr. Hunt and Bridget approached. "Sir, would you be wanting me to escort Miss Bancroft home now?" Bridget asked.

"I'm afraid I will have to answer that one, miss," Captain Ryan said. He inhaled. "We'll be needin' the four of you to stay for more questioning."

"Why is that?" Mr. Marks asked.

"As far as we can surmise from our preliminary inquiries, especially after talking at length with Mr. Galvin, each of you had a reason to possibly wish Mr. Avondale dead. And because the medical examiner here said he died from multiple stab wounds, some shallow enough to have been delivered by a woman, all of you are suspects."

"No!" Lydia said in a panic. "No! I was asleep."

"We will still need to talk with you privately, Miss Bancroft," Lieutenant Howard said.

"But this isn't right." She turned to Sebastian. "Sebastian, can't we try to explain to them what we were doing?"

"I'm afraid we need to follow their orders, dear. Don't worry."

"But—"

"I'll be okay, Miss Bancroft," Bridget said. "You will be too."

Lydia felt a cold chill trickle up her spine as she glanced from Sebastian to Bridget to Vincent Hunt.

What she saw on their faces made her wonder if Captain Ryan had been completely correct. Each of the three other people's faces was devoid of emotion. Carefully blank.

And not a one of them attempted to deny Captain Ryan's accusations. Not a single one.

For the first time since she'd woken from her faint, she was truly afraid. It seemed that as much as she'd thought she trusted Sebastian,

Bridget, and Mr. Hunt, she really didn't know them at all. She'd never thought to ask about their pasts or their reasons for working in such a disreputable part of the city.

That had been a very big mistake.

CHAPTER 20

After all the customers and the majority of his employees left, leaving only their small group standing around a dead body on the marble entryway, Sebastian Marks realized he hadn't felt so helpless in a very long time.

It was as if the Lord written about in the Bible was offering retribution for every mistake and misdeed he'd ever committed. And he had done more things to be ashamed of than most people did in a lifetime.

The only thing keeping him on his feet was the verse he'd memorized from Psalm 86. *In the day of my trouble I will call upon thee: for thou wilt answer me.*

Perhaps God was attempting to answer his calls right now.

He could only hope.

"Mr. Marks," Captain Ryan began, "we can either interview the four of you down at the station or in separate rooms here. The choice is up to you."

"I'm surprised you can offer such a choice with a straight face."

The captain's expression hardened. "I know where you grew up, Marks, and it weren't too far from me. You'd best think again before you go about putting on airs."

"I would think of doing nothing of the kind." After glancing at Lydia and his two employees, he turned back to Sean Ryan. "I cannot speak for the others in this instance, though it is my preference, of course, that we all remain here."

"Sebastian?" Lydia whispered.

His heart hammered in his chest as he fought to remain unaffected by her fear. "Miss Bancroft, the choice is up to you. You will have more privacy here, but you might feel better at the station."

"Where will you be?"

"I will be wherever you would like me to be," he replied, realizing that he meant that in so many ways.

"I think I'll stay here then. With you."

Captain Ryan stared at Lydia for a moment before turning to Bridget and Vincent. "What are your preferences?"

"I'll stay here, sir," Bridget said.

Hunt nodded. "I will as well."

"Now that that is settled, please come with me, Miss Bancroft," said Lieutenant Howard.

Sebastian stepped forward. "Where are you taking her?"

"To one of the private rooms downstairs."

"I would like to be near her."

Howard glared. "I will only remind you of this once, sir. This is police business. You are no longer in charge."

The idea of giving over his authority in his own club chafed him something awful. Only knowing that Lydia had absolutely nothing to do with club business or Avondale's dealings and his murder allowed him to nod. "I understand."

"Miss Bancroft, may we begin now?" Howard asked. "The sooner we get started, the sooner you may go home."

With a swirl of her skirts, Lydia slowly followed the lieutenant down the short flight of stairs. In short order, two uniformed officers escorted Vincent and Bridget to two separate rooms on the second floor.

Only then did Captain Ryan speak. "Where would you like to do this? Here or in your office?"

"It makes no difference to me. As your lieutenant pointed out, I am not in control."

"Let's go to your office then."

Sebastian followed him up, unconsciously straining to hear conversations from Bridget or Hunt. But of course no sound filtered through. His building was nothing if not well built.

When they entered his office, Sebastian motioned to the chairs. "Care for a cigar, Captain?"

"Thank you, no."

He sat down. "Very well. Now, how may I help you?"

"Tell me about your relationship with Lydia Bancroft."

"Surely that isn't any of your concern."

"Don't be naïve," he retorted sharply. "Everything in your life is now my concern." Pulling out a small notebook, he said, "Now, please answer my question. What is the exact nature of your relationship with Lydia Bancroft?"

"I am Miss Bancroft's friend."

"Nothing more?"

"Of course not."

"Oh? Somehow, out of thin air, a bluestocking librarian and the owner of one of the city's most notorious gambling institutions have struck up a new friendship?" Sarcasm laced every word. "Forgive me, but the two of you seem like an odd pairing."

"You are right. We are. However, I believe you also know what it's like to befriend a woman who is far better than you."

Ryan shifted. "Touché," he murmured.

"Sounds as if I'm not the only person in this room intent on bettering himself."

"This is true." Ryan's eyes glittered. "However, you are the only person in *this* room who is suspected of murder."

Seeing that he was not about to gain the upper hand anytime soon, Sebastian relented. "I have spent most of the past year visiting Miss Bancroft's lending library in the afternoons."

"Because?"

"Because I like to read, Captain. I am also fond of libraries. Like you, I did not have a great many books in my home growing up."

Ryan raised his eyebrows. "If you had a real house, you had more than I did."

"I had the floor next to wherever my mother was plying her trade."

"Difficult."

It had been worse than that. "I learned to use my fists at a young age. Eventually, I learned that the smarter a man was, the better his life was. And that is how I discovered the library."

The policeman's expression was far more somber now. "Which brings us full circle."

Sebastian had no desire to continue down this road of bad memories, but he was willing to do whatever it took to walk out of his club—and to ensure Lydia did as well.

"You are right. I started visiting the library again for the books, and then because I admired Miss Bancroft. I thought she was pretty. I liked the way she always had her nose in a book. I liked the way she constantly adjusted her glasses and genuinely was delighted when new patrons asked for library cards. I liked the way she seemed to forget that a real world existed beyond her library's walls."

"She meant something to you."

"I didn't know her. Rather, I was intrigued by her."

"And then?"

"And then one day I saw Avondale mistreat her in the lobby of my hotel."

"You are referring to the Hartman." Ryan looked up from his leather-bound notebook. "Your home."

"It is where I keep my clothes and sleep." He'd never had a home.

"So, that afternoon when you witnessed this mistreatment . . . What did you see Avondale do?"

Sebastian noticed that the captain had not yet written a single word. He wondered if the man already knew the answers to the questions he was asking or if he merely had an excellent memory. "They were arguing. When she did not comply with his wishes, he grabbed her wrist. Bruised her."

"What were they arguing about?"

"Me."

"Because?"

"Because though we'd never spoken to each other, she recognized me."

"So Avondale was jealous of your relationship?"

"We had no relationship at that time." He hesitated, debated whether to mention the debts, but then decided to be completely honest. "If I were to guess, I would say that Avondale disliked running into me more because he owed the Silver Grotto money than because of my having any association with his fiancée." Actually, Sebastian had known that had been the reason Avondale had looked so nervous. Sebastian had been happy to cultivate that nervousness too.

"You mean he owed you."

"No, I mean the club. Avondale frequented the tables in the basement and had lost—over and over. I had nothing to do with it."

"Beyond the fact that you own the club and run it." His voice was dry.

"I do. But just like how you are not responsible for every man's actions in your employ, I cannot claim total knowledge of each patron's debts."

"But you knew he owed the club money."

"I did." Sebastian paused. "I also didn't care for him."

Captain Ryan straightened. "Why is that?"

"He was a sloppy drunk. Difficult. He lost often and hated to pay his debts." He paused, and added more. "I had also recently been informed that he was abusing women."

Ryan stilled. "Abusing?"

"Beating them. For sport."

Ryan's eyes flickered in distaste. "Here?"

"No. I don't keep women here. At the Bear and Bull."

At last, Sean pulled out a pencil and wrote down some notes. "That's Sergio Vlas's club, isn't it?"

"Yes," Sebastian answered.

"So, getting back to the Hartman. What did you do when you saw Avondale hurt Miss Bancroft?"

"I released her from his grip." He frowned at the memory. "When she went to sit down, a china pot of tea fell. Spilled hot tea on her hand and burned her."

Ryan paused. "Was she all right?"

"She was after I got her ice and bathed her injured hand. Avondale, however, was not pleased, and he told her she had to leave with him. When she refused, he ended the engagement."

"Because of that?"

"I am not privileged to know the workings of either Avondale's or Miss Bancroft's mind. All I do know is that I was glad she was no longer linked with him."

"So you could have her?"

"So she wouldn't be married to a man who used force to get his way with her. She wouldn't have been happy." No, she would have been miserable. He sighed, more than ready to finish the story. "After that we formed a friendship."

"Which was why you brought her here?"

"Definitely not. I saw her at the library. And then, when I discovered she had no maid, I asked Bridget to act as hers."

"Miss Bancroft accepted this?"

"Not readily, but she saw the reason for it. After the Slasher's appearance on our city's streets, and the recent crime spree around these parts, it's not safe for women to go anywhere alone. I had discovered that Miss Bancroft had been going back and forth from the library by herself."

"I thought Bridget worked for you at the hotel."

"She did. Now she works for me at Miss Bancroft's house."

"She didn't mind when you gave her new duties?"

"If she did mind, she didn't share. I pay her well enough to keep her opinions to herself."

Ryan raised his brows. "I see."

"I hope so."

Ryan shifted again, looking like he was finding his well-fitted suit uncomfortable. "Why don't you tell me how Lydia Bancroft ended up here this evening. Did you two become lovers?"

The cop had just managed to shock him, and Sebastian hadn't believed anything could. "Absolutely not," he bit out, appalled. "Lydia discovered that I owned the club and asked me to bring her here." For the first time, Sebastian felt the strain in his voice. "Against my better judgment, I agreed to bring her."

"I heard she ran into some problems on the street?"

Sebastian would have paid a small fortune to learn all that Ryan knew and was keeping close to his vest. "Yes. I stopped to speak to an acquaintance, thinking she would keep walking with my staff the last block without stopping. But she did stop, and a gang very nearly attacked her and Miss O'Connell and Mr. Hunt. Hunt can take care of himself in most cases, but there were too many of them. Then an associate and I caught up with them and we got by." He blew out an irritated blast of air. "After escorting Miss Bancroft inside, I asked her to remain in my office. I needed to check with the floor managers. And," he added wryly, "I needed to cool down. I was angry with her."

"Because she disobeyed your instructions?"

"Because she could have been harmed. People are getting stabbed right and left around here, not that the cops on this beat care," Sebastian snapped. "I don't care about her disobeying me."

"What happened next?"

"When I came upstairs, I discovered that she was sound asleep on the couch. I didn't want to wake her up, so I decided to sit at my desk and work until she awoke."

"You didn't want to simply wake her up? It was unseemly for the two of you to be alone together."

"Captain Ryan, forgive me for being personal, but what did you do the first time you saw Eloisa Carstairs sleeping? Was your first reaction to march over and wake her up?"

Ryan's eyebrows rose, then a small smile touched his lips. "No, I didn't do that. I watched Eloisa sleep." His gaze flickered back to Sebastian's. "But we were married."

"Well, we are not. I stayed in here with her until Hunt pounded on the door and told me there was trouble."

"Which brings us to the present."

"At long last."

"Mr. Marks, surely you have to see that there is a lot of evidence against you. You have motive and no alibi."

"I do have an alibi. I was in here with Lydia Bancroft. She simply happened to be asleep and therefore cannot vouch for my company. Furthermore, I would like to point out that I had no motive."

"How so?"

"Killing Avondale would not get my money back. And he owed me a great deal of money."

"But killing him would make Lydia safe."

"I'm not a fool, sir. The majority of the people in the city could harm Lydia. She is a very naïve woman with a very large brain. As the gang of thugs who circled her outside the club made very apparent, men prey on foolish women. It is the responsibility of men to keep women safe. I did that. I would do that again," he bit out.

"Is that so?" Ryan folded his hands on the table, looking a bit like a cat that has just been given a new bowl of cream.

That look was irritating. After taking a fortifying breath, Sebastian forced his voice to become impassive again. "I did not kill Jason Avondale."

He readied himself for the next probable question: Had he had Avondale beaten? But the detective surprised him.

Ryan leaned forward, one hand dangling from where it rested on a knee, his other still clutching the pencil and notebook. "Mr. Marks, may I offer some advice?"

"If you would like," he said grudgingly. Actually, he couldn't care less about any piece of advice Captain Ryan could offer him.

"Be very aware of the precarious situation Miss Bancroft is in now. A lady's reputation guards her against most all ill will. If the general public learns that she slept alone in a room with you, her reputation will be ruined."

"I was already aware of this." He stood up. "Is there anything else you need to know?"

"Not at this time. You are free to leave the premises."

"I'll leave when my employees and Miss Bancroft are free to leave as well."

Captain Ryan stood up and gave a small bow. "In that case, you might be here awhile longer, Marks," he threw over his shoulder as he walked out of the room.

Unwilling to spend another minute in his office with his ghosts haunting him, Sebastian followed.

CHAPTER 21

Though he had quite the reputation of being a gentleman detective, Lydia had surmised rather quickly that Lieutenant Owen Howard was anything but that. Especially since he seemed most determined to prove that she was not much of a lady.

He had been interrogating her for over an hour. She was growing weary of his continuous questions and even more tired of having to repeat the same answers over and over again.

Which was what she was doing at the moment.

"As I said before, Lieutenant, I fell asleep on the couch in Mr. Marks' office," Lydia repeated with an edge to her voice. "I only awoke when Mr. Hunt knocked on the door and informed Mr. Marks that a body had been discovered."

"I must say I find your explanation difficult to believe," he replied, his cultured voice as elegant as his mannerly way. "You have told me you asked to visit the Silver Grotto, had been stunned to see to what extent it is a rather disreputable gambling club, and had been further taken aback to see just how seedy this part of town is. Yet, you promptly fell asleep?"

"I never said promptly."

"Yet you did sleep not long after you arrived."

"It was late, and I was weary. I fell asleep reading, waiting for Mr. Marks to have someone ready to take me home. What I find confusing, sir, is the fact that you seem to find my story difficult to believe."

"I've told you my reasons."

"You have. However, you are missing the point. It is the truth."

He leaned back and crossed his legs. "Miss Bancroft, what do you intend to tell your mother?"

"I assume I will tell her the same thing I told you. I fell asleep in a place I should never have been in the first place. It is regrettable but in the past now."

His brown eyes flickered, whether because he found her amusing or exasperating, Lydia was not sure. After taking a sip of water, he said, "Tell me again when you first noticed Mr. Marks had entered the room."

She gritted her teeth. This was now the fourth time he had asked her this. It was also going to be the fourth time she answered. She was starting to find his interrogation methods a terrible misuse of her time. "Lieutenant Howard, as I stated before, I only realized Mr. Marks was in the room when Mr. Hunt knocked on the door. I was asleep."

"Whom did you think was knocking? Were you afraid it was Mr. Avondale?"

"What?" This question had taken her completely off guard. "Of course not. I didn't know Jason was anywhere in the vicinity."

"I thought he called on you."

"He came to my home not long after our failed tea. But we soon realized it was best that our engagement ended. You see, he had thought I was an heiress. I thought he had money too. I did not—" She bit her lip before she inadvertently told a fib.

He noticed. "Miss Bancroft, perhaps you could expound on this?"

She did not care to, but it seemed she had no choice. "I did not want to patch things up with Jason because I realized that he and I would not make a good match."

"I'm shocked. He is of your class."

"He is of *our* class, Lieutenant," she gently corrected. "I would also like to point out that you did not seek a woman of our class to marry."

"Touché. Why, exactly, did you decide you would not suit?"

After a pause, she decided to blurt the rest. It seemed Lieutenant Howard would wheedle it out of her eventually anyway. "I had developed an affection for Mr. Marks."

"You wanted to marry him?"

He sounded shocked, and she supposed his surprise was justified. Even taking into consideration that Mr. Marks ran a disreputable club, he was also everything she was not. Not only was he extremely wealthy and debonair, he was well-known. Famous, even. He was outgoing and rather forceful.

"Well, I wanted to get to know him better," she corrected.

"I'm surprised your mother allowed this."

Of course, her mother didn't know Sebastian's true colors. "One cannot help one's heart."

"Did your infatuation with Mr. Marks lead you to wishing Avondale harm?"

"Of course not! I did not wish him harm. I simply wished to end our engagement." She sighed. Surely this interrogation would be ending soon?

But like a dog with a bone, Lieutenant Howard continued, circling back to essentially the same subject again and again. "You must have ascertained that you and Mr. Marks would not be a good match."

"I suppose that is true. But we are mainly friends anyway. Who but the Lord knows what our future entails?"

Lieutenant Howard leaned back, crossing one leg over the other, just as if he were sitting in the middle of a club. "If you did not step out into the alley and accost Avondale and you don't believe Mr. Marks did, who do you think murdered him?"

"That's just it, sir. I don't know. I mean, I have truly no earthly idea." Her mind started spinning. "This is the first time I have been in this section of Chicago. Camp Creek Alley seems to be a rather dangerous area. I tried to get a good look around as we were walking, but Mr. Marks didn't want me to tarry."

"That was probably a good idea."

"It was good for him, but it left me feeling like I was walking into a strange world. Why, the only time I stopped, I thought Mr. Hunt was going to be very angry with me."

"What happened?"

"I stopped to look at something, and a gang of thugs, I mean, rough-looking men, practically surrounded us. Mr. Hunt had to talk harshly to them. Come to think of it, Bridget wasn't pleased with me either."

"Bridget is your maid?"

"Well, she's actually Mr. Marks' maid. He simply lent her to me for a while."

His eyebrows rose. "Lent?"

How strange that he was focusing on the odd phrase and word instead of her point. "Lent, perhaps, was a poor choice of word. Mr. Marks asked Bridget to act as my maid when he learned that my current financial situation necessitated my mother and I letting go of our servants. Mr. Marks seems to think that all young ladies need proper escorts."

"He is not wrong."

"Beg your pardon, but in this instance I believe he was."

"How so?"

"I am not all that young, and I'm not necessarily a lady."

His eyebrows rose. "You don't consider yourself a lady?"

"I am not a lady, Lieutenant Howard. I'm a librarian."

Lieutenant Howard stared at her in confusion for a long moment before he laughed. The sound was so out of place, so loud in the empty gaming club, it seemed abnormally loud. "I'm sorry, Miss Bancroft. But you truly are remarkable. My fiancée would adore you. She is a rather forward-thinking young lady as well."

Lydia smiled, liking the idea of the city's gentleman detective finding true love. "My felicitations, sir."

"Thank you. I'm rather thrilled about it myself." Leaning forward, he confided, "I'm going to marry Captain Ryan's little sister."

"My goodness! He must be happy too."

"I think he is. Well, as much as any big brother can be when contemplating a little sister's nuptials," he shared with a wry smile. "It is sure to make family gatherings lively."

She chuckled. "Indeed."

They shared the first genuine smile between them, reminding Lydia that at the moment they were two people meeting someplace neither of their families would have ever imagined their being.

"Wish me well," he said.

"Of course, sir. Um, has the interview concluded?"

"For now, I believe so." He got to his feet. "I'll be right back."

"Take your time, Lieutenant. I'll be fine."

"Yes, Miss Bancroft. I do believe that is true. I think you might be fine anywhere."

Ten minutes later, he returned. "If you will come with me?"

When they arrived at the main lobby, she scanned the area, anxious to see what had happened with Sebastian, Mr. Hunt, and Bridget.

There was no sign of Mr. Hunt or Bridget, but she spied Sebastian immediately. He was standing against the front of the bar. His elbows were propped behind him, as if he was attempting to look rather bored. However, Lydia now knew him well enough to know his pose was a sham. His hands were fisted, and his eyes looked as if they were taking in every single detail that was happening around him. Actually, she rather thought he looked like one of the Siberian tigers she'd read about, ready to pounce on anything he deemed a threat.

When he turned to her, however, his look became less calculating and more concerned. So much so that she felt it like a caress. No matter how frightened she'd been when she realized earlier how little she really knew about Sebastian, she did trust him. She wanted to trust him.

She turned to the detective. "May I walk over to Mr. Marks?"

"You are free to leave, Miss Bancroft. If you would like, I will have one of my men escort you home."

"Thank you. I will just go say good-bye to Mr. Marks."

"Whatever you wish."

Sebastian straightened when she approached. One by one his arms dropped and all pretense left his stance. "Lydia, are you all right?" His voice was rough with concern.

"I think so." She attempted to smile. "It has been an exhausting evening."

"More than that." He nodded to one of the picture windows near the silver doors.

Looking out, she gasped. The sky had lightened. It was morning. "This is the first time I've ever been out all night."

His lips twitched. "You seem excited about that."

"I am, I suppose. This is a new experience for me."

"I hope it won't be anything you ever experience again. I can't tell you how sorry I am about all of this."

Unable to help herself, she reached out and rested a palm on his lapel. It was right over his heart and therefore singularly inappropriate. But she could imagine that she felt his heart beating. Pretending she could feel the warmth of his skin and that it was enveloping her, keeping her cozy.

The muscles in his jaw jumped again. "Miss Bancroft. I fear you are forgetting yourself."

"I have not. We are friends, Sebastian. And friends touch."

"Not like this."

She agreed. Placing one hand on top of his coat pocket wasn't quite what she would consider to be a friendly connection. She would rather hold his hand.

Or, at this time of the morning, she would really rather have his arm over her shoulders and feel as if she was under his protection.

Because he seemed so uncomfortable, she dropped her hand. "What I am trying to tell you, Mr. Marks, is that I know Jason's death is difficult, but I also know you did not have anything to do with it."

"You don't suspect me?"

In his face, she saw both hope and disbelief. "Of course not."

"The police do."

"The police don't know you like I do."

"It's not like we know each other all that well."

"It's not like we don't."

He smiled. "When can you leave?"

"Now. Lieutenant Howard offered to have one of his officers take me home."

"That is a good idea. As much as I would like to escort you myself, it might raise some eyebrows. Plus, I dare not leave until Bridget and Vincent have been allowed to leave."

"You care for them, don't you?"

"They're under my employ."

"No, I think it's more than that. You care about them."

He nodded, barely a flinch of his chin. "I don't want either of them to feel that they have been left out to dry."

For a moment, Lydia considered offering to stay, too, but then she realized she would only be in the way. Instead of giving him support, she would be yet another responsibility.

She stepped away. "I should go."

"Are you worried about leaving with a police officer? If so, I could leave word—"

"I'll be fine, Mr. Marks. Don't worry about me." She took a deep breath, then gave him her best smile. "I will be just fine."

"I'm sure you will. I'll make sure Bridget gets to your townhouse as soon as possible."

"She will need her sleep. That is all I will be doing. Tell her I will see her tomorrow evening, after we have both had some sleep."

Before he could argue, she walked to Lieutenant Howard's side. He had been unabashedly watching and listening to their exchange. "I am ready to leave whenever one of your officers has time to take me, sir."

"He is ready now." Looking over at two uniformed men who were standing together talking, he barked, "Barnaby."

Immediately the taller of the two rushed over. "Sir?"

"Please escort Miss Bancroft back to her townhouse."

"Then return here?"

"No, meet us at the precinct. I don't believe we'll be here much longer."

"Yes, sir." Barnaby turned to her, his expression perfectly blank. "After you, miss."

Lydia started forward, feeling her cheeks heat and burn. The policeman knew she'd been up in Sebastian's office with him. Alone. It was obvious that he thought she was Mr. Marks' paramour. Just as it was obvious that he knew she was no lady.

She walked through the doors of the Silver Grotto, enjoying the rays of the morning sun hitting the pavement in front of them. The effect was bright. Illuminating.

Almost as if God himself were lighting her way home. It seemed fitting, of course. She was leaving the darkness and heading toward the light.

It was really too bad her heart didn't feel the same way.

CHAPTER 22

Bridget hadn't expected Mr. Marks to be waiting for her when she finished her interview with Captain Ryan.

When she walked out of their impromptu interrogation room, feeling more unkempt and exhausted than she could recall being in quite some time, all she'd been hoping for was a quiet place to lie down.

Instead she composed herself and walked to where he was standing. "Sir, I hope you haven't been waiting for me all this time?"

"Of course I have."

"I'm sorry. Has Mr. Hunt finished his interview as well?"

"He has. I just sent him home. He was eager to see Mary."

"I imagine so. How may I help you, sir? Do you need me to escort Miss Bancroft home?"

"She just went home with the escort of one of the policemen."

She was confused. "Then why are you still here, sir?"

Humor lit his eyes. "I stayed here to make sure you suffered no ill effects from your interrogation. I also want to escort you back to the Hartman."

"But what about Miss Bancroft?" Maybe her head was filled with mud, but Bridget was having quite the time keeping up with why her employer was looking out for her.

"She asked that you see her tomorrow. She'll be sleeping, and she wants you to rest too. After you get some sleep at the Hartman today and tonight, go back to the townhouse by tomorrow evening. Meanwhile, I have arranged for someone to watch Miss Bancroft's home to ensure her safety."

"Yes, sir."

Peering at her closely, he said, "Would you like to freshen up before we head to the hotel?"

"Freshen up?"

"Yes." He looked away. "Use the washroom."

"Oh, yes, please."

"While you are, um, occupied, I'll see if I can shoo the rest of these individuals from the premises."

"Yes, sir," she said yet again, then walked upstairs to do as he had suggested. Only when she was out of his line of vision and she was sure there was no one else around did she dare smile. She would never admit such a thing to Mr. Marks, but she actually did so enjoy it when he was flustered.

When she returned to the bar area ten minutes later, the club was completely quiet. Well, except for the faint tapping of the toe of Mr. Marks' well-polished shoe. It was drumming a staccato beat in time with his impatience.

He wasn't looking for her though. Instead, he was staring out the window on the right-hand side of the door. She could only view his expression in profile, but to her way of thinking, he looked rather glum.

"I'm ready now, sir," she said with more false brightness than she had ever imagined she could summon.

"Ah. Very good." He opened the front door and waved her out. In his other hand he awkwardly held a rather large silver ring of keys.

After she passed through the famous silver doors, he pulled them closed and locked them, explaining he'd told Vincent they would be closed for a while.

"It's been quite some time since I've locked this place up myself. Years ago, when I bought the building, I slept here." He looked mildly embarrassed. "I had no employees then, of course. Only a dream."

"You achieved that dream, sir."

"I thought I did. But this evening's events have made me wonder." Staring at the key ring, his voice drifted off.

"Would you like for me to hold the key ring, sir?" She held up her reticule. "I could probably fit it in my bag."

"Of course not, Bridget. I'm not that helpless. At least, not yet." After forcing the key ring into one of his coat's pockets, they shared another small smile as they started walking. Of course, just like always, once the gilded façade of the Silver Grotto faded into the distance, the squalid surroundings of Camp Creek Alley became their only reality.

The alley was as quiet and still as Bridget had ever seen it. Amazingly, she didn't feel any safer. No, the lack of activity so early in the morning only served to remind her that a woman could be attacked without a single witness at a time like this.

"Did the officers treat you all right, Bridget?"

"Yes." She thought about it. "Better than I imagined they would, if you want to know the truth. First an Officer Barnaby asked me questions. Later Lieutenant Howard came in." She smiled at her first impression of the man. "I had heard about the city's gentleman detective, but of course, I had never met him. He certainly takes one by surprise."

"He interviewed Lydia too. I, um, had never thought much of his goals to become a working stiff. I figure that a man who is born to a position of power ought to do everything he can to keep it . . . not going about turning himself into a policeman, of all things." He chuckled. "But he seems to have been gentle enough with Lydia, so I suppose I am grateful for his lowly dreams after all."

Bridget knew Lieutenant Howard had been born and bred to be a gentleman from the papers, where he was often referred to as the Gentleman Detective. His determination to become a member of the police force had taken many by surprise. "He was fair to me. He, um, asked what I knew about Mr. Avondale."

"Did you know him?"

She nodded. "He was the reason I got fired from my previous job."

"I knew a man had been too forward with you, but I didn't know it had been him."

"I never told a soul. I didn't care for him, Mr. Marks. I found him to be everything I hate about the wealthy and privileged."

"I felt the same way." He grimaced. "When he grabbed Lydia at the Hartman, I yearned to kill him." As his words drifted in the air between them, he looked appalled. "I didn't though."

"No, sir. I didn't think you had." It wasn't because she didn't think he was capable of ending another person's life. She had no doubt that he could commit murder, and would, if he felt he had no choice.

But that was the crux of it. In the grand scheme of things, Jason Avondale meant nothing to him. Yes, she'd heard rumors that he owed the club money, but Mr. Marks had more money than he knew what to do with. Everyone knew that.

And he was far more likely to systematically hurt Jason Avondale in all manner of ways in order to get that money back. Killing the man ensured that Mr. Marks would never be repaid.

The only other reason she could think that he would want Jason gone was to protect Miss Bancroft. But he had already done that. Mr. Marks had also moved her into Lydia's life to make sure she was safe—and to let him know if Avondale came around.

As they continued to walk, Mr. Marks took her elbow to make sure she avoided a puddle in the street.

She smiled to herself. It really was endearing how he sometimes forgot that she was used to avoiding puddles and riffraff and didn't need his watchful eyes or courteous arm to do so.

He sighed. "For the record, I don't think you killed him either."

"Thank you, sir."

He didn't catch her sarcasm. Merely continued, deep in thought. "I also have a hard time seeing Vincent as a suspect. He's strong enough, to be sure. I'd even suggest he was brave enough to do something of the sort. But I can't imagine his motive." He paused, then stopped abruptly.

She stopped, too, right in front of a flower peddler. The young girl looked at Bridget hopefully, but Bridget shook her head. "Sir?"

"Did Hunt have a reason to dislike Avondale that I don't know about?"

"I have no idea."

"Sure about that?"

"Well, I heard him once say that he knew a little bit about Mr. Avondale's proclivities from when the lawyers he clerked for had Mr. Avondale as a client. But that was long ago."

"I didn't know about this." He blinked. "How come I didn't know about this?"

"I couldn't begin to guess."

He seemed about to reply but suddenly took notice of the flower girl. Reaching into his vest pocket, he brought out a shiny half-dollar. "Here, child."

She took it eagerly, then proceeded to gather up most of her flowers. "Here, sir."

"I don't need any flowers."

She bit her lip. "But sir, if you don't take them, I'll have to stay out until they're gone. And you've paid for them."

"What would I do . . . Oh, very well. Take them, Bridget."

She hid a smile. "Yes, sir." She waited while the girl wrapped the bouquet in a snug amount of newspaper, then proceeded to carry the large bouquet in her arms. "Shall I give them to Miss Bancroft when I see her tomorrow evening?"

"Of course not. You keep them."

"Thank you, sir."

But of course, his mind had already drifted away from daisies and carnations and back to the topic at hand. "I don't know how the police are going to solve this."

Bridget worried that they'd take a person like her, of no money, no background, no real family, and pin it on her—simply because Avondale had caused her to be dismissed from her job. She would be helpless to defend herself.

"I hope they look for the person who really did it and not simply someone to pin it on."

"I do too."

They continued their stroll down the narrow street. When the next hawker came out, Mr. Marks bought them both a cup of hot coffee. She'd just taken her first sip when a shadow fell over them.

Then it was all she could do to keep her eyes averted. It was Sergio Vlas. The Russian. Though he'd never bothered her before, there was still something about him that she didn't completely trust.

Luckily, he didn't seem of the mind to pay her the slightest bit of attention, not even with the massive bouquet of flowers she was holding.

Instead, his lips were curved into a parody of a happy smile as he eyed her boss, his crooked teeth out on display like a jack-o'-lantern. "Marks. Heard you had some excitement last night."

"I did at that."

"I hope everything is all right?"

"Of course it is. I'm standing here, aren't I?" Mr. Marks snapped.

"What on earth happened?" Sergio's voice was bordering on compassionate.

Mr. Marks heard it too. "Stop the foolishness," he barked. "We both know you've probably got a better idea of everything that happened outside the Grotto than I do."

Sergio shrugged. After letting his gaze drift on Bridget for a moment, he said, "I do understand that the Alley now has one less gentleman caller."

"That would be true."

His lips curved upward again, but this time not in a full smile. This time he looked far more amused. Or, more exactly, bemused. "I also heard word that you were nowhere to be found." He placed a palm on his chest. "Oh, forgive me. You were locked up in your office with a certain woman with auburn hair."

"Where did you hear that?"

"I have my sources."

"Obviously they're on the force?"

"Not everyone wearing a blue uniform is working *completely* for the public's best interest. Some are happy to keep my interests at heart as well."

"I would deem it to be a personal favor if you kept that tidbit to yourself. The last thing I or Miss Bancroft needs is for our names to bandied about in tomorrow's rags."

"Why is that? Does she mean something to you?"

Mr. Marks flinched. "You know she couldn't. Can't."

"Why not? She's almost a lady. You are almost a gentleman."

Bridget stuck her nose in the bouquet. Anything to look as if she wasn't inadvertently eavesdropping. Anything to prevent either man from seeing just how struck she was by both Sergio's allegations and Mr. Marks' reaction.

After gathering himself, Mr. Marks spoke. "*Almost* is the key word, there, *friend*," he said with obvious sarcasm. "But it is not appropriate in either case. Miss Bancroft is a lady, not almost. And I never will be a gentleman."

"If I can be of assistance in any way at all, don't hesitate to ask."

"Thank you, but I doubt that will be necessary."

"One never knows."

"We must be going," Mr. Marks said impatiently, just as he pulled out a coin to give to one of the newsboys selling papers.

Sergio grinned. Then, after a brief, sardonic nod Bridget's way, he pulled a gold timepiece out of his pocket, tapped a blue button, and looked at the watch's face.

Bridget gasped. It was the same watch she'd seen on Avondale's person years ago, when he'd accosted her at the house party, and then again the other night when Vincent was walking her to the Grotto and she'd seen him with Galvin. It was so distinct, she doubted another man in the city had one like it.

Quickly, Sergio glanced her way. When he saw what she was staring at, his expression turned cold, then he slid through the narrow crevice between two brick buildings on the brink of collapse.

It was obvious, to her at least, that Sergio thought he was invincible. Fear curved up Bridget's spine as she realized he was probably right too. No one would willingly do anything to create trouble for the notorious club owner.

"Bridget?" Marks barked.

"Yes, sir?"

"What's wrong? You look like you've seen a ghost."

She shivered. For a moment she considered telling Mr. Marks what she saw, but she elected to keep it to herself. The last thing she wanted to do was make things more of a muddle for Mr. Marks or place him on Sergio's bad side.

Besides, she had never seen Jason Avondale's pocket watch up close enough to be sure Sergio's was just like it. No doubt, her mind was playing tricks on her eyes. There was no reason for Sergio Vlas to be holding Avondale's timepiece. Well, no reason except for one.

"Let's go, Bridget," he ordered, as if they'd been stopped because of her wishes.

"Yes, sir," she murmured.

Less than ten minutes later, he was leaving her at the back door of the Hartman Hotel.

"Now, I want you to sleep and order anything you desire from the kitchens."

"I will."

"I'll be checking. If I discover you only have a meager bowl of soup or some awful leftover concoction, I'll hear about it. And then you will."

"I will do my best to eat as much as possible."

He didn't laugh at her joke though. He was already walking away.

Leaving her to wonder where he was going. Was he going to check on Miss Bancroft?

Go back to the club?

Visit with the police?

Or, by chance, had he, too, seen what Sergio had pulled out before he slipped into the alley—and known what it could mean?

CHAPTER 23

CHICAGO TIMES-COURIER

January 25, 1894—Special Mid-Morning Edition
Reported by Benson Gage

Even this intrepid reporter is shocked by this morning's news. Jason Avondale was found murdered outside the premises of the Silver Grotto late last night, the victim of a stabbing. Currently, our city's finest are combing the dark alleys of Camp Creek Alley looking for the usual suspects . . . as well as some not-so-usual ones.

It is certainly time the recent crime wave was taken seriously. If a man like Mr. Avondale can be murdered in cold blood, truly no one is safe.

Lydia's mother was waiting for her in the townhouse's front entryway when Officer Barnaby bid her good day. Lydia had been thinking about how Officer Barnaby had been an enjoyable escort. He was chatty and prone to blushing.

She was still smiling about his unexpected kindness when she'd quietly unlocked and opened the door. She'd intended to make herself some tea and toast in the kitchen, bathe, then sleep the day away.

But her mother's appearance surprised her.

"Lydia, at last you have returned."

Alarmed, Lydia rushed forward. "Mother, it is very early. Is something wrong?"

"I could ask the same thing of you."

Concerned and confused, Lydia examined her mother. But, as she noticed there was color in her mother's cheeks and she was wearing one of her better day dresses, her concern faded. It was abruptly replaced with curiosity. "You look well. How did you manage to sweep up your hair into a chignon so neatly?"

"I didn't do my hair. Charlotte Williams stopped by almost an hour ago. She brought along her ladies' maid. Baker styled my hair."

"So early?"

"Indeed, far too early to receive guests." Her mother looked down her nose at Lydia. "Which was why when Charlotte arrived at our doorstop, I knew something highly irregular must have happened."

Lydia bit back a comment. Charlotte Williams was known throughout her mother's circle of friends to be a gossip. "Has something happened?"

"Indeed."

"Oh?" She was beginning to hate the turn of conversation. In addition, her mother's very-well-put-together self was in stark contrast to Lydia's disheveled appearance. As each second passed, she began to feel even more bedraggled. She ached to bathe and slip on a fresh gown. "What trouble is that? I hope no one in her family is ill."

"She came here to speak to me about you. It seems that you have been taking advantage of my infirmity."

"Mother, there is nothing wrong with you besides an inability to choose to cope with our present financial circumstances."

As Lydia had expected, her mother took no responsibility for her behavior. Instead, she turned the tables. "You have been keeping secrets from me."

Of course she had. To tell her mother everything meant subjecting herself to endless hours of criticism.

But even though she was right, there was no reason to admit to anything. "What secrets are you referring to?"

"For one, you are responsible for your broken engagement. You angered Jason Avondale in a public place."

"I didn't want to shock you with the details about Jason's behavior, Mother. I promise breaking it off was for the best." Especially since he was, well, dead.

"He was a gentleman."

"He owed a lot of money to disreputable people."

"Mere rumors."

"In addition, Jason had imagined Daddy left us a significant inheritance. He wasn't pleased when he discovered that was not the case."

"Still . . ."

"Plus we didn't suit."

"You could have made it work." Staring at her intently, her mother added, "Women cannot break off engagements, Lydia."

"Mother, he hurt my wrist." He had hurt more than her wrist, of course. He'd frightened her and had made her wonder what kind of life they would have together.

"Men have tempers, Lydia. Furthermore, they never know their strength. It's to be expected."

Lydia wasn't so sure about that. Sebastian was far more muscular than Jason had been. When she'd watched him walk down Camp Creek Alley, she'd realized that he held himself tightly in check for her benefit. Not because he couldn't help himself, but because of the very opposite. He knew his strengths and weaknesses and knew what he was capable of doing.

She'd also witnessed his reactions in several situations and was fairly certain that he didn't do anything without weighing the consequences. He did not "lose" his temper. If he was angry, it was because he intended to let loose his wrath on his victim.

He also had never shown her anything but kindness and respect.

Her mother's sharp tone invaded her thoughts. "Lydia, you need to discover what event he will be attending next and obtain an invitation. Then you may apologize to him in person."

"There's no need for that."

"Of course there is."

"Actually—" Lydia stopped herself just in time. How could she tell her mother that Jason had been murdered without giving away that she had been in the building next to where his body had been found?

"Never mind. Mother, I hate to point out the obvious, but my matrimonial status—or lack of the fact—is no concern of Mrs. Charlotte Williams."

"There is more you need to hear."

Lydia wasn't sure how much more she could take. Walking across their entryway, she took a seat in the receiving room. "I am growing bored with listening to gossip about myself."

"This is not gossip." Taking a chair next to her, she said, "Charlotte told me everyone knows you spent last evening in a house of ill repute."

If Lydia had been sipping the hot tea she so desperately wanted, she would have choked. Redirecting the conversation, she stared.

"How could she know that? How does she even know where those houses are?" A new thought occurred to her. "And Mother, how do you even know about such places?"

"Never mind how I know. I do." Leaning forward slightly, she said, "I believe this establishment is called the Silver Grotto?"

Lydia was so stunned, she didn't even bother trying to deny it. "How did she know I was there?" she whispered.

"She didn't tell me, but if she knows—especially so early in the morning—most of Chicago probably knows or soon will." Her tone turned impatient. "Did you really imagine you could frequent such a place and not be noticed?"

Had she? Had she really been so naïve just twenty-four hours ago? "I am not sure."

"That is no answer. Did you or did you not spend the night in that infamous gambling club?"

"I did."

"Is it also true that you were in the arms of Sebastian Marks?"

"How does Mrs. Williams know all this?" She narrowed her eyes. "Or was she there at the Silver Grotto, and I neglected to see her?"

"People saw you walking with him into that seedy part of town."

"I was not in his arms." She didn't bother pointing out that she had slept on his couch. Somehow she was pretty sure it wouldn't go over very well. "Mother, I might have been somewhere I shouldn't have been last night, but even you can admit that it was the first time I've ever done anything improper." She attempted to smile. "Why, given my age, it's a wonder I didn't do anything worse!"

"You did enough. More than enough. Scandalous news travels fast, which is something you do not need me to tell you." Rather dramatically, her mother pressed her hands to her temples and rubbed them, as if she was fighting off an approaching headache.

"I am beyond disappointed with you, Lydia. You have effectively ruined yourself unless, of course, Jason will accept an apology."

"You are blowing things out of proportion. It is becoming tiresome. I am not going to discuss this with you."

"I think you had better. You and I had only one way to make things better, Lydia, and that was for you to marry well. Instead of doing that, you have thrown yourself off the cliff of anything even resembling good behavior. If Mr. Avondale won't take you back, no one will have you. I doubt even my friends will wish to acknowledge me soon. You have ruined both of us." Her face crumbled into tears. "How can you have done this to me?"

Two raps on the front door saved Lydia from answering.

She rushed to the door and threw it open before checking to see who had arrived. She was fairly sure any visitor would be a welcome diversion.

"Oh," she said in surprise. Quite stupidly, too, for someone who had always prided herself on a substantial vocabulary. "It's you."

There stood Mr. Marks. Sebastian. His pensive expression deepened as he scanned her face. "Lydia, what is wrong?"

She would liked to have shielded him from her mother's stories of gossip, but she had no choice. He needed to know what was brewing in their social circles so he could protect himself.

"Everything, it seems," she said. "My mother was just now telling me she heard about my visit to the Silver Grotto last night." She lowered her voice. "She knows I was with you, but she does not seem to know Jason was killed."

But instead of looking troubled or stunned, Sebastian looked her over carefully. She felt his gaze flit across her eyes and cheeks. Pause on her lips. Carefully continue down to her neck and shoulders.

Obviously searching for some sign of distress. "I see," he said at last as he turned to close the door behind him. "Where is she?"

She pointed to the drawing room. "There." Raising her voice, she prepared herself for the inevitable drama that was about to ensue. "Mother, Mr. Marks is here."

Her mother didn't say a word, but Lydia was sure she could feel her disapproval from across the room.

After several seconds passed, Sebastian reached for her hand. "Would you like to go upstairs, dear?" he asked. "Or perhaps you would prefer to go to the kitchen? You look like you might welcome a cup of tea."

Dear? Brew tea? Unable to help herself, she pulled her hand from his and pressed it firmly in the middle of his chest. "Sebastian, you may not understand, but I am in the midst of a scandal."

"I understand completely, Lydia. And it would be *we*, not *I*."

"Pardon?"

"*We* are in the midst of a scandal."

It was all she could do not to roll her eyes. "You already frequent the Silver Grotto. Your reputation is not in question."

"Everything will be all right. I will make it so." His eyes flickered over her, resting on her eyes before he turned away and walked to where her mother waited.

Feeling a bit like a pet spaniel, she hastily followed after him.

"Mrs. Bancroft. Good morning," he said as he leisurely walked into their modest receiving room, somehow managing to look as if he found their surroundings as attractive as one of the interiors of the fair's white palaces. "I do not believe we have officially met. My name is Sebastian Marks."

Her mother sniffed. "Lydia, please escort this man out immediately."

She was eager to do just that. Not for her mother's sake, but for Sebastian's. Her mother was not going to change her mind about him.

Lydia curved a hand around his arm. "Sebastian, I think it would be best if we spoke another time."

"Chin up, dear. It will be okay. I promise."

She tried again. "Mr. Marks, please come with me."

Ignoring her, Sebastian walked to stand directly in front of her lounging mother. "It has become obvious that we need to talk."

Her mother's eyes narrowed. "We have nothing to say to each other."

"I would suggest you rethink that decision, ma'am. We definitely do need to speak, and I do have a lot to say to you. I promise my remarks will be in the best interests of both you and your daughter."

Lydia was appalled. "Sebastian, that is not necessary."

"Allow me to visit with your mother privately, Lydia. Afterward, you and I will need to have a word as well."

"Sebastian—"

Her mother had sat up and was now eyeing Mr. Marks like he was a new mink stole. Or perhaps as if he were the whole fur salon. "Listen to him, Lydia. He is right. I suspect we do have several things to discuss. Leave us."

Lydia was shocked and dismayed and confused.

But she gave up and walked to the kitchen to heat a kettle for tea. She doubted a soothing cup of the hot drink would help, but at least it might make her wait more bearable.

CHAPTER 24

For a small, housebound woman, Felicia Bancroft could certainly bargain with the best of them, Sebastian reflected as he walked toward the kitchen in search of Lydia.

He'd first arrived at the Bancroft residence because he'd been concerned about Lydia—hoping to catch her before she slept. The previous evening's events had been highly irregular and, he feared, undoubtedly frightening for a sheltered woman like Lydia. Though he had pretended he understood Captain Ryan's caution, however, he hadn't really thought much about her reputation—or her mother's distress when she heard of how that reputation had been damaged in his establishment.

Instead, all he'd cared about was making sure that Lydia was not suffering any undue stress from her eventful night.

All of this, of course, was why he was never going to be good enough for a woman like her. He obviously had no real understanding of what society's expectations were for young ladies.

It constituted a serious gap in his education.

The moment he realized the damage that had been done to Lydia's reputation, he'd known he needed to do whatever he must in order to make things right.

And that, of course, meant his proposal of marriage.

His ensuing conversation with Mrs. Bancroft had been satisfactory. She turned out not to be unreasonable. In fact, it seemed she was focused only on making sure Lydia would never have to worry about her future again.

Sebastian knew it was best to take care of matters as efficiently as possible. Because of this, he nodded and gave in to every one of Felicia's demands, including her request that she stay in the townhouse—refurbished, of course—and that Lydia live in a home grand enough to reflect her new position in Chicago.

Lydia's head turned his way when he walked into the cramped kitchen. She was leaning against one of the counters. Her eyes were wide, and the blue eyes he enjoyed looking into so much were cloudy with worry underneath her spectacles. "Is it over?"

"It is." He paused, unsure of how to proceed. Was he really considering proposing marriage to her in the middle of this drab kitchen?

Looking panic-stricken, she rushed toward him. "What happened? Was she terrible to you?"

"Are you worried about my welfare?" He really wasn't sure how to react to that.

"I'm not worried about your welfare, per se . . ." She hedged. "But yes. I suppose I am."

He lifted his arms. "As you can see, I am unmarred."

"Don't tease."

Another rush of warmth seeped into his heart. Was he so taken by her that everything she said had sweet meaning? Or was it her kindness to him in the face of financial ruin, a broken engagement, a murder, and a marred reputation that moved him so?

"I was thinking a walk might do us both some good, but perhaps it would be best if we merely sat back down here, Miss Bancroft."

"Here?" She looked around and frowned. "Mr. Marks—"

"This is fine." He lifted the corners of his lips. "Besides, it seems we have much to say."

"Oh?" She slid into one of the chairs and looked at him closely as he took the one beside her. While she waited, she clasped her hands in a tight knot on the surface of the table. They almost knocked over the cup of tea she had left there.

He reached for it and planted it securely out of her reach. "Careful now. We can't have you getting scalded again."

"Oh, we both know that was Jason's fault." Her eyes widened. "Oh! I'm sorry. I shouldn't be speaking ill of the dead."

"I certainly don't intend to adhere to that rule. Jason Avondale was no saint."

"He didn't deserve to be murdered."

"Of course not. But there is a broad expanse between deserving to be murdered and being saintly."

He shifted in his chair, attempting to put his rather large build on the rickety surface. "May we discuss something else? I did not come in here to dwell upon your former fiancé."

She softened under his regard. "By all means. Forgive me."

"Always," he murmured.

As he stared at her, he honestly couldn't ever remember sitting at a kitchen table. His mother certainly had never had one, and the moment he could afford it, he had hired a cook to serve him in a dining room at the club.

Now he ate in his suite.

But all of that was about to change.

"Lydia, are you all right? Beyond the shock of Avondale's murder, are you still traumatized by the events of last night?"

Instead of answering him immediately, she paused to reflect on it. Which was her want, of course.

Finally she shrugged. "I am not sure if I am all right or not. I suppose I am, though I feel more than a little numb. Almost as if I had a head cold. I feel as though I am in a fog." She peered at him through her lenses. "Is that how you feel?"

"I don't feel like I have a head cold."

"But do you feel foggy?"

"I do not." He felt relieved that he wasn't sitting in a cell. He would soon visit his lawyer's office and anticipated it to be one of many meetings.

"Oh." She looked strangely disappointed.

Then he realized she was struggling with how she should be feeling. That was what had been occupying her brain. "Anything you feel is acceptable," he stated. Just as if he were the authority on feelings and emotions. "There is no right or wrong way to feel."

"You sound so sure."

"I am."

Exhaling a ragged sigh, she nodded, looking a bit more relieved. "So is all of that what you discussed with my mother? Did you tell her Jason died? Was she heartbroken?"

"No. I did not mention Avondale. Or his passing."

"Oh." She looked at him curiously. "Well, if you did not speak about Jason's demise, um, what did you discuss?"

"Our future."

Looking at her hands, her fingers clenched so tight they appeared in danger of breaking, he gave in to temptation and reached for her right hand.

He clasped it in between the two of his and ran his fingers along her knuckles and fingertips. Smiling as he felt the faint calluses on her fingers from all the writing and cataloguing she did at the library.

"Your hands are cold," he stated, liking the feel of her hands in his. Liking the way their hands fit together. So different, but strangely compatible.

"Are they? I hadn't noticed."

She did sound foggy. He suddenly wished he were the type of man to enfold a woman in his arms to offer comfort, just as he had wanted to in his office earlier that morning. Wished she were the kind of woman who would accept such forwardness.

Knowing that delaying his words was only going to make her feel even more ill at ease, he cleared his throat. "Lydia, your mother and I came to an agreement. You and I need to marry, and as soon as possible."

Instead of looking relieved, she shook her head. "Of course we do not."

"Surely you are not that naïve."

"Naïve?" Her mouth worked. "Mr. Marks, is this about last night?" She wrinkled her nose. "Oh my goodness! Are you concerned about gossipmongers?"

It seemed only Lydia Bancroft was capable of making him feel like the tallest man in the room and a complete idiot all at the same time. "Of course it is. But it is also because the two of us uniting in marriage is the right thing to do."

"I beg to differ, sir." She stood up and went back to the spot she'd been standing in when he'd entered the room. "A marriage between the two of us is undoubtedly the worst thing we could do."

"Hardly."

"Sebastian, we hardly know each other."

"I disagree. I know you as well as I know any of my acquaintances."

She practically leapt upon that key word. "You said *acquaintances*,

Mr. Marks. That means two people who have been merely acquainted. That is telling, don't you agree?"

"I do not. Acquaintances means we are close to friends. It also means we are the exact opposite of strangers."

"Indeed. However, that does not mean we should enter into marriage."

"Enough with the wordplay," he snapped, then just as quickly wished he could begin this conversation all over again. He'd meant to keep his voice soft and his reasoning steady. But seeing her dismay . . . no, seeing her, well, fear made him yearn to be a little more honest. "Lydia, I do not make friends. I do not yearn to befriend others. For most of my life, I've been perfectly happy to live relatively alone."

"Which is yet another reason why you do not need me."

"But I do." Of course, he was willing to say almost anything to encourage her to see his way. But as he heard his words, he realized he was correct. He did need her. "I do need you, Lydia. If life has taught me anything, if that World's Fair in the middle of our fair city has shown me anything, it's that everyone, no matter what their circumstances or bearings or hopes, deserves to be around other people."

"Do you think so?"

He knew he'd struck a chord. "I know so. I may have lived my life on the outskirts of good society, Lydia, but you haven't done much better. You, too, have been perfectly happy to live on the fringes of communities. Instead of becoming involved with other people or even with charities or organizations, you've stayed to yourself and your books."

"That's not true."

"Prove it. Who is your best friend? What do you do when you are not at the library and are not waiting hand and foot on your mother?"

The look of devastation on her face told him everything Sebastian needed to know.

"I don't want a marriage to be another mistake that you need to make better," she whispered. "I don't want to be another liability on your life."

She had no idea about liabilities. She had no idea about pain or embarrassment or anything to do with living in the shadows of hunger and a mother's total sacrifice of everything she was . . . to still feel like she was a failure.

"You won't be a liability."

"But—"

"You will be much better, Lydia."

"Oh."

He saw her wavering. Saw her weigh his words, wonder if he was lying or being sincere. Because he hated to see her suffer, he gave her the nudge she needed. "Your mother was relieved, Lydia. She was thankful to know that you will be taken care of."

"Did she say such a thing?"

"Yes." He waited a beat, then added the words he instinctively knew she would hold close to her heart. "She was also grateful to know that she would no longer have to worry."

Behind her lenses, blue eyes widened. "She said that?"

"Oh, yes. She wants to stay here. I told her I'd rehire Ethel and hire a nurse and a maid. She will be taken care of for the rest of her life."

"That . . . that is very kind of you."

"It is nothing. It is what a son-in-law does." He smiled then, finding both his new title and the strange turn that was transpiring most amusing.

He leaned forward. "Lydia, you are good with words. You have a brilliant mind. You also have a good heart. I know if we stayed here all day, you could come up with a myriad of reasons to refute my reasons. But simply concentrate on one thing."

"Which is?"

"Marrying me is the right thing to do." He inhaled. "I promise to make you happy." At the very least, he would certainly try.

She stared at him a long moment, then opened her lips a fraction.

He prepared himself for a torrent of arguments, each one more logical than the last.

Instead, she merely shocked him out of his skin.

"Will you say the words?"

"Hmm?" He'd say whatever she wanted, but he wasn't following.

"Will you ask me to marry you?"

His cheeks flushed. Not because of what he was about to do, but because he was such a fool that he hadn't remembered what was important. He hadn't recalled what women needed.

Well, at least what this one lady needed.

And because of that, he did something he'd sworn at a young age he would never do.

He stood up.

Walked to the front of her chair.

And knelt down on one knee.

Taking her hand, he gazed up into her eyes. "Lydia Bancroft, will you do me the very great honor of becoming my wife?"

Her lips curved up, the sweetest sight he'd ever seen.

"Yes," she said.

And, by his honor, Sebastian Marks knew that one word had never meant so much.

CHAPTER 25

CHICAGO TIMES-COURIER

January 26, 1894
Reported by Benson Gage

The city of Chicago has put the team of Ryan and Howard in charge of the investigation of Jason Avondale's murder. Readers might recall that this dashing team of detectives solved the Society Slasher case. This reporter, for one, is glad this team is on the case, since there are rumors that quite a number of society's elite were visiting the alley that night . . . including a certain auburn-haired, blue-eyed, former debutant.

Although more than a full day had passed, Vincent Hunt was still chafing from the indignity of having to answer Lieutenant Howard's questions.

Standing in front of his mirror, he attempted to fasten a tie, failed, and then attempted it again. His fingers felt useless, but perhaps that was because his mind kept racing back to last night's interrogation.

"So what do you do, exactly?" Howard had asked, his expression filled with contempt.

"I do whatever my employer asks me to do."

"Give me some examples. What does a man like Sebastian Marks ask a man like you to do?"

Vincent had known Howard had made his tone derisive intentionally. He'd wanted Vincent to get flustered and upset. Infuriated. It was an excellent way to obtain information without having to use one's fists. Vincent had used the same method more than once.

Therefore, he'd stood his ground. "I manage his employees. I confer with the floor managers and compile their reports. I make sure the club runs smoothly."

"Sounds like there hardly needs to be a Sebastian Marks if you do everything."

"I did not mean to insinuate that. Obviously, I do not."

Howard had shuffled through a sheaf of papers. "I looked into your past employment records. It says here that you worked for Sheffield and Towne."

"Yes, I did. I worked for that law firm for eight years."

Pointing to something scribbled in his notebook, Howard said, "It seems Avondale had Sheffield and Towne on retainer."

"Did he? I don't recall," he lied. Mr. Sheffield had in fact given him several of Avondale's papers to proof and copy.

"Are you certain that your paths never crossed there? Mr. Galvin seemed to think perhaps they had. In fact, he said Avondale did not like you."

"If our paths did cross at Sheffield and Towne, he wouldn't have remembered me. I was a mere clerk. He was not only a paying customer but an acquaintance of Mr. Sheffield. And most of the men who owe the Grotto a great deal of money do not like me."

"Why did you leave Sheffield and Towne?"

If Howard was reading Vincent's employment record, he knew why he'd left. But he allowed him his fun. "I did not leave voluntarily. I was fired."

"Because?"

"Because I missed too much work." He'd missed too much work, lost too much sleep, and had botched one of Jason Avondale's financial trusts. Avondale had been furious.

Howard had raised a brow. "Frankly, I'm surprised a man like Sebastian Marks hired you. A record like that is embarrassing," he stated, his voice once again full of derision. "It's nothing to be proud of, certainly."

"That is true." Though it hurt to hear his past reduced to Lieutenant Howard's disparaging terms, he was glad Irene hadn't been mentioned. He wanted to preserve her good name at all costs. At least her memory was spared that indignity.

"Or is that the whole story?"

"You seem to think it is."

Howard had slammed a hand on the table. "Don't play games with me, Hunt. You won't win. Why did you miss so much work? Were you gambling? Experimenting with drink?" He paused, practically leered at him. "Or did you, perhaps, discover other women?"

Each innuendo felt as harsh as a man's fists. "My wife had scarlet fever," he said. "That was why I missed work." That had also been why he'd done such sloppy work on Avondale's documents.

Immediately Howard's expression turned blank. "There was no notice of a wife when I researched you. Only a daughter."

Vincent didn't want to discuss the gaps in the policeman's research about his life. His statement only reinforced everything he didn't like or trust about the police force. They were a bunch of Irishmen who excelled at bending the rules to subjugate innocent people. "I was married," he snapped. "When she fell ill, it was . . . difficult. I was not always able to get to work."

"Did she survive?"

Howard's voice had turned oddly gentle. It was as much a surprise as it was unwelcome, because it forced Vincent to say her name. To not do so would do her a disfavor.

"Irene did not survive," he said at last. "She died." Then, because he'd already shared more than he'd wanted to, he gave in and completed the story. "After she passed, I spent almost my last dollar on providing her with a decent funeral service and burial." He raised his head, meeting Howard's eyes. "It was the right thing to do."

"Of course it was." He paused. "But I imagine Sheffield and Towne didn't approve of your time away."

"Indeed, they did not. I was their law clerk, Lieutenant Howard. When I worked for them, I was expected to blend into the woodwork, doing the work I was paid to do."

"There is nothing wrong with that."

"No. But I was only one of their many nameless faces who organized reams of paperwork into more manageable piles," he stated, bending what had really happened into something that was almost the truth. "And when I wasn't there to do that, when I spent too much time caring for my wife instead, I was easily replaced." Now, as distance afforded a better impression of his past, Vincent knew that his weakness had played a large part of his being let go as well.

He'd never stood up for himself. He'd taken the jibes from his employers, the comments about his tentative nature, the slurs about his less-than-impressive appearance.

Now that man he had been embarrassed him. He hadn't expected anything and therefore thought he'd deserved nothing.

"So that was why you went to work for Sebastian Marks. Because you were desperate and had nowhere else to go."

Howard had been correct, but he'd also been so very wrong. Vincent had gone to work for Sebastian Marks so he could become different. He hadn't even cared if he was going to become a man of worth.

All he'd known was that he couldn't continue to be the man he was.

The interview had continued for another hour, with Vincent sharing far too many details about the running of the Silver Grotto to feel like he could ever look Sebastian Marks in the eye again.

When he'd exited the room, he hadn't wanted to do anything but hang his head in shame. He'd broken his three promises to Marks. He'd lied. He'd gossiped. And though he hadn't actually stolen an item, his hands had felt as dirty as if he had.

But unfortunately, the first person he'd seen was Mr. Marks himself. He'd been leaning against the wall. Somehow, even after being up all night and being interrogated himself, Mr. Marks' suit had looked pressed, his hair perfectly coifed, and his dark eyes alert.

When Mr. Marks had looked Vincent's way, it had felt like he'd seen everything. Furthermore, the man had looked concerned.

It had almost made tears spring to Vincent's eyes, knowing how different he would look at him after he became aware of just how much Vincent had revealed. After ascertaining that Mr. Marks was determined to wait for Bridget, Vincent had left.

He'd only tossed and turned as he'd tried to sleep, though, and now he was determined to go to the club and keep watch over things. Mr. Marks had said he was not sure how long the Grotto would be closed, but all sorts would be sniffing around, waiting for their opportunity to benefit from an empty building.

Vincent would make sure that, at least, didn't happen. He might tell tales against his employer, he might lie about his past experiences with Avondale, but Vincent wasn't about to let some random gang of thugs take advantage of the Grotto.

As soon as his cravat was tied securely, his vest neatly buttoned, and his shoes freshly polished, he exited his bedroom. He would check on Mary and Janet, then get on his way.

Except he found Mary sitting rather disconsolately at the top of the stairs. Her doll was in one hand, but it was dangling from her fist like it was in danger of leaping to its death down the stairs.

"Careful with Willow, Mary," he said. "She's in danger of falling."

She looked up. "Oh. Hi, Daddy."

"What is wrong, sweetheart?"

She sighed. "Aunt Janet doesn't feel good."

"Oh? Is she feverish?" Even after all this time, he still feared fevers.

"I don't think so." She twisted her lips. "When I was downstairs this morning, she was sitting next to the oven. She said I was going to have to be really quiet today. Me and Willow couldn't play outside either."

This was alarming. "I had better go see your aunt Janet."

Mary nodded her head. "I think you'd better, but watch out, on account of her feeling yucky."

"Yucky, is it? I'll do my best." He ran a hand along her dark-blonde curls before walking down the stairs, weighing what the future would bring with each step.

By the time he reached the bottom of the stairs, he was torn between sending for the doctor and quarantining the house. Actually, he'd begun to think both would be the best course of action.

"Oh. There you are," Janet murmured from the sofa in his living room. "I wondered how long it was going to take you to come running to investigate once you were up."

Her sarcasm surprised him. Especially given the way she looked so pale and clammy, and her eyes were rimmed with red. "You look wretched."

"I know. I should, of course. I feel wretched."

"What is wrong? Where is Thomas? Shouldn't he be looking after you?" He couldn't keep his disapproval out of his tone. Usually her husband was attentive, so for him to have sent her over to his house in the condition she was in was surprising.

Somehow her look softened. "Thomas knows I'm fine, Vincent."

"You are hardly that." Before she could interject a word, he began making plans. "Never mind. I'll take care of everything. Mr. Marks' private physician is the best in the city, and for a small price he won't hesitate to pay a house call here." Thinking quickly, he said, "I know a couple of reliable boys at the end of the block. They'll fetch him without much coaxing."

"There is no need."

"Of course there is," he said. "Now, Janet, this is what we are going to do. You are going to lie down right here while I fetch the doctor. Until he gets here, you can rest or sip tea." He pivoted on his heel. "I'll go make you some."

"Tea, Vincent? I'm surprised you even know what such a thing is anymore."

"I know about tea, sister," he snapped. "We'll determine our next steps after the physician gives us his recommendations."

"There's no need for any of that."

He brushed off her concerns. Janet always put herself last. He would put a stop to that. He would also talk to Thomas and see if he needed a gentle reminder about looking after his own wife better. For the first time in days, Vincent was glad of his fearsome reputation and ability to coax all sorts of things with his fists. "Don't worry about the physician's fee. Marks pays me well. Besides, with everything you do for Mary, nothing is too dear—"

"I'm going to have a baby, Vincent," she blurted.

Everything in his world stopped. His feet, his mind, even the time. "Pardon?"

She smiled. "I'm with child. I'm two months along. That is why I am feeling under the weather."

He sat down. "But you don't have any children."

"I know that," she said as she gingerly made room for him to take a seat beside her on the sofa. "Thomas and I thought I was barren."

"But you aren't."

She shook her head. "It would seem I am not. For whatever reason, the Lord decided this was the time in my life to be a mother. We're very happy about it, Vincent."

"I'm happy too." Realizing how stilted his voice sounded, he laughed. "Sorry. I, well, I was so ready to fix your ailment that I now find myself caught off guard."

"So it would seem. Thomas is going to enjoy this tale. It's so very rare to get the best of you these days."

"You got me good." Now that he wasn't worried she was going to become gravely ill, he noticed the look of satisfaction on her face. She was pleased.

He was only concerned about her welfare. "Have you seen a doctor? Do you need to see one?"

"Of course not. Nothing is happening to me that hasn't happened to all the other mothers before me."

"I suppose that is true."

"So now that we have determined that I am merely nauseated and not deathly ill, I'm going to follow you into the kitchen and watch you make me a pot of tea. I've already put the kettle on. And then you are going to tell me what has put such a number of worry lines on your face."

"Nothing you need to be concerned about," he said lightly as he walked with her to the kitchen.

She followed. "What has your employer done now?"

"No reason to sound like that, Janet. He is a good man."

"He deals in drink and gambling. Neither is appropriate for you to be working with."

"I don't serve alcohol, and I don't work at the tables," he said as he checked the kettle. "I run Mr. Marks' life."

"Sometimes I think you also sell your soul to him."

"My soul is very much alive, though I appreciate your concern."

"Maybe it's time you looked for another job."

"That is not possible."

"No, that is inconvenient."

"It is both." When she flinched at his harsh tone, he felt terrible. "Forgive me, Janet. I didn't mean to speak like that with you."

Her expression softened. "Vincent, all I'm saying is that sometimes I fear you've forgotten how to be the man the Lord wanted you to be when you're around Sebastian Marks. It's like you've given up everything about yourself for his money."

She was such a woman. Thomas had probably made sure she never knew the things he did to keep her well fed and warm and snug with coal in the winter, all in their comfortable house. Men had to make sacrifices for their families. They also were expected not to complain about it. Or worry their spouses.

Vincent knew he'd treated Irene that way, and he'd been proud of it too.

When the kettle whistled, he prepared her tea, then brought it to the small table where she was sitting. Though he hadn't intended to burden his sister with the events of the night before, he was more loyal to Sebastian Marks than determined to keep her in the dark.

"There was a murder last night, right outside the club. The police were called in and they questioned several people."

"Even you?" she asked, alarm in her voice.

"Even me." She didn't need to find out he was one of only four people they'd kept.

"Did they discover who did it?"

"Not yet. But it's early still." He shrugged. "I hope they will soon. The club will be closed for at least tonight."

"So you have some time off?"

"More or less. But remember, I don't work for the club. I work for Marks. Which means I need to make sure his assets are taken care of."

"Who died? Some poor gambler?"

"Actually, it was someone rather well-known. Jason Avondale."

Her eyes widened. "You know him."

"I knew him," he gently corrected.

"Weren't you working on his documents at Sheffield and Towne when Irene was so sick?"

He might lie to the police, but he couldn't to Janet. "Yes."

"And he was the reason you were fired."

"He wasn't the only reason. I missed a lot of work." He exhaled, forcing himself to tell the truth. "But yes, he was the real reason. I made some errors in his contracts and paperwork. The fault was my own." He pushed himself to say the last, needing to remind himself that the partners in the firm had had no choice but to fire him. Jason Avondale had been rich and powerful. Vincent Hunt had been nothing. So very expendable.

But of course, when he'd been fired, he'd had nothing. Irene had died, his money had been spent on her funeral, and his reputation had been damaged. He'd been bitter and worried and, for a time, had vowed to one day remind Jason Avondale that he was more formidable than he'd ever imagined.

"I guess like a bad penny, he keeps turning up," Janet cast him a sympathetic look.

Thinking of how Mr. Marks had recently come in contact with him through Miss Bancroft, Vincent nodded. "He did. I just wish he would have turned up somewhere besides the front of the Silver Grotto."

She smiled softly. "Maybe the Lord wanted you to be good and sure you knew Avondale would never turn up again."

"I'll take your word on that one." He stood up. "Now, I'm going to go sit with Mary before I head to the club."

"Off you go. And don't worry about a thing. No matter what happens in our future, we will prevail."

As he walked upstairs, Vincent reflected that Janet had chosen an unusual choice of words.

It almost felt as if she had been giving him a warning.

He wondered what was in store for all of them now.

CHAPTER 26

Sebastian had sent word that he would arrive at two o'clock Friday afternoon to take her out. Though his missive had been only a few lines, he'd been clear that they would not be going to tea at the Hartman Hotel.

Lydia had smiled when she'd read that. His thoughtfulness had surprised her. She would have never imagined that a man, most especially a man like him, would have even thought about how she would not want to revisit a place that had caused her so much distress—twice.

As she carefully pulled on her gloves in preparation for his visit, she realized that she was going to need to rethink what she knew about men, and especially what she thought she'd known about Sebastian. Though she still did not know very much about him, she was learning that he was far more enigmatic than she'd previously imagined. Because of that, she wouldn't have thought that he would ever think to take her sensibilities into consideration.

After glancing out the front window and still seeing no sign of Sebastian, she sat down on the edge of a chair in their receiving room.

"Pacing and fidgeting won't make him arrive any faster, Lydia," her mother proclaimed. "Please, sit still and attempt to relax."

"I am not pacing. And I am sitting still."

"You are certainly not relaxed though."

No, for some reason, she certainly wasn't.

But what was just as much of a surprise was her mother's actions. Instead of reclining in bed in one of her many nightgowns, she was now dressed in a dove-gray day gown and sitting on the couch across from her. Her dark-blonde hair was neatly pinned up. Because Bridget was not expected until later that evening, Lydia had helped her with it soon after she'd awoken. She had color in her cheeks for the first time in ages too.

She looked pretty and far younger than her age of fifty.

It had made Lydia realize just how much her mother had been affected by their financial difficulties and her worries about Lydia's future.

Lydia was also gratified to see that her mother was enjoying a plate of delicacies for her afternoon snack. With his note, Sebastian had sent over several prepared meals from the hotel. Not sure of his plans, Lydia had taken a bite or two as well. She could not be sure she was getting tea on this outing—whatever it was.

Perhaps that was why she was a bit on edge. She still wasn't used to the promise of adventure . . . and maybe a little danger.

Even her mother knew now that Jason had been murdered near the Grotto. It had been in all the Thursday papers. Of course, Charlotte Williams could not wait to tell them Lydia may have been referenced in a *Courier* report about the murder that morning, but only with a vague description that could have been anyone. It was best not to think about that.

Earlier, she and her mother had feasted on bowls of hearty vegetable beef soup, bread and cheese, and a plate of sliced meats. It had felt like a meal fit for royalty. It had also gone a long way toward making her mother feel as if all was right in the world.

"Just think, Lydia, you will soon have your own staff to manage. And you will be eating like this at every meal."

"We shall see, Mother." Her engagement to Sebastian Marks still felt like a hazy, discombobulated dream.

In many ways, she could hardly remember all that had happened. She felt as if his visit yesterday morning had been in the middle of a terribly awkward and scary night—which, since they had not slept, in a way it was.

After delicately wiping the corners of her mouth with a linen napkin, her mother said, "Tomorrow morning we will begin our wedding preparations. How big an occasion do you expect Mr. Marks will want it to be?" she mused. "Perhaps around three or four hundred people?"

Lydia almost choked. "For what?"

"For the reception, of course."

The idea of such a large reception made her cringe. "Mother, I don't even know three hundred people."

"Of course you do. And don't forget, people will be invited who are close friends of our family and Mr. Marks. He is such an important man that I have no doubt he might even have a bigger guest list than ours."

"I certainly don't know three hundred with whom I want to celebrate my nuptials."

"I certainly do. And I'm sure Mr. Marks knows a great many more people than that." Curling into the cushions of the couch, her mother sighed dreamily. "Maybe he'll want it to be even bigger. Just think, Lydia, your picture will be on the society page of the *Tribune*." She paused. "Or at least the *Courier*."

Lydia bit back a caustic retort. She knew such things were important to her mother, so important that she wasn't above seeking the scandalous *Courier* in order to obtain her goals. And she knew such things were second nature to some girls her age. But neither had they the money for such things nor did her manner lend itself to large weddings.

"You know we cannot afford to hold such a grand affair."

"Your fiancé can. That is all that matters."

"But that is not what I want to do. I have no intention of spending so much of his money for such a thing."

"It is hardly a 'thing.' It is your wedding. And of course you will be spending his money." Brushing a stray crumb from her bodice, she said, "Men work so their wives can enjoy the finer things in life. That's what your father always told me."

Lydia heard her mother's words, but more than that, she heard a thick note of bitterness laced with heartbreak.

Her father had probably said such things. Many times. However, he'd also borrowed money, made poor investment deals, and given them things it turned out he couldn't actually afford.

Long ago, she'd come to terms that he'd been living in his own make-believe world as much as she did in her books or her mother did by blatantly ignoring all signs that their way of life was slowly falling apart.

"I'll speak to Mr. Marks, Momma, about his expectations. Don't you say a word."

"Lydia, he is smitten with you. He will do whatever you desire. I'm sure of it."

"That is not how things are between us."

"That's how he made it sound to me."

"Regardless, please let me handle my wedding. At least this next conversation."

"All right." Her words were grudgingly said. "Now, where is that maid?"

"I told you, Bridget isn't coming until this evening."

"Really? I daresay she is already taking advantage of you, Lydia. Maids need to be taught that they work for you, not the other way around."

Lydia frowned and glared out the window, wishing she could will Sebastian to arrive that very minute.

Then, as if she had done that very thing, he appeared on the sidewalk.

"Mr. Marks is here," she said as she grabbed her coat and hat. "I'm going to go outside to meet him."

"Absolutely not. You need to sit down and wait for him to come to the door. Whatever will he think of your manners, Lydia?"

Her mother was giving her directives just as if they were living in their old house and they had a butler to answer the door and a parlor maid to stand prettily in the corner and serve Sebastian tea. But of course Lydia couldn't remind her of that. She couldn't say that her mother was asking for things that didn't really matter anymore.

To put so much out in the open would prove devastating. And, consequently, unintentionally cruel. "It hardly matters, given the fact that we are engaged. He must think my manners are good enough."

Walking toward the foyer, she glanced over her shoulder. "Don't forget to lock the front door after me, Momma."

"We don't need to lock the doors at every turn."

"Of course we do." She'd recently learned that one could never guess what the future would bring. "I'll be back in a few hours."

Sebastian was just a few feet away when she appeared on her steps.

His pace slowed as he caught sight of her. And then his smile faltered. "Lydia, whatever are you doing, coming out to greet me like this?"

"I saw you on the sidewalk and wanted to save you the trouble of coming to my door."

He frowned. "Don't do that again."

"Why ever not?" She couldn't even begin to understand why he seemed upset by her eagerness to be off with him.

"It isn't proper. Or safe," he muttered.

She hated that he was reminding her of her manners—just as her mother had been. "Sebastian, if you don't feel that I am proper enough for you, please don't feel compelled to keep our engagement."

"Why would you make a pronouncement like that?" His gaze hardened as he examined her. "Where did this come from? Are you having second thoughts?"

"I simply don't wish to be reminded of what is proper by my fiancé."

His dark eyes searched her face. "No, it is more than that. What is wrong?"

Unbidden, tears sprang to her eyes, tears that she'd neither wanted nor expected. "Nothing. It's simply nerves. And worries."

"But you have nothing to worry about. I will see to your needs now, Lydia. And your mother's. I promise you that."

She caught the new thread of heat in his expression. And his words. It caused her to take a step away from him. She was as struck by what she saw in his eyes as much as the way she felt by his attention.

"Mr. Marks."

"It is Sebastian. We are engaged now, and no matter what you might think or decide, that fact is not going to change. I will not be breaking off our engagement. I have no wish to do so."

"I don't wish to do that either."

"Then keep that in mind." His voice was clipped. Offended. "And don't call me Mr. Marks again."

His voice was controlled and concise. His expression hard. He seemed to resonate with a dangerous aura. So much so, she was having trouble locating the gentleman she'd known at the library. "Sebastian, are you all right? You seem a bit on edge today. Are you still distressed about Jason's murder occurring outside your club?"

"Not at all." He shook his head as if to clear it. "Forgive my lackluster manners. Now, shall we go?" he asked as he raised his arm for her to take.

She rested her gloved hand on it. "Of course. Where are we off to?"

"It's a surprise."

"A surprise?"

"Don't act like you don't like surprises. Everyone does."

"I don't." And that was true. Lydia liked knowing what was expected and planning for any variation of that plan. She enjoyed thinking about what was going to happen and analyzing most everything she imagined would occur. It allowed her to feel less at risk and more in control.

Which was why she was still mystified that she had gone to the Silver Grotto without first knowing exactly what she was getting into. "Tell me."

The corners of his lips lifted. "No."

"Sebastian."

He chuckled, humor now lighting his face. "You are piqued."

"No, I am affronted," she countered, trying her best to look unaffected by his relaxed, happy expression.

His light chuckle turned to outright laughter. "That's basically the same thing."

"Not essentially." Though, of course, he was right.

"Good manners prevent me from continuing our verbal disagreement. I won't risk offending you."

He had done nothing of the sort. Instead, she'd felt as if he'd given her something far sweeter—an insight to a portion of him that she was sure he rarely shared. "I'd say it was more of a small contretemps."

"Of course, Miss Bancroft."

She arched a brow, knowing he'd referred to her that way just to get a reaction. Therefore, she only smiled sweetly at him. "I am very much looking forward to our afternoon together."

"At the risk of sounding as if I am begging for compliments, I'll ask why."

"Because it seems we are both ready to relax and simply enjoy a few hours together. It will be a nice change. Everything between us seems so complicated."

The light in his eyes faded. "It is."

As if their feelings were conjoined, she felt that same lightness evaporate from her good mood. What were they going to do if their worst fears came to light?

"Don't," he ordered. "Don't think about it. Not yet."

She nodded. He was right.

When a grip car came clanging forward, he held out a hand. "Good. It's right on time."

With his assistance, she easily hopped on. It wasn't very crowded. Also, the few men and women riding seemed happy to give them a wide berth. Lydia knew why. Even dressed in his well-tailored suit and silk-covered hat, Sebastian was a man who emanated power.

She'd never felt more safe in anyone's company.

Since he didn't seem inclined to talk or give her the slightest hint of where they might be going, Lydia contented herself with observing the sights and sounds around them. Day workers were scurrying on errands. Women were pushing buggies, and other women were walking in pairs, holding canvas bags of produce or meat.

Faint smells drifted upward, both from the stockyards and the lake and river. There was a decided chill in the air, made more so by the faint breeze brought on by the grip car's fast pace.

When they stopped again, Sebastian assisted her off, then took her up a flight of stairs to the landing for the elevated train. Soon they were seated in a car, traveling over rails and bridges toward the outskirts of the city.

Fifteen minutes later, they were alighting, and Lydia realized they were at Jackson Park, the sight of the World's Fair that had closed at the end of October.

The fair had begun with all the pomp and circumstance befitting an event anticipated around the world. In contrast, it had ended with little fanfare. Chicago's mayor had died unexpectedly, and several fires had broken out in the White City, mainly due to the nature of the plaster and wood that had made up the majority of the area.

To make matters worse, the Society Slasher had been abducting and killing women there, ending with his subsequent arrest when none other than the Illinois building had been burning down.

These events manifested a certain amount of distaste and fear, and most everyone in the city avoided the grand structures.

They were tainted now. Tainted by time and murders and fire and danger. And, perhaps, by the evidence that the structures' beauty was on the outside only.

Lydia shivered, thinking about how everything that had stood so ethereal and grand had been ruined by a few sparks.

She was also confused. This was definitely not a place where most people decided to come on a whim. "What are we doing here?"

"I thought we might enjoy visiting Buffalo Bill Cody's Wild West show. It's closing this week. Have you been yet?"

"No."

"I'm surprised. An inquisitive young lady like you? I would have thought you would have enjoyed the opportunity to see the real Indians."

"I've been more intrigued by the stories of Annie Oakley," she admitted.

"But?"

"But you know how the prices have been. At the peak of the fair, it cost more to see the show than to get into the fair itself."

"Then by all means, let us rectify this omission."

They walked to the entrance of the Midway. Lydia was struck by the faded glory that it had already become. Several of the main attractions, like the native sword dancers and the infamous Streets of Cairo were already closed. Now there were only some desperate peddlers selling Cracker Jacks, some scantily clad women offering to tell their fortunes, and, of course, the magnificent, looming Ferris Wheel.

After paying for their tickets to the show, Sebastian guided them to their seats and seemed content to simply sit quietly.

She, of course, was far too interested in everything to sit so quietly. As it had been in the grip car and on the elevated train, all manner of people gave her a passing glance, took note of Sebastian, and then kept their distance.

Because they still had some time before the show began, she turned to him. "What is it about you that alarms so many people, even men?"

"I don't think that is the case."

"No, it's true. When men recognize your face, they look scared."

"Hardly."

"What do you do? Do you glare at everyone? Or do they know something about you that I do not?"

"Your question is indelicate."

"I agree. But I would still like to know."

"It is most likely both things. I grew up on the streets, Lydia. I did not grow up imagining that anyone had my best interests at heart."

She shuddered to think how he'd learned that. She knew he had a right to his privacy, but now that they were engaged, she ached to know more about him. Even his dark secrets. "What was it like?"

"It was nothing you need to be concerned about."

"I'd rather learn something more about you. Did your mother never shield you?"

His lips pressed together. "She had no choice. For that matter, she did more for me than many. Many young boys and girls made their living as veritable mud larks, combing the banks of the lakes and rivers for debris that could be sold."

"Did you ever do that?"

"From time to time." His voice sounded carefully controlled.

"I am sorry."

"Don't be," he said lightly. "I learned long ago that life is full of peaks and valleys. It takes both to build character. And, if the Lord is good, one has years to experience both."

His words made sense and spurred a memory of something she'd heard long ago. "My father used to say that we are not living in heaven."

His eyes lit up. "That is correct. We can't expect only happiness here on earth. One must experience a bit of dirt and grime. Builds character, you see."

She knew she shouldn't press him. Knew it was foolhardy to ask for more than he was offering, but against her better judgment, she asked, "How do you feel about your life now? Are you in a peak or valley?"

He lifted her hand and slid his fingers in between hers. "There was a murder outside my club two nights ago."

"Yes." She was such a fool for asking.

"The police consider me a suspect."

"Forgive me." She looked at the seats around them. Men and women from all walks of life were filling them. A few children were there as well, their hands holding containers of popcorn. This was neither the time nor the place.

He continued. "Your reputation is in disarray, and furthermore, you've been put in danger. Both of those things are my fault."

"No, I am to—"

"But in spite of all of that, I do believe right now, at this moment, I am at the top of a mountain."

"Sebastian? Truly?"

He looked at their surroundings, as if truly noticing the horses at the edge of the stage, the Western riders in their chaps and tall hats, the, well, the incredible grandeur of it all.

Then he stared at their joined hands and smiled. "I am engaged. To you." His voice held a note of surprise. As if he couldn't believe his good fortune. "And because of that, my life has never been so good. Though things might change in a day, even in an hour? For this moment, I am grateful."

His words stole her heart. All her life she'd felt awkward and disjointed. Never good enough, never right.

Until now.

"I feel as though I am at a pinnacle as well," she said quietly.

"That makes me happy."

It made her happy too. Even though there was much she didn't know about Sebastian, and some of what she did know made her rather uneasy, she completely agreed with his assessment of their situation. No matter what might happen in the future, for now, things were good. And that was something to be grateful for and to never take for granted.

Even if that moment could be gone in practically the blink of an eye.

CHAPTER 27

CHICAGO TIMES-COURIER

January 26, 1894—Special Edition
Reported by Benson Gage

Aided by a new and strong police presence brought on by Jason Avondale's murder, Camp Creek Alley is now rather safe to visit. However, as long as Sebastian Marks' famed Silver Grotto is closed, there is little reason to go.

Look who the cat brought in," Gwen said when Bridget emerged from her room at the Hartman Hotel late in the afternoon.

Once again, Gwen and Mabel were loitering outside her doorway, looking as eager as ever to chat and gossip. And, no doubt, collect some tidbits to relay to the other staff members.

"Good afternoon to you both," Bridget said, wondering why she'd ever been such good friends with them. Was it because she'd had no one else? Now that she was spending more time with Miss

Bancroft and getting to know Vincent better, the women seemed to be nothing but trouble.

Mabel smiled. "What have you been up to? We heard you've been holed up in there for a solid day."

"I was tired. That's all." Of course, it was so much more than that. She could only pray that Gwen and Mabel didn't know about Mr. Avondale's murder . . . and the fact that she was a suspect.

Seconds later, Gwen squelched that hope. "Is it true what people are saying about *him*?"

"You know I don't gossip about Mr. Marks."

"Well, just to let you know, people are saying he killed the gent Jason Avondale right in his own club!" Her eyes glittered with excitement. "Did you see his body? Was it awful?"

She suddenly felt faint. No doubt it was because she had seen Avondale's body, the sight of which was more than awful. Then, of course, had come the questioning, which had been terrifying. "I didn't see anything," she lied. "I wasn't even there." She was never going to talk about that evening again if she could help it.

The girls exchanged glances. "Now, that's where we know you are lying. The newsboys are saying that the police have found several people of interest, and one was a certain brown-haired maid." Gwen cackled. "I told everyone in the kitchen that had to be you."

Bridget smiled tightly. "Thank you for filling me in. However, I must be on my way."

Mabel reached out and squeezed her shoulder. "You know we're simply teasing you, dear. Are you all right?"

"Of course I am. Now, if you will excuse me, I really must be going."

"Sure you do," Gwen proclaimed as she took a step back. "We know you ain't got time for us no more."

Bridget felt bad. She knew she'd hurt Gwen's and Mabel's feelings.

Furthermore, she knew they hadn't meant any harm, and they really had been only trying to be friendly. The right thing to do would be to stay with them a little longer and attempt to apologize.

But the truth was she was so disturbed by everything that had been going on, she hardly trusted herself any longer. It was likely that she wasn't worthy of friendship, or even capable of it. Her past had also told her that sometimes the very worst things happen even when one has the best of intentions. There was a very good chance that she was only going to make things worse between the three of them if she lingered.

Therefore, with one last look of apology, she turned away and crept down the back stairs, holding her purse tight against her. She couldn't afford to let anyone in her life right now.

That was why she was going to Miss Bancroft's house that afternoon instead of waiting to report back that evening as Mr. Marks suggested. She needed to keep her job there. If she succeeded, that would be enough.

Feeling better about her plans, Bridget headed toward the Bancrofts' townhouse with a determined spring in her step. She was going to be fine. She had to be.

When she passed a man selling warm pretzels, she gave in to temptation and purchased one. And she had just swallowed her first bite when Sergio Vlas stepped out of a nearby crowd and smiled her way.

She knew he and Mr. Marks were contemporaries, but that was where the similarities ended. Whereas she trusted Mr. Marks with everything she had, and even though Vlas had been nothing but kind to her on the rare occasions she'd seen him, now she suspected Vlas could be far more dangerous than she ever imagined.

He had that watch. And he had looked at her so strangely when she'd noticed it when Mr. Marks walked her to the hotel.

She slipped the pretzel and its paper wrap into a pocket and then gripped the lapels of her coat tightly together as he fell into step beside her. "Ah, Bridget. I thought that was you."

"Mr. Vlas. Hello."

"No reason for us to keep so formal. You should call me Sergio."

She smiled tightly, unsure of what to say next.

Evidently, he didn't suffer from such problems. "I am glad we ran into each other." Stuffing his hands into the pockets of his bulky wool coat, he grinned openly. "The sun is almost shining through the clouds today. If it wasn't so cold, it would be a nice day to be outside."

"Yes, sir," she answered politely, but even as she did, Bridget glanced around, getting her bearings. The Hartman was now three blocks behind her, and the Bancroft townhouse was still several more blocks to her east. Though they were on a main street, she felt as if she was vulnerable in a no man's land. "Though the day is nice, it, um, makes little difference to me. I am on my way to work."

"Yes. To Miss Bancroft's house, I believe."

She stumbled. "You know Miss Bancroft?"

He reached out and steadied her arm. "Careful," he cautioned before continuing. "I know you were escorting her through Camp Creek Alley the other night, but of course I don't know her. A fine woman like that would never want anything to do with a man like me." After removing his hand from her person, he brushed a stray piece of yarn from his overcoat. "I don't blame her for that." He laughed sardonically. "I wouldn't want to know me either."

She certainly wouldn't be too eager to be talking with him if she didn't have other people around. "Well, then . . ."

"But I've made it my business to know most everything that happens along Camp Creek Alley," he declared, his accent becoming more pronounced. "And since she was at the Silver Grotto, she is now a person of my interest."

Remembering how they'd seen him the evening of the murder, how he and Mr. Marks had joined forces against those men, her footsteps slowed. The bit of pretzel she'd just eaten suddenly felt too big for her stomach. "Why is that?"

"Well, she is a suspect in the killing of Jason Avondale. But of course you know that." He leveled a look her way. "Since you are of interest too."

She shivered. "I am unsure how you know all of this."

"It is worth my time to know." His voice came low and his lips curved upward, showing his distinctive crooked teeth. "Don't worry, Bridget. You don't have anything to fear from me."

She was beginning to feel like she had most everything to fear from him. He knew too much, and he was stepping by her side, and he was leering at her as if he knew a strange and dark secret that even she did not know. "I had nothing to do with Mr. Avondale's death."

"Of course not." He whistled under his breath. "A woman like you? Of course you didn't."

They were only feet away from the Bancroft home now. Bridget stopped walking, causing Vlas to slow and turn toward her. She had to know what he was getting at.

"Mr. Vlas, I am not sure what you are trying to tell me."

"Sergio," he corrected. After a beat, he spoke again. "Only that it is better to forget and forgive than to dwell on things you cannot solve or fix."

"I am still confused."

He stepped closer, his hulking body looming over hers. "Darling, there will come a time when you might find yourself out of a job again," he said slowly. "You might find yourself alone and desperate. Maybe you will even feel as if you have no choice in anything, and that it is better to attempt to hide than to reach out to others." He exhaled. "If that happens, remember that you can always come to me."

Gazing up at him, she felt her cheeks heat, just as the rest of her body felt as if she were being frozen stiff.

"Are you offering me a job?"

"If that is what you want." His light-gold eyes shone.

She knew why he hired women at the Bear and Bull. "Thank you for the offer, but I have no desire to become a prostitute."

He laughed. "I am not offering you that, Bridget. Never that." He looked then at the townhouse ahead of him. "I wouldn't want to share you with another man."

She gaped at him. His interest was of a personal nature? But what kind?

He met her gaze, then blinked, looking a bit dismayed. "I know it's hard. I know I'm not easy to look at. I'm not handsome and debonair like your Sebastian Marks. But you might find my rough looks helpful one day. And if not that, then perhaps you will find my devotion worthy of your attention."

Bridget wasn't sure if he was being honest or telling her tales. She wasn't sure if she was relieved to hear his offer or sickened by it.

But she did know that for whatever reason, he had gone out of his way to find her. And to offer what small bit of support he could.

"Thank you," she blurted. "Thank you for what you just did."

A new vulnerability flickered in his eyes. "Of course, Bridget. Of course," he said.

As a rush of crowd surged around them, men holding satchels in their arms and women walking with children and their escorts, Bridget watched him depart, his pace much faster than it had been by her side. As he turned the next corner, she saw him unbutton his coat and pull something from his vest.

She saw the gold chain, the one attached to the pocket watch that had looked exactly like Jason Avondale's.

After the Wild West show, Sebastian guided Lydia to the White City. Just a few weeks ago, someone had ordered the remnants of the city to be surrounded by chain-link fence. The fence was poorly executed and even more haphazardly placed in the ground, in no small part, he imagined, because of the time of year. The winter's cold had settled into the ground in earnest, and driving so many stakes into the solid earth had to feel like one of the trials of Hercules.

The fires that had claimed so many of the buildings had been fickle ones. Some of the fires had ravaged through entire buildings, leaving nothing but black ash on the ground.

Just a few yards to a burnt building's right, other structures had remained looking as pristine as the day of the opening ceremony.

The main difference, of course, was the complete emptiness of the parks. No one was there, save for the occasional policeman on patrol or band of vagrants. And, on this afternoon, only the two of them were in sight.

Just as Sebastian pulled back one of the broken sections of chain-link fence, Lydia shivered. "I was never one to entertain fanciful thoughts, but this park now feels filled with danger."

"There's no danger here, Lydia. Merely the remnants of a very grand affair."

"I know you are right. But still, I don't feel entirely comfortable."

A true gentleman would escort her away from the area as soon as possible. A true gentleman would have never taken her to such a place in the first place.

But the novelty of having her to himself was too pleasant to disrupt so quickly. Besides, he was growing fonder of the great White

City, with its Grecian columns and overwhelming visuals now that little remained of them.

"Did you know the mayor feared this fair would be a great failure?" he asked, almost rhetorically.

"I had not heard that. I must admit that I'm surprised."

"The Columbian Exposition was enormously expensive. Federal monies didn't come in as quickly as they were promised," he explained, remembering the talk he'd heard among the gentlemen at his club. "Initially, the planning committees feared the crowds wouldn't appear. Or that the trains to get people here wouldn't work. Or that it wouldn't be finished in time."

"Their worries were for naught of course. This had some of the greatest crowds of any World's Fair in recent memory. It even gave Paris a run for her money."

He did so love her mind. "I didn't realize I was speaking to such an authority on the subject."

She laughed. "I'm not much of an authority. I merely read a lot. I have had access to the newspapers, you know."

"You read both the *Tribune* and the *Times-Courier*?"

"I read the *Tribune* by choice and the *Courier* when its headlines are unavoidable."

He wasn't shocked, but her admission was a bit surprising. Even now, on the brink of a new century, most women were prevented from reading newspapers by their husbands.

She looked worried. "Are you shocked, sir? Are you going to stop me from reading the news after our vows?"

"While I'd love to shield you from the *Courier's* luridness, I would never stop you from reading whatever you want. I like that you are smart, Lydia. That is one of the things I admire about you."

She looked at him in wonder, her blue eyes looking even bigger through her lenses. Looked as if she was trying to speak, then stopping herself.

He was taken aback. "What is wrong?"

"Nothing. Nothing at all." She clasped her hands together. "It's just that your words mean a lot to me."

"I am glad, but I have to admit that I'm at sea. What did I tell you that affected you so?"

"You are the first person who has told me anything of the sort."

"Surely not. I know Avondale wasn't the type to appreciate brains, but weren't your parents pleased with your intelligence?"

"My father was, perhaps. I'm not sure. He wasn't the sort to want to spend time with a daughter." Still not meeting his gaze, she added, "My mother has been so intent on gaining me a husband, I fear she's never considered any of my irregularities to be worthy of note."

"Being smart does not mean one is irregular," he said slowly, wondering if it was true that no one at all before him had made an effort to show her how worthy she was. "What of your governess? Surely she appreciated a bright pupil."

"I fear I wasn't her favorite student." She looked away. "I had the unfortunate habit of correcting her. Governesses don't care for that, you know."

He laughed. "I don't know, but I can imagine that wouldn't go over well."

"I'm glad I made you smile at least. I do love to hear your laugh."

"I haven't smiled so much in ages. And as far as laughing goes, well, let's just say that is a foreign experience."

"Then I am happy for our time together. I want to make you smile. You are a very somber man, Sebastian."

"I haven't had much choice in the matter, I'm afraid." He'd been serious because he'd had to be. He'd learned at a very young age that life was serious. Boys who didn't realize that rarely lived to learn from their mistakes.

Not eager to go down the path of his past, he pointed to the Manufacturers building. "Care to enter?"

She wrinkled her nose. "It is very large. It also looks completely intact. How could we get inside?"

"There are ways if a person truly wants to go."

"You sound cryptic."

"Not at all. I've been inside recently."

She looked tempted, but he knew no doubt her straightlaced manner was holding her back. "I'm still not sure. Is there anything within? I thought everyone took their things back home."

"Some did. But some found it too expensive. Or they didn't have the need. Or maybe they simply didn't care. Looters have raided some buildings, but not this one."

She hesitated, staring at the building dubiously. It was as obvious that she wanted to peek inside as it was obvious that she was more than a little bit afraid of what she would see.

"Lydia, it is merely suggestion. Not an order."

"You will stay by my side?"

He heard the question in her voice. Detected the yearning for his company. Noted that he meant something to her. It was one of the sweetest sounds he'd ever heard.

"Of course I will stay with you. I will never leave you."

After all, she was his. And the sheer knowledge of that, he realized, was something more profound than anything he'd ever experienced in his life . . . or ever learned from a book.

CHAPTER 28

Lydia could list at least a dozen reasons why going inside one of the fair's abandoned buildings was a bad idea. All the reasons, by her way of thinking, were legitimate ones. It was dangerous. It was illegal. It was completely inappropriate for someone who was supposedly trying to safeguard her reputation. She should be concentrating on details about her engagement to Sebastian, not exploring abandoned buildings.

But there was something about Sebastian Marks that made her want to do things that weren't proper. She felt like she was living for the first time when she was with him. Instead of merely reading about things in her safe library world, she was collecting memories to hold close to her heart forever more.

"I would love to step inside," she said at last.

"I confess that I'm surprised. But I'm very glad as well." He held out his hand. "Let's go."

She slid her gloved hand into his and let herself be guided through an opening in the chain-link fence. Then he pulled her alongside the Manufacturers building.

Tall and imposing, it loomed above them. A shiver rushed through her as she became more aware of just how isolated they were.

In a city like Chicago, where hundreds if not thousands of people were working and living together in each city block, the sheer fact that they were completely alone was hard to fathom.

"Wait here," he murmured as he let go of her hand, then tried the handle of the door in front of them. "Hmm. Last time I was here this door was unlocked."

Nerves set in. "Perhaps we should leave?"

"Of course not." Smiling at her, he gave the door a push. When it didn't budge, he simply kicked it in.

She gasped and looked around in alarm. She half expected police officers or security guards to come running.

"Don't worry. I promise there's no one here." He wiggled his fingers. "Let's go."

She had no choice. With great reluctance—and a secret amount of excitement—she walked toward him and stepped inside.

And entered what she could only describe as a magical, mysterious world.

The cavernous space was so very large. Easily the size of a city block. And though she'd been inside before, it had felt cozier when surrounded by hundreds of people and artifacts from all over the country.

Now only the remnants remained. Abandoned boxes, empty wooden crates, sawdust, chunks of plaster. Debris littered the floor.

"It's quite the place now, isn't it?" Sebastian asked. His eyes glowed.

She realized he was enjoying the wickedness of it all. He liked that they were somewhere forbidden. He liked that they were standing somewhere that broke every rule of both society and its laws.

As for her?

She liked it too.

After a lifetime of merely existing in her world of books, she liked actually living.

"It is wondrous," she replied.

He looked like he was on the verge of chuckling. Obviously, her wonder pleased him. "Wait until you see what's over here. Come along."

She followed him down one of the aisles. She couldn't resist peeking at the remainders of various exhibits.

Then, situated in the far corner of the building was the most surprising sight. The Yerkes telescope, some of which lay on the ground in pieces. Next to it were a number of wooden crates filled with shredded paper and more assorted parts of the telescope. During a previous visit, she'd learned that the telescope was the largest in the world. It had been built on two axles so it could be rotated to point in multiple directions. She'd seen it in its glory. But now, seeing it in sections on the ground? It seemed even bigger.

Sebastian motioned her forward, suddenly looking like a child on Christmas morning. "You want to touch it?"

"We aren't allowed. It is a frightfully expensive invention." She remembered hearing that Mr. Yerkes had donated the frightful sum of five hundred thousand dollars to the University of Chicago for its construction. She was amazed that it was still in the abandoned building.

"No one is here to see, Lydia. Do what you want."

She tentatively ran a finger along the smooth steel but was unable to do anything beyond that. "It's too valuable and special, Sebastian. I simply can't."

Instead of pushing her further, he stepped away. "Come, let's explore some more."

And that they did. He showed her the remnants of the displays from Brazil, Austria, Japan, and Russia, as well as from various other countries around the world. Some exhibits were stripped bare. Others were still filled with cases and assorted tools. One case was still completely full, looking as if its workers had merely stepped out for lunch.

She fingered the cloth draping the table. "Thank you for bringing me here, Sebastian. This is a day I will never forget."

"Nor I."

He held out his arm, his expression soft. She could tell he was so very gratified that he'd pleased her.

And that knowledge made her optimistic for the first time since he'd announced his intention that they marry. "Sebastian, do you think this will be our life when we're married?"

"Touring abandoned buildings? I think not."

"No. I mean the two of us exploring together."

"I want to make you happy. If you want to explore new things, I think we should." He held out his arm for her to grasp. After she did, he continued talking as they walked, wandering along abandoned aisles like they were strolling along a beautiful boulevard. "You haven't asked, but I will tell you that you will never have to worry about money again. I have enough to let you follow any whim you might have. We can travel, if that is something that interests you."

Of course it interested her. She ached to see the world. Now that she was becoming used to the idea of actually participating in adventures instead of reading about them, she ached to experience everything she could.

But she didn't want to do it at his expense. "Does it interest you?"

"Being by your side interests me. We can have a good life together, Lydia. It might not be the life you intended, but perhaps it will be a better one."

"I suppose I shall have to get used to being the wife of a notorious club owner," she said, in jest of course. She didn't care what he did for a living. Not really.

"I've been thinking about that. Perhaps it is time to make a change."

"Change, how?"

"I must still own my club, but I am thinking of closing down the gambling part of the operation."

"Why would you want to do that?"

"It is illegal to gamble, Lydia."

"But hasn't it always been that way?"

"The police never cared about my business. They've always had bigger fish to fry, what with the Slasher and the fair and the immigrants coming into the city like flocks of birds. But with a new century upon us, and the police force becoming stronger, I fear circumstances will be changing. There's a very good chance the police won't feel free to turn a blind eye on my club for much longer."

"I suppose that makes sense."

"You suppose?" He raised an eyebrow. "I would have thought you would have been excited about this. Don't you want a husband you can be proud of?"

"I never intended to change you. I already feel guilty about you having to marry me, Sebastian."

"There is nothing to be guilty about."

"I forced my way into your club."

"I allowed you. You have to know by now that I rarely do anything I don't want to."

"But still . . ."

"I am happy about our pairing, Lydia. Allow me to be happy."

She smiled at him, her heart warming. He was right. She needed to look forward to their future. Imagine a life together filled with books and adventures. And happiness. "You are right. Of course I want you to be happy."

His lips curved. Just before his expression turned cold.

"Sebastian? What—"

The rest of her words were cut off by a hand at her neck. She cried out—and attempted to turn—but the ruffian behind her simply increased his pressure on her throat.

"Say another word, and it will be your last," a harsh voice whispered into her ear.

She realized then that she couldn't say a word. She couldn't say a thing. Because then she realized Sebastian had just fallen to the ground, bleeding.

And then she felt a harsh grip, a sting in her arm, and then nothing at all as she, too, fell to the cement floor of the impressive Manufacturers and Liberal Arts building.

Where no one was supposed to be.

And where no one knew they were.

CHAPTER 29

Sebastian awoke with a start. Clawing the floor underneath him, he attempted to pull himself up.

Only to receive a hand pressed to the middle of his upper body.

"Don't move, sir," a uniformed policeman ordered as he continued to press a cloth against Sebastian's chest. "We've got a physician on his way."

"Lydia?" He craned his neck in a poor attempt to find her. Unfortunately, his head was pounding with such force he felt almost blinded by the action. "Where is she?"

"Lydia?" the officer asked. "Sir, is she the lady you were with?"

"Yes," he bit out impatiently. "I am speaking of Lydia Bancroft. My fiancée."

"We found her as well. She is doing a sight better than you." He frowned. "The bullet only grazed her arm."

For the first time in his very long life, Sebastian feared he was on the verge of losing all control. Though his head was aching and he could feel the sting of the multiple knife wounds on his chest and leg, only one fearful word penetrated his brain. "Bullet?"

The officer winced. "Sorry for my, uh, blunt way of speaking, sir. I was under the impression that you'd seen she'd been only grazed before you passed out."

"No." Literally, even uttering that one word was a challenge.

The young officer, his face a myriad of pockmarks and freckles, looked abashed. Then, as if he was remembering his position, he gathered himself. "From what we can discern, sir, some gang probably attacked you both. By the looks of your clothes, I'm assuming you was taken to be an easy mark. And you might notice any watch and wallet are gone, sir. So is your lady's purse."

He frowned as he continued, traces of his Irish accent coming through. "Don't feel bad, sir. The gangs loitering about here are some hardened sorts. Criminals, they are. Nothing a gentleman like you would be used to."

Each word was an insult.

It seemed as if his transformation was complete. He was now an easy mark. A target. Useless. The very idea made him want to hit something. Made him yearn to curse a blue streak. He might have if his head wasn't pounding, his shirt wasn't stained with blood, or he wasn't being looked after by a youthful policeman who was so green he didn't even realize he was staring at the infamous Sebastian Marks.

If there wasn't one person whose safety overrode all feelings of revenge and anger. Lydia.

"Officer, I need to see Miss Bancroft. Now."

"I'm sorry, sir. I am. But I have my orders. We can't risk moving you. Not only are you bleeding something fierce, you've received quite the blow to your head, you see." As he stared at him, the officer swallowed. "You might not even be aware of what you are saying. No offense."

No offense? "This is important." He attempted to say more but the rest of his words became muddled in his head. He reached up to feel the back of his skull and almost blacked out again from the pain it caused him.

"It's important you stay still, sir. Your wound's going to need to be stitched up." The officer watched him with a look of sympathy. "We were worried that you weren't going to wake up for a while there."

"For a while? How long was I unconscious?"

"Can't rightly say," he said as he pulled out a timepiece. "We only found you a half hour ago, when one of our group came around on patrol. The woman, I mean Miss Bancroft, was just coming to when we got here. Took us a while to calm her down, it did."

He'd brought Lydia to this place and had foolishly led her into the abandoned building. Because he'd wanted to entertain her.

No, that was a lie. He'd brought her to the abandoned building because he'd wanted to show off, to show that he could make her happy by doing something daring. She hadn't wanted to be there, but she'd done it to please him.

To appease him.

He'd known the risks. And instead of heeding them, instead of keeping her safe, he'd let down his guard. And because of that he'd nearly gotten her killed.

But what had happened? Every awful scenario rushed through his head as he imagined her being in pain. And worse, being at the mercy of a gang.

Bracing himself, he pushed up to a sitting position. The new pose pierced his head, making him grimace with unease. Queasiness. With a glare, he grabbed the soiled handkerchief and pressed it to his own chest. "I can see to myself now."

The officer sighed. "Not hardly. I know you're impatient, but it's really better for you if heed my warnings. It's for your own good, you see."

"I'd save your breath, Carrew. Sebastian Marks is the last man in Chicago to abide by another's rules."

Sebastian saved himself further pain by keeping his head in one place. But he didn't need to turn his head to know who had just arrived. "Captain Ryan. It seems you are constantly witnessing me at my worst."

Ryan moved so Sebastian could see him. "I would rather not be seeing you like this, if you want to know the truth. It's lucky that you're alive." He knelt down. "You look pretty bad."

"I'll be fine. I need to go check on Miss Bancroft."

"Howard is with her."

"I need to see how she is faring." It was driving him mad to not be able to pick her up and carry her someplace safer.

"I'm afraid you can't do that."

"Surely you don't think I had something to do with this."

"At last," Ryan said, standing up. "Doctor, he's conscious now."

Sebastian forced himself to lie still when the doc knelt down beside him. "Easy now, Mr. Marks. When I stopped by here a few minutes ago, you were practically dead to the world."

"As you can see, I am alive. Go attend to Miss Bancroft."

"I have. She's going to be fine."

"She was shot," he pointed out. Obviously, she was going to be anything but fine.

"It was merely a graze. Little more than a severe burn. I cleaned it well and bandaged her. After a day or two of rest, she will be feeling right as rain."

He was surrounded by fools. She'd been *attacked*. "Doctor, please help me up. I need to see to her."

Instead of helping him to his feet, the physician pressed a hand to Sebastian's chest. "Men in love are truly the most foolish. Lie down."

"Love?" Ryan asked from where he hovered, his tone disbelieving.

"To be sure," the doctor replied with a smirk, just as if they were in the building for a party. "He and Miss Bancroft are engaged."

Ryan stepped closer. "Is that true?"

"It is." He also was in no hurry to discuss said engagement, but if it was going to help him get his way, he attempted to look beseeching. "Obviously Lydia is in distress. I need to get to her."

"Sir—" the doctor began.

"I am fine."

"You are bleeding. Your shirt is sporting a sizable stain," Ryan pointed out.

"Sebastian?" Lydia called as she rushed to his side. The moment she knelt by him, tears formed in her eyes. "Oh Sebastian, what did they do to you?"

Now, of course, he wished he would have kept his peace. It seemed that the only thing worse than knowing she was hurt because of him was having her see him looking so poorly and worrying about his welfare when she should be having someone look after her.

This was all his fault. All of it.

If he'd ever needed a sign from the good Lord above, telling him that he was single-handedly ruining Lydia Bancroft's life, this was it.

"I am fine, Lydia. Please, go rest." Of course, his words were at odds with every protective instinct that was coursing through him.

She reached out and carefully brushed back a lock of his hair from his forehead. "Of course I am not going to leave your side. You need me here."

"I will rest easier if you are resting. You've had a fright."

Her eyes widened. Just then, he realized how he could see them so well. She wasn't wearing her spectacles. "Where are your glasses?"

She wrinkled her nose. "I'm not exactly sure. I think they're broken."

It was yet another thing he'd done to hurt her. "Do you have another pair?"

"I have some old ones at home."

It was time to do something, anything to make things right again. "Ryan, is there someone available who can take Miss Bancroft home? Immediately?"

"Of course. If that is what you would like."

"I would."

Lydia leaned forward, bringing with her the faint, fresh scent of her perfume. "Sebastian, I do not wish to leave. Please, let me stay with you."

"Absolutely not." He needed her as far away from him as possible—as quickly as possible—so he wouldn't do something foolish and tell her that he loved her.

"But—"

"Lydia, this is difficult enough without you being in the way," he interrupted. "Please, do as I say."

She stared at him for one long moment, her beautiful blue eyes cloudy with hurt and unshed tears. Then she stood up. "Captain Ryan, I'll wait over by the wall until someone is free."

"There is no need to wait. I'm sure Lieutenant Howard won't mind seeing you home."

When they left, the doctor leaned forward. "I think it would be best to simply cut off your shirt, sir, so I can see to your wound."

Closing his eyes, he said, "Do whatever you need to do."

The man fished in his kit and pulled out a small glass bottle. "Would you care for laudanum first?"

"Absolutely not."

"It'll take the sting off the pain."

Sebastian knew the pain he was feeling was not going to be eased by any opiate. "I won't flinch. I promise I've suffered far worse."

After the doctor cut off his shirt, he studied Sebastian's bare chest. "It seems you have, sir," Then, opening his black bag, he pulled out a number of instruments.

As he promised, Sebastian never flinched.

But then, of course, he didn't know if it was possible to feel anything at all. Losing Lydia, he might as well be dead to the world. He certainly felt as if his future was gone.

CHAPTER 30

After suffering through seven stitches to his chest and leg, and a careful examination of the cuts and bruises on his head and arms, Sebastian was allowed to stand.

By this time, Lieutenant Howard had returned. Luckily for Sebastian, the officer was in no mood to share any news about Lydia. Instead, he stood by Ryan's side as Sebastian approached.

"Anything else?"

"We would like you to come down to the station with us. We would like you to give us a statement about your attack."

Sebastian ached to refuse but didn't dare. It was obvious with each passing minute that the Lord had had enough of his ego and selfish ways and was finding multiple ways for him to pay his dues.

"Very well. Lead on."

He slowly followed them to the awaiting carriage and climbed inside it with the greatest reluctance. The carriage didn't look well sprung, which meant the ride to the precinct was going to be full of jerks and bumps. No doubt his head was going to feel as if it were going to explode before they were halfway there.

He was not wrong. By the time they'd gone a mile, Sebastian felt as if he were in a medieval torture chamber and was tempted to say anything to put an end to his misery.

Both Ryan and Howard looked at him with expressions of sympathy.

"I've grown to hate riding in a horse and carriage," Howard said. "It feels outdated and thoroughly inconvenient. Sorry for the ride, Marks."

"Not your fault." Truly, even saying those words felt like too much.

After gazing at Sebastian for a moment, Ryan turned to his partner. "Did you encounter any problems taking Miss Bancroft home?"

"No." After pausing to ascertain how Sebastian was faring, Howard continued. "Miss Bancroft seemed fairly upset of course. Today's events were traumatic. Luckily, her maid was there."

"That's Bridget O'Connell, yes?" Ryan asked.

"Bridget has a kind heart. She will see to her needs," Sebastian said before he remembered that he wasn't supposed to care about Lydia anymore.

"For what it's worth, Miss Bancroft certainly seems to care about you. I would say that you two are a very unlikely couple, but it's not any more surprising than my courtship of Eloisa," Ryan said. "It seems our hearts develop minds of their own."

Sebastian grimaced, then used his pain as an excuse to end the discussion. He had no desire to dwell on the multiple reasons he should have never said even one word to Lydia. He especially didn't want to hear how happy the other men were with their supposedly opposite women.

He certainly didn't want to think about how anyone but him would have known that he was so far below her on the social and moral scales that it would have been ludicrous to even think they should try to make a life together work.

So he sat and stewed and prayed that the rocking, uncomfortable coach would cease rocking before the new century.

It seemed no matter what happened to him, he couldn't stop hoping.

—

"Oh, Miss Bancroft," Bridget gasped as she helped Lydia undress and step into the deep, white-footed bathtub in the small bathing room off the kitchen. "Look at your poor arms and legs. And the rest of you! I fear that you have become a dozen shades of black and blue."

As she stood with only her feet, ankles, and calves covered by water, Lydia looked down at herself with a bit of trepidation. Her hips were rather bruised. As were her thighs. And arms. "Indeed, I am looking fairly multicolored. Isn't that something?"

"It's a shame, that's what it is."

"Well, it's over now." Gingerly, she sat down into her half-filled, cast-iron tub, then stretched her legs out with a sigh of relief. The warm water felt so soothing. Closing her eyes, she imagined herself to be one of Jane Austen's cosseted heroines, reclining in her bath without a care in the world.

"Of course you hadn't noticed anything," Bridget said as she poured more warm water into the tub. "You are suffering from a gunshot wound."

Lydia eyed her heavily bandaged arm. It was starting to feel like an awful lot of trouble when compared to Sebastian's injuries. "Hardly that. It is a very small wound, you know. In fact, the physician said it was merely a graze."

"I don't think there is such a thing as a small gunshot wound, miss," Bridget said as she poured the last pitcher of warm water into the tub. "You are lucky to be alive, you are."

"I am. Lucky and blessed." With a ragged sigh, she at last allowed herself to let down her guard. "However, my nicks and bruises are nothing compared to the injuries Mr. Marks sustained."

Bridget's voice floated through the bathing room, sounding as if it came from a long, deep, and dark tunnel. "Miss Bancroft, what did happen to Mr. Marks?"

"He sustained many wounds." Still keeping her eyes closed, Lydia tried to catalog all of the injuries. "Though he wasn't shot, he was stabbed in several places and may have some cracked and broken ribs, and most likely has sustained a concussion."

The maid gasped. "A concussion? That is an injury to his brain, isn't it?"

"His brain? Oh, yes. The word *concussion* is derived from the Latin word *concutere* and it means to shake violently. It's a traumatic brain injury." The feeling of pleasure that had come from remembering that tidbit faded as the memory of seeing Sebastian lying so still on the floor returned with a vengeance.

She blinked hurriedly as her eyes began to tear up. After pressing one wet hand to her face, Lydia attempted to compose herself. "It was a very frightening experience. He was unconscious for a time. Even the police were worried about him. The physician made me wait before I could go by his side."

"Did he wake up?"

Bridget's voice had a tremor. Opening her eyes, she was stunned to notice the maid sitting on a stool next to the white tiled wall. She had her arms wrapped around her body and was biting her bottom lip while staring out into space.

Though her image was blurry, on account of the fact that she was without her glasses, Lydia could tell Bridget was obviously troubled.

Her pain was vivid enough to make Lydia forget her own. "Yes," she said at last. "He did awake."

"Where is he now? At the Hartman?" Bridget's voice had turned frantic. "Does Vincent—I mean, Mr. Hunt—know about this? Is he attending to Mr. Marks?"

"I'm so sorry, but I have no earthly idea. Mr. Marks wanted me to leave the fairgrounds as soon as possible. And though I protested, I soon realized that my presence was only making him more agitated." She ached to tell Bridget more. Ached to describe how it had felt to be ignored and pushed away as if there was nothing between them and had never been.

But those hurts were even more painful to come to terms with than her bandaged arm or many bruises. "I am sorry I don't have any more information."

Bridget got to her feet. "Yes, miss." Looking studiously above Lydia's head, she said in a monotone voice, "Would you like me to help you wash your hair? My mother used to swear that a thorough hair wash was the answer to most any problem."

It had been far too long since anyone had helped her take care of her long hair. And Bridget's mother's promise was so very tempting.

At the moment, she would do just about anything to ease her mind.

"Thank you, Bridget. I would like that very much." Seconds later, Bridget began to soothingly massage the soap into her hair, then helped her rinse it and massaged some oils that smelled delicately of lavender and lemon into her scalp.

The massage was relaxing and rejuvenating. And very much appreciated.

Closing her eyes, Lydia soon forgot everything but the warm water, the heavenly scent, and the fact that both she and Sebastian were safe.

That wasn't everything she needed, but it was certainly enough for now.

CHAPTER 31

CHICAGO TIMES-COURIER

From December 1893
Reported by Benson Gage

It should be noted that the Columbian Exposition of 1893 has been closed for some time. This is for good reason. The abandoned buildings have been ravaged by fire and are in various stages of disrepair. One should only enter at his own risk.

The minute Bridget knew Miss Bancroft was asleep, she went to her small room, pulled on a fresh dress, donned a coat, and hurried out the back door.

She knew if Miss Bancroft or her mother discovered she was leaving without saying a word she would be in very big trouble. But they were both asleep, and she owed no one other than Mr. Marks her loyalty. He'd saved her life, and he was continuing to save it, time and again.

Though the streets were now dark, she hurried along the quickest paths and alleys to the Hartman. It might have been safer to stay on Michigan Avenue, but Bridget only cared about helping Mr. Marks as soon as possible.

When she reached the Hartman, she let herself in the servants' entrance, turned a sharp left, and pattered up the stairs. It was bad form to enter in that manner. Common courtesy dictated that she stop and say hello to any of the staff that was milling around, but she didn't dare take the time. Her heart was pounding as she continually imagined the worst. She'd heard of a gentleman who had fallen asleep when he was concussed and never woke up.

What would she do then? She'd never forgive herself!

By the time she reached the third-floor landing, she was nearly out of breath. Only habit allowed her to take the last few steps toward Mr. Marks' door in a calm and dignified way. When she thought her face was not quite as flushed, she unlocked his suite's main door and stepped inside.

"Mr. Marks? Are you here, sir?"

No voice replied, but she heard faint footsteps. This was not like Mr. Marks. Not at all.

She stiffened and braced herself. She needed to be ready for anything.

"Bridget," Vincent said. "What are you doing here?"

"I could ask the same of you," she retorted. "I came to check on Mr. Marks." Craning her neck, she asked, "Is he sleeping?"

"I doubt it."

"Why don't you know? Will he not let you inside his bedroom?" She knew he was notoriously private, but surely even Mr. Marks knew when it was time to accept help.

Vincent flinched. "I'm sorry, Bridget. It seems that you have not heard."

"I haven't heard what?"

"Mr. Marks was taken to the police station."

"Why? He was injured!" She was beyond incredulous. "Surely they don't imagine that he's tried to hurt himself?"

"Of course not. I believe it is simply to make a statement about today's attack."

"You'd think the police could wait for that."

"One would think. However, we both know Mr. Marks is also a man to fear. He is also known to not always follow the law."

"That could be said of half of Chicago."

"Yes, but few have his past."

While that might have been true, it still didn't explain why he would have been hauled down to the police station. Then a sudden thought occurred to her. "Vincent, what if the police are still trying to pin Avondale's death on Mr. Marks?"

Hunt's expression tightened, though Bridget couldn't decide if it was from worry that Mr. Marks was being falsely accused or fear that she was right. "You are letting your imagination run away with you," he said after a moment's thought.

"He was injured, yet they still took him in for questioning."

With a weary look, he sat down on the arm of an elegant wing chair, upholstered in a fine gray brocade. "I couldn't begin to guess what the police are thinking." After a moment, he said quietly, "Don't forget that he's a legitimate suspect for Avondale's murder. We may need to come to terms with the idea that he could have had something to do with it. Miss Bancroft was asleep. He could have left the Grotto and then slipped back inside. Or he could have paid someone to do it."

As she stared at Vincent, she felt as if she had never known him. "You can't think that. *Do* you think that?"

"I don't want to," he said slowly. "But you have to remember that he is not a well-born, sheltered gentleman. He has grown up from the streets. It's very likely that he's killed before."

She didn't want to contemplate such a thing. But, just as strongly, she knew she had to face the fact that desperate people were capable of doing terrible things in desperate situations. She feared that she was capable of many crimes that she would not have imagined committing when she was a naïve, sheltered girl.

But that didn't mean she was going to abandon her boss. "Vincent, we can't simply wait for him to be released and give us further instructions. That seems like a terrible way to repay a man who has done so much for us."

"I agree, but I don't know what else we can do."

"Perhaps we should go to the police station and ask to speak to him privately." She was rather proud of how calm she sounded about that.

"Definitely not. And besides, what would we even say?"

"We could ask if he needed any help."

Vincent rolled his eyes. "Sure. He is simply going to start telling us what to do, right there in front of the policemen."

"I'll find a way."

One eyebrow arched. "How?"

"I'll think of some way when we get there."

"Bridget—"

"Don't brush me off, Vincent. I want to help him. And even if he can't be helped . . . well, I want to make sure he realizes he's not forgotten. I don't want him to think he's all alone."

"Bridget, your job is to wash his shirts and look after Miss Bancroft. He won't thank you for neglecting your duties."

"I've become more than that to him. I'm his friend." Her mind still working, she quietly added, "And you know what? I don't think he's completely alone right now either."

His expression tightened as he stared hard at her. "That is exactly right. And that's also something he needs to remember. We are there for him. But there is also someone far more able than you or I to help in his times of trouble."

His words were everything beautiful and yet, also everything she'd forgotten about for so very long. "You're . . . you're speaking of God, aren't you?"

He nodded. "I think I am." He shrugged. "I'm ashamed to admit that my faith has become quite rusty."

Feeling stunned, Bridget sat down on the sofa. "I fear I have done much of the same thing. I'm afraid I have been shouldering my burdens like they were weights of gold." She shook her head in wonder. "Why, it's almost as if I've been afraid to realize that I don't have to rely only on myself!"

Vincent sat on a chair and leaned forward, resting his elbows on his knees. "We have been a sorry trio, haven't we? All three of us have been struggling through our hardships and grasping for happiness like someone is going to pull it out from under us if we're not careful."

"All this time, I've been thanking Mr. Marks and feeling lucky that our paths crossed. Perhaps I should have taken the time to remember that our meeting hadn't happened by coincidence."

"I've given thanks that I have a job where I can garner respect, even though it's the type of respect that's laced with a healthy dose of fear."

"Who knows what Mr. Marks' prayers are?"

"Or if he's ever prayed."

"If he hasn't, I wonder if he feels just as alone as each of us does half the time."

"I hope not." He sighed. "All I do know is that we need to pray. And we need to do what you said."

"Go to the police station?"

He nodded. "You are right. No matter how Mr. Marks might feel about it, we are more than just two employees of his who expect a paycheck. We are his friends."

Bridget smiled at him then. A wide, beaming smile that told tales of how pleased she was that they were about to do something—and so very pleased that she and Vincent were on the same page.

Getting to his feet, Vincent held out a hand. "Shall we go?"

"Mr. Hunt, I thought you would never ask."

———

Sebastian had rarely been at a loss for words. But seeing both his assistant and maid sitting in a small room near the lobby of the police station did just that.

Their heads had popped up as he was escorted into the room by Detective Howard. And their twin expressions of worry and relief would have brought a smile to his cynical heart if he wasn't so pleased—and relieved—to see them.

"I didn't know we were going to meet here," he tried to joke. Really, he was so touched to see them there, so late at night, he was torn between wanting to hug them both, give them raises, or berate them for putting themselves in this situation.

As always, Vincent took his comment seriously. "I tried to go upstairs to see you, sir, but they wouldn't allow you to have visitors."

"Well, I wasn't brought here for a social call." He clapped Vincent on the back. "Thank you for coming."

"Of course, sir. Though, um, well, it was Bridget's idea."

Sebastian turned to his maid. Though she was as lovely as ever, she looked on the verge of tears. "Bridget, are you all right?"

"No, sir."

Concerned, he took Vincent's vacant seat. As eager as he was to see the last of this place, he wasn't going to do anything until he saw that she was all right. "What is wrong? Do you need a physician?"

"Of course not, sir."

Her voice was wobbly. Growing even more concerned, he looked at Vincent. His expression was serious too. "Bridget, talk to me."

"I am fine, sir."

Again, her words sounded as if she was forcing them through her lips. "Miss O'Connell, I fear we both know that is a lie. And as happy as I am to see you, I must relay that you look especially bad."

"Oh, Mr. Marks," she cried.

Then, to his horror, she threw her arms around his neck and began to weep. Bridget plastered her face to his shoulder and proceeded to dampen it.

Now thoroughly alarmed, he looked for Vincent.

His man was standing a few feet away, arms crossed over his chest. However, he didn't look concerned. Instead, he looked rather entertained. He was also speaking quietly with Lieutenant Howard, who had just entered the room, no doubt to see what all the commotion was about.

Happy that Vincent, at least, didn't seem to feel there was a reason to worry, Sebastian sighed and remained still as the maid clung to him a little more tightly. Like a barnacle.

Remembering that women appreciated words, he said, "There, Bridget. There, now." When she simply continued her waterworks, he added gruffly, "Hush. That's enough of that."

Unfortunately, his tepid attempt to calm her did little good. She continued to cry.

Again, Sebastian looked helplessly toward Vincent, but his usually attentive assistant was still talking with the lieutenant. What was going on?

As the wetness from Bridget's tears continued to dampen his shirt, Sebastian came to the realization that stronger measures were in order. He pulled away and hardened his voice.

"Miss O'Connell, I must ask you to desist. You are now causing me great distress and, for that matter, truly soiling my shirt. It's going to take you hours to launder it."

He looked around the room. Instead of looking appalled, Howard seemed intrigued.

And Hunt? Well, he had gone from looking entertained to looking impressed.

Impressed? Not a bit about this visit made sense. Including the fact that Hunt and Bridget had gained admittance at all.

"Miss O'Connell, I trust you have calmed yourself?"

"I am trying."

Sebastian looked to the men for help, but now even Howard was gone. The three of them were alone in the room. "Hunt, do you care to explain to me what just happened?"

After glancing at the door, Hunt said, "Bridget wanted to come help."

"By dampening my shirt?"

"I'm sorry about that, sir," Bridget said. "It was just a shock seeing you like this."

"I was not arrested. I was only asked to make a statement about this attack."

"So I heard," Vincent said. "Lieutenant Howard just filled me in on the latest developments. He was rather vague, but seemed to be saying they may have some other leads in the case."

Things were starting to make sense. "Did you two actually come here to get information?"

"We had to do what we could, sir," Bridget said. "I didn't want you to imagine you were alone."

He wasn't sure what Vincent could have found out or what was going to happen next. But an idea occurred to him. Perhaps Bridget had created a diversion so Vincent could get some answers. It was a heartwarming thought.

Surely few men could claim to have such loyal employees.

No, that wasn't right. They were more than that. They were his friends. They were genuinely concerned for him.

"Sir, perhaps you'd like to return to the hotel?" Bridget asked hesitantly.

"I'm not sure if I can leave yet."

"Lieutenant Howard said he was going to go sign the paperwork so you could leave as soon as possible, sir."

Sebastian stood up. "I would like to do that. Very much."

Five minutes later, they were allowed to walk out of the station. The cool air felt like heaven on his skin. He'd never been so thankful for freedom.

As they walked back to the Hartmann Hotel, he turned to Bridget. "Tell me about Lydia. How is she faring?"

"Right enough, I think. I left her sound asleep, sir."

"She is all right? She wasn't suffering any ill effects from today's disastrous events?"

"Not that I could discern. I helped her bathe, then gave her some warm, honeyed milk to drink. Minutes later, she was sleeping like a baby."

"At least there is that," Sebastian said. Even though all of their lives were slowly falling apart, at least Lydia was going to be all right.

That gave him no end of comfort and almost made him happy.

Despite that he was about to break his own heart.

CHAPTER 32

The voice came again. Persistent.

"Miss Bancroft? Miss Bancroft, I'm sorry, I am. But you really must awaken."

Lydia opened one eye, then two. Though everything was fuzzy, she knew Bridget was standing by her bedside. "Bridget?"

"Yes, miss." She smiled. "I'm so glad you roused."

She was not. "Thank you for waking me up, but I'm afraid I'm very tired this morning. I'm going to sleep in a bit longer."

She closed her eyes and was just about ready to flip to her stomach and back to her cheerful, happy dreams when the maid cleared her throat. And then reached out and gave her shoulder a firm push.

"Miss Bancroft? I'm sorry, miss, but you really must get up now. You have company."

That forced her eyes open again. "Who has come calling?"

"Well, um, quite a few people actually." In an apologetic voice, she continued. "Mr. Marks is here. As is Mr. Hunt."

Surely her head must be in a fog. "Sorry?"

"Mr. Marks is determined to see you, miss. You know that he's not a man to say no to. Please get up."

Thinking about Sebastian in her house, about everything they'd gone through and what he must want to speak to her about, she shook away the cobwebs in her head, pulled back the covers, and jumped to her feet.

Bridget heaved a sigh of relief. "Oh, thank you, miss. You were beginning to worry me, you were."

"What about my mother? Is she aware of this?" *Please say no. Please say no.*

"I'm afraid so. She is downstairs too."

Lydia raced to her wardrobe, pulled out her blue-and-white striped shirtwaist.

Bridget neatly pulled it from her hands. "I think your lavender day dress will be more appropriate."

Lydia shook her head. "It's hopelessly out of fashion; I never had it updated. And there's a tear in the hem. And, um, a stain on the bodice."

"I cleaned the stain, mended the hem, removed the lace, and refashioned the sleeves, miss. It will be just fine for today."

"You are a marvel. I would love to ask when you had time to see to that, but I think we had best hurry downstairs before my mother makes things worse than they already are."

Bridget, as usual, was already two steps ahead of her. Holding up Lydia's chemise, she said, "I think that's a good idea, Miss Bancroft."

Less than twenty minutes later, Lydia was walking into her small receiving room, Bridget on her heels. She was so nervous about the group assembled that she didn't even ask why Bridget was coming downstairs as well.

The moment Sebastian saw her, he crossed the room and took her hands. "Lydia. How are you feeling this morning?"

"Confused. What are you doing here? And shouldn't you be in bed? Sebastian, you look terrible."

He brushed aside her concern. "I am perfectly fine."

"But, Sebastian—"

"I am glad you didn't keep me waiting long. Hunt and I have several matters to attend to."

He was making it sound as if she were one item on his list of chores. "I see." Glancing over at her mother, she said, "Good morning, Momma."

"Lydia." She didn't sound especially happy. Or well.

"Sebastian, what is it?"

"I came to tell you that we mustn't see each other anymore."

She blinked. "Pardon?"

"You heard me." His voice, like his expression, was devoid of emotion.

"You are doing this here? And now?" She wanted to add that the least he could do was speak to her privately and save her from embarrassment.

But then she remembered that Sebastian Marks did little without extreme forethought and care. "What kind of game are you playing?"

"It is for the best. I have realized that I've put you in grave danger. I have also been unpardonably selfish. I should have never tried to be your friend. It was wrong of me."

"But we are engaged." Terribly aware that Bridget, Mr. Hunt, and her mother were all listening, she said, "Can't we discuss this later? Or at least someplace else?"

"There is no reason." He backed up. "You may continue to have Bridget working here. I will be happy to pay her salary."

She felt as if he'd taken his hand and slapped her across the face. She was so confused and hurt—and stunned.

"Of course I will not have Bridget here." Feeling painfully awkward, she turned to the pretty maid. "Thank you for caring for me and my mother, but I will no longer have need of your services."

"Yes, miss." Bridget nodded, her face an impassive mask. "I will get some things together immediately. I may have to send for the rest."

"Bridget, no," Sebastian ordered.

"This is still my house," Lydia countered. "Now, please leave." Without a word to her, Bridget walked out of the room and up the stairs.

Turning back to him, dozens of questions burst forth, questions that she had hoped to keep tamped down and hidden. "Why are you doing this?"

"I have already answered. Surely you haven't already forgotten?"

"I haven't forgotten one thing. I haven't forgotten how you wanted to be friends. How you begged me to marry you. How you single-handedly convinced me that everything was going to be all right, even in the midst of so many things going badly."

"That is why it is best if we never see each other again." He swallowed before settling his gaze on her again, pure ice in his expression. "This is for the best," he stated, his voice clipped and eminently formal. "Perhaps one day you will understand."

"I understand well right now," she replied, her throat feeling as thick as if a jar of molasses had been poured down it. She continued, barely trusting her voice, but trusting herself to be completely honest with him at a later date even less. "Don't forget, Mr. Marks, although I have many flaws, the Lord sought to provide me with an exceptionally good brain."

"Did he? Because you seem to be deliberately misunderstanding the situation. You must agree that I am right."

She didn't agree with him at all. But she also knew him well enough not to try to change his mind. "Be sure that I understand everything you are saying."

"Lydia, you cannot allow this to happen," her mother said. "You are going to be ruined."

"I know," she replied softly, just as Bridget returned downstairs, her small valise in her hands. "But Mr. Marks no longer seems to care about my reputation."

Without sparing Lydia a glance, Bridget said, "Mr. Marks, I'll wait for you outside."

Still not looking directly at Lydia, he said, "There is no need to wait. I am ready to take my leave now." He turned on his heel and walked out to the door, opening it without a second's pause. Or looking back at her.

It was as if he couldn't wait to leave her side. It was as if everything that had occurred between them had never happened.

"Miss Bancroft, I almost forgot to give you this," Mr. Hunt said as he handed her a thick envelope. "Please accept this with, uh, Mr. Marks' regards."

"What is it?"

Looking pained, Mr. Hunt said, "It's several thousand dollars."

She almost dropped the envelope. It was a princely sum. "Please say you jest."

"Mr. Marks wanted to make sure you are taken care of. Open it, miss."

Though she didn't want to even hold the envelope, she did as Mr. Hunt asked. But when she lifted the envelope's flap and looked inside, she wished she would have dropped it on the floor.

She hoped she never would know the exact amount it represented. Because its contents were merely proof that she had not only made a bad mistake to ever reach out to Sebastian Marks, she'd made a very terrible mistake to ever think she could trust him.

"I could never accept this," she announced, practically shoving it back into Mr. Hunt's hands.

"You should keep it, miss. He is determined to make sure you are compensated for your time."

Her heart was crushed. "Absolutely not," she replied, drawing out the words so that every single syllable was enunciated with force. "Please inform him that I will never take his money."

"This will not make Mr. Marks happy."

"That is none of my concern." Feeling remarkably brave, she added, "You may tell him that too."

Mr. Hunt looked pained. "While it is none of your concern, I must tell you that I would rather do a great many things than relay that message."

"Keep it," Sebastian bit out from the doorway. "You need it."

Despite his gruff tone, she thought perhaps he had returned to apologize for how badly he had treated her, but seeing the displeasure in his face, she shivered. No, he wanted to ensure she'd take the money from Hunt to make himself feel better. Then she reminded herself that she had not ended things between them. He had. He was the man who sought her friendship, led her to believe that she was worthy of his time, and then promptly tossed her to one side. "I do not."

"Lydia, you have nothing."

Oh, but his words stung.

He was right. Now that he'd left her alone, now that her reputation was ruined, she would soon have no job. The library board members would undoubtedly let her go. Her mother was upset with her, and why wouldn't she be? Soon they would have no home.

Finally, most important, the one man she'd ever loved would soon be gone forever.

She did, indeed, have practically nothing. Except for one very important thing.

"I have my pride," she uttered.

He laughed.

And because he laughed, and because she wished to hurt him

as much as she was bleeding inside, she added, "How dare you even think to give me such tainted bills?"

He stilled. "Tainted?"

"Tainted. It means spoiled. Ruined. Polluted."

"Don't you dare start defining words to me."

"You don't have the right to tell me anything anymore. But you should know that the very last thing I'll ever want from you is money made from other men's gambling and vices."

His eyes lit. "What was the first thing you did want, Lydia?"

She had wanted him. "You are right, Mr. Marks," she said quietly. "I was better off not knowing you. Please leave."

His lips pursed as she felt his glare sear into her very soul before he at last turned and strode through the front door, his assistant on his heels.

The moment the front door slammed, her mother stood up.

"I hope you are happy," she announced, her voice filled with barely suppressed rage. "You have now embarrassed me to no end. Not only have you been dropped by not one but two men, you have left us destitute. We are going to lose our home. I am going to lose my home." With shaking hands, she pressed them to her face. "How can you be so cavalier? How could you do such a thing to me?"

"You don't understand what is happening."

"I understand enough."

Lydia rushed to her side. "Mother, please. Let me tell you what Sebastian Marks is really like. Then you'll understand. Then you'll understand why—"

"Does it matter, Lydia? Does casting your airs and judgments really give you that much satisfaction?" As each word sliced into all the places where Sebastian's hadn't yet reached, Lydia clenched her fists at her side. "You have given up my maid and any hope we had of paying

our bills. You have ruined your reputation. You have cost us everything. Everything. And yes, our pride too. You are fooling yourself
even more than you usually do if you imagine that we have that. So
what, then, do we have now? What in the world do we have left now?"

Before Lydia could fathom an answer, she turned and gingerly
climbed the stairs, each step bringing her to the safety of her bedroom.

Each step serving to make Lydia feel that she had never been
more alone.

Or maybe, now that so many people had left her side, she realized
for the first time that for most of her life, she had always been that way.

She had always been alone.

CHAPTER 33

I am certainly glad that is over," Mr. Marks bit out as he practically pounded each step with the point of his umbrella as they descended the Bancrofts' front steps. His expression was hard while his dark eyes looked almost black.

Vincent glanced warily at Bridget. He was worried about her safety. Their employer was looking as rough and dangerous as any of the dockworkers on the river. Though he'd never treated his workers with anything but cool respect, Vincent also realized that Sebastian Marks had also never received such a letdown before.

Well, at least not in Vincent's hearing.

"Bridget, are you all right?" he murmured.

Before she could reply, Mr. Marks seemed to catch sight of her suitcase. "Take Bridget's valise, Hunt."

Vincent took it. "Where to now?" he asked as Mr. Marks started walking down the street. "The club or the hotel?" That was about the only safe thing he could think to ask.

Everything else running through his head was either inappropriate or would reveal too much about himself and his feelings. All he did know was that he didn't feel good about what had just happened.

Miss Bancroft had looked crushed. And his employer? Well, his employer was no doubt crushed on the inside.

"I am going to take a walk."

"Yes, sir." Vincent glanced warily at Bridget. She looked just as taken aback.

"Hunt, you will see Bridget back to the hotel."

"Yes, sir."

"Mr. Marks? Shall I return to my duties, sir?" Bridget asked hesitantly.

"Hmm?" Mr. Marks stopped and turned to face her. His expression was completely blank.

"At the hotel, sir," Bridget explained. "Would you like me to return to my duties there?"

"Yes, I suppose."

"All right. I'll do that." She tried to smile, but anyone on the street could have guessed that her heart was neither happy nor at ease.

In fact, Bridget looked as uncomfortable as Vincent was starting to feel. Not only was Mr. Marks behaving badly, he was also behaving oddly. The combination caused a foreboding knot to form in his insides.

Therefore, he did the only thing he could think to do. Offer to be of service. "I'll go to the club after I drop her off."

"The club?" Mr. Marks stared at him vacantly. "There's no need for that." His throat worked as if he was trying hard to speak. "You might as well simply head home."

"Home?" This was beyond irregular.

Marks looked at him inquisitively. "Don't you ever miss your child, Vincent?" he asked. "Her name is Mary, yes?"

"Yes, sir. I mean, yes, that's her name." And because he sounded so flustered, he added, "Yes, I do miss her."

Mr. Marks made his usual impatient, waving motion with his hands. "Then go on with you. I'll see you on Monday."

"But it's Friday. You mean tomorrow, yes? So we will be open for the weekend?"

He shook his head. "No, I mean Monday. With the murder and the police around, we need to keep the club closed. The police have always known there was gambling, but something tells me that it wouldn't be wise to push it in their faces right now." He smiled weakly. "Spend some time with your daughter."

"Sir, are you heading back to the Hartman?"

"I've told you before not to question me, Hunt."

"Forgive me." Vincent barely had time to answer before his boss had turned away. Almost immediately, he turned down an alley and disappeared from sight.

"Poor Mr. Marks," Bridget said as she stared at the spot where Mr. Marks had disappeared. "I've never seen him like this."

Vincent hadn't either. "Perhaps he simply needs some time to himself."

"He's not heading to the Hartman. Where do you think he's off to?"

"I couldn't begin to guess. The only time I've ever seen him dart down that alley is when he had business down in the tenements." He shrugged. "Perhaps he has some business we are unaware of," he added as they resumed walking.

"Now? I doubt that."

"Well, then, maybe he is going to reconsider things," Vincent offered, though he didn't really believe that.

"He's not," she said firmly. "Mr. Marks doesn't change his mind. Ever."

Bridget was right about that. If there was anything Vincent knew about Sebastian Marks, it was that he stayed on course. No matter what, he didn't look back. He didn't have regrets, and he didn't try to second-guess himself.

"There isn't any use in guessing what's going to happen or worrying about things," he said, attempting to interject a note of confidence in his words. "Come Monday, things will be back to how they once were."

"I don't know if I can go back."

"You mean to the hotel? I'm sure it will be fine. You seemed happy enough there."

"I mean any of it. I don't know if I can become nearly invisible again."

"You enjoyed being a ladies' maid that much?"

"No. But I enjoyed talking to Miss Bancroft. I even enjoyed listening to her mother's stories and complaints. I was needed. Needed in a way Mr. Marks will never need another soul."

Vincent was surprised. Not that she felt that way but to hear her admit as much. He refrained from commenting on it however. After all, one of them had to be the voice of reason, even if it was silent.

Vincent hadn't expected to feel so empty inside. When he'd first witnessed Mr. Marks' infatuation with the librarian, he'd been both relieved to see that the man was human and did have a need for relationships. Then that feeling had given way to dismay and irritation.

Vincent hadn't appreciated the way Lydia Bancroft had disrupted their finely organized life. She'd thrown a wrench into their wheel and in doing so had changed his boss, his boss's priorities, and even Vincent's friendship and relationship with Bridget.

But now that Mr. Marks had ended things with Miss Bancroft and the three of them were a tightly woven unit again, Vincent felt empty inside. Hollow, as if someone had taken an integral part of him and thrown it away. What was missing? He wondered. Was it Miss Bancroft? Or was it that feeling that nothing mattered except work?

He was suddenly coming to the conclusion that everything mattered, and he somehow had forgotten that over the last couple of years.

"Here we are," Bridget said unnecessarily as she took her valise from him. "I'll, um, slip in through the back entrance like I always do."

Seeing her slim arm clutching her belongings like they were in danger of being snatched, her brown hair looking as beautiful as ever . . . and her matching brown eyes looking as desolate as their employer's, Vincent could no longer prevent himself from asking the question on his lips. "Will you be okay, Bridget?"

She blinked. "Yes."

Her affirmative answer should have been enough. "Sure?"

"Sure enough. I, uh, decided something while we were walking."

"What is that?"

Her chin lifted. "I'm going to quit. And then I'm going to find something different to do."

The thought of the loss of her was almost too difficult to grasp. "Like what?" he scoffed. "What are you qualified to do?"

She flinched. "You may not think I'm good for much besides cleaning chamber pots and ironing shirts, but I have most of my money saved. I was smart enough to put it in the bank and it's a good sum. Good enough to find a room in a boarding house for a couple of months while I figure things out."

"But what about Mr. Marks? You're simply going to abandon him?" He was really thinking of himself.

"Of course not. If he'll let me, I'd still like to be his friend."

"He has no friends."

"He has you and me. That's a start, don't you think?"

"If you want to remain his friend, then why are you leaving?"

"When I first started working for him, I was desperate. I clung to my job like the lifeline it was. But I feel stronger now."

He still didn't understand. Or, maybe more to the point, he didn't want to understand. If he did, he would have to allow her to move on. "Bridget, think about what you are considering."

"I am." Though a muscle in her jaw jumped, she spoke in an even voice. "Mr. Marks told me over a year ago that I owed him nothing, and in fact never had. I was the one who always felt that I couldn't leave."

"But now—"

"Now I know I can't stay." Grimacing, she added, "I can't simply live my life in fear."

"I didn't know you were afraid." Alarm coursed through him at someone even contemplating hurting her. "What are you afraid of?"

"I've been afraid to face facts, Vincent. For too long, I've been afraid to imagine what else I could do. I was even afraid to remember that I have self-worth. God didn't make just some of us worthy and others of us good for nothing beyond being barely invisible."

"Will I still see you Monday?"

She nodded. "I'll report to Mr. Marks Monday, and then I'll give him a few days' notice. Plus I'm going to have to find a different place to live."

"For what it's worth, I'm happy for you. You deserve a better life than simply staying on the sidelines and blending in."

"That's what I'm good at."

But she never had blended in to him. From the moment Mr. Marks had hired Bridget O'Connell, Vincent had been aware of where she was, what she was wearing, and how she seemed to be feeling. He hated the thought of her disappearing from his life altogether.

"Good-bye, Vincent."

"Not good-bye yet," he corrected. "Simply good day."

"Yes. Good day."

As he walked away, Vincent knew he'd think of her smile for the rest of the day. And what the loss of it was going to feel like for the rest of his life.

———

"That was a very sweet scene," Sergio Vlas said as he stepped from the shadows of the Hartman Hotel. "Better than some of the shows that played at the fair. I'd clap, but I fear it might hurt your feelings."

Bridget's mouth went dry as she stared at the man who was both Mr. Marks' competitor in business and reluctant "friend" in life. "Ah, Mr. Vlas, hello. I'm sorry, I didn't see you standing there."

Her words seemed to amuse him. "I didn't expect you to. I doubt Marks' able assistant would have wanted anyone to witness your pretty speech. He's always struck me as being quite attached to you."

Tilting his head to one side, Sergio slowly let his gaze slide from her eyes to her lips. Then lower. "So, tell me. Was your soliloquy sincere? Or was it merely something to tell Mr. Vincent Hunt to let him down easily? I wasn't sure."

As usual, she felt as if the Russian was seeing too much. And was he jealous?

"Did you need something, Mr. Vlas?"

His eyes softened. "Though seeing you always has its benefits, I actually came here to offer you my services. And please, call me Sergio."

She was stunned. And a little frightened. "I am not certain what services of yours I might need . . . Sergio."

"We both know that you're lying now, Bridget," he said as he stepped closer to her. His expensive cologne wafted toward her, reminding her that he had almost as much money as Sebastian Marks.

He had never courted society however.

Which was just as well. No matter how many years passed, he spoke in a careful, clipped way that spoke volumes about him. She'd always wondered if he was so careful with his enunciation because English was his second language, or if that was simply the way he enjoyed speaking.

His golden-colored eyes fastened on hers. "Bridget, with all the drama at the Silver Grotto, I suspected that you might be leaving Sebastian Marks' employment. I came here on the off chance that you might need me now."

"That . . . that is very kind of you," she said, eager to say anything to end the conversation and move away from him.

"I am many things, Bridget. However, I am never kind." When she shivered, he blinked slowly. "Forgive me, I misspoke. I am never kind. I never feel kindness toward anyone. Except for you."

Shocked by his declaration, her lips parted. "Sergio—"

He stepped closer, then softly pressed three bare fingers against her lips. "Don't say a word, Bridget. I know you are too good for me."

"Too good? Mr. Vlas, I am merely a maid." She wasn't even exactly that. She was almost a secret employee of Mr. Marks, doing his bidding in the shadows of his life.

"You are more than that, dear." He smiled then, showing off his shocking display of crooked, gleaming white teeth. "At least, you've been that way to me. Just remember that you are not alone. Remember that I am always available to you. No strings attached."

She wondered if he meant such a thing. Did men ever do anything without an expectation for something more? A tingle ran up her spine. To cover up her confusion, she said brazenly, "You sound as if you know something I don't know."

"I simply know that it is a good thing that you've decided to move on. One never knows what will happen in one's future, especially since it seems as though your employer has suddenly decided to revisit his past."

Without another word, he walked away, and as she watched him go, she caught sight of the pocket watch. And realized he had just turned down the same alley Mr. Marks had.

Though she knew better, she rushed forward and followed. It was a foolish decision and a dangerous one. But she had no choice. There was no way she was going to abandon Mr. Marks now.

CHAPTER 34

Sebastian had promised himself that when he left the tenements, he'd never go back. Yet, that promise wasn't all that easy to keep. Every couple of years, he found himself back in the area. Though he had a new name and a new life, sometimes he needed to remind himself of who he really was.

The son of a prostitute who had once been willing to do anything and everything to change his circumstances. Maybe he still was willing to do most anything.

The place smelled the same. The terrible stench of the stockyards mixed with the sharp tang of blood, machinery oil, coal, and unwashed bodies. There was a time when he'd hardly smelled it. Now he was sure he was going to have to give all his clothes away to remove the odor from his being.

However, it had never been the smell that had bothered him as much as the constant noise. The braying of cattle, the squeals of swine. The men complaining. Women yelling at their men and children. Too many children crying. Encasing it all was the continual din of the machinery, the trains arriving, the clang of boxcars opening and shutting, the screech of brakes.

That irrepressible noise had stayed with him his whole life. It was why he worked in a club where gentlemen's voices floated upward, where the noise of dice and cards and chips clicked in an orderly way. The clink of glassware and the ribald laughter were far preferable to hear than all the sounds that struck nerves and summoned images of heartache and pain.

Of course, nothing could match the beauty of the quiet solace he'd found in the library. There, the rooms smelled of dust and Lydia Bancroft's faint lemon and lavender scent. So clean. So fresh. And the words he'd found in the books were like nothing of his past.

All of that was why he'd used his fists and his brains and his wits and his determination to give himself a new life. He'd adopted the name Sebastian because it was a character from Shakespeare's *Twelfth Night*. He'd taken the surname Marks because he liked how deceptively simple it was. It was also, of course, a play on Marx. Simply a more gentlemanly, acceptable name.

He'd sworn to himself that he would never again be known as the skinny, pale Samuel Marx, the bastard son of a two-bit prostitute who died far too young and left him with nothing.

But "never" was proving to be an elusive state in his world.

"Samuel Marx," an elderly woman cackled from her stoop. "As I live and breathe. I hardly recognized you."

He forced himself to stop. "But yet you did."

She pointed one gnarled finger to the corner of her right eye. "It's the eyes. One always thinks you've got near on black eyes . . . until you see them up close. You always did have too pretty eyes for a man. Pity."

He racked his brain, but he couldn't recall ever meeting this woman. "Do we know each other?"

"I knew you when yous was just a babe."

He had no time for this. He walked on.

"I knew yer mother too! Fed her a time or two when she was a young girl."

He felt the breath knocked out of him as he turned back around and stared. "Say again."

She smiled, showing several gaps in an otherwise surprisingly pretty smile. "Yer mother, she was Adelaide, weren't she?"

"Yes."

"Adelaide grew up here. Her father, yer grandfather, died when they were building the tunnels. She was a happy child." She shrugged. "Then one thing happened and she weren't so happy no more." She smiled again. "But that didn't stop her from coming by here once and showing you off."

He blinked, hoping the sudden wetness in his eyes had less to do with the woman's story and more to do with the soot in the air. "She showed me off."

"Sure she did." She laughed. "She swore up and down that you were a smart child. Smartest boy in the city, she used to say."

He hadn't heard that. He'd never imagined such a thing. "I never knew she thought that." With effort, he swallowed the lump that had formed in his throat. He didn't want to admit that the pride of a common prostitute meant something to him.

But when that woman was his mother, how could it not?

"Perhaps it's good that you returned then, ain't it? I mean, you never know what you will find in yer past."

He was in the process of agreeing with that when he saw a woman and man struggling barely a block away. At first he was as tempted to ignore the fray as the old woman was. But then he realized he knew both people involved—Sergio Vlas and Bridget.

As he raced closer, he saw that Sergio was gripping Bridget's arm and saying something to her.

She looked frantic and scared to death.

"Bridget!" he called out.

As Sergio stilled, Bridget looked his way and started yelling. "Mr. Marks, it was him! It was Sergio who killed Jason."

Ignoring the pain in his ribs and the sting of his cuts, he picked up his pace, just as Sergio slapped Bridget hard and she fell onto the street with a cry.

A few scruffy-looking men and women appeared, some practically hanging out of windows, others walking out on the street. But not a one of them made a move to either help Bridget or assist him.

After quickly ascertaining that Bridget was not too badly hurt, he grabbed Sergio by the collar. "What have you done?" he yelled.

"I stopped him," he replied, panting hard. "I did what you were too weak to do."

"Avondale did nothing to warrant his death."

"Of course he did. He owed all of us money. Thousands of dollars. My men beat him, warned him. His promise to pay his debts after he married your Miss Bancroft was no good anymore—and that was *your* fault, Marks, when you took up with someone well beyond your station. But Avondale arrogantly thought handing over that watch was enough to buy him more time. Well, it wasn't. Something had to be done. Someone had to make him an example for all the other deadbeats."

"But why kill him? We'll never get the money back now."

Vlas waved off Sebastian's comment, illustrating that his final act had never been about only the money. "He beat my girls. He beat everyone's girls. But what would you care about that part of our businesses?"

Sebastian stilled. "You should have taken him to the police."

Sergio grinned. "The police? Listen to you, all high and mighty. There's no police for the likes of us. No cop is going to stay on our side. It's better that he's dead. In fact, Marks, I followed you here thinking it would be best if *you* were dead. Underneath, you've always been too soft for Camp Creek Alley. And now you're worse than ever. Besides, I'd just as soon have your customers and Bridget here for myself—"

Sebastian barely heard the threat on his own life. Knowing how close he came to being arrested for Avondale's murder, knowing how frightened Lydia had been, seeing Bridget hurt . . . He grabbed the man's shoulders and shook him hard.

Sergio twisted and then slammed his fist into Sebastian's jaw. Sebastian retaliated, just before they both fell to the ground. Their fight continued, and suddenly, Sebastian was ten again. Fighting for food, for shelter, for his life. His punches became harder. Little by little, Sergio stopped fighting.

"Mr. Marks, stop!" Bridget cried. "Stop! You'll kill him!"

The air stilled and reality returned.

Struggling to his feet, Sebastian swayed, then noticed that the crowd around him was looking at him with grudging respect. "Bridget, are you all right?" he asked.

She nodded. "And you are too, Mr. Marks. You are too."

Breathing hard, both from his exertion and the realization of what had just occurred, he blinked.

Then, as the seconds passed, he breathed deep—and almost smiled—as three police officers came running up. Everything was, indeed, going to be fine after all.

NINE DAYS LATER

Lydia was discovering that it wasn't too difficult to get through each day if she simply concentrated on each task that needed to be completed instead of how she felt about doing it. Simply taking all emotion out of every activity made most anything possible.

Her heart certainly appreciated that fact.

She'd been able to return to the pawnshop not once but two times. Now it hardly bothered her at all that the man there knew her name but pretended to be surprised to see her each time she walked through his front door.

Simply not thinking about the fact that the rest of their paintings had been in her father's family for generations made it almost painless to sell them. The same could be said for pawning her mother's heirloom jewelry.

And all she had to do was imagine creditors knocking on her door to not feel guilty about selling their townhouse.

She'd come to the conclusion that sentimentality was an overvalued emotion.

She'd clung to this belief when she visited various boardinghouses in the city. She'd stepped into each one determined to only see the benefits to such establishments. That was far easier than imagining how her mother was going to cope while living in one.

After all, one needed to be fed, warm, and safe. That was what was important. All she had to do was ignore the worn furniture and the rather ragtag addresses and focus instead on locating someplace reasonably clean and almost respectable for her mother.

By remaining numb, she'd been able to sign a leasing agreement for her mother and pretend that she had a chance of living there longer than a few weeks before dissolving into a fit of tears. That her mother wouldn't alienate herself so quickly that the landlord was very likely to send her packing in less than a month.

Yes, if she simply concentrated on duty and obligation instead of heartache and disappointment, she could accomplish most anything.

It was impressive, really.

At last Lydia's list was almost complete. All she had to do was talk to Priscilla about which date should be her last day of work.

Then Priscilla would completely take over the lending library and begin running it to the best of her ability.

And Lydia could at last meet with the director of the employment agency and accept one of several offers that had come her way since she'd begun her employment search.

At the moment, she had three job offers from three very good addresses. It seemed though most of society frowned upon women falling from grace, mothers of school-aged children were pleased to take advantage of that fact.

Her worst fear had become her easiest accomplishment. She now had her choice of children to teach for the rest of her life.

It was ironic, she supposed, that the very last thing on her list—the matter of leaving her job at the library and securing a new position as a governess in another family's home—was far more difficult to accept than losing her own home.

Or perhaps it wasn't ironic at all. Merely something of a sad statement on her life.

Perhaps that was because she had felt so at home at the library. Her job had been everything to her. She'd enjoyed the books, the peace and quiet, and most of all the happiness the hours spent in the pages of the novels had given her.

She doubted she'd have either the access or the time to read so many books ever again.

She already knew that visiting this library, even on her afternoons off, would be almost unbearable. Especially since, well, Priscilla was very nice but not very bright. Or hardworking. Lydia was fairly sure the girl would mess everything up in no time.

"Do you have any more questions about cataloging or ordering before I leave for my appointment, Priscilla?"

"No."

"Are you sure? Because you look upset. What don't you understand? I promise no question is too small. It's how one learns after all."

"I simply hate the thought of you leaving this place. As much as I've liked working here, I know it will never mean what it does to you."

Priscilla was no doubt correct. Unfortunately, that didn't make Lydia feel any better. Instead of making her feel proud of the work she'd done, it simply brought home the knowledge that she'd spent most of her adult life giving her heart and soul to a building and the books inside. At the end of the day she would have nothing to show for it.

"It's for the best. Everything has a time and a purpose."

Priscilla looked doubtful. "Maybe. But it still seems like a shame."

"That's because it is one." She tried to smile but knew her effort looked sickly. Therefore she made a great show of examining her timepiece. "My goodness. It's after one. I had better hurry, or I'll be late."

"Of course, Miss Bancroft. Don't worry. I'll handle everything here."

After leaving the building, Lydia drew in big breaths of air. Anything to soothe her frayed nerves.

She regretted her impulse soon after she started walking however. It was snowing, and the wind was even more frigid than usual. Everywhere she looked, people were bundled up and walking with force, obviously trying to get to wherever they needed to go as quickly as possible.

She was in the minority, as she had over an hour to waste before appearing for an appointment. She was standing outside a small café, debating the pros and cons of going in and having a bowl of soup, when Vincent Hunt approached.

"Mr. Hunt?"

He tipped his hat. "Miss Bancroft, good afternoon." He smiled. "I was hoping it was you."

She was torn between hugging him like an old friend and brushing him off as quickly as possible. In the end, she did neither. "How are you?"

He rubbed his hands on his arms. "Cold."

"Well, it is February."

"Indeed." He paused, then forged ahead. "Have you eaten? May I join you?"

"I don't know if that would be advisable."

"Please? I have some news to share, and I'd prefer to do it someplace where my teeth weren't chattering."

"All right then."

He led the way inside and after greeting the proprietress, asked for them to be seated close to the roaring fireplace.

After they both ordered bowls of split pea and ham soup and cups of tea, she leaned back with a sigh. "Thank you, Mr. Hunt. You gave me the push I needed to step inside here."

"What are you doing out on such a blustery day?"

"I have an appointment with an employment agency."

To her surprise, he looked pleased. "Will you be hiring some servants at last? Did your financial situation turn around?"

"Actually, I am seeking employment."

"But you have your job at the library."

"It gave me much enjoyment, but not so much in terms of actual income, Mr. Hunt. I am applying to find a governess position." She was almost able to speak of the job without stumbling over the words.

"But you can't do that."

"Why ever not?"

"Mr. Marks needs you."

"You were standing in my foyer over a week ago when he told me in no uncertain terms that he did not want me to be in his life."

"He was lying. I'm sure of it."

Their bowls of soup arrived, and Lydia was grateful for the reason to halt the conversation. She dug into her meal, enjoying the hearty flavors and satisfying warmth.

When Vincent was about halfway through with his soup, he said, "I suppose you know Sergio Vlas killed Avondale."

"Yes. It's been in all the papers. It seems he didn't appreciate Jason's ongoing debt, but especially his beating his . . . the women in his employ."

"He had also realized that Avondale had no ability—and probably no intention—to pay him back, so there was no reason to keep him alive."

Lydia frowned. "I never would have imagined that money would play such a part in someone living or dying. Obviously, I was wrong."

"People are killed for all sorts of reasons. That isn't a surprise. The reporter from the *Courier* had his own bizarre reasons to have people killed. Can you imagine? Benson Gage was so determined to force authorities to pay more attention to Camp Creek Alley that he would convince a gang to accelerate their criminal activity just so he could write about it."

Lydia nodded.

"It is hard to imagine, but I am so glad Captain Ryan was able to find and arrest the gang leader and learn the truth. When Lieutenant Howard came to the townhouse to tell me the whole story, he said the man was quite willing to help the reporter in his quest, even with unnecessary murders, despite the inevitable increased police interest. He knew their takings from the fair crowd would soon be depleted, and he was more than willing to steal money and jewelry from wealthy men returning to Camp Creek Alley after being distracted by fair events."

"I know Mr. Marks was relieved to learn the man actually had too much respect for him to do any more harm than he did when they followed you to the fairgrounds that day at the reporter's request. When you were not killed as expected, the reporter was afraid you or Mr. Marks had seen your attackers, people Mr. Marks might have recognized. Even as Mr. Marks was giving his statement at the police station, Gage was already asking the police questions that tipped them off about his possible involvement."

Eager to change the thread of conversation, Lydia asked, "Have you heard from Bridget? She told me the last time I saw her that she was going to leave Mr. Marks' employ." She was much safer to ask about than Sebastian.

He smiled. "Bridget has found a new place to live and has allowed me to call on her."

"Call on her? Are you going to court her, Mr. Hunt?"

"I am."

"That is truly wonderful."

His cheeks flushed. "I think so too. I came to my senses when I realized I could have lost her. Thank goodness."

Lydia felt tears prick her eyes. "I wish you many blessings," she said sincerely. Both Vincent and Bridget deserved the happiness they had found in each other.

"Thank you. Mr. Marks is slowly recovering from all the excitement too."

"I'm glad he's suffered no ill effects."

"Actually, the experience has caused him to rethink some things. He closed the Grotto."

She set down her spoon. "Truly?"

"He's not going to get out of the bar business for good. He's going to open a new club but with no gambling. This one will be near the financial district and be far more upscale."

"And he is happy with this decision?"

"I think he's happy to be on the right side of the law."

"How do you feel about this?"

"I'm happy too. I don't want to work for anyone else. Now I'll have more normal hours. I'll get to spend more time with my daughter. And with Bridget too."

"That is a blessing. I am happy for you."

"Thank you."

"Please convey my felicitations to him. I am glad things are working out for him."

"He misses you terribly, Miss Bancroft."

"I haven't heard a word since he told me good-bye. Therefore, the evidence proves different."

"He is a proud man. He is also very insecure."

"Are we speaking of the same man? I've never met anyone with more confidence."

"That is what he has in common with you, Miss Bancroft. He used the Silver Grotto as a cover for his worries."

"That is a bit much."

"It is true. There, in the dark, people went to escape their realties. But he used it as an escape too. As long as he played the part of Sebastian Marks, gambling club owner, he didn't have to come to terms with who he is."

"You believe that to be the case?"

"I do. Just like you also lived in your make-believe world of books in the library. There you could immerse yourself in other people's hopes and dreams instead of dealing with real people, real places, and real emotions and problems."

"I fear you've forgotten yourself."

"And I fear you've forgotten how much you have been giving up.

You need to go see Mr. Marks and assure him that you haven't forgotten him."

"I fear you, too, have been living in your fantasy world, Mr. Hunt. I tried to be his friend. I was his fiancée. He pushed me out of both places."

"I think you are afraid."

"I am. I don't want to get hurt again."

"But—"

"If he wants to see me again, he will simply have to find me."

"Stay at the library then."

"I cannot."

"Make an exception. Stay another week. What's one more week, Miss Bancroft?"

It was a lot. She needed to move forward and put the past behind her. However, she knew walking away was going to be one of the hardest things she'd ever done. She loved the reading room.

She loved the memories made there even more.

She sighed. "All right." Because after everything they'd gone through, one more week was really nothing at all.

CHAPTER 35

CHICAGO TIMES-COURIER

February 1894

Reported by K. J. Ryan

So many changes have occurred in Camp Creek Alley, it is difficult to note them all. Perhaps it is best to dwell on the fact that things are changing in the area. And all of it is for the better.

He'd come back.

It was nearly five o'clock, and the library was empty. She'd sent Priscilla home over an hour ago and had spent the last hour happily reshelving a variety of religious texts and sermons. Every once in a while she would open one and read it, then read it again, using the time to think about God's Word and ponder God's grace. He made so many good things happen even when people didn't deserve it.

As she stared at the line of neatly aligned books, Lydia felt her throat tighten. She was truly going to miss her life here in the reading room.

And then Sebastian Marks walked through the door.

"What brings you here today?"

His gaze flickered over her slowly before he raised his brows. "I'm in need of a book. Obviously."

"Of course." She shook off her disappointment, at the same time chastising herself for even imagining that he would have another reason to return. "May I be of assistance? Or perhaps you would rather peruse at your leisure."

"I am most assuredly in need of your assistance."

She walked around the counter and stood in front of him. Then wished she had not. He smelled of the outdoors and his expensive cologne. Once again, she found it hard to ignore.

In addition, he seemed taller. Or perhaps it was merely his aura? She found herself having difficulty looking away from his face to the rows of books.

"What type of book are you seeking? Fiction or nonfiction?"

"Nonfiction."

Too ill at ease to stand still, she started toward the stacks on the south wall. "What type of nonfiction book do you seek? Biographies? Medical? Geographical? Philosophical?"

"Poetry."

She stopped. "I'm sorry, sir, but that is not possible."

"What is not?"

"The poetry is found in fiction."

"You sure?"

"Very sure. Poems are made up, you know."

"Ah." He waggled his fingers. "Lead on then."

She did an about-face and walked him down one aisle, then up another. Until, at last, they stopped in front of a variety of poets, some well-known, others far less. "Any poet in particular?"

He stood next to her, eyeing the titles in front of them. "Surely you jest?"

"Pardon?"

"No one goes looking for poetry by the author, do they?"

She blinked. "How else would one seek what they are looking for?"

"By need, of course."

She was off-kilter. "Need?"

"Are you able to help me? Do you know your poetry?"

"I will try. What, uh, subject are you interested in?"

He looked her way. "Love."

"Love?" It was a wonder she didn't choke, her utterance spoken around a gasp.

"Are you familiar with the topic?"

She couldn't lie. "Yes." His expression warmed, making her skin flushed. She stepped away. "Well, now. Um, there is Longfellow. Shelley."

"Tennyson?"

"Not usually. Homer is not usually one known for poems of love and beauty either."

"Shakespeare?"

"To be sure, he writes beautiful works about love."

"Shall I compare thee to a summer's day?"

"Thou art more lovely and more temperate."

He looked delighted. "You know it."

"You do too."

"It is a favorite of mine, though even the best poems have never done justice to what I've felt in my heart."

"Words are mere words."

"You know, I came here thinking that I needed to find the perfect way to tell you what is in my heart. But perhaps I should simply say the words. Even though, to be sure, words are mere words."

She swallowed. "Sebastian?"

"You see, something happened to me when I saw you the first time. I walked in here, saw you at that counter right there, nose in your book. You were oblivious to everyone."

She remembered the first time she'd seen him. "Not quite oblivious to everyone and everything."

"You were reading *Little Women* as if Miss Alcott told a hundred stories you were unfamiliar with."

"That is a fair assumption," she said with a smile. "I was an only child, you see."

"I was charmed."

"That, I never knew."

"I didn't want to know you. Because I knew if I did, I wouldn't be able to forget what I felt like in your presence. Therefore, I tried to ignore you."

"You did a good job. I wasn't aware that you knew I existed."

"And then at last we talked."

"And we became friends."

He reached out, took her hand. "And then became engaged."

"Until you broke things off."

"I was frightened. I feared I was hurting you. Instead, I discovered that you had made me better. You lifted me. And now, I find myself adrift. I need you back in my life, Lydia. I need you to be mine once again."

"Sebastian. I know you are responsible for saving my townhouse and securing my pay raise here."

"It was nothing."

"It was everything."

"If you had left your home or this library, how could I have found you? Chicago is a big city after all."

"Why did you come here?"

"To stumble and prevaricate and tell you that I have fallen in love with you. That I want you to be my wife. I want you near me for every reason I said before. And none of those things."

Her pulse was racing. "Why, then?" she asked, hoping that he wouldn't realize just how much what he was saying affected her.

"Simply, because. It seems that you were right, Lydia. Words are only words. Sometimes they are not enough."

She was starting to realize that she had been very wrong. His words were enough. Everything he said had claimed her heart. Encouraged her to believe.

"Oh. Before you give me your answer, I brought you something to try to sway you."

"You didn't need to do that. I have my answer."

"Wait." He unbuttoned his jacket, fished in the pockets, then at last brought out a felt bag. "Here. I decided that nothing will prove my love to you like this."

She took the bag with shaking fingers, carefully slid out the contents, and gasped. And laughed.

For inside was the most beautiful, exquisite pair of eyeglasses she'd ever seen in her life. Gold, embedded with jewels.

"You see, now, when you look through these, everything will be beautiful."

"How could it not be?" Carefully, she pushed the lever, and the lenses popped open. She removed her regular glasses and set them on a shelf, lifted the jeweled pair to her eyes, and saw exactly what he'd said she would. Through those, everything was beautiful. Perfect.

Because all she saw was him. "Sebastian, my answer is yes."

He smiled, then carefully pulled the glasses from her face and set them on the shelf next to her other pair. "What did you do that for?"

"You won't need glasses for this, love. For my kiss, you won't need to see anything at all."

As he pulled her into his arms and at last kissed her, she knew he spoke the truth.

There were no words to describe it.

She only felt loved. And needed.

Everything.

DISCUSSION QUESTIONS

1. Is Sebastian Marks a hero? Why or why not?

2. What were some of Lydia's strengths? How did she prove to be a capable heroine for a novel set at the turn of the century?

3. All four main characters have spent most of their lives trying to find the right place to fit in. Do you think this is a common occurrence? Does everyone have to search at one time in his or her life?

4. The theme of friendship runs throughout the novel, even with Sergio Vlas. How did the need for friendship drive the characters' actions?

5. In what ways are Lydia and Sebastian alike? How are they a good match?

6. What did you think about Vincent Hunt?

7. One of my favorite things about the writing of this novel was the characters' love of literature and libraries. How have books enriched your life?

8. What do you think the future holds in store for Bridget and Vincent? What obstacles, if any, do you feel they will have to overcome?

9. Each character in the novel eventually comes to terms with the fact that they have been attempting to solve all their problems by themselves. How has prayer and faith helped you over the years?

ACKNOWLEDGMENTS

I am so grateful to have had the opportunity to write the Chicago World's Fair trilogy. Writing each book in the series was truly an adventure in itself! I loved having an excuse to learn more about Chicago's history as well as discover all kinds of information about the 1893 Chicago World's Fair.

I am sincerely grateful for all the folks at Zondervan and HarperCollins Christian Publishers for their belief in me and in these books. They guided my writing, pushed me when I needed to be pushed, and helped me craft three novels of which to be proud.

I am especially thankful for the careful eyes of Natalie Hanemann and Jean Bloom in the crafting of *Whispers in the Reading Room*. I had a vision and a goal for this novel. However, this book definitely needed quite a bit of fine tuning, and I'm indebted to them for their guidance. My editor Becky Philpott also patiently encouraged me as well. Becky, I'm so grateful for you.

I also am grateful to my critique partners, especially Heather Webber Blake, for their help, to Lynne Stroup for reading this book as quickly as I could email her chapters, and to my Buggy Bunch street team for reading the series and in turn telling everyone and anyone about it. Thank you, too (and a big hug) to my friend Julie Stone-who toured Chicago not once but three times so I could do all the research

I needed. Discovering Chicago's past wouldn't be the same without you, Julie!

I should note that I made several allowances in this novel. First of all, there was no actual Camp Creek Alley. I based this area on some of the research I did on Chicago's more dangerous areas. And, while there were many bars and illegal gambling clubs, I also made up the Silver Grotto, as well as the other establishments. Perhaps the greatest change I did was to have Sebastian and Lydia visit the Wild West Show after the Fair had closed. While some entertainments were still available after the closing of the fair, Wild Bill's Show had actually closed and moved on by the time my novel took place. As an author, however, I couldn't help but feel particularly fascinated by the show and the vast amount of entertainment that was available on the Midway. I simply couldn't end the series without a scene taking place there.

In closing, I wanted to share that I am always so grateful to God for giving me the gift of writing. I am blessed to spend my days making up stories, and I know the words are possible through Him.

Thank you for picking up the book! I hope you enjoyed the novel.

Blessings,

Shelley Shepard Gray

ABOUT THE AUTHOR

Photo by The New Studio

Shelley Gray is a *New York Times* and *USA Today* bestselling author, a finalist for the American Christian Fiction Writers' prestigious Carol Award, and a two-time HOLT Medallion winner. She lives in southern Ohio, where she writes full-time, bakes too much, and can often be found walking her dachshunds on her town's bike trail.

She also spends a lot of time online. Please visit her website: www.shelleyshepardgray.com.

Find her on Facebook at Facebook.com/ShelleyShepardGray.

Enjoy the first two books in Shelley Gray's
Chicago World's Fair Mystery Series

Available in print and e-book.

The Chicago World's Fair Mystery Series
is also available as an e-book collection!

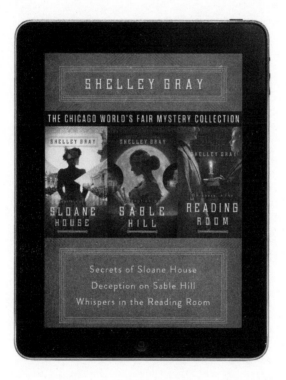

Available in e-book only May 2016.

Enjoy an excerpt from
Robin Lee Hatcher's upcoming novel,
The Loyal Heart

CHAPTER 1

GALVESTON, TEXAS

JANUARY, 1868

At times, the pain was so intense, she wanted to die.

With a new sense of resolve, Miranda Markham skimmed a finger along the second-floor window pane just outside her bedroom door. As she did so, frigid drops of condensation slid across her fingers, moistening them . . . transmitting tiny bursts of pain along her skin. The glass wasn't thick, surely no more than a quarter inch. It seemed, to her eyes at least, that the frame was rather rickety as well.

It would be so easy to break.

Miranda wondered what it would feel like to perch on the edge of the windowsill like one of the gulls that rested on the weathered wood from time to time. She wondered what it would feel like to open her arms. To finally let herself go, to lean forward into nothingness.

To be free.

Perhaps she would feel nothing beyond a cold numbness, accompanied by an exhilarating rush of fear . . . followed by the blessed relief from pain.

Did pain even matter anymore?

The iron latch was icy cold as she worked it open. Condensation sprayed her cheeks as the pane slowly edged upward. Tendrils of hair whipped against her neck as the winter wind seemed to beckon.

She breathed deep.

If she could just garner what was left of her courage, why, it could all be over. Within minutes, in seconds, even, she'd no longer be awake. No longer be reminded. No longer be sad.

She'd no longer be afraid to rise each morning.

And wasn't the absence of fear, that intangible notion of confidence that children enjoyed and the elderly remembered, worth everything?

Reaching out, she clasped the metal lining the frame. Felt the iron bite into her palm as she edged closer. At last, it was time.

"Mrs. Markham? Mrs. Markham, ma'am? Where should I put the new boarder?" Winifred called up from the base of the stairs.

Slowly—too slowly perhaps—one corner of Miranda's dark cloak of depression lifted. She realized she was still standing on the landing at the top of stairs, the window open.

Winifred's voice turned shrill. "Mrs. Markham, do ye hear me?"

Miranda dropped her hands. Turned. "Yes. Yes, of course." Peering through the maze of mahogany spindles, she looked down. Blinked as her elderly maid came into focus. "A new boarder, did you say?"

Winifred stared back. "Yes, ma'am. E is here a wee bit early. A Mr. Truax, his name is. Mr. Robert Truax." Her voice held the slightest tinge of impatience now. She was a reluctant transplant from England, and seemed to always stare at her surroundings with varying degrees of shock and dismay.

"Remember?" Winifred added, raising her voice just a little bit higher, as if she was talking to a child. "We got the telegram yesterday that said he were arriving today?"

She didn't remember much after receiving another threatening letter in yesterday's post. "Yes, of course."

"I been working on his room all morning, I have." Looking pleased, Winifred added, "It sparkles and shines, it does."

"I'm glad," she said absently.

Until Phillip's family ran her off, she was in charge of this house. With that came the responsibility of at least pretending she cared about the running of it. With a vague sense of resignation, she turned back to the window. Set about cranking it shut before locking it securely.

"Mrs. Markham, he's cooling his heels in Lt. Markham's study. What shall I do with him?" The maid's voice now held a healthy thread of irritation. "Do you want to do your usual interview for new guests or would you rather I take 'im straight to his room?"

Miranda truly didn't care where the man went. Any room would do, the further away from her, the better. But she had a responsibility to the rest of the staff to at least meet the man she would be allowing to lodge in the house for a time.

Phillip would have expected her to do that. Summoning her courage, she murmured, "Please escort him to the parlor. I'll be down momentarily." Stepping forward, she smoothed the thick wool of her charcoal gray skirt.

She avoided glancing at her reflection as she passed a mirror.

Though she was out of mourning and no longer wore black, no color appealed. Hence, gray. The general consensus among her four employees was that the hue didn't suit her any better than unrelieved black. Actually, Cook had remarked more than once that she resembled a skinny sparrow.

Continuing her descent, she said, "Please serve Mr. Truax tea. I believe we have one or two muffins left from breakfast as well?"

"We do. Since you didn't eat."

Miranda almost smiled. "Today it is most fortunate I did not."

Grumbling, the housekeeper turned away.

When she was alone again, Miranda took a fortifying breath. Realized that a fresh scent wafting from the open window had permeated the air. Salt and sea and well, something tangy and bright.

It jarred her senses, gave her a small sense of hope.

Perhaps today was not the day to die after all.

The story continues in Robin Lee Hatcher's,
The Loyal Heart, available July 2016.